I'm an Irish author who is addicted to writing romances featuring damaged, moody, book boyfriends searching for their happily ever after.

Visit K.A. Finn online:

www.kafinn.com
(trailers, excerpts, artwork, playlists etc)

Facebook: kafinnauthor

Instagram: kafinnauthor

Additional links: linktr.ee/kafinn

Also by K.A. Finn

Nomad Series (Space Opera)

Ares

Nemesis

Perses

Chaos

Mania

Cronus

Talos (TBA)

Blackjacks Series (Paranormal Romance)

Breaking Phoenix

Reviving Davyn

Defying Shep

Defending Rhain (TBA)

Broken Chords (Rockstar Romance)

Broken Rock (Tate)

Fractured Rock (Gregg)

Split Rock (all band members)

Crushed Rock (Luke)

Shattered Rock (Dillon)

Damaged Rock (Gregg - TBA)

Twisted Legends (Folklore Retelling/Romance)

North Bound (Nick/Santa)

Shadow Bound (Damon/The Boogeyman - TBA)

Broken Chords #5

SHATTERED Rock

K.A. FINN

Cover design by Deranged Doctor Design
www.derangeddoctordesign.com

Photography by CJC Photography
www.cjc-photography.com

Cover model
Eric Lamb

Published by Cooper Publishing
cooperbookservices@gmail.com

ISBN: 978-1-914177-65-1

Shattered Rock Playlist

Although I haven't mentioned any song lyrics in this book, that doesn't mean music didn't play a MASSIVE part in its creation.

This playlist was on every time I wrote, edited, or just read the book.

The bands, the songs, or the lyrics remind me of Dillon and Ash in some way. It's still a playlist I listen to regularly and it always reminds me of Dillon's story.

If you want to check out the playlist that I had blaring in the background while I was writing **Shattered Rock,** you can find it on my website (www.kafinn.com/shatteredrock), by scanning the QR code below, or by searching the following songs.

Just make sure to play it LOUD!

We Fall Apart– We As Human
Make Believe – The Faim
Call You Mine – Daughtry
Livin Right – The Score
Broken Heart – Escape the Fate
Live, Learn, Let Go – Go Radio
Forget the Lies – Quietdrive
Yours Again – Red
Can't Forget You – My Darkest Days
Monster – Reid Henry
Love You For All Time – Gareth Emery, Annabel
You Broke Me First – Conor Maynard
Back To You – Blair
Going Home– The Score
Something to Someone – Dermot Kennedy
Somebody – Gareth Emery, Kovic
What If – Five For Fighting
Dreamer – Dermot Kennedy
Hurtless - Acoustic – Dean Lewis

Dear God – Avenged Sevenfold
Limit – Citizen Soldier
Satellites – No Sleep for Lucy
All For You – Ciam Ducrot, Ella Henderson
Wreckage – Nate Smith
Don't Forget Me – Dermot Kennedy
Where Do You Run – The Score
I'll Be Waiting – Cian Ducrot
Everyone Who Falls In Love – Cian Ducrot
Breathing Underwater – Hot Milk
Go To Sleep – Blame My Youth
Was It The Wind That Stirred The Trees – Boy North
Lifetime – Three Days Grace
I'll Never Need – Charlie South
Here (In Your Arms) – Gregory Dillon
Sunday – Dermot Kennedy
Whiskey Lullaby – Drew Jacobs, Caitlynne Curtis
Part Of Me – Cian Ducrot
Will You Wait For Me - Acoustic – Royal Bliss
Paranoid – Royal Bliss
Drink My Stupid Away – Royal Bliss
Ruin – Moncrieff
ERA – The Faim

Well, enough from me. I'll leave you in Dillon's more than capable hands. Good luck – you'll need it!

Intro

This series is based in the Republic of Ireland. The timescales, procedures, and context are reflective of local practices and policy.

Content Information

This book contains strong subject matter that may not be suitable for all readers, including scenes that may depict, mention, or discuss:

- abusive relationship
- alcohol and drug use
- anxiety
- assault
- emotional abuse
- physical abuse
- rape
- sexual abuse
- sexual assault
- suicide
- violence

To everyone who loves the tortured bad boy.

Dillon

Dillon Ryan stands on the stage next to his three best mates and eats up the applause. Yeah, he loves the music. Loves performing. But the buzz he gets from the fans is what he can't get enough of. It's what he lives for. It's what he needs. What he craves, like a drug. Unlike Tate, Gregg, and Luke, he'll take the attention, lap it up, and come back for more.

There's nothing quite like adoring fans screaming your name. It's one of the few things he still enjoys in life. One of the few things that makes him truly happy.

Fuck knows he hasn't had a lot to be happy about in the last few years.

He kicks the misery to touch, before it can ruin the moment for him. Tonight is a little more reserved than a sell-out concert, but with the chat show televised all over the world, the numbers will be more impressive.

After he gives his final wave, he follows the rest of the band down the corridor to their dressing rooms.

'I reckon I was on fire tonight.' Their drummer, Gregg, beams widely as he nudges lead singer Tate in the side. 'Did you see me? I was epic.'

'I was kind of paying attention to singing, so no, I can't say I noticed.'

'You saw me, Luke?'

Dillon's best mate and guitarist Luke, shakes his head. 'Sorry.'

'Damn it! Dillon?'

'Why the fuck would I be looking at you? All you do is bang a couple of sticks on a drum.'

Gregg lifts his middle finger. 'I really don't like you.'

'Not many do, Gregg,' he replies, grinning to make him think he wasn't being serious. But he is. He's kind of a *Marmite* type of guy. You either took an instant dislike to him, or stuck around long enough to figure out he's not an ass all the time.

'So, what's the plan?' Gregg asks, as they reach the lounge area next to their dressing rooms. 'We heading out for food?'

'Sounds good. I'm fucking starving.'

'You're always starving, Tate. Fucking giant!'

Tate swats at Gregg, barely missing his head when the drummer dodges out of the way. 'I honestly don't know why I work with you lot. You're all a bunch of animals.'

'I'll pass on food,' Dillon says, ending the squabble between Tate and Gregg. 'I'm beat.'

'Are you sure? You don't usually pass up on food after a show.' Luke is looking at him like there's something wrong, and that pisses him off. Mainly because there is.

His feelings for Luke have diminished a little, but not nearly enough to make being in the same room as him bearable. Not even close. Especially when Luke's new and irritatingly amazing girlfriend, Maeve, will no doubt be there too. All the wives and girlfriends joined them on the trip to the UK. He's the only band member still flying solo. Completely his own fault.

He's still pining after Luke, and it's messing with any interest he might have had for anyone else.

'I just didn't sleep great last night. Could do with getting a few hours before we head back. You guys go and have fun.'

Tate and Gregg nod, then head over to their own rooms leaving Dillon with Luke. Great! Just what he needs right now. He could do without any *up close and personal* with his friend.

'What's going on?'

'I told you. I'm just tired.'

'You've been off with me since I came back from Wales a few weeks ago. Have I done something to upset you?'

You left.

'Fuck's sake! I'm just tired. What's with the third degree? We're fine, Luke.' He keeps the smile on his face until it nearly hurts, but thankfully Luke nods and drops the intense look. 'Okay. If you're sure? I'll see you in the morning?'

'Sure.'

Before Luke can pressure him, or even look at him again, Dillon makes his escape to his changing room and shuts the door. He can't keep doing this. It's not fair on Luke, or the other guys. He's being a moody shite and it's going to start impacting on the band if he's not careful.

The problem is, he has no idea how to make things better, and he's tried. He really has, but it's not that easy. Tate and Chloe are married with a son. Gregg and Bria will no doubt be heading down the aisle any day, if they keep going the way they are. And Luke...

He's happy. That's all that should matter. Luke has finally found someone who really cares about him for being himself. His abusive wife is locked away where she belongs, and he's living his life.

But he's living it with Maeve. He's in love with Maeve. He's looking forward to a long and happy life with Maeve.

Not *him*.

Fuck! If he keeps brooding about this, he'll just drive himself crazy. What he needs to do is to stop being a dick and get on with his own life.

But he doesn't know how.

Instead of leaning against the door in his dressing room for the rest of the night, he grabs his phone from his bag and calls his bodyguard. 'Hey Jace. I'm ready to head back to the hotel.'

Ashling Hughes combs her hand through her short blonde spikes, as she sits back in her chair. Her latest assignment has been edited, and the photos are ready for the world to see.

'Oooh, sexy!'

She laughs and takes the cup of coffee from her friend, Charlie. 'Me or the pictures?'

He pulls up a chair beside her, then looks from her to the photo of the happy couple on the screen. 'You, definitely.'

'Thanks, but you're full of shit as usual. They are a stunning couple though.'

'With all due respect to the couple, you can make anyone look stunning. It's part of your gift. Speaking of which, Megan would like to see you when you're done. Something about a new and exciting assignment.'

Ash makes sure she's saved her work, before closing the file. She was due to have a few days off from the magazine. She loves her job, but it's been full on the last few weeks with one wedding after another.

She's had more than her fill of blushing brides and well-dressed grooms to last her a few months at least.

When your own love life consists of a takeaway menu and reruns of sitcoms, the happy couple overload is a bit much to take.

'So much for my time off.'

Charlie shrugs as he scrolls through his phone. 'You don't know the time scale. It could be weeks off. Anyway, I gotta go. Work to do.' He kisses her cheek and leaves her cubicle.

Ash sighs and looks over at her boss' door. Better go and see what fun she has in store.

She's been working for the magazine for two years and loves every second of the job. Her recent promotion means more travel from time to time, depending on where the various weddings were taking place, but she had no complaints. It was something she never thought she'd achieve when she applied for the job.

She waits while Megan finishes sending her email and pushes her laptop aside. 'I just finished your last piece. It's exceptional! Your photography is... no words, Ash. Really.'

'Wow, thanks Megan.'

Megan sits back and crosses her legs. 'So, I realise I had promised you some time off after your last flood of weddings, but something has come up and I honestly can't think of anyone better suited to the job. It's not another wedding,' she adds quickly. 'It's something entirely different, and quite frankly, unbelievably exciting for the magazine. If I was a photographer, I guarantee I'd be all over this myself. To say I'm jealous is an understatement.'

Ash can feel the butterflies building in her stomach. There are at least half a dozen other photographers on the books with the magazine. If Megan is handing this to her, it's a massive compliment. 'Don't keep me hanging on like this. What is it?'

'Okay, so we've been given a once-in-a-lifetime opportunity to shoot Broken Chords on their ten-year anniversary tour. They're doing about a dozen shows around Europe to celebrate a decade of owning the charts. And we've been granted full access while they're on tour.'

Ash swallows thickly and smiles, although it's far from what she wants to do. If anything, she wants to run from the room and throw up repeatedly. Her palms sweat, and her heart races as the panic builds. It's a career changing assignment. She knows that, and Megan is giving it to her above countless other photographers in the company. That is such a huge pat on the back for her.

But she can't take it. No way.

Megan clearly notices her total lack of any excitement. 'You have heard of Broken Chords, haven't you? I mean, you do live on this planet, right?'

'Of course I have.'

'So you know what a big deal this is for both the magazine, and for you as a photographer? You get to spend time with four rather stunning musicians and take pictures of them. I mean, am I missing something here? I know at least a few dozen other people in this building alone, who would jump at this chance - myself included.'

'No, seriously. I'm so grateful you thought of me.'

'But...'

She needs to say no, but if she does, not only would she have a lot of explaining to do, she could also be kissing goodbye to a career she loves. You don't turn down assignments, especially ones like this.

Megan turns her laptop around and points to the screen. She's seen that photo. She's seen all the photos of the band. The four men are gorgeous, no question. Her eyes move to the left of the photo, and her throat closes when she looks into his incredible green eyes.

'Am I sensing a no?'

Ash smiles and shakes her head, still looking into his eyes. 'Don't be silly. I'd be mad to turn this down. I can't wait!' The lie tastes bitter on her tongue, but she's grateful she manages to get it out, full stop. Thankfully Megan buys it, turning her laptop around, hiding him from her again.

'Fantastic! I'll send you all the details. You'll be expected to meet them in Dublin this weekend. Their management team said we can get a peek at a few of their rehearsals too. Okay, I'm still not getting an excited vibe from you. What's the matter?'

'I'm just thinking about who to get as a babysitter—'

'Stop right there. You and I both know Charlie will look after Freya.' Megan clasps her hands together and leans forward. 'I understand this may seem a little daunting, but it is such a huge deal for us and for you. Vox don't usually let anyone get this close to them, especially after all the personal issues Tate, Gregg, and Luke have experienced the last few years. They are extremely protective of them, and rightly so.

'Luckily for us, their manager Ellen, is a friend of mine, so she's trusting me with this and with the band. And now I am trusting you. But you will have to be sensitive. If the guys want you to back off, you will have to do just that.'

'I understand.' She's very surprised Vox have agreed to this at all, full stop. Luke, Tate, and Gregg have been through the mill the last few years. It's no surprise Vox are protective of them after all that.

'So that's a definite yes from you?'

'Of course! What reason in the world would I have to say no?'

'Perfect! I want you to spend the next few days online. See what others have done when they've photographed the band. See if you can come up with something no one has done before. Something to really stand out.

'I want this to be the *real* band - four friends on the road doing what they love. Not that I'm complaining, but the theme when they're photographed always seems to veer towards the topless side of things. It might be different to see them with their clothes on!'

Ash nods, the forced smile still plastered on her face.

'Great! Off you go then. Get some ideas together.

Ash leaves the office and walks on autopilot to the meeting room. Charlie appears behind her and shuts the door, locking it behind him.

'Oh dear. That's not a happy face.'

Ash slumps into the nearest chair and buries her face in her hands. 'It's not. I'm so fucked, Charlie!'

He drapes his arm around her shoulders and taps the side of her head. 'Talk.'

'I'm being sent around Europe to photograph Broken Chords' ten-year anniversary tour.'

Charlie's screech doesn't help to lighten her mood. He's got a serious crush on Gregg. Has for years, which didn't help her put distance between herself and the band. Charlie was constantly searching for pictures of him.

'Why are you all depressed about this?'

'I can't do it, Charlie. What about Freya?'

'I'll look after her. Next excuse?'

She rests her head on the table and groans, then looks back at him again. 'Okay, this has to stay between you and me. I mean it, Charlie. I will kill you if you tell anyone about this.'

'Of course. What's wrong? You got a massive crush on one of the band?'

'You have no idea how close you are. I may have been in a relationship with one of them for a while, years ago.'

His face is blank as he stares over at her. 'Who?'

'Dillon.'

He raises his eyebrows, and his mouth opens and closes a few times before he finds the words. 'You were seeing Dillon Ryan?'

'Not just seeing him. I was engaged to him, Charlie. We were going to get married.'

Dillon

He should be tired. The weekend in the UK had followed a busy week of promoting their new album, and too many interviews to count. They'd been working long days with barely a few hours to themselves.

But while his body may be tired, his mind won't shut down. Dillon rolls over and buries his head under the pillow. After a few minutes he gives up on that position, throws the pillow on the floor, and turns onto his back again. He can't get comfortable.

He looks at the display on the clock and groans. It's heading to five in the morning. He crashed around midnight and managed about an hour of sleep. He's knackered, and his mood is already heading towards the foul side of the scale. No change there. That's where it's been for months.

No point staying here and getting deeper into the grump. He has to be up in an hour anyway to meet with the band. They've got a big milestone heading their way in a week.

Broken Chords has been going for ten years!

He can't believe they made it past one year, let alone a decade. The four of them still being alive and kicking after all the shit that had happened, is something worth celebrating. For a while there he thought he'd be saying goodbye to three of his friends. Tate had been so deep into heroin he nearly killed himself, Gregg's stalker had tried to kill him, and Luke's bitch of a wife abused him and drove him to attempt suicide.

And he's overcome his own demon or two. He still drinks far too much. Still uses painkillers as a survival tool. But he's sleeping with random strangers less than he used to. He's not so sure that's a good thing though. It was something he enjoyed. Something that made him feel... well, anything at all.

But he's lost his taste for it. Not for sex. He still does that from time to time, although recently it was more *vanilla* than he'd like. He prefers extremes. Always has - especially when it came to sex.

Or did.

Now he's not sure what the fuck he wants anymore.

He kicks the duvet off his body and pushes onto his elbows. Unless he's going to knock himself out with drugs, he might as well get up. If Ellen wasn't expecting him to come in for a meeting, then that's what he would do. Wash them down with a bottle of whiskey. Really knock himself out.

He'd tried to back off the drugs a little, but maybe he's more addicted than he wants to admit? He thought he had a hold on it, but at times like this, it feels like it's the other way round.

Things have just been hitting him more over the last few weeks. All the shit he's gone through with Luke, mixed with his arrest and time inside, has thrown him off track. Having been targeted by some inmates while he was inside, had made that month one of the longest and most painful times of his life.

A time he'd brushed off, as far as everyone else is concerned. There's no fucking way he'd tell anyone he dreads sleep because of the nightmares. That he replays the beatings, hating himself for not fighting back, and doing everything he could to hide the bruises from the guards.

He lived each minute in constant fear and dread, always on edge, always waiting for someone to take too much interest in him. When he was released from prison, he swore to himself he'd lay off and take it easy on drink and drugs. That promise only lasted a few weeks. Maybe less. Better than nothing, but that's an excuse.

After seeing what Tate went through and then Luke's intentional overdose, he should be steering clear, but he's weak. That's what it boils down to. He's weak and pathetic and can't get through a measly fucking day without using one or the other, to either get himself out of bed, or to try and silence the nightmares.

As he uncovers his legs, he tries to avoid looking at the tattoo on the inside of his thigh, but like every fucking morning, his eyes fix on it.

He should have the damn thing removed. Should have had it removed years ago. But he can't bring himself to do it. The name had been part of his body for ten years. It's not like getting it removed would change a thing at this stage. He's only glad he didn't use standard letters when it was designed. Instead, he'd picked an old Irish text called *Ogham*. The slanting lines look like gibberish, unless you know what you're looking at, and what letters the lines stand for.

Her name.

Ashling.

It's only one small tattoo considering the massive one covering his back, but it has the biggest impact on him. Maybe he should sleep with boxers on? Waking up naked every day and it being the first thing he sees, is just adding to the daily misery.

His dick springs to life, the three bars piercing the tip digging into him as her face comes into his mind.

'Yeah, and you can fuck off too!'

He gets up and turns the shower to cold, hissing as he steps under the powerful spray. That soon takes care of any wayward thoughts his body might have had.

After throwing on a pair of shorts and a tank top, he leaves his house and heads down to the beach. Thankfully it's deserted, so he has a long run followed by a swim, then heads back to his house for a slightly warmer shower.

He sits at the counter, eating his breakfast and drinking a strong coffee, as he looks out at the sea.

People would probably be surprised by his choice of house. The deceptively large cottage is on the coast in Wicklow, a short drive from Tate's parents' place. It's far from where you'd imagine a decently well-off musician would live. And that's why he loves it.

The paintwork on the walls outside is chipped. The garden a little unkempt. But that's a disguise. An armour he put in place to keep prying eyes away. *Rock star Dillon* has the typical bachelor pad in town. That's where he takes people. That was where he had too many one night stands to count. Or did, before this unplanned dry spell.

The cottage is only for him, the rest of the band, their partners, and his sisters. No one else had or would ever set foot in it. It's the one place he can be himself. The one place where he doesn't have to put on a mask, or a front, or an act. Here, *bad boy* Dillon Ryan, is just Dillon.

His phone buzzes, signalling an incoming text. His sister Clara wants him to come around for dinner tonight. Thanks to a full-on schedule recently, it's been a few weeks since he'd seen either of his sisters. They like to keep an eye on their baby brother and make sure he's eating right. Clara insists on having him over for dinner at least once a week when he's around. You'd swear he doesn't eat when he's alone!

Which is sometimes the case. He's an amazing cook. Downright fucking brilliant in fact. But he doesn't do that anymore. He used to cook for *her* all the time, but he can't bring himself to do it since she left.

It's how he copes with things. Something goes wrong, or reminds him of something painful, he locks it away and ignores it. If he ever sat in front of a therapist, they'd have a fucking field day with him! He's all about ignoring the problems. But it works. It's kept him alive so far.

It will all come back to bite him in the ass at some stage but, for now, it's working...mostly.

He fires her back a quick message saying he'll be around at six, then dumps his dirty dishes in the sink. Time to find out what fun and games their manager Ellen has planned for them.

As long as it's nothing too crazy he'll be happy. He could do without any drama for the next few weeks. Fuck knows he needs a break. Being stuck on a tour bus with Luke for week is going to be hard enough to deal with.

That's just another issue he needs to lock away. He's in love with Luke. Luke is in love with Maeve. She wins. Same old fucking story.

He can deal with the whole Luke situation. He's been dealing with it for years. At least now Luke is happy and not having the shit beaten out of him by his wife.

His best friend had been living in Wales for the last six months. The guitarist is worth millions but decided to live in a camper van with his new girlfriend, touring around the country while she worked as a dance teacher.

He's happy for Luke and Maeve. He really is. The whole campervan thing is a bit extreme, but what the fuck would he know? Luke seems to be enjoying himself.

13

Maeve is completely out of the box and couldn't be more different to Luke's ex-wife Pippa if she tried. But that's what makes her so perfect for Luke. She's carefree and lives each day to the fullest. She brings out all the best parts of Luke. He smiles now. Dillon didn't realise until lately how little Luke had been smiling the last few years. Until Maeve arrived on the scene and changed Luke's world for the better.

He picks up his phone when it vibrates again.

I'll be with you in half an hour.

His bodyguard, Jace, is a decent enough guy, but having a personal babysitter isn't something he enjoys. It's part of the deal though, so he just has to try his best not to cause the guy too many problems.

Over the years working together, he's managed to set some boundaries with regards to his bodyguard. Jace will do what he's supposed to do, but when Dillon needs space, he backs off. Not all the way, but enough to give him some privacy.

And he needs that today. He wants to drive himself. Just him alone in his own car with his own thoughts. No small talk or awkward silences.

I'm driving myself. No detours. Vox, then Clara's for dinner.

He watches the screen, waiting for the reply. Jace will either accept his request or argue.

No detours!

Thank fuck for that. After making himself a coffee to go, he swallows a couple of pills, then grabs his keys.

Time to get his game face on. All this *woe is me* crap is staying in the car. Being in Broken is the best thing that's ever happened to him. Nothing is going to get in the way of that - especially not himself.

Ash

Charlie lies down beside her on her bed and tries to find the spot on the ceiling that's captured her attention. 'This is really bad, Charlie.'

'The ceiling?'

'No! Not the ceiling. Keep up. How am I going to spend a few weeks with Broken Chords? With him? On a damn bus!'

'A bus?'

She hands him the file she printed out from Megan's email. 'They're taking their tour bus with them. That'll be used to get around between venues, and I'm expected to join them on it. Apparently, I'll get some great photos while on the road travelling with them.'

'Oh. Cosy. Are you sleeping on it with them?'

'No thank God. I'll be booked into the same hotel as the crew. The guys prefer to stay under the radar and avoid the hotels where possible. It'll just be the long hours on the road that'll be a living hell. I honestly don't have a clue how he's going to take seeing me again.'

'I'm still trying to get my head around the fact you know him, full stop. You are a dark horse. Why have you never mentioned you were engaged to him? It's a really big deal.'

Ash shrugs. 'You haven't talked about all your exes.'

'Yeah, but I didn't date Dillon sexy ass Ryan, thank you very much. So, I'm taking it things didn't end well then?'

'Not really. I broke it off with him and please don't ask me why. It's a long and painful story.'

'Was he a dick? I've heard he can be a bit of a dick. Not someone you get on the wrong side of.'

Ash shakes her head. 'He did nothing wrong. Quite the opposite in fact. He was sweet, protective, an amazing man. And yes, he can be a little hostile at times, but only when he's provoked. I was crazy about him, Charlie.'

She's still crazy about him. Ten years later and her feelings for Dillon haven't diminished in the slightest. 'What am I going to do, Charlie? It's going to completely blow up in my face. I'll lose my job. Lose the biggest opportunity of my career. Lose the apartment.'

'Dramatic much! It might not be that bad.'

She turns and stares at him. 'Not that bad! I'll be spending a few weeks up close and personal with someone I abandoned. Someone I left a damn letter for! I just walked away from him and told him I didn't love him. Oh God!'

'Ouch. A letter? Sorry,' he adds quickly when he sees the look on her face. 'Why did you lie?'

'Lie?'

'Any fool can see you're still totally in love with the man. So, why did you lie to him and say you didn't love him?'

'I told you I'm not going to talk about why.'

He opens his mouth but thinks better of it and shrugs. 'It's your life Ash.'

He pauses then frowns as he spots a photo of Freya on the bedside table. 'Hang on. Ten years. Is he Freya's... Is he her...?'

'No!' she says, cutting him off before he can finish his thought. 'Freya has nothing to do with Dillon.'

Charlie shrugs. 'Fair enough. Maybe this won't be as bad as you think? Maybe he's moved on? He's massively successful with adoring fans all over the world. I think he's doing okay.'

Ash lifts the iPad from her bed and hands it to Charlie. 'According to all this, Dillon isn't doing okay. Far from it. He's got a criminal record, been in prison, is rumoured to have a drink and drug problem, and is sleeping his way through his massive fan base.'

She leaves Charlie to read some of the articles, while she goes back to staring at the ceiling. The Dillon she's read about is a far cry from the man she loved. But then again, she had taken his heart and kicked it as hard as she could. Since she turned her back on him, he seems to have gone from one night stand to one night stand.

He hadn't found one person he was happy with, and that breaks her heart. She lost track of the countless men and women he's been associated with over the last few years. Is it her fault he can't settle?

'Yikes! Busy boy. Did you know he was bisexual when you were with him?'

'Yes. He came out when he was a teenager. I don't think he's had any serious boyfriends though. Don't think he's had anything serious at all for the last few years.'

'Okay. Let's break this down. Forget Dillon and all your history. Is this a good career move?'

'Are you kidding? Broken Chords are huge! I'd be an idiot not to jump at this chance.'

'Excellent! So, there's your answer. Dillon is in your past. Without meaning to sound cruel, you're in his past too. From reading these, he's doing fine, well apart from the prison thing, which we won't mention. Anyway, he's got an incredible career, and he's got many more years of that ahead, if things keep going like they are. And he's fucking gorgeous! Was he really that hot when you were together?'

'He didn't have the piercing in his lip or nose, but yeah. That's how he looked.' *That's my Dillon.* The thought hits her completely out of the blue. But he's not hers anymore.

'Very nice indeed!'

'You're not really helping at all.'

'Oops! Sorry. Forget everything I just said about the fucking gorgeous part. Go there. Wow everyone with your professionalism, then come home. Trust me. He's moved on.'

Ash wishes it could be that easy. Ten years may have passed, but she still knows Dillon. Knows the real man he desperately tries to hide from the rest of the world.

The side of him that's hurting and has been for too many years.

17

She knew that about him when she left. She knew he'd been rejected by people who should have loved him. She knew all that about him, yet she still walked away.

Ash pulls her bag from the top of her wardrobe and dumps it on her bed. He's not going to let her forget that. If she knows one thing about him, she knows that, at the very least, he's going to make things *interesting* for her.

But Charlie is right. It's a career defining job. She'll just have to deal with whatever Dillon throws at her and try to remain professional. She'll leave the tears until she's alone at night.

3

Dillon

The coffee isn't touching his tiredness. Not the first, not the second, or even the third cup. As the elevator carries him up to the top of the building where their label Vox operates from, he swallows more painkillers. Without them he doubts he'll get through the meeting.

The elevator door opens, and he comes to a stop when he spots Jason sitting in a chair in the lobby, reading a paper.

'What are you doing here? I said I'd be grand driving myself.'

'I'm not driving you. I'm driving myself in the same direction you're heading. I'd like to make sure you get everywhere you need to go without being stabbed. You have form.'

'Hey! I was stabbed once.'

'Yeah. On my watch. That won't be happening again.' He lifts a takeout coffee cup from the low table beside him. 'It's your usual.'

The small smirk his bodyguard gives him as he takes the coffee, doesn't improve his mood.

'Have a fun meeting.'

Dillon walks down the corridor to the meeting room and pulls out the chair at the far end of the table, instead of sitting beside Luke. It's not a conscious move, but he sees the look that crosses Luke's face.

Ellen's assistant, Sam, smiles at him as she flicks through a file in front of her. Both Sam and Ellen love their brown files. Files on the band, files on the individual members, files on songs, albums, appearances. He's surprised the place isn't falling down under the number of files they seem to have.

His file would probably be one impressive read. He's not exactly a model client. Between losing his temper a few times, his public and very colourful sex life, and the bout in prison, he's certainly kept their legal team on their toes.

Fuck it! It's not like they don't get a healthy cut of what the band brings in. Broken is massively popular, and fingers crossed, it stays that way for another while at least. He's just turned forty. A few more years in the limelight wouldn't do his bank balance any harm.

He stretches out and tries unsuccessfully to stifle a yawn.

'Late one?' Luke asks.

He shakes his head no. 'Couldn't sleep for some reason.'

'Aw. You all excited about the tour?'

'What can I say Gregg? I just can't wait to be stuck in the back of a bus with you again.'

Ellen smiles at them as she closes the door behind her and takes the seat at the head of the table. 'Well, this is a good start. We're all here on time. Quite amazing!'

She directs her gaze towards Gregg who smirks and shrugs. 'Trying to reform my ways. I guess I just needed the love of a good woman to kick me into shape.'

'Remind me to thank Bria next time I see her. So, I thought I should call you in before the photographer arrives tomorrow. Go through a few bits and bobs with you. Make sure you all know what the plan is.'

'Photographer? What photographer?' Dillon can be a bit hit and miss reading emails from Vox, but he's sure he didn't see anything about a photographer.

Ellen sighs dramatically as she clasps her hands in front of her. 'I knew it was too good to be true. Judging by the look on Luke and Gregg's faces, they read my email. On the other hand, by the look on your face and Tate's, I would say that, as usual, you didn't.'

'What email?' Tate asks, earning a stern glare from Ellen.

'What is it with you two and emails? Gregg and Luke have mastered the technology. Is it really that difficult to click on an icon and spend a few minutes reading and assimilating the information?'

'You send a lot of emails.'

'Yes, Tate. I do. It's my job. To reduce it to a simple sentence you might listen to, there's a photographer coming over from the UK to spend time with you while you tour. She will have access to your rehearsals, promos, interviews, anything you have planned during the month. Bit of a behind the scenes photo spread. We thought it would be interesting to show you from a different angle.'

'I'm still absolutely sure my front angle is the best one.' Tate whacks Gregg on the chest forcing a yelp from the drummer. 'Oi! Watch it. I bruise easily.'

'Oh, you'll bruise all right, you twit!'

'Ah you love me really.'

Dillon laughs as Gregg tries to pull the much bigger Tate into a hug, failing miserably and nearly being decked in the process. 'Get off me! Hang on a sec,' Tate says, turning his attention back to Ellen. 'Did we all agree to this?'

'Yes, Tate. You did.' She opens one of the many files in front of her and passes him a piece of paper. 'Remember that?'

Tate reads the sheet and grimaces. 'Fuck! Yeah. I guess we did all agree. Can I blame it on baby brain?'

'You can try, but considering you've never read any of my emails in a timely fashion before you became a father, I don't think Brandon is a valid excuse.'

'Worth a shot,' Tate mumbles, flopping back in his seat.

Ellen smiles and taps the file in front of her again. 'Anyway, she arrives tomorrow and will pop in while you go through your rehearsal the following day.'

'How much access are we talking about?' Tate asks, looking a little unhappy about the whole situation. Not that Dillon can blame him. It's not something he's overly thrilled about either. In fact, he's as far from thrilled as you can get. Being photographed is part of their life. That's not the bit that's bothering him. It's the amount of access she's being given.

The four of them value their privacy. Always have done. For the most part, the public see only what they want them to see. That'll be harder to keep track of with an interfering photographer hanging around, sticking her camera places they don't want it to go.

'Free access to the rehearsals and tour, but when you say stop, she will leave you alone. I've already made that clear, and I intend to say it again when I meet with her. I don't want any of you to feel like you're under a microscope. That's not what this is about. She will be blocked from any access to you when you need private time. I mean that. You three,' she says, pointing to Luke, Tate, and Gregg, 'will have your calls with your therapists as planned. Nothing changes there, okay?'

Dillon never thought he'd be the only member of the band who isn't seeing a therapist. With all the shit he's dealt with, it was a sure bet he'd end up there first. He must have a better hold on the shit than he thought. Or he's just so used to what's going on in his head he couldn't give a fuck about it anymore.

With Tate, Gregg, and Luke all in regular meetings with sponsors, therapists, or both, they need that extra privacy - for the sake of their health more than anything else.

'Good.' Ellen says, bringing Dillon back from his thoughts. 'So, try to make her feel welcome. That means no glowering or glaring Tate.'

He glares at her, and she smiles sweetly at him. 'Yes, less of that please. And Dillon. Just behave.'

'What exactly do you mean by that?'

'You know full well what I mean.'

'She means keep it in your jeans, mate.'

Dillon flicks Gregg the bird. 'Asshole.'

'Love you too, Dillon.'

Before he can get a word out, Clara wraps her arms around Dillon's neck, squeezing him hard. 'I can't believe you actually came!'

'Of course I did. I said I would.'

He grunts when she slaps him on the chest. 'Where the hell have you been? It's been ages. C'mon in.'

'I don't know. You going to keep hitting me, or is it safe?'

'Stop being a baby. Get inside.'

He squeezes by her, but she stops him and points towards the driveway at Jason sitting in his own car next to the Mustang. 'Is he coming in or staying in the car?'

'He's staying put.'

'Fair enough.'

He follows Clara into the back garden and crouches down to play with her dog, Rocky. The Labrador licks his face and climbs all over him, covering his t-shirt in sandy coloured hair. Clara hands him a juice when he finally extricates himself from the dog and sits on one of the wooden benches. 'So, how's work?'

'Good. I'm heading away for a few weeks on Wednesday.'

She sits opposite him, then pats the seat next to her allowing Rocky up on the bench. 'Oh yes. The big ten-year European tour. I can't believe you lot have been going ten years. That's amazing Dill!'

'You're telling me. It's probably the only thing I've stuck at for longer than a month in my life.'

She smirks as she sips her drink. 'What's so funny?'

'You. I'm just thinking how that sentence could be applied to most situations in your life.'

'Fuck off!'

'Love you too. So, do you need me to look after your houses?'

'I'm not bothered about the one in town. But if you're around to check on the cottage I'd appreciate that.'

'No problem at all.'

He takes a drink, then waves at his brother-in-law, Marcus, when he sticks his head out the back door. 'Hey Dillon! Dinner will be ready in five.'

'Thanks, love,' Clara says, blowing her husband a kiss before he disappears back inside again. 'So, how have you been?' Clara asks when Marcus has gone.

Dillon smirks at his sister as she looks over at him again. 'You're fucking transparent, you know that?'

'What? I'm just asking how you are.'

'No. You're asking how my love life is.'

She smiles at him. 'Fine. Yes. So?'

'Still the same.'

'Yeah. That's what I was afraid of. I love reading about my baby brother's sex life in every magazine I pick up. Makes me feel all warm and fuzzy inside.'

'Yeah, well that's your fault. I've told you and Eva loads of times not to read those things. Whatever you read is your fault.'

'I know, I know, okay. You just seem to be all over the place since you dated Ben. I liked him.'

'Seriously? This again? Yeah, Ben was great, but it wasn't this deep and meaningful relationship. It just kinda fizzled out.'

'You were with him for two months. That's a lifetime for you. How can you say it wasn't deep and meaningful?'

'Because it wasn't, okay? We wanted different things. He was all set for the quiet settled life, and I wasn't ready for that. And it was three fucking years ago!'

'And now?'

'Now what?'

'Are you ready for the quiet life yet?'

'Clara, seriously. Stop stressing about me. I'm fine. I'm happy, okay.'

'You can't blame me for worrying about you. It's my job as your big sister.'

'Have you seen them lately?' As changes of conversation go it's downright lousy, but he can't help himself. He just has to keep picking at the wound his parents left when they disowned him.

Clara nods once. 'Last weekend. I tried again, Dill. I did, but...' she shrugs and sighs loudly. 'Stubborn fools.'

'You don't have to keep trying. They're not going to change their mind about me at this stage. Are they okay?'

'Same as always. I did find something interesting though. Dad has a copy of your latest album.'

'He what?'

Clara nods. 'I found it in his car when I was looking for his sunglasses. It was hidden in the glove box, but it was unsealed. They still love you, Dill. But they're stuck in their ways.' She reaches across and squeezes his hand. 'Stop making that face.'

'What face?'

'That sad face. I hate when you look sad. That's not who you are.' She pulls her bench closer to him. 'In spite of what our stubborn old-fashioned parents did, you've grown into an incredible man, and myself and Eva are so proud of you. You hear me?'

He smiles and squeezes her hand. 'I know.'

'I love you.'

'Love you too.'

She smiles and wipes tears from her eyes. She may hate when hearing about his parents upsets him, but he hates that she cries when she talks about it. Hates what he's done to their family. Hates not knowing what he did to make his parents hate him so much.

'Okay. What's wrong? I mean apart from Mum and Dad. You're not yourself. You seem a little subdued.'

'I don't know. I...' he sighs and slumps back on the bench. 'I guess I'm a little lost. I mean the guys all seem to know what they're doing. They all have plans for the future or are at least getting things in place. I'm just wandering.'

'In what way?'

'Well take Tate for example. You know what he was like, Clara. I didn't think he'd settle down, ever. Now he's found Chloe, he's married, and he's a father.'

'Bit different to the Tate from a few years back, I agree. But that's a good thing, right? He nearly killed himself Dillon.'

'I know, and I'm not begrudging him, believe me. He deserves to be happy. Gregg and Bria are all gooey eyed with each other. And my best mate is happier than I've seen him... well ever.'

'So what? You're not going to start measuring yourself against what others are doing, are you? Cause that's not what my brother does. If he did, he'd still be living a lie, pretending to be someone he's not.

'Don't let what the guys are doing put pressure on you to try and do the same. It's not like any of them were expecting to find a partner when they did. It just happened. It will for you too.

'Though I will say, that sleeping your way through half of Ireland, probably isn't the best way to find someone you can build a future with, but it's your life. Do what's right for you. Not because you feel like you have to be with someone, just because your friends are.'

26

Dillon curses and shakes his head. 'Fuck! I don't do this. What the hell is wrong with me?'

'Nothing. Your friends are settling down. It's bound to make you think. Listen, I'm a firm believer in the whole *meant to be* thing. The right person is out there for you Dill. He or she, is just waiting for you to find them. And you will. When the time is right. Until then, stop stressing about it, and enjoy being an international superstar.'

He grins at her. 'You're right.'

'I always am.' She pauses, pursing her lips as she looks around her garden.

'What?'

'Are you still coming to my birthday drinks?'

He'd give anything and everything not to go. Fuck, he'd even thought about asking Ellen to invent something he had to go to. But that would be bailing on Clara, and he's not going to do that. 'Sure.'

'Wow! That was enthusiastic.'

'I'm sorry. You know me and family events. I'm all for getting attention, but not at family events.'

'I know, but Mum and Dad won't be coming until later. I promise. You come first. Stay for an hour max, then make a run for it before they arrive. It won't be so bad. I've invited a few of the cousins, but just be the aloof, standoffish celebrity with them. It's your thing.'

He laughs, not feeling in the slightest bit reassured. When his parents disowned him, the rest of the family had kept to themselves. Aunts, uncles, cousins - they all buried their heads, leaving him alone. Fuck the lot of them, but it's Clara. He can never say no to her. 'You want an aloof celebrity, you got one.'

Ash

She stands outside the door and closes her eyes, taking a few deep breaths to calm her stomach. She's going to throw up. No question. Her first major, worthwhile assignment and she's going to hit it off by throwing up. Fantastic start.

He's in there.

Behind the unassuming wooden door is the man she adored. The man she wanted to marry. The man she left. Does he know she's here? Maybe Ellen hadn't told them her name? Not that he'd recognise it. She'd taken her grandmother's maiden name Hughes when she left. She doubts she'd ever mentioned that surname to him, and even if she did, he wouldn't have looked for Ash Hughes.

This is ridiculous. She has to go in. Charlie is probably right anyway. He's a megastar. Why would he still be hung up on someone he dated for a few months, years ago?

She takes another deep breath and pushes the door open. The venue is monstrous. A surge of pride hits her. Dillon is playing venues like this. Not only that, but the band also sell out venues like this. She lingers at the side door, searching the faces setting up on the vast stage.

Then she sees him.

He's sitting at the edge of the stage playing a guitar. Ash grips the side of the raised seating area beside her and watches him for a few minutes. She'd seen so many pictures of him over the years. It was hard to avoid seeing him. But seeing him in person is so different.

The few changes to his appearance in the last few years, have done nothing to detract from the stunning man he is. His light brown hair is shaved tight to his head at the sides, the top bit swept back from his face and the black ring piercing his lip is drawing attention to his mouth, which isn't helping her in the slightest. He looks bigger too. Even from this distance she can see the thick muscles in his arms shift as he plays.

He's incredible.

'Can I help you?'

She jumps as a deep voice startles her. She spins around and comes face to face with Tate. Or more specifically, face to chest with Tate. She knew the lead singer was tall, but he's seriously tall. She takes a step back so she can look at his face. His dark blue eyes narrow as he stares down at her. Seriously tall, seriously attractive, and seriously intimidating. 'Hi.'

He frowns but doesn't say anything.

'I'm Ash.'

'Right.'

'I'm a photographer. Ellen arranged for me to—'

'Right,' he mutters again, interrupting her. 'She said something about that. What are you doing lurking around back here?'

'I just arrived. I didn't want to interrupt.'

Tate steps out from the passageway and stops a few feet from her. 'Sam!'

Ash jumps as his shout echoes through the space. A woman with dark hair tied in a ponytail appears from the back of the stage and climbs down, hurrying over to him. Tate points to Ash. 'The photographer. I'll leave her with you.' Tate glances over at Ash, before he joins the rest of the band at the stage.

Sam smiles at Ash and holds out her hand. 'So pleased to meet you. I'm Sam. I look after the band with Ellen.'

'Ash. Great to meet you.'

'Apologies about Tate. He can be a little gruff. He's a big teddy bear really, once you get to know him.'

'I'll take your word for that.'

Sam laughs and shuffles the clipboard she's carrying to the bottom of her pile. 'Yeah. It's well hidden.' She finds the paper she was looking for and reads through some information. 'Okay, so Ellen met you yesterday and gave you the run through of what you can, and can't photograph?'

'Yes. She went through everything. I understand the need for privacy in certain situations. I'm not here to irritate any of them. I promise.'

'That's good. I work closely with Ellen, so I know the guys fairly well. They can act like a bunch of children at times, but they're professionals. You shouldn't have any trouble with them not cooperating... or at least I hope you won't. If you do, I'll be travelling with you. Just let me know and I'll sort them out. Do you have any idea what you're hoping to do?'

'I was planning to go for a more natural theme if possible. No posed photos. Maybe just take pictures while they're doing their thing. A lot of the photographs I've seen of them tend to be posed. Usually dark and moody. I thought a different angle could be refreshing.'

Sam smiles widely and nods. 'I like that. They will too. They're well used to being photographed, but there's only so much posing they'll tolerate before they get grumpy. Like I said - bunch of kids. That's probably why photographers veer towards the dark vibe. It's easier than getting them to smile. So, I probably should introduce you to them. You ready?'

Ash smiles and nods, although she'd much prefer to bid Sam a fond farewell and make her escape before he sees her. Instead, she allows Sam to lead her over to the stage. Each footstep only adds more weight to the rock in her gut. She can do this. She's a professional.

Not that it means a thing right now. In that moment, she's a decade younger, eyeing up the stunning man from across the room.

When she first met him, she'd wanted to speak to him for a good hour, before he finally took the decision out of her hands and introduced himself. He wasn't famous back then. Broken Chords existed, but they hadn't yet found the epic fame they so rightly deserved.

But that didn't matter. This tall, gorgeous, slightly cocky man had ignored all the other women in the restaurant with her and talked to only her. When the night ended with him kissing her then asking her out, it had been incredible.

Now it's her turn to approach him. If only the circumstances were anywhere near the same. Suddenly she's standing in front of the stage with Sam next to her. Ash barely hears Sam call the guys. Her own heart is pounding so loudly it drowns out everything else. Keeping her eyes straight ahead, Ash says hello to Tate, Luke, and Gregg as they walk over to the edge of the stage.

Beside them, Dillon is still playing his guitar. She can't look directly at him. Can't bring herself to meet his eyes. Sam makes the introductions and Tate nods, while Luke and Gregg say hello to her.

Dillon, however, doesn't say anything. He doesn't need to. Without turning her head, she knows he's looking at her. Or more specifically, glaring at her. She can feel the weight of his gaze.

Ash finally turns her head to look at him. Yeah, he recognises her. His clear green eyes have targeted her, and it doesn't take a genius to figure out he's less than happy. He's downright furious, but also confused.

Luke slaps Dillon on the shoulder and points to the stage. 'You going to sit there all day? C'mon.'

'Yeah. Right.' Dillon climbs to his feet and walks away from her. No comment. No hey. Nothing. Ash wipes her clammy palms on her jeans and swallows. She's not sure if that went better or worse than she thought it would. He didn't shout at her, so that's something. She was expecting something more though.

Sam walks over to a table against the stage and passes her a bottle of water. 'There are other refreshments on the table. Help yourself. They're going to run through the show in a bit. Make sure the guys and the crew know what's what, before we do the live shows. Have you seen them perform before? Ash?'

'Sorry. No. No I haven't. I've heard they're amazing.'

Sam nods enthusiastically. 'You're in for a treat.' She hands her a plastic folder. 'This has my contact number in it. Also numbers for Liam, Andy, Jason, and Ciaran.'

She points to the rather large men drinking coffee at the front of the stage. 'They're the band's security team. We don't let the guys out alone after what happened to Tate and Gregg. Nasty business. They'll be assigned to you while you're travelling with us. There's also a pass and schedule in there. Do not lose the pass. It'll give you access to everywhere we go. Without it you're stuck out with the rest of the fans.'

'I understand. Thank you.'

'You'll be travelling with the band on the tour bus. There's a party tomorrow night in a local club before they head off. I've included the details for you in your information. You've been put on the guest list for that too.'

'Thank you. I really appreciate all of this.'

Sam smiles again and shrugs. 'Of course. Well, I'll let you get on with it. I'm sure you want to get started.'

'Of course. Thanks Sam.'

She disappears onto the stage with her clipboard, leaving Ash alone at the front of the massive venue, not sure what the hell she's doing. Why did she think this was a good idea? What possessed her?

Accepting the assignment had nothing to do with her career. Not deep down. It was about torturing herself by bringing Dillon back into her life for the next month. Self-sabotage at the highest level.

But on some slightly off-kilter level, she doesn't regret it. Seeing him again for even a moment is worth it. Ash lowers her camera bag onto one of the chairs and risks a quick look at the stage again.

She'd seen so many pictures of him over the years. As much as she tried not to look, he was everywhere. But nothing had prepared her for seeing him in the flesh. He's a stunning man, always has been. The years had only served to refine what she had found attractive about him in the first place.

She's still in love with him but, because of what she did, he hates her.

Dillon is glaring over at her. In fact, he's giving her such a cold look it actually gives her chills. Ash swallows thickly and bites the inside of her cheek to keep the tears at bay. This can't be about her feelings for Dillon. She needs to make it about work - full stop.

Ash picks up her camera and walks around the venue as the band gets ready to begin. She takes a few shots from the end of the room, while they talk to members of the stage crew, or each other. The last thing she wants to do is launch into full face shots so soon. Especially with Dillon.

This isn't about him. It's about the four band members. She needs to see him as a member of Broken Chords and not Dillon. *Her Dillon.*

Like that's helpful in the slightest.

But it's hard to forget about him when he's looking at her from the stage. Thankfully they begin their rehearsals and, once engrossed in what they're doing, she feels a little of the pressure on her ease.

Sam was right. It's only a rehearsal, but hearing Tate sing in person is incredible. His voice is spectacular, but again, it's their bassist who captures her attention. Watching Dillon play, sends shivers through her. When he sings with the others, she can easily recognise his voice from the rest of the band.

He used to sing to her when they were together. She'd fall asleep in his arms, while he ran his fingers through her hair and sang to her.

Ash lowers her camera and wipes her eyes. This is the worst start to her assignment ever. If she can't even be in the same room as him without crying, she's in for a fun-filled four weeks.

5

Dillon

He's far beyond wasted, but he really couldn't give a fuck. He needs something to silence his brain and the whiskey is doing a fine job.

He glares at the empty glass on the table, before nodding at the bar tender to order a refill.

Ashling!

Of all the fucking people on the planet, why did it have to be her? Ten years of nothing, ten years of wondering why she left him, then she just saunters back into his life like nothing happened. Like she hadn't killed a part of him when she left him like she did. She toyed with his feelings, made him fall in love with her, then upped and left.

She was his entire world for those few short months they were together. They had a future - or so he thought. They were planning a life, but then one day she was gone. He still has the letter she left for him, telling him she didn't love him and didn't see a future for them.

He pulls the chain out from under his shirt, watching as the ring twirls in front of him. The diamond on the ring isn't huge, but it was the best he could afford at the time. She'd screamed when he proposed to her. Then she cried as she hugged him, saying yes close to half a dozen times as she hung on to him. She seemed to want it as much as he did.

At the time.

Which only means one fucking thing.

She'd been lying to him the whole time. He doesn't know or care why. Not anymore. He's lost too many hours wondering what he did wrong. Why she left him like she did. But no answers ever came to him. It didn't matter how long he brooded over it. How long he thought about every minute of their time together, he still couldn't figure it out.

Whatever the reason, she didn't think it was worth talking to him about it. It was obviously easier to walk away, than fix whatever was wrong.

He shoves the chain back under his shirt. She fucked him over in the worst possible way, and he can never forgive her for that. He can't even imagine two minutes alone in a room with her, let alone a month.

How the hell is he supposed to give his best on stage when he's getting off his head to try to deal with being near her again? She's fucking with his career now, and he doesn't appreciate that.

His personal life is one thing. His career is a whole other matter.

Why did she even take the job? Did she hate him so much that she didn't care how he'd feel about her showing up again? Maybe. It'll certainly add an edge to her story to document watching him falling apart.

He'll just have to ignore her. Completely blank her. Pretend she isn't there. But she will be. She'll be there with her fucking camera taking pictures of them. Always there, watching him. Looking fucking stunning. That shouldn't have been the first thing he noticed, but it was.

God, she is gorgeous. Her short blonde spikes are a little longer than she wore them when they were a couple, she's removed some of her earrings, and her make-up is tamer, but she's still out of this world. He's still attracted to her. She still manages to draw him to her like no other woman has been able to do either before, or since, he met her.

He's still deeply in love with her. He still hates her. Talk about a love/hate relationship. He desperately wants to see her again but can't bear to lay eyes on her. He's in his own fucked up hell.

He glances up as someone sits beside him and slides a glass of water across the table. He doesn't bother looking at Luke, just pushes the glass back towards him and reaches for the whiskey instead. 'How did you find me?'

Luke points to the far end of the bar to Jason, his fucking newspaper still in his hand, as he talks to Luke's security, Andy. 'He called me. It's what happens. You get drunk and refuse to move leaving Jace with two options. One, he drags you out kicking and screaming or two, he calls me. So, how much did you pay the owner to shut it, so you could drink yourself silly alone?'

'A few thousand. Can't remember. At least I'm not drinking myself silly with loads of people around. The integrity of the band is safe.'

'I'm not worried about the integrity of the band. I'm worried about you. What's wrong Dillon?'

Dillon leans back in the corner booth and turns the whiskey glass in his hand. He knew he should have stayed home and drank himself into a coma there. He should have locked himself away in private and kept the rest of the band out of his business. 'Nothing. I'm grand. Can't you tell? Living the dream.'

Luke drapes his arm across the back of the chair and examines him across the table. He doesn't say anything which irritates the fuck out of Dillon. This new confident Luke is taking some time to get used to.

The once crushed man is now sure of himself. He's stronger, standing up for himself more than he did. Fair enough, he still has a way to go before he's over the years of physical, emotional, and sexual abuse he suffered at the hands of his bitch of a wife, but he's getting there.

The problem with all that is, that he's not so easily brushed off anymore. Luke's not taking any more of his shit.

Dillon licks his lip ring as he examines Luke over the rim of his glass. He's looking healthier too. The dark rings have disappeared from under his eyes, he's not pale or sickly looking any longer. Not living in constant fear of being beaten has made a massive difference to the guy. He looks downright gorgeous. Helpful thought he kicks aside as soon as it comes to him.

'I'm allowed to have a few drinks. Get off my fucking case!' He's not really pissed off at Luke. He's just an easy target because he's in front of him.

'Who is she Dillon?'

'Who's who?'

'Stop being awkward. You know who I mean. The photographer. From the second you were introduced, you've been throwing daggers at her. You're seriously pissed off and I want to know why.' He tries to lift the glass again, but Luke pushes his arm back to the table. 'I think you've had enough.'

Dillon pulls his arm away from Luke, spilling some of the whiskey on the table. 'I think you need to fuck off, Luke! I'm a big boy. I know when I've had enough.'

'No Dillon, you don't. That's the problem. You never know when you've had enough.'

'Oh seriously, Luke? Get off my fucking case! Or better yet, just go away.'

He should know better than to try to push Luke away. It never works and that's probably a good thing. Thanks to Luke refusing to leave him, he's saved him from too many embarrassing nights.

'Who is she, Dillon?'

Dillon finishes his drink, then shoves the glass across the table. 'What the hell is this, huh? You've finally got your life sorted, so now you decide to stick your nose in mine? You're the last person who should be giving relationship advice, so I'd appreciate if you keep your opinions to yourself.'

Even in his drunken state, Dillon knows he's gone too far. Luke's face goes blank, and he plays with the piercing under his lip as he stares at the table.

'Fuck! Sorry. I didn't mean that the way it sounded.'

'It's okay.'

'No, Luke. It's not.' He scrubs a hand over his face and glares up at the ceiling. 'Fuck! That was beyond low.'

'It's fine, Dillon. Really. But you're right. I am happy now, so I do know you're far from it.'

Dillon still can't believe he said what he did. His friend barely survived what Pippa did to him. But Luke stood up to her and still needs support, not a dig. He didn't deserve that. 'You're right. I should call it a night.'

'My car is outside. I'll give you a lift.'

Dillon allows Luke to help him outside, but swats the bodyguards away when they try to help. Luke manhandles him into the passenger seat of his Range Rover, then takes a few steps away from the car to speak to Jace and Andy.

Three guesses what the topic of conversation is.

While Luke gets into the driver's seat, Dillon watches the bodyguards climb into Jason's car. Looks like they'll be going in convoy.

Luke pulls out of the car park and heads towards Dillon's Dublin apartment with Jace keeping to their tail. He'd prefer to go to the cottage in Wicklow, but that's a half hour drive versus five minutes. He's already insulted his mate. He's not going to push his luck.

'We having a party at my place?'

Luke glances at him before focusing on the road again. 'They're just making sure we get back to your apartment okay. I've told them I can take it from there. I've had enough practice.'

Something about the way Luke says that last sentence hits him. He's right. Over the years he's called on Luke so many times to bring him home, when he's been too drunk to do it himself.

'When did I become such an arse hole?'

Luke smiles as he pulls up at a red light. 'You've always been an arse hole.'

'Fuck you! I am sorry for what I said.'

'I know. Forget it. So, you going to tell me what's going on? I'm just going to keep asking, so you might as well stop fighting.'

Dillon rests his forehead against the passenger window and closes his eyes. 'Maybe later. I'm tired.'

Thankfully Luke takes the hint and doesn't ask any more questions. Luke parks in the underground car park, then half drags, half carries Dillon over to the lift. Dillon stares at the buttons, unsure which floor his apartment is on, which is fucking ridiculous.

Thankfully, Luke is on the case again, as always. He's lost count of the number of nights they've gone through this routine. Dillon would get drunk, or high, or both. He'd either find someone to go home with, or bring them back to his place. Otherwise, Luke would do the honours and drag his sorry ass home.

Dillon struggles to get his key out of his pocket, so Luke helps him out again and deals with the front door. He brings him into the bedroom and Dillon flops back on the unmade bed. He tries to kick off his boots, but doesn't get anywhere, laughing to himself when he realises he needs to unlace them first. For some reason that fact seems a lot funnier than it actually is.

Luke reappears and places a glass of water on his bedside table. 'You going to be okay?'

'Yep. Absolutely peachy, mate. Top of the fucking world.'

Luke just shakes his head and closes the blinds. 'I'll stay on the couch tonight.'

'What about the delightful Maeve? Won't she be wondering where you are?'

'I sent her a text. You want anything else?'

Dillon pats the bed beside him. 'You can sleep here. I'm not planning on puking, or making a pass at you.'

'Nice imagery. Thanks, Dillon.'

He shuffles aside, grateful when Luke sits on the edge of the bed, instead of staying on the couch. He doesn't want to be alone tonight. Sleeping with Luke is no doubt another bad idea, but why not add another one to the list.

Luke deals with his own boots, then leans over to take off Dillon's, before he lies back beside him. Luke pulls the duvet over them and turns on his side to face him. 'Who is she, Dillon?'

'Remember when I was living in the UK, just before we got signed?' He wasn't planning on telling him, but he wants Luke to know. He needs someone to know. Or maybe he just needs to get the words out for the first time ever. He's never told anyone about what happened between himself and Ash. It's a pain he's kept to himself for the last decade.

But it's not something he can keep to himself much longer. She's back and, like it or not, she's going to be around for the next few weeks. The guys will know something's up after a few days. Hell, they probably already guessed something is wrong.

'When you were working as a chef?'

Dillon nods but keeps his focus on the ceiling. 'I was seeing someone. Had been for a few months.' He laughs and runs a hand over his hair. 'I was in love with her, Luke. I'd never felt like that before about anyone.' Not until he fell for Luke, but he keeps that comment to himself.

'Anyway, just after we were signed, we had to go away for a week. Seems she got bored waiting for me. I came home to a *Dear John* letter. She didn't love me anymore and didn't want me to contact her again. Not that I could. She'd vanished.'

'Oh God. Ash? The photographer is the woman you were seeing back then?'

'Yeah. That's her. She left me.'

'Why didn't you tell us what happened?'

'I didn't want to talk about it. It hurt too much. Anyway, our old manager, Louis, reckoned she left because of my sexuality. That she couldn't deal with what I was.'

'He said that to you?'

Dillon nods. 'He probably had a point. Not about my sexuality so much. More about me as a person. I mean, I know I'm no prize at the best of times, but I really fucking loved her, Luke. I would have done anything for her if she'd given me the chance.'

He rolls over to face Luke. 'You know the way you look at Maeve? Like she's the only one on the planet with you? No one else exists. I've seen you do it loads of times. You could be in a room with dozens of other people, but then you see her, and you smile. Your whole face lights up. You can see how much you love her in that one look.'

Luke nods. 'Yeah. I know what you mean. You felt that way about Ash?'

'Didn't make a difference. It wasn't enough. I wasn't enough.' Now he's getting all *woe is me*, a clear sign he's had too much to drink. 'Fuck her! I'm just glad I found out before we got married.'

'Hang on. Married?'

'I proposed to her before I went away. She'd said yes. I was going to tell you guys when we got back the following week. We were going to announce it to everyone. But she obviously changed her mind. She was gone when I got back. All she left was that letter, and the engagement ring I'd given her the week before.

'That was the last I saw of her, until Sam introduced her to us at rehearsals.' He scrubs his hands over his face. 'Fuck, Luke. It's messed me up. I don't know how to be near her without losing my shit.'

'Of course it's thrown you, Dillon. But getting drunk won't help you deal with this.'

'Oh yeah. So what will?'

'I don't know. Maybe talk to her? We're going away in a few days. You can't tour while you're like this. Have it out with her, then do what you do best.'

'Fuck up you mean?'

Luke shakes his head. 'Stop it! I mean, get on stage, and give the fans one hell of a show. Why are you beating yourself up like this?'

Dillon rolls over, putting his back to Luke. 'I'm tired. Goodnight.'

He hears Luke sigh, but he doesn't push him to talk. Dillon stares at his wardrobe door listening to Luke breathing.

He shouldn't have asked Luke to stay. The entire situation between them is still too raw for him. Luke was never his to begin with. He belongs with Maeve.

They began Broken with him being the only one in a relationship. The only one settled and truly happy with his life.

Now the tables have flipped and he's the only one still scrambling to find something to make him happy. Tate and Chloe have Brandon and are married. Gregg and Bria are living together, and Luke has Maeve. He's got whiskey and whatever painkillers he can get his hands on. It's like he's a shadow. He's here, but also not. He can't explain it, but he's drifting from day to day without any plan or purpose.

What's worrying him the most is what he sees in his future if he keeps going this way, and it's not the happy ending he desperately wants.

6

Dillon

He has absolutely no interest in getting out of the car and going into the house. He'd rather have a fucking root canal done instead, if it meant he didn't have to get out of the car.

Dillon looks in his rearview mirror at Jace's car parked a little further down the road. Jace knows some of the Ryan family history. Not all the details, but enough to convince him to stay in the car and let Dillon do this alone.

It's going to be weird enough having to be in the same room as his relatives without dragging his bodyguard around with him.

Dillon peers out the window of his Mustang at the unassuming house. There's nothing scary about it in the slightest. Clara and Marcus both have good jobs, so it's a decent sized home. It's what's going on inside right now, that has him leaving his engine running.

He's still in two minds about going inside at all. But he promised Clara he'd make an appearance at her birthday party. He can be an ass at the best of times, but he's not going to let her down... as much as he wants to in this situation.

'Fuck!'

Dillon jumps when the passenger door opens, and his sister Eva slides in beside him. Shows how far in his head he was. He hadn't even noticed her pull up behind him in the X5 he bought her last year for her birthday.

Over the years he's lost track of how much he's spent on cars for both of them, but it's the least he could do for the two most important people in his life.

She gives him a crushing hug, before finally releasing him so he can breathe again. 'You wouldn't be hiding out here, would you?'

Dillon smiles, but he knows it falls short. 'I'm not sure this is such a great idea. Is Leon inside with the kids?'

She nods. 'They are indeed. I'm impressed that you remember his name it's been that long since you've seen my husband.'

That's one way to give him a kick. She's right, but he doesn't need reminding about it. He's not intentionally staying away from her, her husband, and their kids. He should make more time for them, but it's difficult. 'I know. I get it okay. Sorry, it's been hectic lately.'

She pushes him on the shoulder. 'Relax! I wasn't having a go. Okay, so I wasn't having a serious go. I can't help it if I miss you. Now, are you going to sit in the car all day, or are you coming in?' She reaches over and takes his hand in hers when he doesn't immediately leap from the car. 'It's been over twenty years, Dill. Maybe it's time to—'

'Don't say bury the hatchet. Wouldn't put it past Mum. Then again, there would be a fuck load of witnesses. Might put her off.'

Eva punches him playfully in the shoulder again. 'Stop being dramatic. Clara told them to hold off coming until later. They're not even in there. It's just other random family members, and I'm sure

45

you're more than capable of ignoring them. Come on, Dill. It's Clara's birthday. She's not going to turn fifty-five again. Pretty please! Just come inside and sit down. Or even stand if you'd prefer. You don't have to say anything. Just be there for Clara.'

Dillon looks back at the house, still not in the slightest bit interested in doing anything except flooring it and getting as far from the place as possible.

'I'll mind you.'

He hits his head against the headrest and sighs. 'Fuck.'

'That's the spirit!' Eva gets out and walks around the car, opening the driver's door. Dillon turns off the engine and slowly gets out. He adjusts his top, second guessing his choice of outfit. He hadn't made much of an effort. He should have dressed a little less like a degenerate rock star.

His ripped black jeans are tucked into combat boots. The t-shirt is probably too tight for his uptight family and shows a fair bit of his chest. Might be best to leave his leather jacket on and zipped up.

Eva takes his hand and has to pretty much drag him up the driveway. Clara smiles widely at them when she opens the door, then pulls him into a tight hug. 'So glad you came.'

'Didn't want you on my back if I ditched it.'

Clara drags him and Eva into the downstairs bathroom, ignoring their protests. She locks the door behind her and leans back on the sink.

'What the fuck, Clara?'

'Mum and Dad are here.'

Eva drops down onto the toilet lid and Dillon curses. Well, isn't this just fucking perfect!

'I thought you told them to come later?' Eva says, while he's still getting his brain in sync.

'I did! They came with Uncle Reggie. I could hardly tell them to go away and come back later, could I?'

46

'It's fine,' he says, finally back in control of his voice. 'I'll go.'

'No! Please stay. I know Dad would want to see you. He misses you so much.'

'Then maybe he should have stepped in when Mum called me *disgusting*, then disowned me.'

'I know. Okay, so this is far from ideal, but will you please stay? Just for a few minutes. It's my birthday, Dill. I would never have intentionally put you three in the same room, but now you're all here, I'd love to have even a few minutes with my whole family together again. Please!'

There goes his escape plan.

Fuck! Why is he even contemplating this? He hasn't seen his parents since he was seventeen. That's twenty-three long years with no contact.

'You don't have to do this.'

He looks over at Clara, knowing full well he's going to stay. Clara, Eva, and the guys are all he has left. His only family. But more than that, he feels guilty. He's put his sisters through so much over the years. Fucking guilt is going to have him agreeing to whatever Clara wants, even though all he wants is to get back in his car and do a runner.

'I'll give it a few minutes, okay?' He forces the words out, each one twisting at his gut. If he gets through this without throwing up, he'll be shocked.

She nods, then hugs him. 'This means the world to me. Thank you.'

'Yeah well, just don't leave me alone with them.'

'I promise I won't.'

She opens the door and walks into the sitting room followed by Eva. At least it's not just the family. There must be a few dozen people in the house. All of Clara's friends will help dilute the tension a bit.

Or so he thinks, until every single person in the room goes on mute and turns to look at him.

Fucking perfect!

Hopefully, the reaction is down to the fact he's a celebrity, and not because he's the disowned, bisexual, black sheep of the family. It's probably a little of both. Usually, he couldn't give a fuck what people think about him - well, in public at least. But this is his family. For some reason it hits a little harder. Hurts more.

Clara turns up the music, masking the awkward silence a little, then introduces him to a few of her friends. He nods politely, taking the compliments with less enthusiasm than usual. They're getting a toned-down version of him today. The version that hides in the corner trying not to be noticed. Far cry from the person he is most of the time.

Marcus hands him a coke, which he sips as he makes his way to the back of the room, near the patio doors. If he has to, he can make his escape out the side gate. Fuck it, he'll just climb over the damn wall if he needs to. Just one wall between this hell and his car.

Then he spots them. His parents.

They're in the garden, talking to some relatives of his he vaguely recognises. He's lost track of his extended family over the years. Not one of them had reached out to him when he was younger. Fuck them all!

His parents look the same. Few more grey hairs. A few more lines on their faces. They're laughing, something he's not used to seeing. They didn't do that much around him while he still lived with them.

He should have left as soon as he found out they were here. If he had any plans of ever meeting with them again, it wouldn't be at Clara's party with loads of spectators. Fuck that, he wouldn't have planned it at all. He'd survived so far without them in his life. Now isn't the time to attempt this grand reunion.

Dillon swallows back the bile and checks his watch.

'Planning to run?'

He jumps as Clara nudges him in the side. 'Fuck! Don't sneak up on me like that. You scared the shit out of me.'

'Sorry. How are you holding up?'

'I'm fine,' he lies. 'Stop worrying about me and enjoy your birthday. Oh, before I forget.' He reaches into his back pocket and pulls out a card. 'Happy birthday.'

She hugs him and kisses him on the cheek. 'Thanks, Dill. Glad to see you kept it simple this year. I don't need another car.'

'You can never have enough cars, believe me.'

'Not everyone collects them like you do. Which is a complete waste of money. You only ever drive the Mustang and your bike.'

'The others are contingency cars. Just in case.'

She laughs and shakes her head as she opens the envelope. Clara pulls out the card and reads what he wrote. 'Love you. That's it? Not even a happy birthday message.'

'Open the fucking piece of paper and stop whinging.'

She frowns at him as she takes the paper from inside the card and unfolds it. He watches her expression as she reads what's on it. Clara slowly lifts her head to look at him. 'Are you fucking kidding me!'

'You give out to me for cursing.'

She waves the page in his face. 'Two fucking weeks in Antigua! All expenses paid. Seriously!'

He shrugs. 'I thought you and Marcus could do with time away together. And you banned me from getting you another car, so I didn't have a lot of options.'

She wipes the tears from her face, then hugs him tight. 'You are the best, you know that. I've always wanted to go there.'

'I know. I do listen... sometimes at least. I haven't booked any specific dates, but when you decide when you want to head off, just let me know and I'll sort it out.'

'Thank you, Dill. Really! I don't know what to say.'

'I'm just glad you like it.'

She folds the piece of paper and slides it back into the card. 'I love it, Dill. You don't have to go so mad with myself and Eva. We'll still like you even if you don't spoil us rotten.'

He laughs. 'Just shut up and take it. It's got nothing to do with the fact I need all the help I can get with keeping people on side.'

'Thank you. Really. I love it. Speaking of keeping people on side, do you want to say hi?'

'No. Not in the slightest.'

Clara's face drops and he instantly feels like a dick. 'You never know. This could be what you all need. The kick to get our family back on track.'

It's going to be a kick all right. A kick to his gut. He has no more interest in being within spitting distance of his parents, let alone talking to them. But he's never been able to say no to Clara.

Seeing the resignation on his face, she takes his hand and leads him outside. With each step towards his parents, his throat tightens, the invisible vice like a collar pulled too tight, choking him. He's forty years old. He can do this. He's not a scared little kid anymore.

His dad smiles at him as he approaches, but Dillon isn't fooled for a second. It'll take more than a smile to put all the shit behind them. Then his mother looks at him, and he's instantly transformed into the scared little kid again. His father might be on board with this fucking painful meeting, but his mother isn't.

'Dillon! I'm so glad you're here. You look well.'

He nods at his father, but his attention is on his mother and the clear undisguised disgust on her face.

'Doesn't he look well, Valerie?'

Nothing. Well, nothing except for the daggers being hurled in his direction.

'Mum, please,' Clara says. 'Can you at least be civil? It's my birthday. Please!'

His mother takes a few minutes to examine every inch of him. Take in every piercing. How he's dressed. Dillon feels like he's being dissected. He drops his gaze, unable to take the way she's looking at him. He's strong, confident, not afraid to face up to anyone. But in front of her, he's an insecure kid and he hates it. His mother terrifies him, takes all that confidence - fake or otherwise - and stamps it into the ground.

He wipes his clammy hands on his jeans as she slowly picks him apart with her eyes. The silence continues, so he lifts his eyes from the ground.

As soon as he looks her in the eyes, she shakes her head. 'I'm sorry. I can't do this.'

Twenty three years and that's the best she can do.

'Mum please...'

'I can't, Clara,' she hisses, as if he can't hear what she's saying. 'I've tried, but this is impossible. I can't even look at him.'

'Mum. Don't talk about him like that!'

'I have tried this, for your sake, Clara. I tried every single day for seventeen years. How can you ask me to accept him? From the moment he was conceived he's been a blot on this family. Everything about him is wrong. I won't accept him.'

With those words, Dillon is seventeen again, sitting at the table facing his parents when he came out. The hurt, the shame, the utter loneliness. It all hits him again, leaving him frozen to the spot, staring at a patch of grass while his family argue about him yet again. It was the story of his fucking life for too long. He thought he was past it.

But that's never going to happen. As much as he wants to tell himself he's over it, he never will be.

He doesn't take in what's being said, but he knows Clara and Eva are defending him, as they always do. He's got to give it to his sisters. They take protective to the next level. Always have when it comes to him - especially Clara. But they're wasting their time. His mother hates him and that will never change.

Moving on autopilot, Dillon turns and walks back into the house.

He pushes past family and friends of Clara, ignoring the pity on their faces. He makes it as far as his car before Clara catches up with him. 'Dillon! Please, stop! I'm so sorry—'

He shrugs away from her touch, instantly regretting it. 'I'm sorry. This isn't on you. I'm going to head. I don't want all this crap ruining your party.'

'Okay, just give me a sec. I'll grab my bag and come with you.'

'Don't Clara. I'm grand, okay? I knew that would happen. It's not a surprise and it's not getting to me.' It's getting to him more than he thought it would. He needs to get out of here and beat the crap out of something. 'Stay and enjoy your birthday.'

'I can't if you're not there. I love you, Dillon. So much. I want you here.'

'I love you too. You know that, but I can't... it's too hard, Clara.' He wipes his face, so angry to feel tears on his cheek. 'I can't let them bring me down again. I can't afford to feel like this again.'

She hugs him. 'I know. And I'm so sorry for all of this. I shouldn't have forced you to talk to them. I just thought... I don't know. I hoped it would be different.'

He smiles, but it's for her benefit. All he wants to do is scream. 'Hey, I'm a big boy. I'll be fine. I'm not heading off with the band until the day after tomorrow. How about I treat you to lunch tomorrow?'

She looks back at the house, shaking her head. 'This isn't right.'

Dillon pulls her into another hug. 'It's how it is. Go and enjoy your party. I'll ring you later and I'll pull some strings. Get you a table wherever you want.'

'I'm worried about you.'

'I'm fine, Clara. I'm not going to do anything stupid. I promise. I'm just going home.'

'I'm holding you to that.'

He gets into his car, then drives away as fast as legally possible before she can say anything else to him, with Jace following closely behind. He's on the edge and the last thing he wants is for her, or any of his fucked-up family, to see him fall apart.

He drives back to his seaside cottage on autopilot. Seems like that's his default mode lately. Get up. Pretend to be okay. Go to bed. Then repeat again. And again. And again.

He can't remember the last time he genuinely smiled. Can't remember the last time he had a reason to smile. Or to be happy, full stop. It's all fake. Fake smiles. Fake laughing. Fake living.

He's a fake.

After parking his Mustang in the garage, he waves towards Jace, dismissing him. He doesn't need an audience. No fucking way. Once he's safely inside his house he walks straight to the gym.

Dillon takes off his jacket, dumping it on the ground, then attacks the boxing bag hanging from the ceiling. Every ounce of anger, of humiliation, of misery, is taken out on that bag as he beats it. Blood stains the bag, but he doesn't stop. It's not the first time he's torn his fists to bits on the bag.

By the time he runs out of steam, his hands are a mess, his t-shirt is stuck to his sweat-soaked skin, and he's out of breath. Clinging on to the bag for support he breaks down. He's so tired of crying about his family. So fucking tired of it all.

Tired of feeling alone and unwanted.

He pulls his wallet from his back pocket and takes out the bag of pills, swallowing two before lying back on the floor and examining his fists. He rubs the blood from his knuckles, smearing it along the back of his hand. They need to be cleaned, but that would mean hauling his ass off the floor.

He can't be bothered moving, so he just stays where he is, watching the blood drip off his knuckles onto the floor.

Ash

After thanking the driver, Ash gets out of the car, stifling a yawn. The dreadful first meeting with Dillon had kept her awake all night. She couldn't get his expression out of her mind. Couldn't stop thinking about the hatred she saw in his face.

More than once, she had to talk herself out of contacting her boss, Megan. But if she backs out of this assignment, she can pretty much kiss her career goodbye. Not to mention that she'd then have to explain why she wanted to be reassigned. There's no way she wants her past with Dillon made common knowledge.

So, she's going to give it her all. No matter how painful or uncomfortable he makes things for her, she will do her best to be professional. Her job is to photograph Broken Chords - all four members. If one isn't going to play ball, that's on him. She's sure Tate,

Gregg, and Luke will be more cooperative.

Unless Dillon tells them about what she did, and they all boycott her.

Ash shakes her head. That's one hurdle she'll cross if it happens. Right now, she has work to do. She faces the monstrous tour bus and takes a deep breath. She wants to have a look around while there's no one else on board, to familiarise herself with the layout. The guys will be moving in tomorrow and after that, it'll be full of rowdy rock stars - one of whom hates her.

Ash tries not to dwell on that one major point as she walks over to the impressive black bus. The security guard checks her ID before unlocking and opening the door. She climbs up the steps and is immediately struck dumb.

The bus beats her apartment any day. It's all black leather and chrome everywhere she looks. There's a vast sitting room towards the front, with a comfortable kitchen, then the bunks and bathroom towards the back.

As she wanders through it, she checks the cupboards and fridge. It's all stocked up for the guys. Ash runs her hand over the bags of sour apple laces waiting for Dillon to consume like they were going out of fashion. He always smelled of apple when they were together. Even to this day, the scent reminds her of him. Of them.

She slowly closes the cupboard and moves down to the bunks. Each one is roomy, with plenty of head and leg room. But with four guys all over six foot they'd have to be.

She glances over her shoulder as the door opens and someone big steps on to the bus.

'What the fuck are you doing here?'

She swallows thickly as she stares at the person glaring at her.

Why him?

Of all the people who could have come to the bus while she was on it, why did it have to be him? 'I just wanted to familiarise myself with it before we left. I have permission.'

Dillon leans back on the table and glares at her, arms crossed. As usual he's wearing black. But it suits him. It always did. His ripped jeans tucked into combat boots enhance his long legs and the fitted t-shirt shows off his incredible chest and arms. Two platinum chains hang around his neck, whatever is on the end, hidden by his t-shirt, with matching platinum and leather bracelets around his wrists.

When they were together, he was always clean shaven, but she really likes the tight beard on him. She really likes everything about him in fact.

But then he slaps her back into reality.

'Why are you here?'

'I'm just leaving.'

He grips the edge of the table, the muscles in his arms bunching under his skin. 'Not on the fucking bus! The tour. This assignment. What the fuck possessed you to show your face anywhere near me?'

At least he kept those comments to himself when they were at the rehearsal. It would have left her with some explaining to do. 'Would you like me to quit? Is that what you want?'

'Yes. Thanks for offering.'

'I'm not quitting, Dillon. I made a commitment and I intend to stick it out.'

His lip twitches when she says his name. 'A commitment? Are you taking the piss?'

Of all the words she could have used, that was the worst one. 'I didn't mean—'

'You made a fucking commitment to us! To me! Didn't stop you from walking away. Why don't you see if you can do it again?'

'Please—'

'You're enjoying this, aren't you?'

'All the hostility? No, not especially. What I enjoy is getting paid and this is my job. This pays my bills. I can't afford to say no to it.'

He points his finger at her. 'It's my fucking job too and you being here is screwing with it!'

'How? You blanked me from the moment Sam introduced me at the rehearsal. You should just continue doing that and everything will be fine.'

'I'm trying to ignore you, but it's kind of hard to when you're always there. You know what? Maybe this time I'll do the leaving.' He stands and turns back to the door.

'Dillon. Wait!'

He stops but doesn't look at her.

'This is ridiculous. You can't keep ignoring me. We have to work together for the next few weeks. We have to at least try to be civil to each other.'

'No, we don't. And it's better I ignore you. Believe me,' he responds, keeping his attention in front of him rather than looking at her.

'Really? You're going to keep this up for the whole tour?' She should drop it and let him leave, but this needs to happen sooner rather than later.

He slowly turns to face her and a hand clamps around her heart. She was expecting him to be angry, but it's not anger she sees in his face. It's sadness. He quickly masks it again, then shrugs, dropping his hands to his sides, his shoulders slouched like he has the weight of the world on them.

'What exactly do you want me to say? You want me to say it's all okay, is that it? You want me to say I forgive and forget? That we should be mates and get a drink together?' He takes a step closer to her, that familiar apple scent assaulting her. 'You want me to say I forgive you for leaving without any explanation and breaking my fucking heart?'

Ash swallows and licks her dry lips. She knows that's what she did, but hearing him say it makes it seem so much worse. 'No. I don't expect—'

'Then what do you want from me?' He looks away, and she knows he's trying to get himself under control. When he looks back at her, his green eyes hold so much hatred, she wants to take a step back from him. 'What the fuck do you want me to say to you, so *you* can feel better about yourself? Because clearly that's what's going on here. It's all about *you*. All about making *you* feel better. It's got fuck all to do with me.'

'Dillon... it's not—'

'Don't! You walked out the door and left me a fucking note!' He steps closer, but she holds her ground. Even furious with her, she can't help but marvel at the man in front of her. He is hands down the most spectacular thing she's seen for too long. All the muscles, tattoos, and facial piercings have elevated him from hot to scorching. The attraction never went away. Not even for a second.

But none of that matters.

She left him and, by doing that, she hurt him. He'll never forgive her for that, and she understands. Why should she expect him to forgive her when she can't forgive herself?

He licks his lips, giving her a fleeting glimpse of the piercing in his tongue. Her mind instantly hits her with so many unhelpful images of what he could do with that. What he probably does to the people he sleeps with. That thought is sobering. She can't think of him with anyone else.

'Dillon, I'm sorry...'

'I don't care! If you really wanted to do me a favour you should have stayed away.'

'It's complicated.' That weak statement isn't going to help him understand why she left. She barely understands it herself.

He laughs harshly. 'Complicated? Right. You know what, I really couldn't give a flying fuck. I mean that. I'm not going to mess this up for either of us. I'm not a complete dick. I'll pose and smile or do whatever the hell I need to for this shoot. But when you're done with this job, you get the fuck away from me and stay away this time. That's all I want from you.'

Then he turns again and leaves her alone.

Ash stares after him, the hollow feeling in her gut threatening to swallow her whole. Unable to keep a hold, she sits on the end of the couch, looking at the spot where he stood less than a minute ago.

In some deep, dark part of herself, she had held on to a fleeting thought. It had surfaced when her boss gave her this assignment. It wasn't a planned thought. But the seed was planted. A seed that he just tore from the ground and destroyed.

She laughs to herself. She shouldn't have let the thought take root. No way. Dillon was never going to forgive her. Never going to do more than barely tolerate her presence. He'll never want to be with her again.

But it's what you see in those corny movies all the time. Separated lovers reunite, realise their true feelings for each other, and live happily ever after.

The only thing Dillon wants to do is get as far away from her as possible.

She's lost him.

Forever lost the only man she's ever loved.

The tears break free, and she lets them fall. It's not the first time she's cried over Dillon, and it won't be the last.

God, she looks terrible. Ash grimaces at her reflection in the mirror over the sink. She hadn't slept a wink all night. The painful reunion with Dillon had gone over and over in her mind until the early hours.

'What exactly did you expect, huh? That he'd run into your arms and say all is forgiven?'

Her reflection offers no answer, so she turns away and steps into the shower. The band is heading out to a club in two hours, before beginning their anniversary tour. After that she's going to be trapped with a man who, quite rightly, hates her guts. What fun!

After a quick shower which does nothing to re-energise her, she sits on the end of her bed and contemplates heading down to the restaurant for a real coffee, or risking one of the instant sachets stuffed into the small container on the counter.

She's going to need something to help get her through the evening. She needs to be there tonight, camera at the ready, even though she'd prefer to be hiding under the duvet in her room.

Spending the evening in a nightclub watching Dillon catching the eye of too many people isn't appealing to her in the slightest. Especially since she knows it's a certainty he won't be going home alone. He never does.

Maybe she can go for an hour, take some quick pictures, then run before he does anything with anyone? An early night is preferable to spending the night in the club, then leaving mid morning, exhausted.

Like hiding is going to do her any good! She can hardly do her job while hiding from the man she's meant to be photographing. As soon as she gets on that bus with them, she'll have to get to work. Whether he's throwing daggers at her or not.

And he will be throwing a serious quantity of daggers her way - there's no question of that.

Too miserable to venture out of her room, she boils the small kettle and empties a sachet of instant coffee into one of the mugs.

Her phone rings, and she smiles when she sees her home number on the screen. 'Hey.'

'Hi Mum. Where are you?'

Even hearing her daughter's voice instantly brightens her mood. Freya could always do that to her. 'I'm still in the hotel. I don't leave until tomorrow.'

'Did you meet the band?'

'Yes, I did.'

'Are they nice?'

Ash smiles, hoping it carries through to her voice. 'Yes love. They're all really nice. So, are you behaving yourself?' she asks, desperate to get off anything to do with the band.

'Of course I am. Charlie is making me do all my homework before I can watch TV.'

'I should hope so! I miss you.'

'I miss you too, Mum. Oh, I better go. We have to leave for drama class.'

'Have fun and I'll talk to you soon. Love you.'

'Love you too.' Freya ends the call, leaving Ash staring at the screen, a knot forming in her stomach as she looks at the photo of her daughter on the background. Freya is laughing, but then again she usually is. Her ten-year-old daughter has a bubbly personality.

But it's her eyes that always harden that knot in Ash's stomach. Every single time she sees them, the guilt and shame take hold, threatening to crush her.

Ash picks up her camera, scrolling through the handful of photos she took of Dillon. She zooms in on one, focusing on his eyes. Those crystal clear, dark green eyes that, to this day, she gets lost in. Then she looks at the photo of Freya, seeing the exact same eyes.

And that knot in her stomach hardens a little more.

She could easily sit here for the rest of the night going over all the mistakes she made in her life. But Freya isn't one of them. Freya is the one thing she did right. The one thing she's proud of. She just wishes...

Ash shakes her head. There's no time for that now. As much as she'd prefer to do pretty much anything else, she needs to get dressed up and spend the evening with Dillon. Or spend the evening watching Dillon with other people.

Dillon

He shouldn't go tonight. All he has to do is pull a sicky, or just not show up. It wouldn't be the first time. No one would bat an eyelid. He'd pulled shit like that too many times over the years.

Except this time, if he doesn't show, she'll know it's because of her. That he's trying to avoid her. Which he is, but there's no way he's going to give her the satisfaction.

He'd leave the fucking country to avoid her if he could. But that would mean walking out on the band and, apart from his month in prison, he's never missed a performance. There's no fucking way he's going to let her fuck things up for him. Not again.

He storms into the bathroom and glares at his reflection as he chews on his lip ring. He thought after a good night's sleep he'd be calmer. But he didn't have a good night's sleep. He tossed and turned all fucking night as he relived every single minute of his short, but deep relationship with Ashling. Including the day he came home from their first Irish tour to find her gone and a letter on the table.

He pushes back from the sink and slams the door, then sits on the end of the bed. He went to the bus today to load some of his stuff in it, but when the security guard told him she was there he'd left it in his car.

So, why did he still go into the bus? Why didn't he just get back in his car and leave? Why did he confront her, knowing that it would open that old wound again and mess with his head?

Which it has. Tonight he'll be running on painkillers and a lot of whiskey. That part isn't her fault. That's all on him, but she didn't help.

He pushes to his feet and angrily paces his bedroom. Four weeks with her in his face! Taking pictures of him! Watching his every fucking move! It's going to drive him insane.

It's already put him on edge, and that's never a good thing. Without that control over his life, he feels as if he's free-falling.

He grabs a black, long-sleeved t-shirt from his wardrobe and a pair of jeans. He'd usually put a lot of thought into what he wore, but his head is elsewhere tonight. Once dressed, he checks his reflection again. Not too bad considering. He wouldn't call himself vain, but he likes to look good. His image is another part of his armour. If it's not in place, he doesn't feel right.

After sliding his wallet and phone into his back pockets, he grabs his keys then locks his penthouse after him.

Jace is waiting in the underground garage for him when he gets there. His foul mood is barely under control, and Jace knows it. After working together for so long, his bodyguard knows when to keep his mouth shut, and when it's safe to talk.

Jace manoeuvres the car through the late evening traffic. The club is only about ten minutes away, but with the number of cars on the road, it'll take about twenty tonight. He closes his eyes as the blur of headlights suddenly makes him dizzy.

'Are you okay? Dillon? Hey!'

He grabs onto the door handle as the world continues to spin around him. Then Jason is at his side, crouching beside the open passenger door. When did he stop the car?

'Dillon? Can you hear me?'

He pushes Jason's hand away from his face when his bodyguard taps him on the cheek. 'Fuck off! I'm fine.'

'You're far from fine. You drifted off on me for a bit.'

Jace is right, but he's not about to admit it. He feels seriously rough. Dillon unfastens his seat belt and begrudgingly accepts Jace's help to stand. Once out of the car, the world seems to right itself again.

Whatever that was, it's passed now. He's probably just over tired. Sleep and him haven't been on the same page for too long.

'Look at me, Dillon.'

'I'm fine! Will you just leave me alone. I didn't eat much today. It's probably just that. Can we get in the car and go?'

Jace looks at him long and hard for a minute without saying anything. Just when Dillon thinks he's going to refuse, he curses and gestures to the car. 'Fuck knows you'll do what you want anyway!'

They drive the rest of the way to the club in silence, but Jace won't stop looking over at him, checking he's still conscious. If he was in better form, he'd tell him to back off, but he doesn't have the energy.

As they pull up at the club, Jace turns around in the seat. 'Are you sure—'

Without replying, Dillon knocks on the window, climbing out when one of the attendants opens the door for him. He steps out into a barrage of flashing lights, and people screaming his name. It helps to pull him out of his head, letting rock star Dillon take control again.

This is what he lives for. This is where he thrives.

All the crap with Ash gets pushed to the back of his mind, along with all the other shit he keeps buried there. For the next few hours, he'll put on a show. And if that means Ash sees a side of him she hasn't seen before, so be it. If he's going to survive this, he needs to let the asshole side of himself out to play.

Ash

The club is packed. News of the band's expected appearance brought in the crowds tonight. At least, being part of their group, she didn't have to fight through the hordes of screaming fans. The VIP area is not only protected by security provided by the club, but the four bodyguards will be here in a few minutes with the guys.

With Dillon.

Ash thanks Sam for her drink and settles into the comfortable seat.

'How are you enjoying the assignment so far?' Sam asks, her voice raised to be heard over the crowd.

'I'm loving it,' she replies, hoping the lie is convincing. 'I'm used to doing weddings. This is a whole new area for me.'

'I'm sorry about Dillon.'

'What about him?'

'He's giving you a bit of a hard time, isn't he?'

Ash takes a sip of her drink before answering. What exactly is she supposed to say to that? She doubts he would have told Sam about their past. 'He's fine, really.'

'You don't have to lie. I know him. He can be awkward at times. Under it all he's genuinely lovely.'

Ash nods. She knows that. Under the shell, he's loving and caring. But he's defensive, always pushing people away before they can hurt him. Just like she did. 'I'm sure he is.'

'He'll fall in with the others though. He's just taking time to get used to having you around. When he gets on the stage, he'll be a different person, Trust me.' Sam nods towards the entrance, as the crowd goes crazy. 'I presume the boys have arrived.'

It's silly to feel excited, but Ash can't help keeping her eyes locked on the stairs, waiting for him to appear.

And then he does, the excitement turning to regret when she sees him.

Like the others, he's in black as they always are in public as a group. The tight-fitting jeans hug his long legs, and the long-sleeved t-shirt shows off every ridge of his broad chest. His light brown hair is brushed back from his face, his green eyes targeting everyone in turn as he walks up the steps.

He is gorgeous. No other man in this club can hold a torch to him, even on their best days.

Those interrogating green eyes lock on her, and his face hardens. It's not difficult to see why he's got the reputation he does. He's got an air about him. A *don't you dare mess with me* vibe that only makes him even more attractive.

He deliberately turns away from her and speaks to Tate. Ash sips her drink trying to push down the hurt at his reaction. But what did she expect? She's going to have to get used to it. She's got a few weeks of this level of *fun* heading her way.

The night improves slightly when Chloe, Bria, and Maeve join her on the couch. It's difficult not to warm to the other women. She especially likes Maeve, her carefree personality instantly drawing her in. The conversation flows easily between them, even when their celebrity boyfriends and husband join them.

She discretely glances around her, spotting Dillon talking to the bartender, a stunning guy who is looking at Dillon like all his dreams have come true. Which they probably have. He's got Dillon Ryan eyeing him up.

Ash excuses herself, making a controlled, but speedy retreat to the bathroom. She hasn't even left on tour with them yet and she's already hiding in the bathroom, avoiding playing spectator to Dillon, as he gets up close and personal to anyone who looks at him the right way.

After ten minutes, she decides it's time to stop hiding. Locking herself away in the bathroom isn't giving Sam a professional view of her. She checks her make up, then nods at her reflection and heads back to the others.

But life is clearly all about kicking her at the moment. Just outside the bathroom, in a corridor to the left, is the man she's desperate to avoid. And he's not alone.

Seems the guy behind the bar is having one hell of a night. But it's the way Dillon is kissing the guy that hits the hardest. The guy's arms are pinned back against the wall, Dillon's hands keeping them firmly in place by his side as he fucks the guy's mouth with his tongue.

He either hasn't noticed her, or he doesn't care. She's hoping it's the first but knowing him it could be either.

'On your knees.'

The guy does as he's told, and Ash feels sick. She needs to go. She can't see what's about to happen. But she's stuck. If she moves, he'll see her, and God knows what his response will be.

Dillon unfastens his belt, then opens his jeans. 'You can suck it next if you want.' Dillon smirks at her over his shoulder. 'But you'll have to ask me really nicely.'

She has no reply for that. She turns and walks away from the scene. She feels physically sick. She doesn't recognise him anymore. That's not the man she used to love. Dillon always had a healthy sexual appetite, but this is bloody ridiculous.

Ash grabs her drink from the table, desperately wishing it had alcohol in it, but everyone had stuck to the no alcohol rule around Tate. She completely appreciates that, but right now, it's not doing her any favours.

'Are you okay?'

She jumps, then smiles at Maeve. 'Sorry. You scared me. I'm fine.'

Maeve grabs her by the hand and pulls her over to the side of the room. 'What did that insensitive dickhead do?'

'Excuse me?'

'Dillon told Luke about you and Luke told me. Don't worry. No one else knows about you and Dillon. And I promise I'm not here to judge you. It's in the past and we all have one of those.'

Ash doesn't talk about Dillon. She never has. But there's something about Maeve she can't help but like. The problem is, Luke is Dillon's best friend. 'I don't know. I don't want to put you in an awkward situation with Luke.'

'Just because I'm madly in love with dickhead's best mate doesn't mean you can't trust me.'

'Why do you keep calling him dickhead?'

'Because he is.' She grins and sweeps her long black and purple hair behind her shoulder. 'Don't get me wrong. I love Dillon to bits. I really do, but he can be a massive asshole when the mood takes him. Which is most of the time at the moment.'

'It is?'

Maeve nods. 'He's going through a rocky time. We're looking out for him I promise, but he's not the most receptive to help. I'm sure

68

you know that.'

Ash laughs. 'That's such a polite way of putting it.'

'So, what's up?'

'I'm thinking of quitting to be honest. I thought I could do this, but he hates me, Maeve. He just... forget it.'

Maeve crosses her arms and stares at Ash.

'I walked out of the bathroom, and he was about to get a blowjob from a guy. He...well he offered me a go next if I asked nicely. I don't want to see that. I can't see that.'

'Ugh! That's disgusting - even for him.' Maeve taps her foot against the ground and glares over at the bathroom door. 'I won't, but I want to smack him. How about we head back to the hotel?'

'No, stay with your friends. I'll head back and get some sleep.'

'Nonsense! Just give me a sec. Stay put.'

Maeve hurries over to Luke and straddles him. She speaks in his ear, and he turns his attention from Maeve to her. Oh God! She really hopes Maeve didn't tell him about what happened.

Maeve kisses her boyfriend and climbs off his knee before joining her again. 'Right. You good to go?' she asks as she slips on her jacket. 'Andy will take us to the hotel then come back for my man.'

'Seriously. It's—'

Maeve presses her finger to Ash's lips, silencing her. 'Shush. We're going to go back to your room and have a good bitch about dickhead, then I promise I'll have you in bed early - alone. Don't go getting any ideas,' she adds with a wink.

'You know what? That sounds great. Thanks, Maeve.'

Maeve links arms with her, then waits until Andy joins them, before they walk arm in arm down the stairs. As they round the corner at the bottom, Ash feels someone looking at her. When she turns, she sees Dillon leaning on the railing, staring straight at her.

He smirks at her, then turns away. Seems he just made a point, and it's a point she's not going to forget in a hurry.

Dillon

She left. Again. What a shock!

Okay, so he drove her away this time, but fuck her. If she can't take it, she needs to find a new job. When they're on the road this is what he does, so she had better get used to it.

He leans on the bar and turns his whiskey glass on the polished surface. He doesn't feel bad about what he did. Doesn't feel great either.

'You are a complete asshole.'

He sips his whiskey, ignoring Luke's dirty looks from beside him. They promised to lay off alcohol tonight, but in the heat of the moment he forgot.

'Why did you do that?'

'Lay off with the judgemental looks, okay!'

'You let a guy suck you off knowing Ash would see you. That's cruel, Dillon. You're not like that.'

The glass hits the bar a little harder than he planned. 'My dick is my business!'

Luke shakes his head. Fucking perfect. The old disapproving look he's well used to. 'I'm not talking about your dick. I'm talking about you being a dick. It was downright cruel.'

He turns to face Luke, squinting when his friend blurs out of focus a few times. 'What exactly does any of this have to do with you? She's nothing to any of us. Vox hired her to take some pictures. That's it. What are you getting your neck out of joint about?'

'Because she *is* something to you. You were going to marry her Dillon. That's kind of a big deal.'

He waves at the barman and points to his glass. If he's going to do this, he needs more drink in him. 'That was a lifetime ago.'

'Oh come on!'

He shoves Luke in the shoulder, driving him back a step. It's the wrong thing to do. Luke is the last person he should be pushing around. But he's pissed off and Luke is going to get the brunt of it.

Or is, until the massive form of Tate gets in the way. They're roughly the same build, but Tate has about an inch on him. He's also stone cold sober which gives him the advantage. The lead singer easily manoeuvres Dillon away from Luke, forcing him into the corner and pinning him against the wall.

'What the fuck was that? You're pushing Luke around now?'

He tries to push Tate off him, but the brute won't budge. 'I didn't mean to. He was getting in my face.'

Tate leans closer to him. 'Now I'm in your face. You want to try your luck with me? You want to push me around?'

He's gone up against Tate in the past, but they were either both drunk or both sober at the time. A sober Tate is going to pound him to mush without having to try too hard. He holds up his hands, admitting defeat.

Not that he was really going to go up against Tate or Luke. He looks around Tate to Luke, talking to Gregg at the bar. Bria and Chloe are giving him some of the dirtiest looks he's had thrown at him for a while. He probably deserves it.

'What's wrong?'

He shakes his head, but Tate gives him a sharp shove against the wall.

'What's wrong?' he asks, a little more forcefully.

What's right? That would be the easier question to answer. Tate grabs a chair and pushes Dillon onto it. 'Stay there!'

The whiskey buzz has died down, leaving him tired and fed up again. A few minutes later, Tate taps him on the shoulder and points to an open door to the left of the bar. 'C'mon.'

He traipses after Tate to a staff room. He's not usually so compliant, but he's worn out and can't be bothered arguing back. Tate gestures for him to go into the room, but they're not alone. Gregg and Luke are in there, looking at him.

'Fuck!'

'Sit down.'

Tate's tone doesn't give him any choice. He sits on one of the plastic chairs and crosses his arms. So what if he's giving off defensive vibes. He's fucking defensive.

'What's wrong, Dillon?'

He glances over at Luke who nods at him. Of course he wants Dillon to open up. Faced with three mates used to talking for hours in therapy, this is a losing battle.

He leans back and drags his hands through his hair as he glares at the ceiling. 'I was in a relationship with the photographer about a decade ago. We were... I asked her to marry me and she said yes. She left me a touching letter while we were on our first Irish tour. Didn't see her again until she showed up at our rehearsal this week.'

One fell swoop and it's all out. Or as much of it as he's willing to release. It's enough to get Gregg and Tate off his back.

'And you had no idea who she was before you saw her?'

Dillon looks over at Gregg as he shakes his head. 'No fucking clue. I saw her and I just froze.'

'Have you spoken to her one on one?' Tate asks.

'I went to put some stuff in the bus and walked in on her checking it out. We spoke, but it wasn't a friendly chat. I laid into her. Told her to quit and get the fuck away from me.' He shakes his head as he clenches his fists. He stops just short of telling them that he doesn't know how to deal with this. That he doesn't know how to be near her without going fucking crazy.

The silence hangs for a few minutes until Gregg finally breaks it. 'Do you want to go to Vox and tell them?'

'No way! Having you three know the truth is too much as it is. I told her on the bus that I wouldn't be a dick about this. Didn't get off to a great start, but I know how I'd feel if someone messed with my career because of personal reasons. She stays until the assignment is done.'

'You sure you can deal with that?'

He shrugs at Tate. 'I don't know. It was a shock seeing her again. I'll get used to it. I'll be fine.'

They look as convinced about that as he does, but thankfully Gregg and Tate nod, while Luke continues hitting him with an intense look.

'We've got your back,' Tate says. 'Whatever you want we'll support you. Run interference if you want us to.'

'Thanks.' And he means it. 'Sorry about tonight. I fucked it up for everyone.'

'Night is still young,' Tate says, getting to his feet. 'How about we blow this off and head back to my place. Stick on some music, get some really unhealthy chips, and just chill for a bit.'

'You know what?' Dillon says, pushing up in the chair. 'That sounds great.'

'I'm in,' Gregg says, jumping up and clapping his hands together.

'Me too.' Luke walks over to him and, in a move that takes him completely by surprise, jabs him in the chest. 'You push me like that again and next time I'll push back.'

'Yeah. Got it.'

Gregg and Tate look after Luke as he opens the door and goes back into the club. 'Well, that was different,' Gregg says. 'Seems our quiet Luke is getting himself a bit of a backbone. I like it!' He points to the door. 'Are we going to just stand here or follow him? I'm hungry.'

Ash

Another lousy night's sleep, but at least this time the coffee is from a real coffee shop, instead of an instant sachet from her room. She'll need the real stuff to face the day ahead of her.

After what happened in the club last night, the looming tour is filling her with dread. And today is only the first day of what could be a very long month of heartache and sleepless nights.

She will say one thing though. Maeve is probably the nicest woman she's ever met. Luke found himself an amazing girlfriend. It's no wonder he's coming out of his shell more and more.

Of the three women linked to the band, Maeve is the one she has the most in common with. They're both a little alternative, both like to be themselves no matter what.

After having Freya, she had toned things down slightly, but is still hanging on to her platinum spiked hair, and piercings up both ears. She's had both elements since she left school, and that style is a part of who she is. Just like Maeve and her purple hair.

It's hard not to be upbeat and happy with her around.

A stark contrast to Luke's best friend, who, right now, is owning the dark brooding personality.

She sips her coffee and tries to focus on her assignment, instead of Dillon again. They're all going to the ferry port separately and meeting there. At least that's one less awkward journey for her to worry about.

A sleek black car pulls up at the door of the hotel and she groans to herself when Jason climbs out from the driver's seat.

Please, please, please don't say that Dillon is there too.

She fixes the smile on her face as she walks over to the car, relieved to find it empty. 'Am I the only one you're collecting?'

'Ciaran is driving the bus, I'm picking you up, Liam is with Tate and Gregg, and Andy is collecting Dillon and Luke. Not too keen on seeing Dillon, are you.'

'Excuse me?'

'You blew out a pretty impressive breath.'

Well, that's not even a little bit embarrassing. 'Why would I be relieved he's not in the car?'

Jason puts her bags in the boot, grinning as he slams it shuts. 'I'm his bodyguard. I know what he's like. I also heard what he did last night. Word of advice?'

'Go on,' she says as she slips into the backseat, partly dreading what he's about to say to her. Surely Dillon wouldn't have told his bodyguard about what went on between them.

Jace climbs into the driver's seat and pulls away from the hotel. 'Avoid him when they're out in situations like that. It makes life easier.'

She nods and smiles at him in the rear-view mirror but doesn't respond. What can she say to advice like that? Avoiding him full stop would be the better solution.

But less than thirty minutes later, Jason pulls up into Dublin Port and she instantly notices the sleek black bus at the far side of the car park.

And so it begins.

A silence filled awkward assignment.

Jason pulls up around the back of the terminal building and opens the car door for her. He leads her into the building, carrying her bags for her. With every step along the corridor, the nerves escalate.

Then she spots Andy and Liam standing outside a door. Show time. They open the door for her, and she is shown into a large room furnished with comfortable looking couches, a bar with various drinks dispensers and snacks lined out on the counter.

Tate and Gregg are slouched on one of the couches, but there's no sign of Dillon or Luke yet. Both men smile at her, but it doesn't take a genius to figure out that Dillon has told them about her. The way they're now looking at her is different to yesterday.

Perfect!

She helps herself to another coffee which probably won't help relax her nerves, but she needs something to hold. When she sits on the couch at the far side of the room, Tate and Gregg's eyes are still locked on her.

'He told you, didn't he?'

Gregg nods, but Tate just continues to target her with his cold blue eyes. 'Yep,' Gregg says. 'But it's all good.'

'It is?'

He nods again, his hair falling over his face. 'Whatever happened between you two is your business. You're here to do a job. He doesn't want to mess that up. So, like I said, it's all good. You won't get any trouble from us. Right Tate?' He nudges Tate on the arm when he doesn't immediately respond.

'Yeah. No trouble. But if I were you, I'd keep a wide berth. Don't make this harder on him than it already is.'

Gregg may be willing to let it go, but Tate isn't. 'Of course. I'm here to take photographs. That's it. I don't want to cause any trouble for anyone.'

He nods and sits back, finally dropping his glare.

The uncomfortable silence diminishes a little, until the door opens again, then it jumps right back up a level when Dillon walks in with Luke and Andy. The former glances at her, but his eyes are hidden behind a pair of impenetrable glasses. Luke smiles and grabs a coffee, before sitting on the last of the couches beside Dillon.

Luke, Tate, and Gregg talk amongst themselves while Dillon focuses on his phone. She follows his example, checking her camera equipment is set up. Which it is, but she needs something to do. She risks a quick look at the bassist. He looks pale, but no doubt he had a late night.

Then she catches a glimpse of something that confuses her so much she has to force herself to stop staring at him. On the middle finger of his left hand is a heavy platinum ring. She knows that ring so well. She had taken a long time to pick it for him for their month anniversary. The thick Celtic band had screamed Dillon to her when she saw it in the shop. It was him and he had loved it.

But why is he still wearing it? It makes no sense.

Ash takes out her phone and puts his name in the search engine, picking the image tab. Oh God! He's wearing it in all the photos. How hadn't she noticed that before? Every single picture of him, whether on stage, on album covers, on nights out, the ring was on his finger. The ring she gave him.

Any further thoughts of the ring get pushed aside, as Sam opens the door and peeks her head inside. 'Time people. Let's get you lot on the ferry.'

Ash hangs back with Sam, letting the band go ahead of her with their security. As Dillon passes her, she is hit with the intoxicating scent of his cologne, and it instantly takes her back a decade. But he doesn't even look in her direction as he walks past. Not even a small glance at her.

And that hurts.

Dillon

In hindsight, drinking an entire bottle of whiskey while on a ferry probably wasn't his best idea, but it's a little late to worry about it. Dillon dumps the empty bottle on the bed and stares out the porthole at the sea. It's going to be a fucking rough crossing if those swells are anything to go by. Yeah, necking a full bottle of whiskey is going to make this an interesting ride.

It's all her fault. Again. Most things are. Well, maybe not, but she is to blame for a lot of it.

Spending a few hours with the guys last night had been just what he needed. For a short time at least, he'd been able to stop thinking, or over thinking in his case. Going over the same things again and again is tiring.

But as soon as he stepped into the lounge and saw her, the thinking began again. And the regret.

He honestly hadn't planned on having her catch him about to get a blow job. Not consciously at least.

What does it matter? Why is she getting to him like this all over again? He feels guilty about her finding him like that. How messed up is that? What the hell does he have to feel guilty about?

He's just living his life the way he wants to. So what if she walked in on that?

He stumbles over to the bed and drops down, landing on the empty whiskey bottle. 'Fuck!'

This whole tour is going to be a fucking nightmare. How is he meant to get on stage with her looking at him, taking pictures of him, laughing at him?

He loved her so fucking much. He would have done anything for her. Anything. He's trying to get his life straight, then she decides to come back to kick him in the heart all over again.

He pauses, then laughs out loud. Who the fuck is he kidding? He's never going to get his life straight. What the fuck does that even mean? His life has been a fucking disaster since the day he was born. He was destined to live a short, painful, miserable lonely life. Destined to be hurt repeatedly, until he's got nothing left to give.

Fuck it! He's already there.

There is nothing left to give.

He's given it all and all he's got in return is pain.

He picks up the whiskey bottle and glares at it. It's still empty. Fuck!

He throws it against the wall, but it doesn't break. Damn cardboard walls in the cabin.

Is he really supposed to just get on with it and be all nice and smiley with her? Fuck that! He's not renowned for being particularly friendly, but she's going to see a whole other side to him.

But first he needs to throw up.

When he stumbles out of the bathroom, Luke is sitting on his bed holding the empty bottle. 'Give me a fucking break, please.'

'You drank all this?'

'Why are you in my room?'

'My room is next door. I heard you throwing this against the wall. Bet you were ticked off when it didn't break.'

Dillon lies back on the bed, shoving Luke out of the way with his knee. 'Go away.'

Luke turns to give him one hell of a disapproving look. 'Are you going to be like this all tour?'

'Maybe. Won't that be fun?' Luke thumps him on the leg. 'Hey! What the fuck was that for?'

'Stop being an asshole, Dillon. I get Ash turning up like this has thrown you, but drinking this much whiskey in one go isn't the answer.'

He buries his head under his arm. 'Yeah, well it worked. I've stopped thinking about her. Or had, until you came in being all helpful.'

'Oh, knock it off. You're not fooling anyone. You're hurting, Dillon. Talk to me about it. I can't help if you drink and get angry.'

'I don't need your help, and I sure as hell don't need to talk about it. I just want to sleep. Go away and leave me alone.'

When he hears the door closing behind Luke, he feels shittier than he felt a few minutes ago. He can't keep pushing Luke away. One day he'll push too hard and he'll lose him.

Then he'll be left with no one.

Ash

As she tucks into an incredible dinner, Ash has to force herself not to look at him. Dillon is sitting at the far end of the table, talking to someone she doesn't recognise. Then again, the same can probably be said for everyone at the table.

Apart from Sam and the guys, she has no idea who these other thirty or so dinner guests are. They all have something to do with Vox in some way or another, but Ash lost track of the names and titles when she was initially introduced.

The only one she remembers is Zane, the man sitting beside her. He's in his mid to late thirties, is attractive, and absolutely someone she would go for on a normal day. But this isn't a normal day. With her ex at the far end of the table talking away to his own attractive guy, this is a situation she'd prefer to be far from.

But it's for work.

That mantra keeps going around in her head as she makes pleasant small talk with Zane, who has manoeuvred his chair closer to hers.

God, she wishes he would go away. She should be lapping up the attention this stunning man is giving her, but with Dillon so close she can't. It's not like she's doing anything wrong. She's single and fully allowed to speak to whomever she wants. What Dillon thinks about that shouldn't concern her - especially after his display outside the toilets in the club back in Ireland.

The trip from Ireland to the hotel in Scotland had been uneventful. Dillon hadn't acknowledged her existence for the entire journey. In fact, he hadn't shown anyone much attention at all. She's fairly sure he was drunk by the time they boarded the bus in the UK. He wasn't much of a drinker when they were together, but clearly that's changed.

A lot has changed.

The best thing she can do is focus on her job and leave him to it. They'll be performing here tomorrow night, before heading down to London for a show, then across the channel to France the following day. No doubt he'll be busy with band stuff during that time. Hopefully he'll be too preoccupied to glare at her.

Much like he's doing right now from the far end of the table.

She's just talking to Zane, not doing anything sexual with him. And even if she was, it's got nothing to do with Dillon. He's hardly given her feelings a second thought all evening, so why is she worried about him?

So, ignoring the daggers being thrown at her from further down the table, she puts on her best smile and gives Zane her full attention.

Not only is he attractive, but it turns out they have quite a lot in common. After a few minutes she becomes engrossed in their conversation, completely forgetting about everyone else.

Not only is the company enjoyable, so is the meal. Vox had booked the entire restaurant for the evening, celebrating the first night of what they hope will be a successful tour for the band. And they haven't spared any expense. While there is no alcohol, there is plenty of incredible food for them to enjoy, the waiters continuously filling plates and topping up glasses with various non-alcoholic drinks.

That's something she finds particularly touching. The fact that everyone here completely supports Tate like that, says a lot about the group of people.

As the evening wears on, people leave the main dining table, spreading out to the different seating areas set up around the restaurant. Zane continues to hold her attention for the most part, but every now and then she can't help but be drawn to Dillon again. Like a pathetic moth to an irritatingly powerful flame.

He's still talking to the same man and, if she knows the look in his eyes like she thinks she does, he'll be taking him back to the hotel after they're done here.

Leave him to it. It's none of her business.

So why does it tear at her heart?

Why does she have to bite the inside of her cheek to hold back the tears?

She gave him up. He can talk to whoever he wants. Dillon glances over at her, his smile fading briefly, before he turns his attention back to his companion.

He's enjoying his night. She might as well follow his example and do the same.

Dillon

He finishes his drink, then slams the empty glass on the counter a little harder than necessary. The guy he picked up at dinner is walking around the hotel suite, his mouth open as he takes in the vast room. They're staying here for one night before heading off to the first venue in the morning. He'd tried to get out of the dinner tonight, but Sam had insisted they all go. Everyone from Vox was going to be there because of Broken Chords. The least he can do is show his face.

So he did. He sat at the table and made pointless small talk with too many boring people. They all work behind the scenes for the band, but he couldn't have been less interested in meeting them. It's not that he's ungrateful for their efforts. He'd made sure to politely voice his appreciation for all their hard work like a good well-trained boy.

He has no idea what efforts they made. He's pretty fucking sure Tate writes their music, and he performs the backing vocals and all the music with Gregg and Luke. It's the four of them that make Broken Chords so successful. Just the four friends. Everyone else at that table was riding their coattails.

Including his companion. What part he plays in the grand scheme of things he has no fucking clue. Nor does he care.

'This is incredible. I don't think I've ever been in a room this fancy.'

Dillon smiles but wishes the guy would shut up. He didn't bring him back here to talk. He shouldn't have brought him back here, full stop. The only reason he's here is to provide a distraction.

From her.

The entire meal was spent trying not to look at her and that asshole who was drooling all over her. It didn't help that said asshole was fucking gorgeous. Ash was lapping up the attention he was throwing at her.

The entire evening was a joke. He was all over whoever this guy in his room is, just to show Ash he'd moved on. But he was only all over this guy because he wanted to make her jealous. Not exactly the actions of someone who didn't give a fuck.

Watching her flirting with that guy had been like a knife to his gut. A knife she kept pulling out and shoving back in every time she smiled at the dickhead.

He wanted to hurt her back, so latched on to the first prospect he found. And now he's stuck with that decision walking around his fucking room.

She's probably having a fun night with that gorgeous guy. Why would she be in the least bit bothered by what he was doing? If she cared about him in the slightest, she wouldn't have left him years ago.

What the hell is he doing?

Ross or Russ or whoever, walks over to him and takes a sip from the other glass. 'I can't believe I'm in a hotel room with *the* Dillon Ryan.'

Dillon pours himself another drink. He's going to need the alcohol to get through this. This is always the problem when he takes fans back with him. He wants a fuck, not someone to massage his ego. He takes another drink to kill any residual doubts and shame, then crooks his finger at Russ or Ross, who smiles and walks over to Dillon.

He kisses Ross. He's fairly sure his name is Ross...well, mostly sure. What does it matter? After this he won't be seeing him again. Not until the next awkward Vox get-together.

Dillon pulls off the guy's t-shirt then guides him back towards the bedroom. He takes off his own shirt and Ross steps back. 'Oh wow!' He gingerly runs his hands over Dillon's chest as he stares at him. 'Your body... it's incredible, Dillon.'

Oh, put a fucking sock in it!

He pushes Ross' hand away from his chest. He's not a fan of being touched. Unless he gives permission or an order, he prefers people to keep their hands to themselves.

He doesn't have the time, or the interest, to tell Ross how he works in explicit and clear detail as he usually would. The sooner he gets what he wants, the sooner Dillon can show him the door.

He steps closer and tilts Ross' head back so he's looking at his face instead of his chest. 'I'll give you two options. You can either leave right now, or you can shut up, get on all fours on the bed and let me fuck you. Which one?'

Unsurprisingly, Ross picks option number two and jumps on the bed like the floor is made of lava.

Might as well get this over with. Not the best thought to have in this situation, but he's off his game tonight. So much so, that nearly an hour later, he's still fucking Ross or Russ.

He's an expert at holding himself and his partners back as long as possible. But he's not trying tonight. If anything, he wants to come so he can get this over with. He's edged Ross a few times, drawing it out for him, so it at least appears like he's trying. He's got a reputation to uphold. No good sending him on his way after a five-minute session, but this is getting ridiculous.

Ross will come soon. He'll make sure of it. But as for himself... well, he's facing a situation he never thought he'd have to face.

There's a strong chance he's going to have to fake it.

Whatever is going on in his head is fucking with his dick. He's ploughing into Ross, riding him hard, but his own orgasm isn't even hinting at making an appearance. There's nothing. He's hard but that's it.

'I'm... close...'

Dillon grinds his teeth, doubling his efforts. This is a fucking nightmare. He's never had this problem before. Dillon reaches around, fisting the guy's dick in his hand, pumping it hard as he slams his dick into Ross' ass.

'Oh God... I'm coming...'

Lucky fucker.

Ross tips forward, only being supported by Dillon as he comes, covering Dillon's hand as he groans, riding out his orgasm. Dillon could keep going, but he's bored now. He's not going to come. He could be here for another hour and still be in the same messed up situation.

So he fakes it.

He grips Ross's dick and hip in his hands, making all the right sounds as he shoves into him, slow and steady, giving an award-winning performance.

While Ross is still quaking under him, he pulls out, quickly taking off the condom before Ross notices it's empty.

Leaving him to recover, sprawled out on the bed, Dillon locks himself in the bathroom and glares at his reflection. What in the name of fuck was that? He didn't think it was possible to hate himself more than he already does, but he was wrong.

He faked an orgasm to end sex.

Dillon clenches his jaw, his reflection giving as good as it gets glare wise. God, he's so fed up with all of this. Fed up living from one night stand to one night stand. Fed up locking his emotions away, fucking for the sake of fucking, just to get the release. Always taking the lead. Always in control. Always the one making the decisions, planning, and executing to make sure his partner left his bed satisfied.

But what about him? When is someone going to care if he's satisfied?

He lets his head drop to his chest. He loves being in control. But just for once in his life, he'd like to know what it feels like for someone else to look out for him. For someone else to take that control away from him - even for a short while. To take away all the thinking and second guessing out of his hands. To show him what it's like to get carried away in the emotions and feelings.

To sweep him off his feet, tie him down, and fuck him for a change.

His dick has been inside too many people to count. It's not something he's necessarily proud of, but he doesn't regret it either. No point. Having sex with random strangers helps dull the pain... for a while at least.

None of those partners has fucked him. He's only had one person who's done that to him. With him.

For him.

Ash had taken control of him while they were together. She'd tamed him, been with him in a way no one has even come close to doing since. And he missed it. He needs it.

But no one else has even tried or asked to dominate him. To give him a chance to be the one taking, instead of always giving.

It requires trust and he doesn't have a massive supply of that. He used to trust Ash, before she left him. Apart from his mates and his sisters, he trusts no one on the fucking planet. That doesn't give him any options. Which leaves him stuck in a cycle he fears is slowly sapping the life from him.

Seems his body is tired of it too.

His dick is still painfully hard. He needs to come, but he's not interested. For the first time in his life, he honestly can't be bothered.

Ignoring his dick, he opens the bathroom door, but just then something catches his eye in the bathroom mirror. The diamond reflects the light, taunting him even more.

It's the engagement ring he had given Ash a decade ago, which she then threw back at him, with her farewell note. For some unfathomable reason, he has been wearing it on a long chain around his neck, where it sits over his heart, and has done for ten long years.

He's never taken it off, except when he went to prison. But now, he needs to remove it again. He can't risk her seeing it, or bear to see the pity in her eyes. He is pathetic enough as it is. So, he takes off the chain with the ring, to put away in his wallet for at least the next few weeks while she is here.

He leaves the bathroom, then comes to a stop when he sees whatever his name is. The fucker is stretched out on his bed, face down, snoring.

It's probably a compliment. Dillon wore him out. But it's also a fucking irritation. He'd usually show them out the door once he's done, before they were tempted to fall asleep.

He's never been a fan of sleeping with someone else in the bed with him. It just doesn't feel right. How can anyone possibly get a good night's sleep with another body taking up space in the bed? Touching them. Hugging them. It didn't appeal to him in the slightest.

Well, unless it's Luke.

Or her.

He thumps his fist against his forehead, trying to ram those unhelpful thoughts from his mind. What the hell is wrong with him? If other people aren't fucking with him, he's doing it to himself. Thinking about Luke is seriously painful. Thinking about Ash is so much worse.

He needs to get out of here.

Dillon showers to get rid of all traces of whatever his name is from his body, then grabs a clean pair of boxers from his bag. He takes his wallet, then puts the chain and ring into the zipped section at the back of it, alongside the slightly dog-eared photo of Ash, which he's been carrying around for a decade.

He lies on the couch in the living area and turns on the TV, making sure to keep the sound low.

What the fuck is he doing with his life? Clara is right. He is sleeping his way through the population of Ireland, the UK, and beyond. Not that it's doing him any favours. He's earned himself an impressive reputation for all the wrong reasons, and he's still alone.

He pulls up the leg of his boxers and looks at the tattoo of Ashling's name. He thought he'd found the right person when he was with her. He had loved her. Deeply loved her. When he'd asked her to marry him, it had felt right. To him anyway. Just a shame she hadn't felt the same in the end.

Fuck this! He needs to work off this tension. If he can't do it sexually, he'll have to find another way.

11

Ash

It's useless. It doesn't matter how long she stares at the TV, it's not going to help her switch off her mind.

Dillon left with the man.

She knew he would, so it shouldn't bother her. Zane had hinted he wanted to join her in her room, but she wasn't going to mix business with pleasure. Seeing Dillon leave with his date had left a sour taste in her mouth. After seeing that, the only thing on her mind was going back to her room and hiding under her duvet.

Had Dillon really changed that much? She knew there were stories about him and his sexual exploits on pretty much every gossip site and page out there, but a part of her had assumed, naively, that some of that was exaggerated. After seeing what she had tonight, and back in the club in Ireland, she has no doubts most of it is true.

She's lying on her own watching the TV, while Dillon is probably showing that guy the night of his life. Sex with Dillon had always been incredible. 'Oh, stop it!'

She gets up and throws on a pair of shorts and t-shirt. She's too wound up to sleep, and if she stays here any longer, she's going to replay moments with Dillon she doesn't need to replay.

Ash grabs her room key and pass, then leaves her room and walks through the deserted hotel down to the gym. There are certain perks to working with the band like this. Because the guys liked to work out a lot, the gym had been locked to regular guests while Broken were staying for the night. With the guys either asleep or having sex, she should have the place to herself.

Ash holds her key card up to the scanner and the light changes, unlocking the door. She smiles and looks around the impressive gym. More importantly an empty gym. Ash starts with the treadmill, turning her music on loud as she runs. After twenty minutes, something catches her attention. She looks up and there he is.

Dillon.

He looks as thrilled to see her as she is to see him. She thought he'd be busy for another few hours yet. Then he turns to leave the room and Ash switches off the treadmill. She pulls off her headphones then grabs her bag. 'Wait!'

He stops but doesn't turn to face her.

'I'll go. You stay and do your workout.' But instead of letting her leave, he blocks the doorway, refusing to move. 'Can you get out of the way?'

He peers down at her, just silently throwing his weight around as he's so good at doing. She realises it's the closest she's been to him, and his scent hits her like a punch to the gut. It's familiar, and comforting, and she desperately misses it.

She braces for the argument that's about to begin, accepting that this is the way things are going to play out between them.

But instead of verbally attacking her, he takes a step closer and licks his lips. Ash doesn't have a clue what's going on. All she knows is that her heart is racing. He's looking at her the way he used to. That same possessive look she was never able to resist. His green eyes lock on hers, drawing her in.

She wants him. She always has, and all this tension between them is impossible to ignore. He's angry and upset, but under it all, he wants what she does. He needs what she does. Needs to have that release.

Dillon peers down at her, clearly trying to figure out what the hell is going on. He needs to get this off his chest. He's so angry at her and the only way he can release some of that is to do this. It's how he operates. He was like that before she met him and while they were together. It's not a stretch to believe he is still like that.

Sex is his therapy, his way of blowing off all that steam he forever keeps trapped inside. He doesn't talk. Rarely opens up about what is going on in his complicated head. It keeps him on the edge all the time. Always teetering between losing his control or keeping that weak grip on it.

Dillon pushes her against the wall, his eyes never leaving hers as he pins her back with his body. He slowly takes her wrists in his hands, keeping her in place as he fights a huge internal battle. One she doesn't want to interrupt.

Or at least that's her intention. Having him this close is doing things to her body she hasn't felt since she left him. She widens her stance, opening her legs. His attention drops to her crotch briefly before he looks back up, his eyebrows drawn in confusion.

When she playfully pulls against his grip, it removes any of the lingering doubt. He leans down and kisses her. In that moment, she is brought back through time. Ten years apart and he still feels, still tastes the same. The addition of the piercings in his lip and tongue is too good. She's turned on and she's not alone. His dick is pressing against her stomach through his shorts, thick and hard, and she wants it.

So badly.

Dillon pauses for a moment, releasing her wrists so he can pull off her t-shirt followed by his own. Then her shorts are pushed down her legs with her underwear. His hand brushes along her side, his fingers rough from hours playing guitar. God, she missed that. Missed how his hands feel on her.

She doesn't fight back when he takes both her wrists, holding them above her head in one hand, while his mouth and free hand explore. He groans against her mouth, his kiss becoming more frenzied as his hand moves down her body. She spreads her legs, letting him brush against her.

He was usually more talkative when they were together, giving orders and commands which she lapped up. But this is different. This is raw emotion. It's ten years of pent-up feelings they both need to release.

His hand leaves her body so he can deal with his own shorts. She drops her gaze to his dick and the piercings she's been curious about. The three thick curved black bars cross the head, each of the ends topped with a solid ball. It must have been painful to have done, but she likes it. Quite a bit actually.

He doesn't give her any longer to marvel at his piercings. Dillon wraps his hand around her chin, holding her head in place so he can kiss her again. He's in control, in charge, and she's in ecstasy.

She wants to be with him again. Is desperate to feel him even just once more. But she's afraid to tell him. If she speaks now, she could tip the scales, scare him off.

Or maybe bring him to his senses.

Dillon

In some distant part of his brain, he knows this is a bad idea. The worst fucking idea in a long life of bad ideas. But that's what he's all about. He lives for the bad ideas he can beat himself up about later. It's kind of his thing. He'll do this, go back to his room or the bus, and wallow at the bottom of a bottle of whiskey. Then wake up and get on with life.

But he needs to do this.

As much as it's going to demolish the wall he's built around all his feelings for Ash, he needs to be with her again.

He's not going to make the mistake of letting her get to him though. He's going to fuck her. No emotions at all. Just a guy having sex with a girl. No big deal.

That all went to shit when he kissed her.

The instant his lips touched hers, he knew he was fucked.

What he should do is back off. Pull away from her, apologise for coming on to her, then leave. One of them needs to back off and put a stop to this before they both do something they'll regret.

But it won't be him. His self-sabotaging side is going to force him to stay and see this through.

He wants to see it through.

How fucked up is that?

He's about to be with the woman who seriously hurt him.

Hell, he's naked in front of the woman who broke his heart. His fingers are brushing along her pussy.

She keeps her eyes on his as he slides a finger inside. She's the only person who's ever been able to look him in the eye the way she is now. Goading him on, begging him to continue, just by looking at him. And why does that have to turn him on so much? Why does that get his dick so hard it hurts?

She moans softly, her hips circling so she can grind against his finger, pushing him deeper. He grips her wrists tighter, holding them against the wall when she fights him. It's all part of the game. All adding to his growing need to fuck her hard.

But she might not want this. Not really. He pulls his finger out, but she isn't on board with that. Ash wriggles against his hold, desperately trying to get close to his hand again. 'Fuck me!'

He pushes against her wrists as he leans closer. 'Don't fucking move.'

She nods, so he releases her and grabs his wallet from his bag. Once he's slipped on a condom he grabs her wrists again, her sexy, mischievous smile like a shock to his dick.

He picks her up, slowly sliding his dick inside as she wraps her legs around his waist. Dillon supports her weight as she lowers onto him. Fuck, she is so tight. The long groan she releases when his piercings push inside her is so hot.

That's part of the reason he got them in the first place. He loves that initial reaction when they slide in.

He wants to go hard, but he holds himself back. Personal feelings aside, he always puts his partner first.

It doesn't matter what he's doing to them, they have to enjoy being with him, and they have to come first. Every single time.

He feeds off that energy, off the fact that he's in control of their pleasure, that he can bring them to orgasm, or hold them on the brink.

'Oh God...'

Her moans of pleasure are like a drug. And it's *her*. It's *his* Ash, and that makes it so much more intense – both the pleasure and the pain that will hit him later.

But not now. Now he's going to fuck her. Give her everything she wants.

As soon as she relaxes and takes a deep breath, he knows she's ready for him to take over. With the first thrust, her short fingernails dig into his shoulders, gripping him hard as she hangs on.

To stop himself from doing something stupid like kissing her again, he turns his head to the side, moving away from temptation.

Ash moves against him, desperately trying to get him deeper. He grips her tightly, then moves from the wall to the floor, lowering her gently onto her back.

But her mind is on another track. She pushes him on the shoulder. 'Lie down. I want to be on top.'

Shit!

He doesn't know why his first thought is to freak out. It's what he wants. It's what he's wanted for so long. Before she changes her mind, he rolls onto his back, watching *his* stunning Ash straddle him, her face full of pleasure as she slides onto his dick.

He needs to look away as he bites the inside of his cheek. He's so close to coming already. Being pinned under her is enough to have him struggling to keep hold of himself.

But she barely gives him a chance to think about it. Ash rides him, sitting back with one hand on his leg to prop herself up. He doesn't want to look at her, but he can't resist.

And fuck does she look so beautiful! Her lips are parted, her eyes closed, small gasps and heavy breaths of pleasure mixing with the slap of their flesh.

How can a change in position do so much to him? She's not holding him down, not keeping him from doing anything, but he feels powerless under her.

'Fuck...'

When she cups his balls, holding them firmly as she picks up her pace, he can't hold back the shout.

'Not yet. Hold it.'

Hold it? He's never been told to hold himself back before. Not once, and it's something he could easily get used to.

Her pace quickens, and even though every fibre of his being is screaming at him to move, to thrust into her, he doesn't. He lies there, as the woman who knows him better than anyone on the planet, takes control from him.

Ash falls forward, one hand against his chest as she pushes both of them towards the edge. Not that she needs to do much. He's struggling more than he's ever done before.

'Now! Dillon now!'

His own shouts are drowned out as Ash comes, her orgasm tearing through her , squeezing his dick so hard it's nearly painful.

His own orgasm hits before she's even finished saying the words. He grips her hips, holding her in place, desperate to draw this out as long as he can.

Ash flops onto his chest, her body still shuddering on top of him as she comes down. He's still inside her, still feels her body gripping his.

She still feels so right against him, around him, near him. The scent of her sweat, the feel of her racing heart against his chest, the sound of her low moans. It's all familiar.

Having sex with her was an impulse. It was meant to kick him out of the past so he can move on. Instead he's put himself right back in that amazing but painful time in his life.

And as fucked up as it sounds, he'll take that pain if it means another five minutes with her like this.

Once she gets off him, he'll lose her again.

Ash

For a long time, she lies on his chest, listening to the comforting sound of his heart. For a moment, she could almost imagine they are a couple again. Cuddled up in bed together, holding each other as they did so many nights. Sleep had always been something she struggled with. But not with him. There was something about Dillon that instantly soothed her, made her feel safe.

But then he decides to put her right back in her place, tearing her from her memories and throwing her into the real world.

His entire body turns to stone beneath her. 'Get off me!'

His tone gives her no doubt he's as serious as you get. Ash pushes off him, sitting back on her legs as she looks at him. But he won't meet her eyes as he pulls his boxers and shorts back up.

When he stands and reaches for his t-shirt, she realises he's shut her out again. It shouldn't surprise or hurt her, but irritatingly it does. She knew when she went into this that it would mean nothing. But that didn't stop the hope from creeping in. And it doesn't stop the almost physical flinch when he rejects her.

'So that's it? You're just going to get dressed and not talk to me?'

He finishes dressing before he acknowledges her again. 'Talk about what? This wasn't about talking for either of us. It was a quick fuck, nothing more.'

That really hurt, but she hides it as best she can. 'Right…'

'Don't go making this into something it's not. You scratched an itch. That's it. I'm kind of guessing the same can be said for you, or do you orgasm like that all the time?'

'No. I'm not going to say I didn't get something from that either. But that's not what I'm talking about. I'm talking about trying to clear the air between us, so the next few weeks are a little less painful.'

He approaches her again, but there's nothing friendly in his smile. 'Clear the air? Did you really think spreading your legs for me would begin to put everything right between us? It was good. I'm not going to deny that. But it changes fuck all. It just adds you to a very long list.'

He smirks and Ash wants to throw up. 'That's right. I forgot you fuck anyone who shows you even the slightest bit of attention.'

'Like you just now? Seems the same can be said about you.'

She bites her tongue before another comment comes out. This could go on forever. Without getting into the argument they probably should have had to begin with, she grabs her clothes, suddenly embarrassed to be naked in the room with him. He watches in silence as she covers up, grabs her bag, and makes her way over to the door.

'What? No thanks for the orgasm?'

She stops and turns to face him. 'You're right. I do owe you a thanks. Thank you for helping me realise exactly what kind of person you are. You've saved me a lot of trouble.'

'Oh, fuck off! Don't go all holier than thou on me. You wanted to fuck too. Don't make me out to be the whore of the group, like everyone else does. I only have sex with people who want to have sex with me. Even with all this shit between us you wanted that. You're no different to me, so don't you dare put this on me.'

'That's not what I'm doing. I was just hoping... I don't know.'

He leans against the wall and crosses his arms. 'Hoping for what? A hug. An *I forgive you?*' She tries to hide the truth from her expression, but it's too late. He's seen it.

He narrows his eyes and stares at her. 'Fuck! Is that what you want?'

She is about to admit that yes, it is exactly what she wants. Tell him exactly how she feels about him. But then he breaks out laughing. God he's as frustrating as ever. 'Forget it. I'm tired. So, thank you for the amazing orgasm. You clearly haven't lost your touch. Well done you. Good night, Dillon.'

She hurries away to the sound of his laughter behind her, barely making it to her room before she breaks down in tears. She's such a fool. Why did she think doing what she did would make the slightest bit of difference in the long run? It's just made things so much worse.

When she was with him, she saw him relax, saw a bit of the old

Dillon she knew and loved from years ago. But then the hard exterior came back.

Perhaps it's a lost cause. Maybe she should do herself a favour and use this time to finally have some closure. She broke up with Dillon. She ended things with him. Whatever the reasons, he won't be able to move past that one fact. She let that amazing, if not slightly irritating, man go, and it's time she lives with the consequences of that decision. No matter how much it hurts.

Dillon

Forgive her?

Did she really expect that? Or even want it?

As he paces the gym, still laughing away to himself like he's lost the plot, he can't move past that one point.

He wasn't being serious when he said that to her. He was pissed off that he let her get to him so much he had sex with her. All he wanted to do was get dressed as fast as possible and leave, so he could kick himself in private. But then her face dropped, and he knew it was what she was hoping for.

Tough fucking luck! She could get down on her fucking knees in front of him and that wouldn't change. He can't forgive her for leaving like she did.

So why did he fuck her?

He kicks the side of the treadmill in frustration.

He can still taste her. He lifts his hand to his face and curses. He can still smell her.

Being with her was so right. Being with her filled the hole in his chest. He'd forgotten what it was like to feel like himself. For even those few minutes, he was at peace.

His mind was clear, his thoughts calm.

All the darkness that is on his heels every fucking day of his life, pushed that little bit further away.

But now it's back, stronger than ever. And this time it's his fault.

He used her.

He fucked her like she was someone he picked up in a bar, then discarded just as fast. A part of him wanted to hurt her. To lure her in, then throw her aside like she did to him. It was meant to make him feel better. All it's done is add to his shame and disgust.

He sinks onto the end of the treadmill, pulling at his hair, as the last half hour plays over in his head.

Why did he do it? Why?

The answer doesn't come to him, even when he beats his fist against his forehead. Fucking idiot!

The second he touched her, all that crap between them disappeared. It didn't matter. He was with the woman he loves. But once the sex buzz had worn off, all that crap came back, and he threw her aside.

It's a lost cause. He's never going to be able to get over what she did. It doesn't matter how badly he wants her, that will always be between them, bringing doubt and mistrust with it.

She left him once. What's to say she wouldn't leave him again? He's still the same person under all the bravado. Still the same man she left. Still the same man she couldn't love.

Who is he kidding? If anything, he's less of a prospect now than he was back then. Financially he's sound, but everything else about his life is more unstable than ever.

At least years ago, he was sober. At least back then he didn't have a criminal record. At least back then he was someone she would have been proud to be associated with.

Enough of feeling sorry for himself. She left, so fuck her! He had managed to build a decent life for himself without her in it.

What he needs to do is consider what just happened as a decent shag with a nobody, have a workout, then go back to his room.

Fuck! That Ross guy is still sleeping off their session in his fucking bed. There goes that idea. He'll work that part out later. Right now, he has to move, or he's going to spend the night sitting on the treadmill regretting what he just did with Ash.

Or wishing he could do it over and over again.

Ash

In less than five hours, Broken Chords will take to the stage, ready to give their London fans one hell of a show. As Ash sits at the back of the venue, watching the crew set up the stage for the concert later., her attention is drawn to Dillon more than she'd like.

Stealing glances at him every few minutes between taking shots of the rest of the band is becoming tiresome. Not that she doesn't like looking at him, far from it. But every time she does, she's taken back to the gym and what they did.

It was incredible. It always was with him. She'd had a few boyfriends over the years, but none had compared to Dillon. He was on another level completely. A level that no one could come close to.

She hadn't spoken to him since he laughed in her face two days ago. If anything, she'd gone out of her way to avoid him.

Embarrassment had been the main reason, but she was also less than eager to have him bring it up again. She doubts he would. He's not like that, but he'd also never made her feel so utterly mortified as he did in the gym.

Having sex with him had been a foolish thing to do. It wasn't like sex would put everything right between them. There's a chance nothing can.

Who is she kidding? Nothing she does can ever change how he feels about her. Though watching him on stage with his friends, she can't help but think he appears more relaxed.

It's probably just her imagination. Her mind playing tricks on her, seeing hope where there is none. The performance in Scotland last night had probably released some of his tension. The guys barely stood still for a second while they were on the stage.

At least she'd been able to get quite a few amazing shots of the band, even Dillon, which makes a change. He usually has a sixth sense when it comes to her and her camera, disappearing whenever she's around. Not great when both the photographer and the celebrity are doing what they can to avoid each other.

But it is what it is, and she's just going to have to do the best she can.

To take her mind off the steamy gym scene her mind is refusing to stop replaying, Ash wanders through the stadium, taking random shots of the set up. She'd been to so many concerts over the years, but never realised how much work goes on behind the scenes. The number of crew and vast amounts of equipment that follow the guys around is astounding.

She climbs the steps to the stage, keeping to the side to avoid getting in Dillon's sights. There's only so much glaring she can take from him. Leaving the band to their preparations, she steps backstage to explore the space, so she knows the layout for later when the show is on.

But then she hears something that stops her. He's singing. She'd know his deep, rich voice anywhere. Moving slowly, she makes her way around the back of the stage, until she's beside him, but still hidden behind a stack of metal boxes. Dillon is sitting on the edge of the platform where Gregg's drums are being set up, playing his bass, singing to himself.

He used to sing to her a lot. She'd spent so many nights falling asleep in his arms as he stroked her hair and sang to her. His voice is deeper than Tate's and is absolutely guaranteed to send a shiver through her body every single time.

She risks a quick peek. His eyes are closed as he sings quietly to himself. Singing had always been a way for him to relax. Before they were signed, they spent a lot of time promoting themselves, desperate for someone to take notice of them. He'd enjoyed that time, but the stress had got to him occasionally. He'd come home to her and just sing to her as he cooked dinner.

Food was another of his passions. Or at least it used to be. She can't remember ever seeing a mention of it in the many interviews she'd read over the years. She'd met him when he worked as the head chef in a restaurant she went to with her friends. It was a birthday party and they had booked the chef's table as a special treat.

And what a treat it was.

When she had seen the chef in question, her attention had been on him for the rest of the night. Dillon is an exceptional chef, each meal he prepared one of the best she'd ever tasted. After he'd prepared their meal, and all the other diners had gone home, she'd stayed in the restaurant, talking to him for hours.

Everything about their relationship was more than she could ever have wanted or wished for. Dillon was protective, and caring, and put her before himself so many times. All that mattered to him was her happiness.

And the fact he is utterly gorgeous, doesn't hurt. She's not a fan of tattoos or facial piercings, but they suit him. He was attractive when she knew him ten years ago. This Dillon is so much more.

He stops singing and frowns, as he chews on his lip ring. She's noticed he seems to do that when he's thinking, which he does a lot. He used to get lost in his head quite a bit when they were together. Something he still does if she's reading him right.

One of the sound technicians approaches him, pointing to something on a notebook he holds out to Dillon. Seems the grumpy ass act is reserved just for her. He has a reputation, but around all these people, around his friends and the crew, he's being rather nice.

'Sam! What the fuck is this?'

Okay, maybe not all the time. She bites back her smile as the technician takes a step back, putting distance between himself and Dillon.

Sam hurries over to him, listening intently as he has a go at her about something or other. The frazzled assistant nods repeatedly, then walks quickly away from him, sliding past crates of equipment blocking her escape. The poor girl needs hazard pay dealing with that lot.

'Is everything all right?'

Sam jumps, holding her hand to her chest when she sees Ash. 'You scared me!'

'I didn't mean to.'

Sam smiles, waving the apology away. 'Don't worry. I'm just jumpy today. Last minute nerves. This is my first time doing a tour solo. Ellen was here last time. I'm just trying to keep everyone happy, and believe me, that's becoming increasingly impossible.'

'I can only imagine. For what it's worth, you seem to be handling everything incredibly well.'

'I appreciate you saying that, Ash. Would you like to join the band and I for dinner? We're just about done here, so we'll grab some food now before they have to get ready for the show.'

If she hadn't been naked with Dillon in the gym, she would absolutely accept the invitation. However, it's too new, too raw. Sitting at the same table as him, making polite conversation, it's not going to work. 'Thank you, but I really should make sure I'm all set up for later.'

'Are you sure? I promise I'll make sure Tate doesn't eat all the food.'

Ash shakes her head as she laughs. 'I'm not sure how you'd do that, but thanks for the offer. Have a nice dinner. I'll see you later.'

'No problem. We'll meet in the lobby and head over here together later.'

'Sounds good.'

She watches Sam go over to the guys, waiting while they grab their jackets before heading off the stage with her. Dillon stops at the bottom of the steps to glance over his shoulder at her. They hold each other's gaze for a minute before he turns away, dismissing her.

Dillon

He's wired, but not in a good way. They're on stage in a few minutes and she'll be watching him again. There will be thousands of fans watching them perform, so why is she giving him issues? He had been able to ignore her last night, but for some reason, he can't get his mind off her tonight.

What if he forgets the words to a song? Or the chords? Or trips and falls on his arse?

He hasn't done any of those things before, so why is he assuming he'll start today? The Scottish show had been a roaring success. No forgotten lyrics, or bassists falling on their face.

Fuck! Why does it matter so much to him that he makes a good impression in front of her?

Why can't he get her out of his fucking head? Why did he fuck her in Scotland?

He's made some monumental mistakes in his life, but that probably tops the list. After working out in the gym, he'd crashed on the couch in Luke's room. Or at least tried to. The next few hours were spent replaying his time in the gym with Ash. Then every other fucking time they were together. When he finally dragged his sorry ass off the couch for breakfast, he was horny, pissed off, tired, and another healthy dose of horny.

He doesn't do this. He has sex, then moves on. Simple.

But this is different. He's still in love with her and it's screwing with him, big time.

He hates her, but he loves her. The whole situation is pissing him off.

He paces his dressing room as that thought keeps fucking with him.

He can't go on stage while his head is on other things. He's not even ready to go on. He's got jeans and his boots on, but he threw his t-shirt somewhere a few minutes ago when he got pissed off. Again. It's a constant thing at the moment.

He's so tired of always being pissed off at something.

His pacing comes to a stop when someone knocks on his door. 'Dillon? You okay?'

'Yeah, Sam. I'm fine.'

'Can I come in?'

'Sure.' She might be able to kick his ass into action. Fuck knows he's failing miserably.

She stops in front of him, her clipboard in her hands as usual. 'Oh. You're not ready. They need to hook you up.'

'Yeah. Sorry. On a bit of a go slow today. I just need to find my t-shirt.'

She hugs her clipboard to her chest and gives him a look that has him instantly on edge. 'What?'

'Can I ask you something?'

'Yeah.'

'Are you okay? You've seemed... off lately.'

No way he's even going there with her. It's his business. 'Just in a grump. Ignore me.'

'Being in a grump is Tate's job,' she says, grinning at him. She locates his t-shirt against the far wall and passes it to him. 'Should I ask how it ended up over there?'

'I threw it. Bad mood. I'll be fine once I'm on stage.'

'Aren't moody rock stars meant to throw guitars and things like that? I'm not sure what damage a t-shirt is going to do.'

'I think my guitar trashing days are over. I'm not keen on heading back behind bars again.'

'You know what? That's actually a very good idea. None of us want to lose you again. You didn't deserve that sentence.'

He hadn't spoken about his time in prison with anyone from Vox other than Ellen. Truth be told it was fucking humiliating and not something he fancied sharing with anyone. But hearing Sam say that means the world to him. 'Thank you. I mean that.'

'No need to thank me. It's the truth. So, are you planning on putting that t-shirt on?'

He finishes getting dressed, not stopping Sam when she straightens the t-shirt. She adjusts the chains around his neck, making sure they're lying correctly over the t-shirt.

'I'm worried about you.'

'Why?'

'I love your unpredictability. Love the way I have no idea what you're going to do from one minute to the next.'

'Seriously?' That surprises him. It's usually the trait he gets in the most trouble over.

'Yeah. I'm not saying working with the four of you is boring. Far from it. But you especially keep me on my toes. Lately though, you're different. Quieter. Darker perhaps.'

He swallows the lump that suddenly forms in his throat. That blindsided him in a way he wasn't expecting. The hug he gives her surprises him just as much. He's not one for randomly hugging people. Sam hugs him back and it feels nice. Kind of what he needs right now.

He releases her and gives her his best smile. 'I promise I'm okay. You don't need to worry.'

She nods and takes a deep breath. 'I'll hold you to that.' Sam steps back and nods at him. 'You look like the rock star they're waiting for. You ready to give them one hell of a performance?'

He nods. Isn't that what he does every single day from the minute he wakes up? 'Always.'

'C'mon then. Let's get you on stage.'

He follows Sam out of the dressing room and does his best to push any thoughts of Ash from his mind. He's Dillon Ryan, bassist and singer for Broken Chords. For the next few hours, that's all he should be focusing on.

For a few minutes, as she watches one of the biggest bands in the world perform a few feet from her, she becomes lost in the music, lost in Tate's voice and his lyrics.

Being at the front of the stage with the security and other venue personnel, Ash has an unobstructed view of the guys doing what they do so well.

Of Dillon in his element.

Which has her in a strange mixture of heaven and hell.

She can't get over how incredible he looks right now. The black tank top shows off every splendid and well toned inch of his arms, the rhythmic movement of the muscles under his skin intoxicating as he plays his bass. The fine sheen of sweat on his skin glistens under the spotlights, a few strands of his hair sticking to his forehead.

He used to be hers.

Ash slips through the door to the side of the viewing area in front of the stage, climbing the steps to bring her out to the side of the stage itself. She takes a few pictures of Gregg and Luke, moving around behind the scenes to the other side so she can get Tate and Dillon.

She's doing her best not to distract them. The last thing she wants to do is throw any of them off by waving her camera in their faces. So far it seems to be working. None of them have even cast a glance in her direction.

But as soon as she comes level with Dillon, all thoughts about taking a picture of him fade away. He's even more mesmerising up close. She lowers her camera, letting it hang around her neck as she just takes time out to watch him.

This is what she should have been doing for the last ten years. She should have been beside him, watching and admiring him as he performed. Supporting him as he travelled the world doing what he loves. She would have been more than happy to spend hours on the road, following him from concert to concert.

Instead, she'd allowed herself to be scared off. To be driven away from him. But seeing him right now, she knows it was the right decision. If she'd stayed with him, Dillon may not have had the success he has. And there was no way she could have lived with herself if she'd been the reason he lost it all.

This is where he belongs. Even back then she knew singing and performing were what he was meant to do. He's a natural. They all are. But with Dillon, it's his way of showing his emotions. When he sits down with his guitar, he lets that guard down. She never figured out if it was an intentional slip, or if he was just too busy playing and singing that he forgot to keep his mask in place.

Dillon with a guitar in his hands is the real Dillon. The truly happy, at peace man who isn't putting on a front, or trying to be someone he's not.

He's smiling. She can't remember the last time she'd seen him smile like that. It was probably when they were together. Before she took a piece of him and destroyed it.

Then he looks at her, directly into her eyes, as he plays. For the briefest of moments, she's back in their small apartment, listening to him play.

He grips the neck of his bass as the song ends, wiping his forehead with his free hand, his eyes still on her. There's no anger or hostility though. Ash could swear he's sad. For those few seconds his guard is down, those emotions he hides, visible to her.

I'm so sorry I hurt you, Dillon. You didn't deserve it.

His wall comes up again, almost as if he heard her thoughts. His eyes harden as he turns away, waving at the crowd along with the rest of the band.

There's no forgiveness there. Not for her.

13

Dillon

He's tired. Then again, lately he's always tired. Being on the road makes taking pills to knock himself out more difficult to conceal. He's not hiding it from anyone. He'd just prefer not to have that conversation with the guys.

Especially with her eavesdropping on every fucking conversation.

The bus is spacious enough, but she's still too close. Still invading his space. He'll have to remember to thank whoever had the great idea to let her tag along on the bus.

As well as a fucking rotten headache, a stinking hangover, and being exhausted, he has to endure her company while they're on the road. After what they did a few days ago, he would have preferred to keep as far from her as possible.

He's not embarrassed. No regrets either. No point regretting fucking her. If he beat himself up every time he had sex, he'd be doing it all the time.

All he can do is put what happened in the gym to the back of his mind. It was no big deal. She was just another in a long line of meaningless sexual encounters.

He'd told her that. Told her she was just another number. Maybe that's something he wishes he hadn't done, but it's too late to do anything about it.

It'll be another three hours before they get to the French venue, so he just needs to suck it up until then. Grab a few hours to himself without her watching his every fucking move.

He looks down the length of the bus to the seating area just behind the driver's seat.

Ash is chatting away to Gregg and Luke, showing them some of the shots she took last night. Tate is asleep in the bunk opposite him, his arm hiding his face as he snores softly.

It's great to see him sleeping for a change. For a while there, Tate couldn't sleep at all. Maybe Chloe, Brandon, and therapy are making a difference.

Then again, he could say the same about Gregg and Luke. Both are happier, more content than he's seen them for ages.

Great. So, he's the only fucked up one left in the group. Happy days!

He rolls onto his side, tucking his hand under his pillow. He's not going to sleep. No chance in hell. Lying here for the next few hours isn't going to improve his mood.

Admitting defeat, he climbs off the bunk and, after stopping to take a packet of his sweets from the cupboard, sits opposite Ash, stretching his legs out in front of him.

She looks up at him, meeting his eyes for a moment, before turning her attention back to her camera and the guys. Every fucking time they accidentally look at each other like that, he forgets how much she hurt him. It just lasts a second or two, but he can't stop his brain from fucking him over and it's pissing him off.

She walked away. He should be focusing on that, and not the other memories that keep coming back to him. It even happened last night when he was on stage. He felt her looking at him from the side of the stage, and suddenly out of nowhere he was back in their place, singing to her. One fucking look and she got to him, opening the wound all over again.

He flicks through an entertainment magazine on the table as he tries to block out her babbling.

Okay so maybe babbling is a little harsh. Her voice is actually not that bad. Who is he kidding? It's a very nice voice. Unfortunately. Fuck, he's in a right mood today.

'So have you been to any of these venues before?' Gregg asks her, irritating Dillon for some reason.

'No, I haven't,' she replies, putting her camera on the table. 'You've played all over the country, haven't you?'

'Yep. Loads of times. We're kind of a big deal here.'

'Is that right?'

Gregg nods. 'Oh yeah.'

'You think you're kind of a big deal wherever you go,' Luke says, grinning at him.

'That could very well be the case, and for a good reason. I am!'

Dillon zones out, flicking through the magazine until he comes across a picture of himself. *How is the bad boy of Broken Chords surviving life after prison?*

Fuck! Just what he wants to be reminded of right now. Worst month of his life. He still has nightmares about being locked up. He turns the page, but it's a four-page spread. Flattering to get that much publicity, but he'd prefer it was because he's a talented singer and musician. This bad boy image he's earned for himself is getting old.

And he's forty years old. Being referred to as a *bad boy* is ridiculous.

But that's his fault too. If he didn't keep getting into trouble, he wouldn't have earned himself that title.

He dumps the magazine back on the table with a loud sigh.

'You saw it.'

Luke isn't asking a question, so he doesn't bother answering. One quick glance up at his friend is enough of a response.

'Saw what?' Gregg asks, pulling the magazine across the table towards him. It doesn't take long to find the article. 'Ah. Nice.'

'Isn't it.' He chews his lip ring as he glares at Gregg, hoping he drops the subject.

'You look good in these pics.'

'Thanks,' he replies, unable to keep the sarcasm from his voice. 'That's the most important thing, isn't it?'

Gregg shrugs, closing the magazine again. 'Better than looking shite and having that article printed.'

'It's actually a very good article.'

Dillon takes a few seconds to convince himself to give her any attention. 'What?'

'Did you read it?'

He narrows his eyes but doesn't respond.

'You should read it. It's extremely well written and, in spite of the title, it's not all about you and prison. The writer took it from a different angle. She's focusing more on the fact that you've thrived and hit the ground running again after what happened. That your fans have welcomed you back and support you. It's very flattering.'

He keeps glaring at her, so she finally gets the message and turns her attention back to her camera.

'Whoa! Death glare.'

'Fuck off Gregg!'

'What? It was a death glare. You'll give yourself some serious frown lines if you keep that up. Or a whopping headache.'

'How about I give you a headache?'

Gregg holds up his hands in defeat. 'Message received.'

He feels Luke glaring at him so returns the favour, dropping it as soon as he sees Luke's face. He's never been good at being pissed off with Luke. He can still diffuse him with just one look. Screw this. He grabs the magazine, before heading back to the bunks and sliding onto his bed.

After pulling the curtain across, he opens the magazine and scans through the article. Ash was right. It's not too bad once you get into it. Apparently, the fact he got out of prison and went back to performing was being praised. Like it was some sort of achievement.

He didn't have a choice. If he didn't get back up on stage as soon as he could, he never would. For a while after getting out, he had convinced himself his popularity would take a hit.

That he'd just be tagged as the drunken ex-con.

But after the truth came out about Pippa abusing Luke, it probably bought him a little sympathy.

Being inside had knocked his confidence like nothing before. It's a knock he still hasn't fully recovered from. Having the shit kicked out of him and not being able to do anything about it, had gone against everything he is.

He fights. He's fought every day of his life. But in there the rules are different. The only thing he was focused on was doing his time, not causing trouble, and getting the fuck out of there as fast as possible.

So, he took the beatings, refusing to fight back in case it prolonged his time by even an hour. He needed to get out.

It's just a good thing he's such a great actor. Or bullshitter. Whatever he is, he'll keep it up.

Dillon dumps the magazine on the bed beside him, then opens the curtain a crack so he can see her. She's showing Gregg some shots from the show last night and, from the look on Gregg's face, he's

117

impressed.

And he should be. Ash wasn't working as a photographer when they were together. It was more of a hobby, something she did in her free time. He's not surprised she took it up full time. She's incredible. Always has been.

She laughs, brushing some hair back from her forehead. She is incredible in more ways than one.

He angrily yanks the curtain back across again. If he doesn't get his head out of the past, he's going to drive himself crazy. Moving quietly, he pulls out his wallet and takes two pills from the packet. He swallows them, then closes his eyes, willing them to work fast.

He needs to sleep, but more than that, he needs to forget, because the memories are killing him.

Ash

After already seeing the band perform in the first two venues, she thought tonight she'd be more focused on taking photos rather than forgetting she's here to do a job and just stopping to listen to them like everyone else in the audience.

But it's a battle she's not winning. She'd lost count of the number of times she had to force herself to stop watching them and do her damn job. It was so easy to get lost in the music, become captivated watching the four men own the stage for every minute they were on it.

Stifling a yawn, she packs away her kit while she waits for Sam and the guys to meet her. How they manage to get on stage and give such an energetic performance after spending all day in the bus on the road, or in a ferry she'll never know. Three shows and she's already feeling worn out.

'Are you with someone?'

Ash smiles at the security guard and holds up her pass. 'I'm actually with the band.'

'That's not quite what I meant,' he replies in heavily accented English. 'I finish work in an hour. Do you want a drink with me?'

'I'll have to pass I'm afraid. I have loads of work to do, but thank you.'

He runs his fingers up her arm, so she takes a step back. 'Are you sure you won't change your mind?'

Whatever answer Ash was going to voice disappears when the guy is pulled away from her and thrown against the wall. Dillon presses his arm against the guy's neck and gets right in his face. 'She said no asshole.'

'Dillon! What are you doing? Let him go!'

'What the fuck is your problem?' With a good foot on the security guard, and a lot of anger in his favour, Dillon manages to hold him in place, even though he's fighting to get free.

'She said no. Get it?'

'Yes! Yes, fine! I get it. Just let me go.'

Dillon slams him against the wall one more time just in case he didn't get the message, then lets him go.

As the guard hurries away, cursing under his breath, Ash faces Dillon, more confused than angry. Not that she's going to let him know that. He's going to get it with both barrels.

'What the fuck, Dillon! What were you thinking?'

'He wasn't leaving you alone.'

'Yeah. And?'

'So, I told him to stop.'

'No, you didn't tell him to stop. You threw him against the wall, then told him to stop. And I was handling the situation just fine without your help. If you could call it help. He could report what you just did.'

119

'Let him try.'

'Unbelievable!' She jams her finger against his chest. 'And what gives you the right to come to my rescue like some fucking thug, huh? It's got nothing to do with you. Fifty men could come on to me and it would still have nothing to do with you.'

'Fine! How about next time I leave you to deal with it yourself?'

'I didn't ask you to deal with it this time, so yeah. That would be great. Thank you!'

Luke grabs him by the arm, but Dillon pulls his arm free. 'Get the fuck off me!'

'Just walk away, Dillon. Come on. We're heading out for some food.'

'I said get off me Luke!'

Ash steps back as Jace and Tate join Luke, leading Dillon away. She considers going in the opposite direction, but she's getting a lift back to the hotel with one of the bodyguards. She hurries after them, but Gregg stops her before she gets to the minibus with Dillon and the others. 'How about you come with me? Leave Tate and Luke to deal with Dillon.'

'Deal with him how?'

'Just calm him down a bit.'

'Is he okay?'

Gregg nods, then leads her over to the second minibus waiting for them. 'He gets like this from time to time. He just needs to blow off some steam. He'll be right as rain in a bit.'

Ash isn't in the slightest bit convinced by that. Even in the van she can hear Dillon shouting. 'How exactly is he going to blow off all that steam?'

'He'll probably hit the gym with Tate. That's what they usually do. Don't worry, it happens a lot. He's more of a make war not peace, instead of peace not war, kind of a guy. But sure I don't need to tell you that. No doubt you witnessed it yourself when you were together.'

120

Gregg has a point there. Dillon had never once lost his temper with her, but she had witnessed him having a go at other people from time to time. 'I take it the anger management classes he was told to take by the court had little effect?'

Gregg laughs as Ciaran pulls out of the private car park and heads towards the hotel. 'You're kidding right? No changing that leopard's spots. But all joking aside, it comes from a good place. He's got a heart of gold under it all. He's just not the best at showing his feelings without getting all in your face about it.'

'You all really care about each other, don't you?'

Gregg runs his hand through his hair, ruffling the crazy spikes. 'Absolutely. Without getting all deep and meaningful or anything like that, we're more than mates. More than family too. We've been with each other through some scary shit.

'As much as they can irritate the hell out of me at times, I wouldn't be without any of them. Well, maybe Tate! Have you ever been to a buffet with that one? He'll demolish it all before you've had a chance to get a look in.'

Ash laughs when he winks and grins widely. She has a lot of time for Gregg. It's impossible not to instantly like him and his carefree nature. 'I can imagine it would be challenging.'

'Challenging! Ha! Greedy more like it. Anyway, I'm getting off the point. Dillon went after that guy because deep down, in some warped part of his being, he still cares about you. Plain and simple. He lashes out because he cares.'

'It's not exactly romantic.'

'No. Not the best way to get his feelings across, but it's all you've got. For the moment at least.'

She looks across at Gregg when he says that. 'For the moment? You think there could be more?'

He shrugs. 'Never say never. That's not a great help I know, but it's better than a definite no. And knowing that awkward fucker - excuse the French — the way I do, it's not a definite no.'

'Thank you, Gregg.'

'Now don't go thanking me just yet. He's not a fan of going with popular opinion. You'll just have to take it a day at a time. Actually, scrap that. Take it an encounter at a time and see where it goes.'

He stretches out and yawns loudly. 'Well, I don't know about you, but I am beat. First though I need food. Fancy joining me for some grub in the hotel? Now I have a girlfriend, so don't go getting any ideas, but if you think you can resist my natural charm, you're welcome to join me.'

'Oh, I don't know if I can resist.'

'Fair point. But according to my stunning girlfriend, I have the table manners of a toddler. I'm sure you'll be turned off after a minute or two.'

Ash laughs as he wiggles his eyebrows at her. 'You know what? That sounds lovely. Not the table manner's part. I would love to join you for dinner.'

He claps loudly, startling her. 'It's a date. A completely platonic one of course. Driver! Back to the hotel as fast as you can. We're hungry.'

Ciaran laughs as he glances at them over his shoulder. 'As you wish, sir.'

Dillon

His muscles are screaming for a break, but he pushes on. He needs to push on. To push himself. To expel the rage that's building inside.

His reaction to that security guard last night was an embarrassing joke. He lost it and it makes no sense. He just saw that guard talking to Ash, and the only thing on his mind in that moment was beating the shite out of him.

He's fucking amazed he let the guy go so easily. Usually, when he's like that, his temper is in full control. It's part of the reason he's the one with the criminal record, while the others can just walk away from situations like that.

He's not a fan of walking away from confrontations.

He'd taken a few classes to try and control his temper and they sometimes helped...for the most part.

With Luke and Tate babysitting last night, he'd worked out for a good hour in the gym before heading back to the bus, and again this morning as soon as he woke up.

It's part of what they do when they're on tour. Performing, interviews, moving from venue to venue, it can be stressful as well as tiring. This was their way of blowing off steam.

And he has a fuck load of steam to blow off today.

There's also a chance he might be putting off seeing Ash again. Fuck, he's dreading seeing her. Having her witness him losing it like he did, is going to give her one hell of a kick. She probably laughed all the way back to her hotel room.

Not that he'd blame her. If he was trying to let on he didn't give a fuck about her anymore, going all caveman with the guard wouldn't have helped his cause.

He drops the weights back in the rack before he does some damage to himself or the equipment. He needs to keep that hurt, the pain she caused and still causes, locked away so she can't see it. He needs to control it better.

What he needs to do is have some mindless sex with a random stranger. Just keep fucking until his mind shuts off and he's lost in the moment.

Like when he was with Ash in the gym.

He shouts, kicking at the bench in frustration.

'It's not working, is it?'

He glances over at Luke, then back at the bench. 'I'm fine.'

Luke sits on the bench as he wipes his face with a towel. 'I've never seen you this worked up before. You have to talk to her, Dillon. Get some of this off your chest before it eats you up.'

'Believe me, talking to her about how much she hurt me won't stop it hurting. I just want to forget about it and get on with my life. Is that too much to ask?'

'I don't think you can move on until you talk to her.'

'Whatever. I'm done talking about it. I just want to finish my set.'

'I promised Gregg I'd go for a run with him. You want to join us?'

'No. I'm good. You head off. Jace can keep me company.' He glances over at his bodyguard who rolls his eyes before focusing on his phone again. He's been pissing Jace off a little too much lately. The guy is going to walk at this rate.

'You sure?'

'Yeah. Go. I'll head back to the bus in an hour or so.'

Luke nods, grabs his bag, and leaves with Andy. He wouldn't have minded going for a run. Might have helped blow off some more steam. But she's there. At the bus waiting to pounce.

Another half an hour here, then he'll face the music.

Ash

He's not here. Thank God for small mercies. She'd been dreading seeing Dillon after what happened yesterday with the security guard in France. Ash closes the door of the tour bus behind her and smiles as she sits down on the couch next to Sam.

'Coffee?'

Ash places her camera on the couch next to her, and gratefully accepts the steaming cup of coffee from Sam. 'Thanks. Where are the guys?'

'Luke and Gregg have gone for a run, Tate is swimming, and Dillon is at the hotel working out, I think. So, did you get any good shots yesterday?'

Ash nods and takes a sip of coffee. 'Yeah.' She looks out the window at the clear water of Lake Zurich, and smiles. 'It's a stunning location.'

Sam nods in agreement. 'It's my first time here, but I have to completely agree. The campsite owner is a friend of Ellen's, so he lets us set up camp here away from everyone else.

'The guys have no problem meeting with fans, but they like to have privacy too. Can't ask for better than this place.' She leans back on the couch and looks out the window at the lake. 'So, is everyone cooperating with you? They're all swimming or working out. You're free to be honest.'

Ash really doesn't want to go there with Sam. She went down to the small beach at the edge of the lake earlier hoping to catch the guys, well, mainly Dillon, but he was proving to be elusive.

Tate had been swimming for the last half hour. She'd dipped her toe in and decided he could have the water to himself that day. Luke and Gregg had gone for a run, but Dillon had vanished. Again.

She's got some amazing shots of Tate, Luke, and Gregg, but not so many of Dillon. 'Yeah. I could do with a few more of Dillon though. He seems a little camera shy.' He's avoiding her plain and simple.

Sam snorts loudly. 'Are you sure we're talking about the same Dillon?'

'What do you mean?'

'Out of the four of them, he's the least camera shy. It's usually Luke you have to coax in front of the camera. This isn't like Dillon at all. Is he giving you the runaround? I can have a chat to him if you want?'

'Oh no, it's fine, really. Please don't say anything. Maybe it's just what I'm doing that's turning him off. It's a little different to the usual photo shoots.'

'Okay, as long as you're sure? But if you need me to step in, please let me know.'

Ash smiles and takes a drink of coffee before she answers. Why did she open her big mouth? Now Sam knows Dillon is causing problems and will no doubt be keeping an eye on him. 'Leave it with me. I'll make sure I get loads of him too. I might just need to convince him

I'm not the bad guy.' Easier said than done, but this is her job on the line. She needs to do something.

Sam smiles and leans over to look out the back window. 'Speak of the devil.'

Ash can hear the distant rumble of an engine. The truck pulls up beside the bus and Dillon gets out along with Jason. Dillon's hair is wet, and he's got a gym bag in his hand.

His face drops as soon as he steps into the bus and sees her. He dumps the bag on his bunk and without a word, leaves the bus and heads down to the water.

Sam grimaces and looks over at Ash. 'Yikes. He's not the chattiest of guys at the best of times, but that was just weird. I'm so sorry about his behaviour. I may have to have a word with him.'

'No, really. I'll go after him. See if he'll talk.'

Sam raises her eyebrows, then looks at the screen on her phone as it rings. 'That's Ellen. Okay, good luck with Dillon.' She answers the phone as Ash leaves the bus. She grabs her sunglasses, takes a deep breath, then heads down to the beach after Dillon.

She finds him in the water. Typical he'd go somewhere he knew she wouldn't follow. Tate is just emerging from the lake, his impressive body pushing through the water. He grabs his towel from the sand and walks towards her.

As intimidating as he looks, she was surprised how nice he really is. It takes a bit to get him going conversation wise, but there was something about him that she likes. He's a decent guy once you get through the wall.

'Hi Tate. How's the water?'

'Fucking freezing! You heading in?'

'After that recommendation, I don't think so. You haven't done a great job selling it to me.'

He laughs and runs his hand over his hair. 'Fair enough. I'm off to grab a shower.'

Ash sits on the sand and watches Dillon swimming. Gregg and Luke appear from a path through the trees, Ciaran and Andy keeping pace with them. All four men are covered with sweat, their faces flushed from the exertion. 'Good run?'

Luke nods and takes a second to catch his breath. 'Don't go running with Gregg. He's like a damn gazelle.'

'Plenty of practice chasing bad guys in my youth,' Gregg says with a wide grin.

Luke sits down beside her and rests his arms on his legs. 'I thought I was in shape.'

'Oh, don't get all broody, buddy. I'm just a hell of a lot faster than you.'

'Yeah, I got that part.' Luke looks over at her. 'You heading in?'

Ash shakes her head. 'It's a bit cold for my liking.'

'Too right. Tate and Dillon are freaks. No question.'

Gregg nods towards Dillon. 'Absolutely. Neither of them feels the cold. It's ridiculous. I stuck my foot in there and I still can't feel it. Anyway, time for a shower I think.'

'Tate just headed back for a shower.'

Gregg groans as he pushes his damp hair back from his forehead. 'Asshole will use all the fucking hot water. C'mon Luke. I'll race you.' He sprints off towards the bus leaving Luke behind.

Luke laughs but stays where he is. 'Leave him to it. Hyperactive idiot,' he mutters to himself. 'Are you okay?'

'Of course! Why do you ask?'

He nods towards Dillon, his powerful strokes moving him quickly through the water. 'He's my best friend so I'm in the right position to say he's one of the most stubborn, infuriating people I know. He's giving you a hard time, isn't he?'

She shrugs, looking back at Dillon in the lake. 'No more than I deserve. I hurt him. I have to accept this is the way it's going to be with him.'

'Do you want it to be more? You can trust me. I won't say anything to him.'

'Why are you so bothered? I don't mean to sound harsh. I'm just curious.'

'Mainly because I'm a really nice guy,' he says with a big smile. 'But I'm also worried about both of you. Neither of you asked to be thrown into this situation. He's struggling and I'm guessing you are too.'

'I didn't think I'd ever see him again. It's just... difficult.'

'He's difficult.'

Ash can't help but laugh at that. 'Oh yeah. But that's Dillon.'

'That's Dillon all right. I don't have any advice I'm afraid. You probably know him as well as I do. And you didn't answer my question.'

'About wanting more?'

He nods.

What the hell. 'Yes. I had this whole scene in my head. You know like they do in those Hallmark movies? We'd see each other again and run into each other's arms.'

'And live happily ever after.'

'I know. It sounds ridiculous.'

'Of course it doesn't. I'm not going to ask why you left. It's none of my business. Dillon still has feelings for you. He wouldn't be reacting like this unless he did. But he'll keep pushing you away. He won't let you in easily. So, you know what you have to do?'

'I have to fight for him.'

Luke nods. 'And fight hard. He assumes everyone will leave him. It's how he's wired. It won't be easy to convince him otherwise, especially since you've already left him once. That wasn't a dig, really.'

'Do you think there's even the slightest chance he'll forgive me?'

'Yes.'

She's surprised by the quick response. 'Really?'

'He loves you. I think he wants to forgive you. He needs to. The hard part will be helping him to realise that.' He nods towards the water again. 'No time like the present to make a start.' Luke stands up, waves at Dillon, then heads back to the bus.

Ash turns to look at Dillon. He's standing in the lake, the water swelling around his chest, but he doesn't make a move to join her. Stubborn git will probably stay in there all day if it means avoiding her. Tough. Two can play at that game.

She gets to her feet and walks towards the water's edge. With each step she can feel his cold gaze boring into her. Ash stands a few feet from the water and crosses her arms, waiting for him to get out.

He slowly stalks towards her, and Ash begins to regret her decision to confront him. Dillon's broad chest is on full display thanks to the black shorts he's wearing. He's spectacular.

She moves her attention from his body to his face, and it helps to quench the heat rising in her body. He's pissed off. But nothing new there. He's been pissed off since she walked into the venue that first day.

'What do you want?'

'Can we talk?'

Dillon rests his hands on his hips and takes a long, steady breath before he answers. 'I told you. Best we don't go there.'

'So, you can fuck me, but you can't talk to me?'

'I fuck lots of people. It doesn't mean I want to talk to any of them.'

She bites her tongue. She won't give him the argument he wants. 'Surely we can talk about this.'

'The time for talking was years ago. I'm over it.'

'Yeah right. Clearly, you're over it. You can barely look at me. People are noticing.'

He moves his hands from his hips, crossing them instead. 'Who?'

'Sam for starters.'

'What did you say to her?' he asks accusingly.

'Nothing, but we need to do something about this. I can't go back to my boss, or to Ellen, with hundreds of pictures of Tate, Gregg, and Luke, but barely a dozen of you.'

'So, you're blaming me for the fact you're not doing your job?'

'I can hardly take a picture of you when you're either hiding from me or glowering. Which you're doing all the time I might add. Including right now! The only time I've seen you look remotely happy is when you're on stage.' She pauses and smiles at him. 'You really come alive on stage, you know that.'

He meets her eyes briefly, before looking away again. His guard has just dropped. Not by much, but she'll take whatever she can get. 'I know you don't want me here, and the last thing I want to do is piss you off more than I have. But this is bigger than you and me. It's our careers at stake.

'If I don't get some amazing pictures of the *four* members of the band, I'm in serious trouble at work. And it's not great for Broken if their bassist is in a grump in each of the photos. I thought you wanted to shed the whole *bad boy* thing you have going on? This isn't helping.

'And you did say you wouldn't mess this up for either of us. How exactly is avoiding me, and making an already awkward situation so much worse, not messing things up?'

Dillon doesn't say anything for a few minutes, then nods once. 'Fine. You're right. About not messing things up for both of us. That's not what I want.'

Ash smiles and relaxes a little. The last few days of being treated like something he scraped off the bottom of his shoe, hadn't been easy, but she wasn't expecting him to back down so easily. 'Okay, that's great.'

He walks past her and grabs his towel from the sand. 'Go back to your hotel. I'll get dressed and pick you up before lunch. We can head over to the venue and you can take as many pictures as you want.'

'Thank you, Dillon.'

He doesn't bother responding as he walks away.

15

Dillon

The first two pills didn't make much of an impact, but the next two did. Especially when washed down with a good few mouthfuls of whiskey. He takes another drink, before dropping the bottle back on the sand. The tree he's slumped against is fucking painful, but he can't be bothered moving.

When he made the arrangements with Ash earlier, he fully intended following through with them. Or at least trying to. But as he watched her being driven back to her hotel, he knew he couldn't go through with it.

He should have cancelled. Should have even sent her a fucking text. But he didn't. Let her wait there for him to arrive. Just like he did for months after she left.

When someone had walked by his door, he was sure it would be her. Every time the phone rang, he had hoped it would be her. Days turned to weeks, then to months. And still he waited. Even when his lease ran out and he had to hand over the keys to the apartment, he still drove by every day just in case she was there.

That continued until he was forced to move back to Ireland when the band took off.

He nearly went mad during those months on his own. He never told the guys about Ash, or what happened, so they had no idea what he was going through, and when he got back to Ireland, he just put up a wall around himself.

She was shoved to the back of his mind. It was all about self-preservation. The only thing he could do was bury himself in work and try to forget...unsuccessfully.

Touring had been the distraction he needed. When his celebrity status grew, so did the attention he received. And he lapped it all up. Too much of it. Every time he slept with someone, it was done to get back at her. To stick two fingers up at her and what she did to him.

Fucking total strangers, then leaving them, was easier than opening up and letting someone do that to him again. Hurt them first, then walk away. It was his MO.

Would Ash still be waiting for him now? Would she be pacing the lobby, checking her watch and wondering where he is? Maybe she's on her way over here? He washes that thought down with more whiskey, then closes his eyes. He really couldn't care less.

That's a lie. Of course he does. He cares too much and that's the problem.

He looks up as someone drops down beside him on the sand. Luke takes the bottle from him and has a mouthful before handing it back. 'Are you going to talk to me?'

'About what? I'm living the dream.' He smiles at Luke but can't seem to focus properly on his face.

'If this is the dream maybe you need a new one. How much have you had? You look wasted.'

He raises the bottle to Luke. 'Cheers for that. Great fucking mate you are. Where are Tate and Gregg?'

'They went out to get something to eat. You do know we're on tomorrow? You might want to ease up on that and get some food yourself. You don't want to face a long show with a hangover.'

'I will in a minute.'

'Dillon...'

'Oh, don't you Dillon me in that tone! I'm forty fucking years old! I can drink if I want, and I can sure as hell be a grumpy fucker if I want.'

'Well, you're succeeding on all points. Well done.'

Dillon could swear he'd managed to restrain the snort, but it clearly broke free.

'Now you're snorting at me. Nice.'

'You know I'm getting fucking sick of you all looking at me the way you do.'

'What way?'

He points the neck of the bottle at Luke's face. 'That way.'

'Well maybe if you stop getting drunk and being a complete jerk we wouldn't have to. I get that Ash showing up out of the blue has knocked you. But dealing with it by drinking like this isn't going to help.'

'Stop making a big deal out of this. I'm not. Her being here isn't bothering me in the slightest.' He wishes he could convince himself that's the truth. Doesn't look like he's managed to convince Luke either.

They both stop talking as Ash storms across the sand towards them.

'Oops. Looks like I'm in trouble. Fucking shock.'

Luke glances sideways at him. 'Jesus, Dillon! What did you do now?'

134

He doesn't get a chance to reply as Ash arrives looking less than happy. He grins up at Ash as she stands in front of him, her hands on her hips. She is seriously pissed.

'Oh hi. How are you?'

'How am I Dillon? I'm pissed off. And you're drunk?' she replies in a tone that grates on him.

'Absolutely. What can I do for you?'

'You had no intention of meeting me today, did you? No, don't bother answering that. I know you didn't. What the hell was I thinking?'

'What can I say, something came up.'

'I thought we agreed we'd try to work together?'

'I lied. You know all about that, right?'

He hears the words, but he's too pissed, and too pissed off to stop them. He did want to meet her. More than anything. But as usual, he's screwed it up. He can feel Luke looking at him and doesn't need to see his face to know he's disgusted. Join the club.

Ash laughs humourlessly. 'Of course. I walked right into that, didn't I? So, is there more payback heading my way, or are you done with the childish tit-for-tat?'

Dillon uses the tree behind him to push himself to his feet. He didn't think he'd had that much to drink, but he's seriously smashed. 'Childish? I haven't even begun yet. You broke my fucking heart!' She glances down at Luke, but Dillon waves his hand in her face. 'Oh, he knows all the gory details. He knows how you said you'd marry me, then fucked off without a word.'

He needs to stop talking. To stop all the emotional shit that's pouring out. Instead of digging himself a bigger hole, he drinks more whiskey to shut himself up.

'Please, Dillon. I don't want to have this talk with you when you're like this.'

He holds his hands out to the side. 'But this is who I am now. I mean you must have read what's been written about me? Drink. Drugs. Anger issues. Prison. Fucking men and women everywhere I go.' Fuck, he really is one disaster after another.

'You're right. You're not the man I fell in love with. He was decent and cared about other people. You're a selfish, drunk, asshole. I want nothing to do with you.'

He points his whiskey bottle at her. 'That makes two of us.'

He drops back onto the sand, as she turns and walks away from him. He glares over at Luke. 'Oh, stop looking at me like that.'

Luke shuffles around to face him. 'What the hell is wrong with you? I don't know who that was, but it wasn't my mate talking.'

'I think I'm allowed to be a little pissed off with her.'

'Yeah, but that was plain cruel. How long did you leave her waiting?'

Dillon shrugs. 'Few hours maybe.'

'And did it make you feel better?'

No. 'Yes. I feel fucking fantastic. Can't you tell?'

'You have to talk to her Dillon. This won't go away until you do.'

'Spare me the fucking sermon Luke.'

'Stop being a dick and talk to me.'

'Can you do me a massive favour? Will you please just go away.'

Luke curses under his breath, something he rarely does, then gets up and brushes sand from his combats. He picks up the drink and takes it with him, ignoring the less than complimentary comments Dillon hurls at him as he walks away.

Alone on the sand, drunk and miserable, Dillon realises he's probably hit rock bottom. Or near enough to it. He's in a fucking stunning location getting drunk like some idiotic teenager.

Luke has put up with a hell of a lot of crap from him over the years, but he's never walked away like he just did. No doubt Tate and Gregg would feel the same.

He pushes to his feet again, pissed off that he needs to support himself on the tree behind him. He's going to have to overload on the caffeine tomorrow if he's to have any chance of getting on stage and giving a half decent performance.

But the thought of going back to the bus right now doesn't appeal to him in the slightest. So he decides to go for a walk. Where, he doesn't know. He just needs to get away from everyone for a while.

If he goes back to the bus he's just going to be heading into another lecture or a lot of dirty looks. Fuck that!

Maybe a walk beside the lake will do the trick. Turning in the opposite direction to the bus, he stumbles across the beach, keeping away from the water just in case he falls. He curses as his phone vibrates in his pocket. Then it rings.

Probably one of the guys ready to lay into him.

And they're not letting up. It must be a good three or four minutes later and his phone is still going nuts in his pocket. 'Fuck it! Leave me alone!'

He tears his phone out from his back pocket, sorely tempted to throw the damn thing in the lake. But when he sees his sister Eva's name appear on the screen, he knows something is seriously wrong. She never called him, preferring text messages to actually speaking to him. 'Hey Eva, can I call you later? This isn't a good time.'

'I'm sorry, but Clara has been trying to get a hold of you. Dillon, it's Mum.'

The hairs on the back of his neck immediately rise. They always do when his parents are mentioned. 'I'm not interested.'

'Dillon will you just shut up for a second.' Eva sniffs and he realises she's crying.

'What is it, Eva?'

'She had a heart attack Dill. She's dead. Mum's dead.'

Luke

When Luke got the call from Clara, he'd been heartbroken for her. But that wasn't the first thing that came to his mind. His first thought was that they had to find Dillon before he did something stupid.

He honestly has no idea how Dillon will have taken the news. Clara said that Dillon had hung up on Eva after she told him what happened, and no one had managed to get a hold of him since. That was two hours ago.

Tate and Gregg had gone one way up the lake with their security, leaving him with Andy and Jason. He can't have gone far without any transport, but it's Dillon. He doesn't need to go far to get into trouble.

He shouldn't have left him on the beach like he did. He should have stayed with him, or at least dragged him back to the bus.

'Over here!' Jason shouts, suddenly taking off down the beach to a dark shape a few metres ahead of them. Luke sees what he spotted. There's someone lying face down on the sand half in, half out of the water.

'Oh fuck!'

He hurries after Jason and Andy, getting to the spot a few seconds after them, wading through the freezing water to Dillon.

'Is he okay?' Luke asks as the men grab Dillon by the arms and drag him out of the water, laying him down on the sand so they can check him.

'He's breathing and pulse is steady,' Jason says, glancing at him over his shoulder. 'Hey! Dillon! Can you hear me?'

Jason taps him on the cheek but Dillon just groans. No other reaction.

'That's something I guess. I think he's just drunk.'

The sickening worry Luke had been experiencing for the last two hours quickly turns to anger, as he stands in wet combats looking down at his wasted friend.

He pushes past the bodyguards and kneels in front of him, slapping him on the face. 'Dillon! Wake up. Do you have any idea what you put us through you selfish asshole! You could have drowned!'

Dillon groans and turns away from Luke.

'Dillon!' No response this time. Luke grabs him by the t-shirt and gives him a good shake, only stopping when Jason pulls him away. 'I get you're pissed off with him. I am too. First, we get him back to the bus, then we kill him. Better plan?'

Luke nods, his fury still solely focused on Dillon. 'We're going to have to carry him.'

'It's okay,' says Andy, moving Luke aside. 'Jace and I have him. You handle the light.'

'I can help carry him.'

Andy grabs one of Dillon's arms while Jace gets the other. 'Nope. You're on stage tomorrow night. We already have one of you less than stage ready. No way we're risking you too.'

They haul Dillon off the ground and get a firm hold on him.

'Now lead the way.'

He wants to argue with Andy, but it's difficult when he's talking sense. Besides, Andy and Jace are both larger than he is. They'll probably be able to manage Dillon better than he can.

By the time they reach the bus it's half an hour later, and they are more than ready to have it out with Dillon.

Gregg is waiting for them, looking about as thrilled as he feels. Tate had stormed off when Luke rang them to fill them in. He's still battling his own demons, and seeing Dillon go through the same is getting to him. Understandably so. Liam had taken him off to stock up on food. Give the rest of them time to get Dillon sorted while Tate was out of the way.

'Where did you find him?' Gregg asks as he opens the door of the bus for Andy and Jace.

'Far end of the beach unconscious in the water.'

Jace curses as they drop Dillon on the bed. 'Fucker is damn heavy!'

'Are you okay to get him out of the wet clothes?' Gregg asks Luke. 'I kinda want to do the whole drink and drug search before Tate gets back.'

'Yeah. And don't just hide it. Get rid of everything. He's going to kill himself if he keeps this up. Enough is enough.'

'Couldn't agree more. I'll make sure the bus is clear.'

Luke stands at the foot of the bed and looks down at his friend. They've all allowed this to go on for too long. They've let him suffer for too long and that's not right.

Dillon was one of the first people to confront Tate about his heroin use. He put his own life at risk, by going after Angel when she kidnapped and tried to kill Gregg. He was even stabbed in the process, but he didn't care. All he was interested in was protecting Gregg.

He stood up to Luke's abusive wife and was arrested trying to protect him. But more than that, Luke owes Dillon his life. If Dillon hadn't found him when he tried to kill himself, he wouldn't be here now. He wouldn't have met Maeve, or known true happiness for the first time.

It's what Dillon does. He protects. If he cares about you, he'll put you first. No question. Even if it means hurting himself in the process. There aren't many people like that.

Luke knows that if he rang Dillon from the other side of the planet and said he needed help, Dillon would be there. No question. No excuses. He'd be there for him as fast as possible.

But who's looking out for Dillon?

As he begins the difficult task of stripping the wet clothes from Dillon, he knows he let his friend down recently. With things going so well between himself and Maeve, he's been neglecting him. He went from seeing him nearly every day, to maybe a few times a month for band stuff.

Touring around Wales with Maeve while she works, is giving him his life back. After everything that went on with Pippa, he never thought he'd feel whole again. He thought she'd crushed a part of him he'd never get back. Until he met Maeve.

But the last thing he wants to do is turn his back on Dillon, just because his own life is finally on track.

He eventually gets everything off, then throws the duvet over him.

'All sorted,' Gregg says joining him in the bedroom again.

'Did you find much?'

'Enough. Actually, too much. I've disposed of it.' Gregg says as he looks at Dillon. 'Did you know it was this bad?'

'No. I knew he was using, but he shot me down when I asked him about it. I guess my head has been elsewhere lately. I should have done something, Gregg. I just walked away and left him to deal with everything alone.'

'Don't do that, Luke. You did nothing wrong. He's a big boy. This is on him.'

'But I haven't even been talking to him as much as I used to.'

'And? Come on. You're in love. You are doing exactly what you should be doing. You and Maeve are living your life together.'

'Yeah, but he had feelings for me, and I've been flaunting Maeve around the place.'

Gregg pulls him away from Dillon. 'Stop that! Like I said - this is on him. No one else. Okay, so he was in love with you. But that's his issue - not yours. You can't live your life worrying about how he's going to react. He wouldn't want that.'

'So what? Do I just let him carry on like this? He's going to kill himself, Gregg.'

'I hear you, but it's Dillon. He's more stubborn than Tate and that's saying something. We can talk to him, but I don't see him accepting anything we say, and that's putting it politely.'

We have to do something. I can't lose him Gregg.'

'You won't. We'll figure something out.' Gregg nods towards Dillon, sprawled out unconscious in the bed. 'I'll sit with him for a bit. You go and get cleaned up.'

Luke nods, leaving Gregg to babysit while he showers and changes. As he walks through the bus, he spots Tate through the window, standing on the grass staring at the moonlit water.

'Tate? Are you okay?'

'I can't deal with this shit, Luke. I can't be around him when he's like this. I'm not strong enough. I want to help him, but I don't know if I can.'

'I'm so sorry Tate. This isn't fair on you.'

'What the fuck are you apologising for? I'm having a go at him - not you. You want to be with him when he's off his head? You enjoy seeing him like that?'

Tate has a point. 'I don't know how to make him see he's in trouble. I've talked until I'm blue in the face. He's not admitting he has a problem. His mother dying is just going to make things so much worse.'

'I hear you. I went off the rails when my dickhead father died. That's what's pissing me off. I've been there, Luke. I've done what he's doing. But every time I try to get something straight in my head to say to him, I just think about my father and what he did, and... I can't. I've been to rehab twice. There is no third chance for me. If I fall, I'm not getting back up. I won't leave Brandon without a father and Chloe without a husband. No fucking way.'

'I understand. We all do. Besides, I honestly don't think any of us can help him. Until he admits he's in trouble, we're talking to the wall.'

He turns to face Tate, instantly noticing the tight lines around his eyes. He's stressed and that's not what he needs. 'Have you spoken about this?'

142

Tate checks the time. 'I've got a call in five minutes. Like I said, I'm not falling again. I love him, but I'm not losing myself again to help him. Same should go for you. You've come too fucking far to let him drag you back. We need to be a little selfish here Luke. We were both given a second chance. Not everyone gets that.'

16

Dillon

He's woken with a headache more times than he can remember, so it's no surprise when the first thing he's aware of is the pounding in his skull. Then his stomach decides to join in, the queasiness and the thumping in his head keeping each other company.

What the fuck happened last night?

His stomach lurches when he remembers the call from Eva. The piddly amount of food he ate yesterday hits the bottom of the bowl that's thrust in front of him, just in time.

Once his stomach is back under control, a glass of water appears in front of him. He sips from the straw, the cold water tasting better than he remembers water tasting. Must be dehydrated after his session.

He manages a croaky 'thank you', before slowly rolling back on to the pillow. Luke's face appears in front of him. Fuck, he looks angry. Luke doesn't do angry. Ever.

'What did I do?'

'What did you do? Are you serious? We found you passed out a few miles down the lake. You passed out in the damn water, Dillon! You could have drowned, you selfish asshole! Then we had to take it in turns to sit with you overnight in case you threw up and choked on your own vomit. Would have served you right. What the hell are you playing at?'

'Right now, I'm trying not to throw up on you, so lay off.'

Luke's face softens slightly as he takes a deep breath. 'Clara called me. I know about your mother.'

Brilliant. Not a topic that's going to help his headache. 'Right.'

'I know you won't want to talk, but I'm still going to offer.'

'You answered your own question.'

'Is that why you wandered off alone like you did? Because it's not bothering you?'

'Oh, fuck off Luke! I've got a raging headache, my stomach is in bits, and I sure as hell don't need you to step in to mother me now that woman is dead. Go find some other sad case to make yourself feel better. I'm not it.'

He closes his eyes as he finishes his downright cruel speech. It's got nothing to do with the fact the room is spinning. He can't bear to look at Luke's face. Not after he just kicked him like he did.

A few minutes pass before the bed rises as Luke gets up and walks away. Serves him right. He doesn't deserve a friend like Luke. Never did.

The bed tips again when someone else sits down, but this person is larger than Luke. Must be Tate. At least he won't want to talk. Tate isn't a fan of deep and meaningful conversations.

'He's worried about you. He didn't deserve that.'

So much for keeping his mouth shut. 'Not now Tate.'

'Yes now. I've been where you are. Do you not think I can't see the fucking signs, Dillon? If you carry on with this shit, you're going to kill yourself.'

'I've got a handle on it. I'm not like—'

Tate's face hardens, clearly picking up on what he tried not to say. 'Not like me? So, you think you're stronger than me? That you won't push it too far and end up on life support with your friends and family worried sick about you?'

'Tate...I didn't mean.'

'Fuck you, Dillon!'

Friend number two leaves him alone. Perfect. Less than five minutes and he's managed to alienate both Luke and Tate. All he needs now is—

'You're being a miserable dick today, aren't you?' Gregg sits beside him, his arms crossed as he glares down at him. 'You going to try for the hattrick? Go on then. Let's see what mud you can throw at me.'

'I'm not trying to do that.' He doesn't want to push them away, but he's pissed off and they're getting the brunt of it.

His mother is dead.

He should be happy, shouldn't he? Or at least relieved. She made his life hell. Thanks to her, he was alone and confused most of his childhood.

'It's normal to have mixed feelings about your mother.'

He pushes himself up in the bed, taking a minute for his stomach to calm down before he talks again. 'I'm angry.'

'That she's dead, or that you're not happy she's dead?'

'Both.' He scrubs his hands over his face. 'Fuck, Gregg! I just want...'

Peace. Just five minutes with nothing in his head but silence.

'Can you go please. I'm tired.'

Gregg nods then walks down the bus leaving him alone with his misery.

Ash

'Luke? What are you doing here?' Ash steps aside to let him into her room, quickly wiping the tears from her face before he sees them. She cried herself to sleep, then picked up where she left off after she woke up.

'Dillon's mother died yesterday. He found out after you left the campsite.'

She drops down onto her bed. 'Oh God. How is he?'

'I'm sure you can imagine,' Luke says, sitting down on the chair by the dressing table. 'Angry. Upset. Confused. Angry.'

'He's always angry, unfortunately.' She falls silent as she has a proper look at Luke. The black rings under his eyes are new. 'What did he do? You might as well just tell me. I can tell you had a rough night. And I'm not trying to be cruel by saying that. You just look tired.'

He nods as he rubs his hands on his legs. 'I'm wrecked. Dillon went for a walk after he got the news and disappeared for a few hours. We found him passed out further along the lake. He was so far gone he passed out in the water. Thankfully his head was out of the water. But that was just down to dumb luck.

'We took it in turns to sit with him all night. Then when he woke up, he decided to pick a fight with all of us. When I left about half an hour ago, he was trying his luck with Gregg.'

'Well that's not surprising. It's what he does. Luke, what's he taking?'

Luke peers up at her, frowning. 'I don't feel comfortable talking about that with you. Please don't take offence. It's his business, and if he found out I told you he'd kill me.'

'I understand. I'm going to guess it's painkillers of some sort being washed down with whiskey. Never mind killing you, he's going to kill himself.'

'We've all tried to talk to him. We push and he pushes back twice as hard. It's how he works.'

'Is he going to the funeral?'

'I haven't been brave enough to broach the subject with him. If she died yesterday, it'll be another few days before everything is organised. Hopefully he'll have his head sorted by then.' He twists the stud under his lip for a minute before he speaks again. 'Did he mention his family to you when you were together?'

She nods. 'Mainly Clara and Eva, but yes, his parents came up too. He just said they never liked him and took him coming out as their chance to finally get rid of him. They disowned him when he was seventeen.'

'Yeah. I can't imagine that.'

She can't either. Most children fight with their parents at some stage. It's part of growing up. But no matter what Freya did, she could never imagine even considering disowning her. It would never cross her mind for a second. 'He should go to the funeral. For himself and for his sisters. They adore him. I know that much. They'll need his support.'

'I agree, but he might not be able to see that through his anger. We'll cross that bridge when we get to it. Right now, I just want him to get sober enough to try and make a sensible decision about what he's going to do.'

'If you need any help I'm here. Not that I think he'll take it from me.'

Luke shrugs as he smiles at her. 'You might be the only one he will take it from.'

Dillon

'We have to cancel the show.'

Dillon shakes his head, refusing to look up from his phone. His lunch is on the table in front of him, still untouched. His stomach isn't ready for solids.

'No way Tate. I'm not cancelling tonight because of *her*. We're going on as planned.'

'It's not a big deal Dillon. We'll have to reschedule the next gig in Italy anyway because of the funeral. We'll just move these two dates. The fans will understand.'

The Swiss and Italian fans shouldn't miss out just because his mother died. It's not happening.

'For the last time, we are not cancelling anything! I need to go on Tate. Do not cancel.' He chews his lip ring as Tate curses to himself. Fuck him. He's not Tate. He's going to deal with his mother's death his way. 'And I'm not going to the funeral so that date is safe too.'

'What do you mean you're not going?'

Dillon flicks through his phone, doing his best to make it seem like he's busy. But, as usual, Tate knows all the delaying and avoidance tactics. He'd used them all himself over the years.

'Dillon. Stop being a dick and put down your phone.'

He sighs and lowers his phone. 'What?'

He's rubbing Tate up the wrong way with his attitude, but he's beyond caring. He's in a fucking foul mood.

Tate pauses as he pulls himself back from whatever comment he was going to shoot back with. 'I have a lot of regrets in my life—'

'Oh, save me the sermon, Tate!'

He just poked the bear. And that's not something you do. Dillon braces himself for the well deserved, and maybe much needed, punch.

But Tate doesn't oblige. Instead, he pushes to his feet and storms off the bus, slamming the door behind him.

'Fuck!'

He scrubs his hands through his hair, pulling at it in frustration. Tate didn't deserve that. He was just trying to help. His abusive, dickhead of a father died a few years ago in prison. Tate hadn't wanted anything to do with his funeral. But he knows it's something Tate regrets. He mentioned it once after the event. He missed out on the chance to stick a finger up at his abuser, and he can never get that back.

The door opens again, and he gets ready to apologise, but it's not Tate. It's Luke. Which could be better or worse, depending on what Luke is going to say to him.

His best mate sits opposite him and twists the stud under his lip.

'I'm guessing you bumped into Tate.'

'Yeah. He's pissed off at you.'

'What's new. It's my thing at the moment.'

'Pushing people away? People who care about you. Who love you. I get you don't want—'

'No Luke! You don't fucking get it! You have the most sickeningly loving family I've ever seen. When we were kids, I would come over to your house for a small glimpse at what a normal family should be like.

'Fuck, even Tate's family gave more of a damn about him than mine did about me, and he's adopted. So, no. Don't you dare sit there and tell me you understand a fucking thing about what that bitch put me through! Cause you don't. I bet your mum told you how much she loved you every single day. Didn't she?'

Luke takes a deep breath which means yes. Of course she did. He knows that for a fact.

'Did she ever tell you she couldn't bear to look at you? That the very sight of you made her skin crawl?'

'Dillon...'

He grabs the bottle of whiskey and takes a healthy swig. Damn stuff has no effect on him anymore. 'Forget it. She's dead. I can move on and have a happy life.' He laughs, hating how crazy it sounds. Maybe he's finally losing the plot?

'Want a drink?' He offers the bottle to Luke, who shakes his head.

'Where the hell did you get that from? Gregg searched the bus and got rid of everything.'

'I asked one of Sam's helpers to get it for me. It's their job to make sure the awkward rock star is kept happy. And this,' he says lifting the bottle. 'This keeps me happy.'

'You know we're being interviewed by a local radio station before we go on tonight? Are you planning to do that drunk?'

He wants to tell Luke to back off, but he has a point. They don't go on unless they can give their all. Plus, he may have completely forgotten about the interview.

Dillon slams the bottle back on the counter and watches as Luke screws the lid on.

'Get changed. We're going for a run.'

'I don't want—'

'Get changed, Dillon! You're coming for a run with me. Then we'll head over to the venue and get ready for the interview and show. I'm not letting you sit here and mope for the next few hours. Come on! Move!'

Luke throws a pair of shorts and a t-shirt at him. 'Two minutes.'

Dillon opens his mouth to argue but Luke leaves, presumably to get changed himself. He looks down at the clothes at his feet. What the hell. Luke is right. If he stays here, he's going to get further into his head.

Over the years she's watched so many interviews with the band. Whether on TV or on the radio, they were always amazing. Tate tended to take the lead, which was his job as front man, but the others got involved too.

She loved hearing Dillon's voice, watching him interact with the interviewers. Each of the guys could hold their own when facing probing questions. No doubt Ellen and her team had been coaching them for years on how to handle those hard to answer questions.

This will be the first time she's going to watch them in the flesh as they are interviewed, and she's so excited.

It's three hours before they go on stage and the venue is already packed with eager fans, waiting to see the guys on stage. But as soon as she steps into the meeting room at the back of the venue, she knows it's not going to go as anyone had planned.

Dillon is drunk. Maybe more than just drunk. One look at him and Ash can tell he's in no fit state to do an interview. From what she's seen of him, he's an angry and hostile drunk. Certainly not a version of Dillon that Vox would want the world to see.

From the look on Luke's face, he knows it too. Let him deal with his friend. There's no way she's going to attempt to take on Dillon - especially when he's drunk.

Luke is as excited about the prospect of confronting him as she is but, unlike her, he doesn't really have a choice. 'Are you okay to do this?'

It takes Dillon a minute to acknowledge the question. 'What?'

'I left you alone for half an hour! What the hell did you do?'

'I'm grand.'

'Come on Dillon. You're drunk. We made a deal. We don't go out drunk or high.'

'How about drunk and high? Have we any rules about that?'

'Seriously! This isn't funny. Do you really want everyone to see you like this? You know the interviewer will notice. Do you really want reporters to jump on that?'

'Jump on what?' Tate asks as he joins them in the suite.

'He's fucked,' Luke says, pointing to Dillon.

'I think I preferred it when you didn't curse.'

'And I preferred it when you didn't need to drink to get through the day, Dillon, but I guess we're both out of luck, aren't we?'

'We're calling this off.'

'No fucking way, Tate! I'm fine.'

'You're slurring your fucking speech so no, you're not.'

'You may be the front man but that doesn't mean you're the boss, Tate. I'm going on.'

Ash guessed the guys would tousle from time to time. It was bound to happen. But she hadn't planned on witnessing or being this close to one of those arguments. When Tate walks right up to Dillon and glares at him, Ash is sorely tempted to make a quick exit and leave them to it.

'You fucking hypocrite!'

'What?'

'You went apeshit when I was going to perform last year after taking heroine.'

'Oh, come on Tate. This is different.'

'How? We made a deal that we always give our best every fucking time we get in front of fans. You were right to pull me last year. Just like we're right to pull you now.'

Dillon squares up to Tate. The lead singer has an inch on Dillon, but right now he's being fuelled by drink and drugs.

'I'd like to see you stop me.'

'Ah now lads calm down.' Gregg's arrival doesn't seem to stop the intense standoff between Tate and Dillon. She doubts either of them have even noticed he's joined them.

'What the hell did I miss?'

'Apparently, I'm too drunk and high to go on. Tate here is trying to pull rank and I'm not on board with that.'

'Fuck...' Gregg mutters to himself. 'Well, isn't this like a blast from the past? I thought we were over all this shit. Tate, calm down and back off. Dillon, you're not going on like this. It's three against one buddy. End of discussion.'

'End of fucking discussion? No, it's not.'

'It's the same rule for all of us. You know that.' Tate takes a step back from Dillon, the heat of the moment seeming to dissipate. 'I'll grab Sam. See if we can reschedule.'

Ash can see what's about to happen a split second before he reacts. She can see Dillon's fist clenching, but can't get the words out fast enough to warn anyone.

He launches himself at Tate, surprise helping him instantly gain the upper hand, sending Tate crashing to the ground with a thump.

Before Tate can get himself together, Dillon is on him lashing at the singer with his fists. It takes Gregg and Luke a few seconds to move in to stop him, but when they do, Dillon goes for them too.

Ash yanks open the door and shouts at Liam and Jace who are chatting further down the corridor. 'Quick! Get in here!'

When the bodyguards join the band, they quickly attempt to get things under control. Jace and Andy tear Gregg off the top of the pile, then go after Dillon, while Liam pulls Tate out from under the furious bassist, and Ciaran helps Luke to his feet.

It takes a good few minutes but they finally pull the men apart, holding each one back as they try to get at each other again.

'What the fuck are you doing?'

Instead of answering Liam's question, Dillon just glares over at Tate. In the few seconds before Tate could defend himself Dillon had caused a bit of damage. Tate's nose is bleeding, his lip is split, and there's the start of an impressive bruise on his cheek.

'Are you okay?' Gregg asks Tate, moving closer to check out the damage.

Tate curses but nods. 'Yeah. I'm fine. What the fuck was that about? Hey! I'm talking to you!' Tate glares over at Dillon who isn't helping things by completely ignoring him.

But when Ash really looks at Dillon, she realises he's not ignoring them. He's blinking strangely as if he's having trouble focusing. 'Jason, is he okay?'

The bodyguard leans back to check him out, then curses. 'Dillon? Are you with us?'

'Yeah...'

Ash grabs a chair and pulls it over to Jace. He lowers Dillon onto it, then crouches down in front of him. 'Look at me Dillon. Hey! Look at me!'

Ash takes out her phone to call for help, but Gregg shakes his head.

'Give him a minute. He just needs to relax.'

'He looks like he's about to collapse.'

'He's drunk and high. He just needs to take it easy and stop picking fights with everyone.' Gregg raises his voice for the last part, earning a stern glare from Dillon. 'What? Do you disagree with something I said?'

'Fuck off, Gregg!'

'Deep and meaningful as usual,' Gregg mutters, turning away from the source of his irritation.

Luke speaks to Tate and Gregg out of her earshot, while Dillon sits slumped in the chair looking spaced out and angry at the same time.

All she wants to do is take him in her arms and hold him. Seeing him like this, so dependent on whatever drugs he's taking, breaks her heart. He's not this person. He's so much better than this, but there's nothing she can do to help him.

'We're going to cancel the interview,' Gregg says, interrupting her thoughts. 'Get some food into him and see how he goes. Can you give us some time to get him sorted?'

'Of course. Is the show going ahead?'

He shrugs. 'Hope so. We just need to load him up with the strongest coffee we can find and stuff him full of carbs. He'll be grand.'

'Do you need any help?' She already knows it's a stupid thing to ask. Dillon will only get more agitated if she hangs around him.

'We've got him,' Gregg says, squeezing her shoulder as he walks past. 'We've always got him.'

Ash

As the band leave the stage to deafening applause and screams, Ash lowers her camera. The show was incredible. But it was Dillon's performance she was particularly impressed by.

Watching him own the stage you would have no idea his mother had just passed away or that he'd been drunk and high a few hours earlier. He gave as much as he did every other time she's seen him perform.

Maybe more so, almost like he had something to prove tonight over other nights. And after what happened with the interview, he probably does. She had been expecting to receive a call from Sam saying that the show was going to be cancelled. But, whatever the guys did to him during those few hours had worked.

Instead of travelling to their next venue in Italy with the band tomorrow, Sam had asked if she wanted to join her in her car which she was only too happy to do. Ash isn't an idiot. It's quite clear they wanted to give Dillon time to himself, and she understands that. He needs time to come to terms with his mother's death.

After she packs away her kit, she heads backstage to the lounge area set aside for the band so she can check the shots from the evening. They'll all be in their dressing rooms getting changed, so she should have the place to herself for a while at least.

The Swiss fans were incredible, and she was able to get some fantastic shots of both the band and their adoring fans.

She stumbles to a stop when she finds Dillon leaning against the drinks table. He looks utterly worn out and defeated. 'Dillon?'

He quickly lifts his head to glare at her. 'Of course you're here! You're fucking everywhere I go! How about you fuck off and leave me alone.'

By the way he's slurring his words, he must have drunk a lot after he came off stage, or perhaps taken some of the pills she's seen him swallow when he thinks no one is watching. Considering he only stepped off stage a few minutes ago, maybe he started in the intermission? 'Gregg told me about your mother. I'm so sorry.'

He pushes himself upright and points a bottle of whiskey at her. 'Not another word about her! Actually, why don't you just stop talking altogether. Do us both a favour.' He stumbles across the room, no doubt trying to get away from her. 'How did you even get in here?'

'I have access to all the places you do.'

'Perfect! No escaping you is there?'

He loses his footing, falling against the table, knocking over the bottles of water and juice lined up on the top. 'Maybe you should sit down before you hurt yourself.'

'Maybe you should mind your own. I don't need you looking out for me. You lost that chance years ago Sweetheart.'

Even so, he sits on the couch. Not that he would ever admit it was down to her suggestion.

He smiles sadly as he lies back. 'Remember when I used to call you that? I called you Sweetheart a lot. You were mine then. All mine. I would have killed anyone who looked at you the wrong way.'

'I know you would have.'

He laughs harshly before glaring at her, his green eyes cold and angry. 'That was a long fucking time ago. Bet you blocked it all from your memory? It's not like it meant anything to you.'

'Why would I want to block any of it from my mind?' In truth, she'd tried and failed so many times. For years after she left, thinking about him had hurt so much. It was like a knife in her chest, making breathing difficult. Then just when she thought the wound was beginning to heal, the band had hit the headlines.

He was suddenly everywhere. Larger than life and in her face no matter where she looked.

He points the bottle at her again. 'Such a fucking liar!' He deliberately keeps his eyes on her so there's no doubt he means what he just said. He wants to hurt her. His go to response was always to fight. Better that, than show his true emotions. It took a lot to get him to crack, but she'd seen that side of him. She'd seen him break down and drop the wall.

But now isn't the time for that. It's not what he needs. He doesn't want sympathy.

Ash takes a few steps closer, then crosses her arms as she glares at him. He straightens, squaring up to her, but his posture is slightly off, thanks to the drink. It reminds her so much of when they would fight as a couple, which they didn't do very often. But when they did, he always lost. She could more than stand up to him.

'You're nowhere near sober enough to even attempt a conversation, so what's the point?'

'You know what? We finally agree on something.'

'You are an asshole. Even worse than that. You're a drunk asshole.'

159

He pauses, slightly taken aback by her comment. 'Nice. Thanks for that. Anything else you want to throw in the mix? I'm having a great fucking few days, so go for it. Make it better!'

'How about selfish?'

That gets him seriously pissed off. 'Selfish? Are you fucking serious! Don't you of all people dare say I'm selfish!'

'What else would you call it? Your mother just died. Have you stopped for one second to think about how your sisters are feeling?'

He silently glowers at her but doesn't say anything, which is exactly what she was hoping for. If he keeps arguing back it can easily go on forever. At least if he's listening, she has a chance of getting through to him.

'They just lost their mother. I know you didn't have a relationship with her, but they did. I'm sure they need their brother with them.'

Dillon turns his attention back to the bottle, lifting it to his lips. But he doesn't take a drink. Cursing under his breath, he slams it onto the arm of the couch. Ash wants to get the bottle away from him but isn't about to send him off again by approaching him.

But then the whiskey becomes the lesser of two evils. Ash watches in horror as he takes some pills from a packet in his jeans and swallows them. He follows that with another fair amount of alcohol from the bottle, before lying back on the couch.

She stares over at him, the despair and sorrow weighing on her chest. 'What did you just take?'

He snorts, but that's as far as his reply goes.

Did she do this to him? Had leaving him like she did break him so much this is the result? Maybe it's a combination of his new career and what happened between them? Maybe it started with his parents and their treatment of him over the years? Whatever the reason, watching him like this is breaking her heart all over again.

He turns his head to glare at her with slightly unfocused eyes. 'You're looking at me like I'm a piece of shit. Stop judging me.'

160

'Dillon, I'm not—'

'Fuck off! I know that look. I've had people give me that look for years. I sure as fuck don't need it from you of all people.'

Ash takes a few steps closer and clears her throat. 'Is this you now Dillon? Is this how you survive?'

'Yep,' he replies as he stares at the ceiling. 'Sex, drugs, and rock'n'roll all the way Sweetheart!' He laughs a little maniacally, then stops suddenly and goes quiet again.

'Do you want me to call Luke?'

'Why would I want you to do that?'

'Because I don't want to leave you alone like this.'

He snorts loudly. 'He's got himself a nice new girlfriend. Doesn't need me bringing him down. He's all awkward around me anyway. Has been since I told him I love him. *Did* love him. I'm over that now. Over you. Over him. Over everything. Fuck it all!'

So, Dillon was in love with Luke. That doesn't surprise her. It just makes the whole thing so much more tragic for Dillon. 'I'm sorry.'

It's the wrong thing to say. She knows it as soon as the words come out. Dillon doesn't do sympathy. It's like a kick to his gut.

He pushes upright and reaches for the bottle again. This time Ash beats him to it, picking it up before he can take hold of it again. 'You've had enough.'

'Is that right? Well, I guess I better stop then, hadn't I?' He holds out his hand. 'Give me the fucking bottle, Ash!'

Hearing him say her name again after all this time brings tears to her eyes. She'd forgotten how it sounds. Missed hearing him say it. 'You know, that's the first time you've called me by my name.'

He chews on his lip ring, keeping up the silence for a minute before he replies, his voice low and laced with exhaustion. 'Just go. I don't need you here. I don't want you here. I just want to be alone. What's so fucking hard to understand?'

Then he turns the heat up again by grabbing the bottle from her hand and flinging it against the floor where it shatters into pieces.

'So, you're going to try to intimidate me into leaving?'

'Is it working?'

'No. I'm not leaving you alone like this.'

'Why not? You've left before. You left and broke my fucking heart! Just walk out the door. Or do you need a pen and paper? You could write me a touching note before you go.'

Ash swallows and nods slowly. 'I deserve that.'

'Yeah. That's why I said it.' He looks over at her. 'Tell you what. I'll go to my dear mother's funeral, okay? I'll put on my best suit and stand in that church with the rest of my fucked-up family, while everyone cries and sobs and comforts each other.

'Who knows, I might even be able to cry a little if I really work at it. Put on one hell of a performance. I'll be the big fucking hypocrite and pretend I give a damn that she's dead. I'll go all out if that'll keep you happy?'

'That's not what I want.'

'Then what do you want? Tell me, cause I haven't got a fucking clue what you want! If I did, you wouldn't have left.' He's raised his voice before, but never like that.

Ash has never ever been frightened of him. Not once. But she's never been one on one with him while he's angry, drunk, and on drugs. It's not a version of Dillon she is comfortable with.

She could argue with him for the next few hours and not make a difference. He needs to sober up first...whenever that will be. Ignoring the comment about her leaving, she tries to steer him back onto the subject of his mother.

'What I want doesn't come into this. It's your sisters I'm thinking of. If you're not there for them now of all times, you might regret it later. You may not care about your mother, and I understand why, but they need you. And as much as you want to think otherwise at the moment, you need them. So does your father.'

'It's too fucking late for him to need anything from me. He made his feelings clear decades ago.'

'Maybe he just wants his son back.'

'He has no son. Got a touching letter from him with those words on it.' He points at her. 'You and my folks would get on well. You both like leaving touching letters that fuck up my life.'

It doesn't matter what she says, he's going to keep bringing it back to that damn letter she left him. She'd love to tell him she'd give anything to go back and redo that time in her life, but he doesn't need to hear something like that now. Maybe never.

'That was over twenty years ago. Things have changed. You've all changed. Maybe this is the time to put all that aside and get to know each other again. To be a family again.'

Dillon pushes to his feet and stalks over to her, bumping off the wall when he loses his balance. 'A family? We'll never be a family. You can't fix what went wrong in the Ryan household, believe me.

'You don't know that—'

'Do you have any idea what it feels like to have your parents look at you like you're some depraved, disgusting thing?' he asks, interrupting her. 'What it feels like to have your parents turn their back on you like you don't exist?'

'Dillon—'

'They've hated me since the day I was born,' he says, completely ignoring her interruption as he moves closer. Ash can smell the whiskey on his breath as he glares down at her. 'And you know the worst part? I have no fucking clue why!

'I watched them hug and cuddle and love my sisters. Spend time with them. Read to them. Talk to them. But every time I went near them, they'd walk away. What the fuck could I have done as a kid that made them hate me so much? I didn't do anything wrong!'

'I know, Dillon...' She's crying now, but there's no stopping the tears. He didn't deserve to be treated the way he was. She knows that much.

'My sisters raised me - not them. They wanted me gone all along. When I told them I was bi, I just gave them the excuse they needed to get rid of me once and for all.'

He stumbles backwards, bumping against the wall, using it to hold himself upright. 'I was only seventeen when I told them. You know what they did?'

Ash wipes her face, then shakes her head. He's crying too, but it's anger bringing it on. Anger and despair.

He leans back against the wall then laughs once. 'My loving parents kicked me out. Gave me one day to pack everything and leave the house. Haven't heard from them since.' When he looks up at her, his eyes are cold and hard. 'So, to be honest, I really couldn't give a flying fuck that she's dead. Good riddance!'

Ash reaches out to touch his arm, but he jerks it out of her reach. 'Don't fucking touch me! I don't need pity from anyone.'

'It's not pity, Dillon.'

'Of course it is. I didn't tell you that so you'd pity me. I told you so you'll understand why I couldn't give a fuck about her dying or making things right with my father. Both of them can rot in hell for all I care.' He gestures towards the door. 'Now fuck off and leave me alone! I'm done with you too.'

She's fighting a losing battle. But if he thinks she's going to leave him alone here like this, he can think again. Once out of his sight, she'll get Jace or Luke. She is about to turn around to leave when his face greys and he sways again.

'Dillon?'

His eyes roll back in his head just before he slumps to the ground.

Ash falls to her knees and feels for a pulse. It's there and steady. 'Dillon? Dillon!' But he's out cold. 'Fuck!' She searches in her pockets for her phone and dials the first number on her recent calls. 'Sam! It's Ash. I'm in the lounge backstage with Dillon. He's collapsed!'

19

Dillon

He feels crap. Worse than crap.

The heartbeat in his head is causing serious problems with his stomach. He's not usually someone who pukes when he's hungover, but this might be a new one for him.

Something cool is placed on his forehead and it's such a fucking relief he can't help but groan. A hand rubs his back, the slow steady circles helping to loosen the knot in his stomach. He doesn't care who it is as long as they keep going.

Over the pounding in his head, he hears soft humming. It's familiar on some level, but he can't place it. All he knows is that the humming mixed with the hand on his back, is lulling him back to sleep. So he doesn't fight it.

When he wakes up again, the pounding has eased a little, and so has his stomach. He's not alone in the bed. He can hear the steady breathing of someone near him. It's probably Luke, babysitting him after whatever fucked up mess he got himself into yesterday.

But it's not Luke.

His breath catches in his throat when he opens his eyes and sees Ash asleep beside him. He's in the back of the bus, on one of the couches that turns into a bed. He must have been too wasted to get into his bunk. Or the guys couldn't drag his unconscious ass onto it.

Her perfume is all he can smell, the fruity scent bringing him back a decade to happier times. To his life with her. He'd been so angry since she arrived, he hadn't allowed himself to look at her. Hadn't allowed himself to admire the stunning woman she is. Ash was always gorgeous. The ten years had done nothing to change that. If anything, she looks better now than she did back then.

He's still attracted to her. Still loves her.

She mumbles in her sleep and grabs his hand tighter. He didn't realise she was holding it until she squeezed it. Her smaller delicate hand looks so fucking right over his.

He swallows as his throat tightens. He's not usually so emotional. Years of practice had made sure of that. Seems he needs more practice. He wipes the side of his face on the pillow. Now he's fucking crying, which makes the level of pathetic drop to all new levels.

He's just so tired.

Tired of dragging his sorry ass from one day to the next. Tired of not feeling good enough. Tired of using drink and drugs to just exist. But more than any of that, he's tired of being alone.

He pushes people away. He's obnoxious and argumentative most of the time. But all he wants is for someone to care enough to fight back. To see through all that and give him a chance.

He looks over at Ash again. She did that.

Okay so he wasn't as obnoxious back then, but he did have a serious attitude problem. She didn't waver though. She gave as good as she got, and he fell in love with her because of that.

She opens her eyes and those beautiful blue eyes lock onto his. Ash instantly tries to pull her hand back, but he hangs on to it.

Ash looks at their hands for a long time not saying anything. Her finger gently runs over the ring he wears on his middle finger. She gave it to him on their first month anniversary and he hadn't removed it since.

Apart from his time in prison, the ring never left his finger. He doesn't skimp on the jewellery, but nothing else he wears comes close to meaning as much as that ring does. Even pissed off at her, he hadn't contemplated taking it off.

'I'm surprised to see you're still wearing that.'

'I like it.'

She smiles and licks her lips as she twists the ring on his finger. 'How are you feeling?'

'Fucking rotten. What happened?'

'You collapsed. Sam brought in a doctor to check you. I'm sure I don't need to tell you what he said.'

'Too much drink.'

'For starters. Luke found the painkillers in your pocket. Those mixed with the whiskey knocked you out. You collapsed on me, Dillon. Scared the hell out of me actually.'

'I'm sorry. 'And he is. He doesn't want anyone to see him like that.

'Do you do that a lot?'

His first instinct is to pull his hand away and get the fuck off the bed. But he stays. Even after all this time, she's able to calm him just by being with him, rein in the anger always brewing under the surface. 'Get drunk or collapse?'

'This isn't funny, Dillon.'

'Sorry.' Fuck it! Why is he apologising again? 'I've been taking different painkillers for a few years. Probably upped my usage the last year though. Drink too.'

She nods, but doesn't comment further, which is a good thing. He's not in the frame of mind for a lecture. He's not an idiot. He knows he drinks too much. He knows he's beyond foul when he's drunk. And he knows he's going to kill himself one day. Not intentionally. More that he'll do something stupid and run out of second chances.

Okay so maybe he is an idiot. He knows all that, yet can't stop himself from fucking up, repeatedly.

'I heard Sam mention rehab to the guys after the doctor left.'

That figures. Of course someone wants to lock him away again. Put him somewhere his problems can be dealt with in private. He's done with all that. Not happening. 'I've got this.'

'No, you haven't.' She shrugs but doesn't push him. She knows better than to do that with him. It gets you nowhere. 'I'll get you some water.'

She pushes onto her elbow, but he refuses to let go of her hand, pulling her back onto the bed. 'Not yet. Stay.'

Ash lies back down. She hasn't got a clue what's going on, which makes two of them. He was a complete dick to her yesterday, and now he doesn't want her to leave. Talk about mixed and seriously fucked up signals.

'You've been here all night with me?'

She nods. 'You're the biggest ass I've ever met, but I couldn't leave you. Clearly, I have a serious problem.'

He smiles and she smiles back.

'How are you?'

What a question. He's not sure. His mother is dead. He should be upset. Maybe a little sad. But there's nothing there. Nothing except the same old sense of emptiness that he always feels when he thinks about his parents.

'It's okay to feel nothing.'

He frowns as he looks at her. Seems she can still get into his head after all this time. 'Don't think my sisters would agree.'

'Your relationship with your parents was difficult. I'm sure Clara and Eva understand. I'm convinced they do. But that doesn't mean you can't feel something for them. Leaving your relationship aside, they have lost someone important to them. I just don't want you to forget that.'

In the light of a new sober day, she's right. Doesn't make it easy to swallow or accept, but he needs to go. He needs to support Eva and Clara as they've supported him so many times over the years. 'I'll talk to Sam.'

'Speaking of which,' she says. 'I think it's best if she arranges for someone else from the magazine to come over and finish the shoot. I don't know what I was thinking when I accepted this assignment. I know you're not going to believe a word I'm about to say, but I honestly can't stand hurting you like this.'

'No! Don't do that. You're right. We're both adults. What happened is in the past. Stay and finish your job.'

She stares at him for a long time without saying anything. Even after all this time, she can look him dead in the eye and have him squirming instead of the other way round.

'Are you sure you can handle me being around? I mean without all the attitude and impressively dirty looks you like to throw in my direction? I understand why you feel that way, but I can't work like that, Dillon.'

'I'll behave.'

She looks down, tracing her fingers along the scar just above his waistband. 'Is that from Gregg's stalker?'

'Yeah. Lucky for me the bitch hit my leather waistcoat. Kept the knife from going in too deep.'

'I wasn't surprised when I read the report on the news. When they said you went after Gregg's stalker all alone, the first thing that went through my mind was *typical Dillon*. It was a stupid but brave thing to do.'

'She hurt Gregg. There was no fucking way I was going to let her escape.'

'You could have been killed.'

He shrugs, trying to play down the seriousness. 'It was worth it. It all worked out fine in the end.'

He shuffles a little closer, closing his eyes for a second when the room suddenly spins. It must have been one hell of a night. He doesn't remember ever feeling so rough. Or so lost.

He wants Ash. He needs her. As fucked up as it sounds, his mind and body crave her as much as he craves the drugs and drink. That's nothing new. She's always done that to him. She always managed to captivate, to possess him, to uncover the hidden submissive, desperate to be dominated.

But now it's different. Instead of soothing him, the hollow in his chest aches so much more when she's close. So much pain. Pain of losing her again. Pain of not being good enough for her.

She closes the gap between them, their clasped hands pressed against their chests as they lie face to face.

He'll go back to Ireland. He'll stand by his sisters as they say goodbye to their mother. They deserve that. They deserve his support. However horrible, or uncomfortable it is for him, he'll be there for them.

Then he'll come back and finish the tour with his friends. Even if it means having to be close to Ash. He's been a selfish dick the last few weeks. Putting himself before the rest of the band and his sisters, just because he can't deal with his own issues. Enough is enough.

He should get up and talk to Sam. Get arrangements made for heading home. But that would mean letting go of Ash and, as much as it's hurting to be close to her, he can't let her go. It's a temporary thing. He knows that. In a few minutes, she'll let go of his hand and leave him again, but in this moment he doesn't care. All he knows is that, for the first time in too long, his mind is silent.

170

Dillon

It's been years since he was at a church. Decades in fact. A part of him fully expects to burst into flames as soon as he sets foot inside the building.

Not that walking into the building is going to be an issue yet. He can't even get himself out of his fucking car. He'd taken his BMW instead of the Mustang, so he wouldn't stand out as much.

That's not what today is about. It's about disappearing as much as possible. Blending into the background. Kind of like he did every day when he was a child.

Dillon loosens the tie around his neck, but he's still suffocating. What the fuck is he doing here? He should have stayed where he was. Should have told Ellen and Sam he didn't need to come back. He let Ash and the guys guilt-trip him into being here for his sisters. Clara and Eva know the situation with him. They wouldn't have held it against him if he didn't show up.

Two days back here to deal with this shit, is two days too long.

The guys had wanted to come back with him, but he'd flat out refused for anyone other than Jace to come with him. It's bad enough having to be here, without having an audience watching the car crash as it unfolds.

Luke had put up one hell of a fight, but in the end knew it was a battle he wouldn't win. Dillon had promised to stay with Clara while he was back. It's not happening, but Luke doesn't need to know that.

And it's not like he's on his own. The ever-present Jace is sitting in his own car a few metres behind him. It's at times like this having a bodyguard is a right pain in the ass. At least he'll stay out here and let him deal with the family shit in private.

So lost in his thoughts, he jumps when Clara knocks on the door, startling him. She sits into the car beside him, then collapses into his arms.

Okay, so maybe Ash was right. Clara and Eva do need him. He's not upset the way they are, but that doesn't mean he shouldn't support them. Fuck knows they've been there for him enough over the years. The least he can do is return the favour.

'You okay?' he asks when she finally releases him.

She smiles weakly and nods. 'Not really. I was surprised when I got your message. I didn't think you'd come.'

'Neither did I. I'm here for you and Eva, not for her.'

She takes his hand and squeezes it. 'I'm glad you're here.' She looks down at his hand and he knows she's holding something back.

'What is it?'

'Okay. I need to talk to you about something.'

'Is Eva okay?'

'She's fine. Well, upset, of course, but it's not that.' Clara looks out the window as she clenches and unclenches her fists on her knees.

'Hey? What is it? You can tell me anything, you know that.'

'Mum... she left a... damn it! Okay, so she left us a list of instructions for her funeral. You know, what she wants hymn wise and flowers. Things like that.'

'Right.' He gets a sinking feeling in his gut.

'Dillon, I'm so sorry, but I only found out about an hour ago. Dad had kept it to himself but... Uncle Gavin, Mum's brother...'

'Yeah. What about him?'

'She had shared her last wishes with him too. Dill, she stated in no uncertain terms that she doesn't want you to attend her funeral.'

The words take a few replays to sink in. He only really believes them when he notices that Clara is staring at him, sobbing.

'I'm so sorry, Dillon. We want you there, but Uncle Gavin said he'd stand at the door and manhandle you out of the church if you do show up.'

He nods slowly, still not quite believing this is happening. His mother hated him so much she specifically added him as a line to her funeral arrangements.

'Dad wants you there, but he also doesn't want to cause any more upset today. I'm sorry, but you can't come in.'

'It's fine.' He doesn't know how he gets the words out, but it's the standard response he's used to giving her. He's not fine. Far from it. Being banned from his mother's funeral shouldn't upset him in the slightest.

So why is it?

Why is it like someone has him by the neck and is squeezing, cutting off his oxygen?

'Go back in there. Be with Eva. She needs you.'

'This is shit!'

'It's what she wanted. I need you to go inside, Clara. Please. Be with Eva. Say goodbye to your mum.'

There's nothing else to say on the matter. They both know it.

'I'll call you later. I want you to come to mine as soon as we're back.'

'Sure.' Not a fucking chance in hell! He's locking himself in his house and getting drunk. Clara hugs him again, then quickly leaves his car without saying anything else. Dillon waits until she's gone inside the church before he slams his fist against his leg and shouts.

'Fuck!'

The pain helps distract him as he starts the engine. Before pulling out of the parking spot he fires a text to Jace. *Change of plans. Heading home. You're off the clock.*

He doesn't care if Jace follows him or not. He just needs to get away before he loses the plot completely.

Dillon takes a drink of beer, then drops the empty bottle on the sand beside him with the other three bottles. He's not drunk though... unfortunately. There was no whiskey in his house and, by the time he drove from Dublin to Wicklow, he couldn't be bothered heading out again to get some.

Luckily there were two six packs in the back of a cupboard from when Luke was last over. He'd carried the beer down to the beach, still wearing his black suit, and proceeded to work his way through them.

His mother's funeral should be over by now. Since becoming a celebrity he'd been invited to too many events to count. But being officially *not* invited to a funeral is a new one, even for him. Trust him to claim that record. Maybe he'll get a plaque to add to the others on his wall?

He glances over his shoulder when he hears someone making their way across the sand towards him. 'How'd it go?'

Clara smiles sadly and nods. 'As well as you'd expect I suppose.

Can I join you?'

He pats the sand beside him, and she sits down, stretching her legs out in front of her.

'Any of those left?'

He twists the cap off a bottle and passes it to her.

'Thanks. How much have you had to drink?'

'Not enough. No whiskey in the house. This stuff isn't hitting the spot as well. Where's Eva?'

'She went back to my house with Marcus and Dad. Leon took their kids home. They're too young to fully understand what today was about. I've been trying to call you for about an hour. I guess you were ignoring me. We'd like you to come too.'

Dillon snorts and picks up the last bottle of beer. 'Not sure I'm in the mood to reminisce about our dear mother.'

'It's not going to be like that, Dill. It will just be the five of us. Everyone else is gone.'

'Everyone else who was invited you mean?' He takes a drink, not missing the hurt on his sister's face.

'I honestly don't know what to say to you. None of us do. If we could have done something to—'

'It's done, Clara. It's not like I was expecting her to give a shit about me when she's dead. She couldn't be arsed with me when she was alive. Can we just drop this please?'

'Dillon, she does—'

'Don't!' He shouts, startling her. 'Don't you dare say she cared! I'm gutted for you and Eva. I really am. But do you want to know the worst part?'

She turns to look at him as she wipes tears from her eyes.

'Now I'll never know why. I spent years wondering what I did that was so wrong it would turn them against me. Dad never liked me, but it was something else with Mum. I honestly think she hated me. I saw how they were with you and Eva. They loved you both to bits. Anyone could see that. Why didn't they love me, Clara? Fuck that, why didn't they even tolerate me? What the fuck did I do?'

He scrubs a hand over his face, surprised to feel tears on his cheeks. Dillon pushes to his feet and picks up a stone, shouting as he throws it in the sea. 'Fuck!'

He crouches down and buries his head in his hands. He swore he'd never get like this over them again. It took years to build up his wall. Years to protect himself against the pain that was always there, whenever he thought about his parents. Now it's all gone to shit.

Clara walks down the beach to him and holds out her hand. 'Please, Dill. Come home with me.'

He sits back on the sand and shakes his head. 'I just want to be alone.'

'Do you really think I'm going to leave you alone while you're like this?'

He wipes his face and takes a long shaky breath. 'I'm grand, Clara. Really. You can go.'

Instead of leaving him to wallow in his own misery, she sits beside him and wipes her eyes with a tissue. They sit in silence for a long time, but Dillon doesn't mind. As much as he says he wants to be alone, he needs the company. He's terrified what he'll do if he's left alone while he's like this.

Clara reaches out and takes his hand. 'I need to tell you something, Dillon. Something I've wanted to tell you for so long but couldn't.'

That gets his attention. 'What?'

'It's about your mother.'

And just like that, he's not interested. 'Give it a rest, Clara! I'm done talking about her.'

'No Dillon. You need to hear this. And I need to say it. The lie has been allowed to continue for too long. It's hurt you too much and enough is enough. It's time to end it once and for all.'

'Now you're freaking me out. What lie?'

176

'Your mother does love you, Dillon. She's loved you since the moment you were born and that's never changed. Never will.'

He laughs harshly. 'Don't know what house you grew up in, but she didn't. Fuck, can we just stop talking about this.'

Clara is quiet for a moment before she speaks again. 'I promise I have loved you since the moment I gave birth to you, Dillon.'

The alcohol probably doesn't help him register her words as fast as he usually would, but when he does, he swears his mind is playing tricks on him. 'What the fuck did you just say?'

Clara smiles a little and sniffs as the tears pour down her face. 'You're my son, Dillon. I'm your mother.'

21

Dillon

He shakes his head over and over again and pulls his hand out of hers. 'No. Stop this! What the fuck are you playing at? Is this some kind of sick joke or something?'

She ignores his outburst and looks at the sea. 'When I was fourteen, I was in a choir at the local community centre. There was a concert planned for that Christmas, so we had to rehearse a lot. I was so excited about it. One of mum's friends was in charge of the choir, so he'd drive me home after rehearsals.' She pauses and tears at the tissue in her hand.

Dillon wants to get the hell away from whatever is going on. He wants her to stop talking. But he can't move.

'It was the last day of rehearsals, so he said he had a treat for me.' She licks her lips and pauses for a minute. 'He drove to a wooded area not far from our old house, then he raped me. I didn't tell Mum or Dad. I couldn't. But then I got sick. Morning sickness, but I didn't have a clue what it was. Mum brought me to the doctor and after some tests I found out I was pregnant.

'I told them what had happened. I still felt like it was my fault though. Like I'd said or done something, and that's why he thought it was okay to do that to me. I was confused, terrified, and facing something no fourteen-year-old should face.

'They both believed me though, and it was such a relief. Mum's friend was arrested and sentenced, but I was a scandal in the area. School was horrible, and I came home most days in tears because of the bullying.

'So, I was sent away to stay with a cousin of Dad's. I stayed with her until you were born.' She pauses again and smiles. 'I fell in love with you the second I saw you. I held you for hours. Just staring at you. In that moment I couldn't have been happier.'

Her smile drops again as she continues. 'It didn't last though. Mum and Dad decided it would be a good idea to get a fresh start after you were born. Go somewhere no know knew us or knew about what happened. And I was all for it.

'But as soon as we moved to Wicklow, things changed. In hindsight I should have seen it coming, but I was too caught up with looking after you. I'd been allowed to name you, to be your mum for those first few weeks, but that wasn't to last.

'Instead of relocating with my parents, my sister, and my son, our family dynamic changed. I moved with my parents, my sister... and my brother.' She sniffs again but the tears are pouring down her face.

'Suddenly, I wasn't allowed to be your mother anymore. I was only fifteen at that stage and I know I couldn't have looked after you alone, but I wasn't allowed to do anything at all. I had to stand back as Mum and Dad raised you.

'I knew they didn't feel the same for you that I did and that killed me, Dillon. It was like every time they looked at you all they saw was what had happened to me, instead of seeing you.'

'My eyes. You all have brown eyes. I'm the only one with green ones. They're his, aren't they? I have my father's eyes.'

'No Dillon, they're your eyes.'

'That's not what I mean, and you know it. He had green eyes, right?'

She nods once. 'I think that made it so much worse for her. I think Mum felt so guilty. Like it was her fault because he was a friend of hers. She couldn't accept you and she tried, Dillon. She really did.'

Instead of responding, he leans over and vomits on the sand. Clara touches his shoulder, but he shoves her hand away. 'Don't touch me!' He wipes his mouth with the back of his hand as he glares at her. 'You lied to me my entire life! What the fuck is wrong with you?'

'I had no choice. I was only fourteen when I got pregnant. I did what my parents wanted me to do. I was completely out of my depth and terrified. The entire situation was far from ideal, and I guess we all did what we thought was best at the time. As the years went by, I thought about telling you, but how could I?'

'Yeah. You all made the best of a bad situation, right?' Clara tries to take his hand again, but he pulls away. 'I said don't touch me!'

'You are the only good thing to come out of that horrific time of my life. The only thing. I have never ever thought about that night when I look at you. Not once.'

'How can you say that?

'Because it's the truth.'

Dillon pushes to his feet, wobbling slightly as he rights himself. He needs to get away from this now before he loses it. Clara stands, but he shakes his head and backs away from her. 'No!'

'Dillon, please.'

'Please what? You expect me to just give you a hug and tell you it's all okay? Do you have any idea how fucked up all of this is? Everything

180

about my life has been fabricated by you. Does Eva know?'

Clara shakes her head. 'She was only five when you were born. She didn't know any different. As far as she's concerned, you are her brother.'

'Except I'm her what? Her nephew? Fuck Clara! I thought Mum and Dad had screwed things up enough, but well done. You've outdone them.'

'I didn't want any of this, Dillon. I wanted to tell you the truth from the start.'

'So why didn't you! Why did you stand by and watch them treat me like shit my entire fucking life, for something that wasn't my fault? You say you've always loved me, but everything you've done for the last forty years says differently.'

'Dillon... please...'

'No, Clara. I can't do this. Get the fuck away from me! I can't even look at you right now.'

He pushes past her and clumsily makes his way up the beach to his house. As he gets to the gate leading to his garden, he glances back at her. Clara is still standing where he left her. She looks devastated. Whatever bit of guilt that creeps out is shoved aside. He's too angry to feel sorry for anyone right now.

Dillon unlocks his front door, making sure to lock and bolt it after him so she can't follow. Once inside he stares at the floor as her words play over and over in his head.

Clara is his mother.

He's Clara's son.

His sister is his mother.

His other sister is his aunt.

His parents are his grandparents.

Each person in his family has been playing a part, like actors in a fucked-up performance he knew nothing about.

He can't process any of it. Can't process what happened to Clara at such a young age. Can't process who and what his father is. He rushes to the sink, barely making it before he vomits again. This time it has nothing to do with the drink. It's down to disgust, revulsion, guilt.

Dillon shouts out, then sweeps his arm across the countertop, sending cups and the kettle crashing to the ground. Then he turns to the other side and pulls open the drawers, emptying the contents onto the floor. As he works his way through his house, tearing it apart piece by piece, he feels nothing. He couldn't care that he's destroying his home. Couldn't care about the damage he's inflicting on the one place he truly felt like himself, because right now, he hasn't got a fucking clue who he is.

Ash

This can't be right? She pulls up outside the address and checks the piece of paper again. It's definitely the right place, although the unassuming detached cottage sitting at the end of a dirt track leading to the beach, doesn't say *super wealthy rock star Dillon* to her.

He'd told her not to come. Made it perfectly clear he didn't want her anywhere near him while he dealt with this. But she can't do that. She'd booked and paid for her own flight back to Dublin. This isn't work. This is personal.

The odds of him needing her at all are slim to none, but that didn't mean she was going to just sit in Italy and do nothing.

She loves him. He may hate her and rightly so, but she's not going to abandon him again. Not when he's just lost his mother.

She gets out of her car and peers into the garage through the small window. It's Dillon's house all right. His bike sits alongside a stunning deep red vintage Mustang Shelby GT500.

Seeing that particular car in his garage brings tears to her eyes. It was the car he always talked about getting when he made it big. She lost track of the number of hours he spent on the internet, searching high and low for the exact model and colour he wanted. She knew he'd get it. Never doubted it for a second.

She walks around the side of the garage to the front door. Before she can talk herself out of it, she rings the doorbell, but there's no reply, so she walks around the cottage to look down the beach. She holds her hood over her hair as the wind tries to expose her to the driving rain. Ash squints against the rain which seems to be attacking her from every angle.

Then she spots him. Or at least she thinks it's him. Someone is running along the beach in her direction. And they're not having a leisurely jog. It's a full-on sprint, his arms and legs pumping as he tears across the sand.

As he nears, she recognises him. It's Dillon all right. But then her smile fades. He looks terrible. Wearing only shorts and a t-shirt, his exposed skin is red from the cold, wind, and rain. But it's his eyes that trouble her the most. He's been crying.

He comes to a stop a few feet from her and gives her one hell of a hostile glare. 'What the fuck are you doing here?'

That was exactly the welcome she was expecting, but it still hurts a little. 'I wanted to see how you are,' she shouts over the wind.

'I'm fine. Now fuck off!' He pushes past her, and she catches a glimpse of what looks like blood on both his knuckles.

'What happened to you?'

He turns on her and she stumbles back in surprise. 'Just because we had a sweet little moment the other night, doesn't mean we're mates or anything like that. I'm not your concern anymore!'

He marches back to his house and, even though she knows he'll go nuts at her, she follows. Dillon slams his front door, but the lock doesn't catch, and the door swings open again. Ash slowly pushes it open then walks into his hallway. She shuts the door behind her and goes into the main room, coming to a stop in the doorway.

What was once clearly a beautiful house, looks as if a whirlwind has been through it. Dillon has destroyed it, throwing plates and cups on the floor, tearing pictures off the walls, emptying cupboards, and turning the couches on their backs.

'Trespassing now too?'

Dillon glares at her from the kitchen, leaning against the counter separating the kitchen area from the living room.

'Why did you do this to your beautiful house?'

'It made me feel better. I need a shower. Shut the door on your way out.'

Without looking at her again, he grabs an apple lace from the bag on the counter and disappears down the corridor leading off the living room. Ash knows she should leave, but she can't. There's something very wrong with him. More than his mother dying, and she isn't going to leave until she knows he's going to be okay.

While she waits for the full wrath of Dillon to be unleashed, she puts on the kettle and sets out two cups he didn't break, then searches his cupboards for the coffee.

She finds a dustpan and brush, then begins the long job of making sure all pieces of broken crockery are swept up. He's managed to break the blinds covering the windows so there's not a lot she can do about that. Although there is something comforting about standing inside while the rain beats against the vast windows and waves crash on the beach.

By the time he reappears nearly half an hour later, the fire is going and she's dishing out the pizza she found in his freezer. With all his plates in pieces, she has no choice but to use a tray, but she doubts he'd give a damn either way.

Instead of having a go at her, Dillon merely stops when he sees she's still in his house, then, ignoring the cup of coffee she's pouring, grabs a bottle of whiskey from a cupboard. He takes a dirty glass from

184

the sink, then, after righting the couch, sits down.

'Are you hungry?' she asks. She doubts he would have eaten anything, the mood he's in. 'I cooked some pizza.'

'No.'

Ash places the pizza on the low table in front of the couch, then sits on the armchair near the fire. One look at him and she knows she did the right thing by staying. He looks terrible. His skin is pale, his eyes bloodshot, and he seems to be shivering slightly.

The joggers and t-shirt won't be giving him much warmth, but he doesn't seem to care or notice. He hasn't even brushed his hair and that's not like him. Even when he was slouching around at home, he always took pride in his appearance.

He pulls his phone out of his pocket when it rings, glares at the screen, then slams it down on the couch beside him.

'Are you avoiding someone?'

He turns his glare on her as he downs the full glass of whiskey in one go. 'Didn't work. You're still here.'

'Dillon—'

'What do you want, Ash, huh? What exactly do you want from me? Cause right now I've got nothing left.'

'I don't want anything from you. I'm worried about you, Dillon.'

He smiles sarcastically, then refills his glass. 'Yeah. Isn't everyone? Fucking touching isn't it! Maybe people wouldn't have to worry about me if they stopped fucking me over. You think that might help?

'You know what? It's your fucking fault this happened. You and the guys. I wasn't going to come here. I told you all I didn't want to come. I was quite happy being on tour, doing my thing, but you couldn't let it go. None of you could. You had to keep going on at me about coming back to do the right fucking thing for my amazing family. Laying on the fucking guilt trip until I said I'd go.'

'Did something happen at the funeral?'

'I wouldn't know. You know what mummy dearest did? As well as choosing what hymns she wanted them to sing, she also popped in a small line banning me from setting foot inside the church.'

Ash curses under her breath. 'Fuck!' She can't believe his mother hated him so much she would go so far as to ban him from attending her funeral. What did Dillon do that was so terrible? What could he have possibly done that would stop her from even tolerating him attending her funeral?

He laughs harshly. 'Yeah. *Fuck* pretty much sums it up. We might finally agree on something.' His phone rings again. This time he answers it, closing his eyes when whoever is on the other end lays into him. Ash can't hear the words, but she can hear a lot of talking.

Dillon stands and walks over to the window. 'I know, okay. Please Eva, I'm fine. I just need some space, okay. No! Stay with Dad. I'm grand, I swear. No! I didn't upset Clara. It's complicated. I just didn't want to come over. Of course I care about you.'

He drops his head and rubs the back of his neck over and over as Eva talks. Ash never met Dillon's sisters, but he had spoken fondly of both of them.

'How many times? Don't come over! I just want to crash. Seriously Eva, just leave it.' He listens in silence as Eva says something to him. 'Yeah. I know. Love you too.' He ends the call and throws the phone onto the couch. 'I'll let you fill in the gaps for the magazine. Just make sure it's juicy.' He finishes his drink and refills his glass again.

'Is that really what you think of me?'

He shrugs. 'Wouldn't put anything past you.'

Ash leans forward, pointing her finger at him. 'I know you're hurting, but don't even consider having a go at me. You know full well I could have made a small fortune over the years selling stories about you. But I didn't. You know me better than that.'

He scrubs a hand over his face and curses quietly to himself. 'Sorry.'

That one word means so much to her. He's not usually one for admitting he's wrong about anything - even when he clearly is. It's just not what he does.

He slouches back, looking so defeated she wants to cry for him. 'I've had a shite day. Really fucking shite and I'm done. I can't...'

'You really should try to eat something.'

He turns his head towards her. 'What?'

She holds out a slice of pizza. 'C'mon. Sitting on the couch eating pizza must be a better option, than sitting on the couch and drinking.'

He takes such a long time to give in, but when he does, he sighs, then takes the slice from her hand.

Without asking, she puts the cap back on the bottle of whiskey and places it in the cupboard out of sight. He surprises her again by not arguing. He's right. He's done. Out of fight.

She takes two bottles of water from the fridge and pops one on the table in front of him next to the cup of coffee. She doesn't care which one he drinks, as long as it's alcohol free.

'How's the pizza?'

He's barely taken a bite but he's trying and that's all that matters. 'Don't have much of an appetite.'

Feeling braver than she probably should, Ash decides to sit beside him. He freezes for a moment but doesn't tell her to get the fuck away as she expects. She turns on the TV, finds the film she was looking for on one of the streaming services, and settles back to watch it.

After a few minutes she risks a quick glance at her companion. He's smiling. The grumpy ass of a man is smiling. 'What's that look for?'

'The last time I watched Lethal Weapon was with you.'

'Do you want me to turn it off?'

He shakes his head, then takes a bigger bite from the slice of pizza. 'No. It's okay. Leave it on.'

22

Dillon

They're on the second Lethal Weapon film, he's forced down about three pints of water which has helped clear his head, and they've polished off the pizza, a tub of ice cream he didn't know he had, and are now working their way through a packet of cookies. Not the healthiest, but neither was a diet of whiskey and bags of apple laces.

It's not the food that's helping the most. It's her. They used to spend at least one night a week doing this. They'd get loads of food and have a movie marathon. It always ended with the two of them naked on the couch, but that was a long time ago. Just being with her like this is enough for now.

As much as he said he doesn't want her anywhere near him, he does. Why else would he have left the catch on the door so it wouldn't close? A part of him needed the company after what happened - even if it was her.

Especially if it was her. In truth, she's probably the only one he can handle right now. She's not connected to his family or his life over the last few years.

Right now, that makes a massive difference.

It's not like having her here can make things worse. Destroying his house hadn't helped. Kicking and beating the shit out of the punching bag hadn't helped. Running on the beach in the rain shouting and cursing the whole time, hadn't helped. He's probably got a cold to look forward to in his not-too-distant future, thanks to that stupid stunt.

He needs a distraction. Something to keep his mind from going over everything Clara had said, again and again. Slowly driving him crazy, as he analyses every interaction with his family over the years. Was there something he missed? Some clue or hint that all wasn't what it seemed?

But it doesn't matter how often he replays parts of his life, nothing would have led him to anything close to the truth. It's so far fetched he doubts he ever would have reached it himself.

But now the truth is out, he's more lost and lower than at any other time in his life. And there have been some low moments.

When he went for the run, he'd planned on coming home, going to bed, and making sure he didn't wake up.

It's been a hell of a time since his thoughts veered anywhere close to that level of darkness. Years since he felt there was no other option but to erase the problem.

But then she was there.

When he saw her standing at his house, soaked and windswept, he couldn't have been more relieved and grateful to see her.

Ash had come to him at exactly the right time.

He's not going to give her an easy break, but he's also not going to kick her out. Having her here is comforting in a way he misses more than he could ever realise. All the crap and bravado seem to fade when she's near. It always did. She's one of the few people who can uncover the real him. She can see the emotional mess he tries so hard to hide.

And he doesn't mind at all. He needs to let that wall down. Not that he can keep it up after what he learned today.

No fucking chance of that after Clara's bombshell. He can't even begin to process any of that right now. He meant what he said to Ash. He's got nothing left.

He finishes his cookie and leans back on the couch looking over at Ash. He doesn't understand why she came to see him. Or why she stuck around. It's not like he had been remotely civil to her in any way. He's been downright obnoxious. And she didn't deserve that.

Nothing he's feeling today is down to her. All she's done is try to look out for him. Make sure he didn't do something stupid as he tends to do. She must care about him on some level. Why else would she be here with him now?

So why did you leave me? Why did you break my heart?

Stop it! Thoughts like that won't help him. What does it matter why she left? All that matters is that she did. End of story. She clearly didn't care about him enough back then to stick around. This now is probably just down to guilt or duty.

But she's still here when he needs her. That must count for something and, as pissed off as he is with the world, that deserves some recognition. She deserves some recognition. 'Thank you.'

She looks up at him. 'Sorry?'

'Yeah, I did just say that.'

She smiles and he can't help joining in. 'All I did was cook a pizza. It's not a big deal.'

He wasn't referring to the pizza, but there's no way he's going to tell her that. 'My plan was to drink until I passed out.'

'Oh. Pizza was probably a better option.'

'Maybe.'

'I'm not going to ask if you want to talk. I'm assuming the answer will be no.'

Too right. Talking about it means that it's real. That everything Clara told him is the truth. Not a fucking chance he's even close to being ready to accept that. He gets up and brings the pizza tray into the kitchen, staring out at the storm still raging.

'I should leave you in peace. I just came to see if you were okay.'

I haven't been okay since you left me. Please don't go again.

She gathers her bag and coat from the couch, ready to leave him again. 'Stay.' Ash is as stunned by his comment as he is. He hadn't planned on saying that.

'What?'

How the fuck does he salvage this pathetic situation? 'It's fucking rotten out there. I'm not having you ending up in the ditch.' It's a valid reason for his outburst - one she seems to buy. Total bullshit, but who cares.

'Are you sure?'

'Yeah.' He points to the door at the other side of the fireplace. 'The spare room is the door at the end of the corridor. There should be fresh towels in the en-suite if you want a shower. Night.'

Like some idiot, he hurries down the corridor to his bedroom, closing and locking the door behind him. As if she's going to follow him and try to get in! He sits on the end of his bed and stares out the window. It's barely ten. He's usually up until well past midnight. Is he going to hide in his room for the next few hours?

His phone vibrates again. Clara asking if he's okay. He slams it face down onto his bed. Fucking ridiculous question! Of course he's not okay.

It's like someone kicked his legs out from under him, and he doubts he'll ever right himself again. How do you, after having your entire world flipped around into something so bizarre you haven't got a fucking clue what the truth is anymore?

He's lost everyone. In that moment on the beach, his family, such that it was, had ceased to exist. The last forty years of his life was torn apart to reveal the lie it was built on.

What he wants to do is go to Ash. To collapse in her arms and tell her everything. To get lost in her embrace, let her hold him while he falls apart. Cry, shout, and scream. Let all this shit out before it drags him further into the darkness.

Instead, he lies back on his bed, watching the rain pouring down his window, taking a small amount of comfort from the fact the love of his life is on the other side of the wall.

Ash

When she came to see him, she had never expected to have dinner with him, let alone stay the night. While she'd prefer to be tucked up in his bed with him, being in his house is a start. Or maybe it just means he tolerates her. Nothing more than that.

He disappeared into his bedroom about ten minutes ago, leaving her in his living room. She could leave, but he might have a point. It's horrible outside.

And she doesn't want to leave him alone. He's in a dark place, lost in his head, lost in his emotions. When she saw him on the beach she knew that much. Seeing the state he made of his beautiful home just confirmed her suspicions.

Ash turns off the living room light and goes into the spare room. Like the rest of the cottage, the room is painted white, with exposed beams, wooden floor, and feels warm and cosy. She showers, then smiles when she goes back into the bedroom to find a t-shirt lying on the end of the bed. She picks it up and buries her face in the material.

It's clean but it still smells of him. Everything around her smells of him.

Ash slips into the t-shirt and climbs under the thick duvet. It is undoubtedly the most comfortable bed she's ever slept in. She turns onto her side and looks at the wall facing her. Dillon is on the other side of that wall.

Is he thinking about her? Is he already asleep, helped by the many glasses of whiskey he had before she arrived? Is he still mulling over what happened with his family? Is he still upset?

She'd never seen him like that before. Something else happened today with his family. She's sure of it. Being banned from the funeral would have hurt, she knows that. But Dillon has had years to deal with his parents' feelings for him. He wouldn't have reacted the way he did just because of the funeral.

She can't imagine a parent being so cruel to their child. Over the years, she's had many heated arguments with both her mother and her father, but they would never consider disowning her. It doesn't take a genius to figure out one, or both of his parents, has a serious issue with his sexuality.

In this day and age, the idea is preposterous, but there's no way she's going to ask Dillon about it. It's a private matter between him and his parents and, after what she did to him years ago, she's the last person he would open up to.

Ash closes her eyes and buries her face in the pillow. She doesn't want to cry over him again. She's had years of crying every single day. Years of carrying around the pain. Years of wishing life had played out differently.

But what's done is done. There's no going back. She broke his heart. He's not going to forgive her for that.

Dillon

One-thirty in the morning and he's still staring at the fucking wall. He doubts he even got an hour of sleep so far. His mind is going at ninety and his body isn't far behind.

He lifts his duvet and curses again. Fucking dick is a traitor. It wants her. Dillon rolls onto his back and laughs harshly to himself. Who's he kidding? *He* wants her. He's always wanted her. And it's fucking irritating.

He shouldn't be thinking about her in that way with everything else going on, but tell that to his body.

He shoves off the duvet and gets out of bed, heading into the kitchen. Maybe a shot of whiskey will help knock him out.

But there she is, standing in his living room looking out the full-sized window at the sea.

She's wearing his t-shirt and looks fucking gorgeous silhouetted in the moonlight. He shouldn't stare, but he's captivated. Just like that first time he met her in his restaurant all those years ago.

The minute he saw her no one else in the room existed. How can she still do this to him after so long? After hurting him so badly.

She turns when she notices him and tries to pull the t-shirt down to cover more of her legs. 'I'm sorry. Did I wake you?'

'No. You okay?'

'I couldn't sleep. Are you okay?'

'Couldn't sleep either.' He somehow manages to get his legs to move him away from her and take him into the kitchen. Instead of grabbing the whiskey he wanted, he fills a glass with water and goes back towards his room. He needs to get away from her before she notices his traitor dick. At least he'd left his boxers on for a change.

'Goodnight.'

He escapes back into his bedroom before she can respond, then slams the glass of water on to his bedside table with more force than necessary, but he's pissed off.

He thought he had a grip on his feelings, but being around her is weakening the wall he'd built. A wall he wishes, in part, he could knock down, but also desperately needs to survive. If he lets her in, she'll just leave again. The first time had nearly killed him. He doubts he'd survive a second.

'Dillon?'

He peers over his shoulder at her, standing in his doorway looking all kinds of sexy and irresistible. Why is she doing this to him?

Why is she just standing there? Why is he moving towards her?

It's the worst fucking decision of his life, but he really couldn't give a damn right now. He wraps his hand around the back of her head, pulling her closer so he can kiss her.

When her arms circle his neck, he lifts her, carrying her over to his bed. He lowers her onto his unmade bed and tugs at the t-shirt she's wearing, breaking their kiss long enough to pull it over her head.

Fuck he can't get enough of her. Right or wrong, he wants this. He's about to ask her if she really want to do this, but stops when she slides her hand down the back of his boxers to squeeze his ass.

Fair enough. He's game if she is.

He doesn't kiss when he's having sex. He's kissed lots of people, but never when he's having sex with them. It just made everything too personal for him.

It was different with Ash. She's the only one he's ever done that with, but things are different now. Kissing her in the gym was a mistake. One he's not going to repeat.

Just sex, Dillon. She doesn't want anything else from you.

If he keeps saying that to himself, he might just get through this without making a fool of himself.

He might not want to kiss her on the mouth, but that leaves a lot more of her body to lavish attention on. He pins her arms over her head, holding her wrists in one hand. He's taking control today. He can't let her do it again. It killed him too much after the last time.

She tries to break free from his grip but he holds her back, reaching down to explore her pussy. Ash lifts her hips, giving him clear access, silently begging him to play.

He slowly slides a finger inside, not surprised that she's already wet for him. Or she's just horny and he's the only option she has.

He shoves that thought aside, concentrating on Ash instead of putting himself down. Why the fuck is he so nervous? Why is he in his head instead of on the bed with her? He never second guesses himself when he's having sex. It's what he excels at.

Ash moans, writhing against his hand when he slides another finger in. Her moans are so hot. She's driving him crazy. She doesn't just turn on his body, she gets his head in the game too and that rarely happens.

He can't keep the emotions out of it with Ash. Being with her means something to him and that's what's throwing him off.

Stop overthinking this!

She moves against him, faster and faster. She's close, her body clenching and relaxing against his fingers.

This is what he does, and does well. Ignoring the feelings he usually bottles up, he concentrates on giving her one hell of an orgasm.

Less than a minute later, she arches off the bed, her hands clenching on the sheet to either side of her as the orgasm tears through her. He doesn't hold back, his fingers sliding in and out, his thumb massaging her clit, extending her orgasm as long as possible.

He's never seen a more beautiful sight than Ash, breathless and mid orgasm on his bed. He could never get bored of looking at her like this.

When she gazes up at him, her eyes glazed over, he falls in love with her all over again.

'Lie down Dillon.'

'What?'

'It's my turn. If you want?'

'Of course he fucking wants. He lies back, his heart racing already. He wants her to take control like she did in the gym, but more. He wants so much more, but he'll never ask her. Never ask anyone. He's known for being the dominant one. How would he even begin to explain what he wants deep down.

Ash straddles him and runs her hands down his arms to his wrists, pinning him to the bed. 'Yes or no?'

He nods quickly, terrified and more excited than he's been for a hell of a long time. She squeezes his wrists hard, holding him down as she kisses his chest, her teeth grazing against his nipples.

'Fuck Ash...'

She straightens, slowly lifting his arms until they're above his head.

Tie me down. Please...

She goes back to his chest, swirling her tongue around his nipples, down the sensitive flesh along his side, and down to this groin.

When she flicks her tongue across the piercings in his dick, he instantly drops his arms to his sides.

Ash stops what she's doing so she can put them back where they were. 'Can I make sure you don't move again?'

'How?'

'Maybe a tie or a belt.'

He knows she used English, but he could swear it was a foreign language by the length of time it takes him to comprehend what she's saying.

'Wardrobe. I have a few ties in there. Belts too.'

She climbs off him and retrieves what she wants from the wardrobe while he lies on the bed trying not to have a fucking panic attack. Can you have a panic attack when something you want finally happens?

As he watches her secure his wrists to the headboard with two ties he wears to awards ceremonies, he does some of that deep breathing shit Tate and Luke do. It's either that or he could pass out on the bed like this. Not the best impression to leave her with.

'Is that okay?'

He nods even though he can't feel his body right now.

'Just say and I'll untie you, okay?'

'Yeah. Okay.'

The smile she gives him is downright sexy and mischievous. She slides down his body, her eyes on his as she kisses her way back to his dick, taking it all in her mouth without any build up.

He's not bigging himself up at all but his dick isn't small by any means. Seeing her take him all the way down her throat has him on brink of coming. He pulls his arms, momentarily forgetting he's tied down.

Not being able to stop her, not being able to move, to do anything other than watch her suck him, is so much more intense than he ever could have imagined.

Her tongue flicks against his piercings sending a jolt of pleasure right through him. The headboard creaks as he pulls against the makeshift restraints. Fuck, he's going to come! He can hold himself back no problem. But this is so different, he's struggling.

Ash wraps a hand around the base of his dick, keeping the pressure on as she sucks him. It helps hold him back, but every other sensation ramps up.

She sucks the tip of his dick, pulling against the piercings.

'Fuck!'

'I like these more than I thought I would,' she says as she slowly licks each of the piercings in turn.

'Right. That's good.'

'Do you have any condoms handy?'

'Top drawer.'

She takes one from his beside drawer, then slides it on him before straddling him again. Ash groans as she slips him inside, moving slowly until he's buried deep inside.

After checking he's still firmly secured to the bed, she rests her hands on his chest, pressing against him as she pumps her hips.

He's going out of his mind right now. He wants more of what she's doing to him, but even having this much is too fucking good. She's so stunning bouncing on him, her short hair sticking up in sweat soaked spikes, her lips parted, her breath coming in quick gasps as she drives him into her hard and fast.

'Don't you dare come yet. Not ready yet.'

Being told not to come by Ash has him nearly whimpering in pleasure. She's in control and he'll willingly do what she says.

It's not going to be easy. He's so close, too close.

Then she slows down and he does whimper. He's never been edged before. He's done it so many times but this is the first time he's getting taste of his own medicine.

And he wants more.

She keeps pushing him to the edge, bringing him back, then doing it again, and again. He has no idea how long or how many times. All he's aware of is the stunning woman controlling him and the restraints making sure he stays where she wants him.

He can't think straight. Lost in the sensations, lost in what she's doing to him.

'It's time now, Dillon. You're going to come for me, okay?'

He nods, or at least he thinks he does. He's not sure of anything right now.

'Look at me.'

He does as he's told, then groans when she picks up the speed again. Then she plays with her clit, putting extra pressure against his top of his dick.

'Oh fuck, Ash!'

'Now,' she mutters as she comes, but he's barely a second behind her.

'Fuck!' His entire body spasms as he comes, and it keeps on coming. Ash rides out her own orgasm which just prolongs his. He closes his eyes, losing himself in the moment.

When his body finally stops shuddering, he feels like he's made of jelly. Usually he'd orgasm, then get up and get on with his day. He doesn't even have the energy to open his eyes.

He feels Ash untying him, but after that there's nothing except peaceful bliss.

Ash

She'd dreamed of this moment so many times over the years. Far too many times. So when she wakes and sees Dillon asleep beside her, sprawled on his back with his arms over his head, she has to pinch herself – just in case.

But he's real. They fell asleep together in his bed after having some of the best sex she's had for years.

She knows he's dominant in bed. Always has been. But she liked to take charge herself from time to time. Not that she'd argue if he tried to control her. Not in the slightest, but something about his mood last night hinted that he might have wanted a change.

She can't explain what it was. He just seemed a little hesitant, and that's not like him. Who knew the life long Dom wanted to submit. Her gamble paid off. And then some. His orgasm was so intense he'd fallen asleep afterwards.

But she didn't mind in the slightest. If anything, she took it as a compliment. She wore out Dillon Ryan. She didn't think that was possible.

The covers have moved down his naked body and she takes some time to just marvel at it, so grateful he always sleeps naked.

His body has changed a lot in the ten years since they were together. The tattoo of the Celtic wings covering his entire back is probably the biggest change, but the piercings circling the top of his dick are without doubt the most extreme addition.

She can't even begin to imagine what it must have been like to have them done. Initially she'd been unsure about them, but after experiencing how they feel inside her, she has no complaints at all.

Even asleep, his dick is ready to go and begging to be touched. But she wants more than just sex with him. She wants Dillon. All of him. She wants to wake up to this sight every morning. To fall asleep in his arms every night. She wants to share his life. But more than that, she wants him to be a father to Freya.

He comes across as someone who couldn't care less about anyone or anything, but the truth is very different. When they were together, she had never felt more loved, more protected, more appreciated than she did with him. He put her first every single day.

And that's why she had to walk away. He would have put her before himself. If he had to choose between her and the band, he would have picked her. She knows that. And that wasn't an option for her. Nothing in the world would have convinced her to force him to make that choice.

So, she had done it for him. Rightly or wrongly, she had left him so he could have the career, the dream he so deserved.

He turns towards her and the sheet slides lower exposing the inside of his leg and a tattoo she hadn't noticed before. After making sure he's still asleep, she leans over and examines the ink.

It takes her a few seconds to realise what he has inked into his inner thigh. Her grandmother had given her a necklace with her name written on it in an old Irish text.

She'd spent hours memorising the lines on the necklace so she could impress her school friends by writing like that. It's been years since she used the text, but she is positive Dillon has her name tattooed on the inside of his upper leg.

She looks at his face and he suddenly opens his eyes. Instead of asking him about it or saying anything at all, she just looks at him. It always amazed her how he could be asleep one second and wide awake the next. There was no in between for him.

'Hey.'

He smiles, instantly brightening up her morning. He's stunning when he smiles like that. 'I thought I might have been hallucinating last night.'

'That was one hell of an hallucination, cause I had it too.'

'Yeah. It was a fucking amazing. I remember you untying me but that's it. Did I fall asleep or something?'

'You were out like a light.'

'Sorry. I didn't meant to do that.'

'It's not a problem, Dillon. I think you needed the sleep. You had one hell of a day yesterday. Are you okay?'

He tucks his hand under his head, then shrugs. 'I don't know.'

She shuffles a little closer, taking his other hand in hers. 'Close your eyes.'

'What?'

'Close your eyes.'

He sighs but does as he's told. Dillon can't talk about how he's feeling. He's never been able to do it. Not eye to eye. He also can't be pushed. When they were together and he was upset and lost in his head, she'd get him to close his eyes and wait. Eventually he'd talk. It always worked.

She runs her thumb over the ring on his finger as she hums quietly. It used to soothe him, to help clear his mind. She knows it's rarely quiet in his head. He may not say much, but that doesn't mean he's not thinking. Always thinking or, more likely, over-thinking.

In time, it would manifest itself in other ways, like losing his temper and landing himself in trouble. The trick was to release some of that steam before it took him over.

She traces her finger over every detail on the heavy ring, still surprised he's wearing it. It gives her hope. More than likely misplaced hope, but any hope is better than nothing.

'I found out yesterday that Clara isn't my sister. She's my mum.'

When he finally speaks, what he says doesn't initially register with her. But when it does, she understands why he is so devastated. 'Your mum? I don't understand...'

He turns his face further into the pillow, hiding from her. 'She was... fuck, she was raped when she was fourteen and I'm the result. The dirty secret they were all keeping for the last forty years. They moved after I was born and raised me as their son. But they couldn't see past what was done to her.

'I have my rapist father's eyes. Lucky me. I was a constant fucking reminder of what happened to their daughter. They couldn't accept...' He curses quietly, then covers his face with his arm.

'They couldn't accept you because of what happened.' As she says the words, she can't hold back the tears. She understands completely. As a mother she understands why his parents... his grandparents, struggled to accept him.

But it wasn't his fault. He was born into a situation he had no control over.

And Clara... she can't even begin to comprehend what she had gone through all these years. Watching her parents constantly being so cruel to her son must have been incredibly painful for her.

'She really wanted to be my mum,' he says, more to the pillow than to her. 'They wouldn't let her though. It's such a mess Ash, and I can't get it straight in my head. It's driving me crazy.'

She brushes her hand along the side of his face. 'You're not going to get it straight overnight. This is going to take a while to process. My God Dillon, it's unbelievable!'

He laughs and finally opens his eyes to look at her. 'I wish it wasn't true. How fucked up is that? All I ever wanted to know was what I had done to make them hate me so much. Now, I'd prefer not to know and just have parents who hate me for no reason. And Eva hasn't got a clue about any of it.'

'She doesn't know?'

'As far as she's concerned, I'm her brother. But I'm her nephew.' He rolls onto his back and snorts. 'It's massively fucked up.'

'That's an understatement. I don't know what I can say to you to make this better.'

'There isn't anything anyone can say. It is what it is. Everything I thought I knew about my life is a lie. I'll just have to try to deal with that. Fuck, I didn't think it could get any worse.'

'What you said a few days ago... about their reaction when you came out. Was that true?'

He nods. 'The kicker is I figured after trying to do right by them for all that time and getting nowhere, I couldn't make it any worse. I mean they already hated me. What else could they do? I'd decided to tell them one evening when I got home from school. I'd been building up to it for ages but picked that day. Fuck knows why? It was as good a day as any.'

He closes his eyes for a moment and chews on his lip ring. When he looks down at her again, she could swear there are tears in his eyes.

'I knew telling my folks I'm bisexual would be a bitch. I knew they'd take it badly. They're old-school parents, you know. Really religious. Good old fire and brimstone kind of religious. But I had to tell them. I was miserable keeping it to myself, so figured anything had to be better than bottling up how I was feeling.'

He shakes his head as he wrings his hands together.

'It was a Thursday. I remember not wanting to tell them at the weekend. I didn't want to be stuck in the house with them while they processed it. I figured if I told them on a Thursday, I'd be able to hide at school the next day. Give them a little time to get used to it. Anyway, I came home from school, sat them down, then told them.

'I didn't beat around the bush. Just said that I'm attracted to men and women. That I'd known for a while I was bisexual and that I didn't want to hide it from them any longer.

'Saying they were horrified is a fucking understatement. My mum... fuck, I don't know what else to call her. Anyway, she started crying and my dad just shut down. He wouldn't even look at me. My parents were still there. Still sitting in front of me, breathing and very much alive. But neither of them said a word. It was like I'd transformed into a monster. Like I'd done something so terrible they couldn't even look at me and couldn't forgive me for it.'

He curses to himself and scrubs a hand over his face.

'I tried to get them to talk to me. Fuck, to shout at me. Anything. But it was like I was invisible. Then Mum stood up and wiped her face. She said she always *expected* there would be something wrong with me. Always knew something would come to the surface at some stage. Then she looked me in the eye and said that I was *wrong*. *Flawed. A disgrace.*

'I've never seen my mum look at me like that - look at anyone like that. She was ashamed of me. Disgusted by me.' He laughs once. 'She even took a few steps back to get further away from me, like I had some disease she was going to catch. They went upstairs to their room and refused to open the door to me.

'So I left. Thought they needed time to process what I'd said, and if I gave them space, they'd come around. I went to Luke's house. Didn't tell him what had just gone on. I could barely get my own head around it. When I got home, they were in bed.

'I bunked off school the next day. Couldn't face it. Just sat on the beach for the day, thinking the worst possible things about myself. That was eight hours of fun.' He wipes the tears from his face before he continues.

She takes his hand, squeezing it as he struggles to get out what he wants to say.

'There was a note for me when I got home that evening. They had gone away to my aunt's place for the weekend. They wanted me out of the house by the time they got back on Sunday afternoon. They couldn't accept me. Couldn't live under the same roof with someone like me. The last line was the killer though. *You're not our son.*'

'Oh, Dillon. I'm so sorry.'

He shrugs and tries to laugh, but it falls desperately short. 'You're not our son. Guess they were telling the truth at that stage?

'I knew they'd be pissed, but disowning me was an unexpected blow. I... I don't remember the next few hours. I just kept reading the fucking letter over and over again. So do you want to know what I did?'

She shakes her head, not sure she wants to know.

He sniffs and wipes his face again. 'I emptied my mother's medicine cabinet and took the lot. I took every pill hoping more than anything that it would be enough to kill me. Would have worked too if Clara hadn't found me a few minutes later.' He laughs harshly.

'She still doesn't know why she called around that night. Mum and Dad hadn't contacted her. I hadn't said a word to her or Eva about it. She just felt like she had to come and see me. Seems I was all out of luck that day. Worst fucking timing.'

He may have said that in a flippant way, but she has no doubts he would have preferred the alternative at that time. 'Oh Dillon...'

'They were able to save me, obviously,' he adds with a weak laugh. 'But I was so angry at Clara for so long after that.'

'Angry? Why?'

'She fucked everything up. It wasn't a cry for help or anything like that. I wanted to die, Ash. In that moment, reading that letter, I knew I wanted everything to go away. I couldn't do it anymore. I didn't want to have to deal with it.'

She wipes her eyes, then squeezes his hand again.

'Clara got me into a hospital that could help. Not that I was interested in getting help, but she wasn't going to turn her back on me. Neither of my sisters were. They paid for my care for the six months I was there. Paid for someone to try to *fix* me. To sort out what's wrong in here,' he says, tapping the side of his head.

'I know I needed to be there, but at the time, and for a long time after, it felt like they'd washed their hands of me too. Like they'd locked me away in there because they couldn't deal with me. And I know that's kind of the truth. Not in a bad way though. I was in a dark place for a long time, and it wasn't fair to have that thrown at them.

'Over time I felt better in myself, but it's not like going in to have a broken leg set. It's not a definite fix. I'm not saying I think about suicide at all now, but my head does go to dark places sometimes. It usually happens at night when I'm trying to go to sleep. That's where the drink and drugs came into play. Helped to knock me out for a bit.

'When I was discharged, I went to live with Clara. It's not like I had anywhere else to go. It was either stay in the hospital or go home with her. It took a while, but I sorted my head out. But even through all that, my parents stayed away from me. I heard nothing from them.'

'What happened with school and your friends?'

'The guys don't know I tried to kill myself. I'm not sure why, but Clara and Eva kept that from them. Maybe they didn't want to freak them out? They just said I'd had a massive fight with my parents, and they needed to take me away.

'We kept in touch a bit while I was away, but it was hard. We probably grew apart for about a year or so. They were getting on with their lives, heading off to college or work, and I was stuck somewhere I didn't want to be, talking about stuff I really didn't want to talk about.

'As for school, I never finished it. I missed my last year and couldn't face repeating it. It didn't work out too badly though. I got a job in a local hotel in the kitchen and managed to work my way up.'

She laces her fingers with his. 'Self made man.'

Dillon turns his head back to her and smiles. 'Too fucking right! I worked my ass off to get where I am. We all did. Broken is my world. The band, the guys, they're everything to me. I fucking love it all.'

'You don't have to tell me. You only have to see you on stage to know that. You own that stage. You belong up there.'

He glances down at her hand. 'It's the only place I feel like I belong.'

You belong with me Dillon.

The silence hangs between them for a few minutes as he keeps his focus on their hands. Leaving him like she did wouldn't have helped his abandonment issues. She's added to his doubt, and she'll never be able to forgive herself for that.

'Are you talking to anyone about it since you were discharged?'

'No. I probably should, but I've managed so far without that, so I'm in no rush to go there. I know it's helping Tate, Gregg, and Luke, but I'm not built like that.'

'Why did you never tell me any of this before?'

He shrugs. 'It's not something I like talking about. Or even thinking about. It's in my past. Like a lot of shit. It's just... I guess it comes back to give me a kick every now and again. Mainly when something knocks me off course.'

He brushes his hand over his face, then smiles, but it's a poor effort. 'Whatever. Sorry for dumping all that on you. I didn't mean to.'

'What are you apologising for? I'm glad you told me. It means a lot that you could tell me.'

He turns to look out the window, calling an end to the conversation. She doesn't mind. The fact he told her as much as he did, that he opened up to her about such a painful time in his life, means the world to her. Perhaps it means he doesn't hate her after all?

If she looked him in the eye and told him she's still in love with him, would he believe her? There's only one way to find out, but now isn't the time. There's too much going on in his life to insert herself in it too. Last night was a way of blowing off steam. It was sex between two consenting adults who are attracted to each other.

Knowing he's still attracted to her is fantastic, but she wants more than that. She wants the emotion, the love. She doesn't deserve it. Not after leaving him the way she did. But selfishly it's what she wants. What she needs.

She fears she's blown her one chance with him. He doesn't forgive. You get one shot and if you mess it up, he walks away. She's seen him do it before. And she messed up her shot in the worst way possible.

He surprises her by wrapping his arm around her to pull her closer. Ash drapes her arm across his chest, just being with him as he looks out the window.

'I'm flying to Italy tomorrow morning. I need to be back in time for the show there tomorrow night. I've got a plane booked for first thing. Fancy tagging along with me?'

'I have a flight already booked.'

'I've got a private plane booked, so screw that. Come back with me. I'll cover the cost.'

'Are you sure?'

'I wouldn't have asked unless I was sure.'

'Okay. That sounds amazing. Thank you.'

He suddenly pulls his arm out from under her and sits up. 'Get dressed. We're heading out.'

'Out? Where?'

He stretches and she's momentarily distracted by his glorious body. 'Stop eyeing me up. There's time for that later. We're going out for a drive. Fuck knows where! I don't really care. I just want us both out of here.'

Then she gets what's going on. 'You're afraid Clara is going to call around?'

'Maybe. But that's not the only reason. I just want to do something that hasn't been planned or organised. Just get in the car and drive. Remember when we used to do that?'

Of course she remembers. Every detail of their short but incredible relationship is burned into her memory forever. 'You know we need food though?'

He grins and it's the best thing she's seen for a while. 'We'll stop somewhere and grab some food. I'll send Jace a text and get him to meet us on the way. Now move!'

25

Ash

A few hours later, Ash is sitting on some rocks overlooking the sea, eating fish and chips with a downright sexy rock star beside her. Absolutely perfect way to spend the morning.

The drive to Port Oriel in Clogherhead had been just like old times. For breakfast, they had eaten bacon buttys in the car, that he had picked up from the local garage on the way. Conversation had flowed easily between them, but she had stayed away from any topic that could put a stop to that.

Today was about distracting him. Taking his mind off his new family dynamic.

And it seems to be working.

'It's beautiful here.'

He nods as he swallows his lunch. 'It's worth coming for the fish and chips alone. But yeah, the scenery is pretty great too. We come here from time to time - me and the guys. Just get on our bikes and escape all the crazy for a few hours.'

'And you don't get noticed?' The rugged coastline seems to be a popular spot. She doubted his baseball cap would provide much in the way of a disguise, but it has been effective so far. He was still drawing attention, but he's not someone you can easily ignore.

Apart from the fact he's a good six-foot-two, there's something about the way he carries himself that demands attention, no matter how disguised he is.

Jace is doing his job, continuously watching everyone within a few metres of his charge. He's digging into his own fish and chips a little further along the headland. Even dressed in jeans, a t-shirt, and a pair of sunglasses, the bodyguard still stands out as much as Dillon does.

At least he followed them here in his own car. He's a great guy, but she wants this time alone with Dillon.

'It tends to happen more when the four of us are together. On our own we can blend in a bit better. Jace is great at not drawing attention to me which helps. And there are enough places here to just sit and get away from people.'

'And there's the fish and chips,' she says popping another delicious chip in her mouth.

He laughs at that. 'Yeah. Can't get better. Gregg had a party a few years back and booked them for the food.'

'Did they come?'

'Of course.'

'I thought with you all being celebrities you'd be enjoying the finer things in life.'

He shakes his head. 'We enjoy ourselves, but we're not stupid about it. Mostly.' he adds with a grin. 'I've splashed out on a few cars and houses, but the majority is invested. Put away for a rainy day. I'm not always going to be this hot.'

He winks at her, and she laughs. 'Well, I have to say you are ageing incredibly well.'

'Is that right?'

'You're owning forty. It's quite sickening really.'

'What the fuck are you talking about? Time stopped for you. You're what - thirty-five now? I'm getting grey hairs, and you look like you're still in your early twenties! You're more beautiful than the day I met you.' He licks his lips and looks down at the food on his knee. 'Sorry. Not sure where that came from.'

'Why are you apologising? You don't apologise for complimenting someone like that. Thank you, Dillon. That means a lot. You haven't changed much either. Well, apart from the metal on your face. I read about the Broken dares. Were they a result of that?'

'Fucking Gregg and his big mouth! The dares were meant to stay in the band. He went and blabbed about it at an interview. But yeah, some of them were.'

'Some?'

'My nose and lip were dares. My tongue and dick weren't.'

For some reason she thought it would be the other way around.

'You look surprised. You thought I wouldn't have had my dick pierced unless someone dared me?' He moves closer and licks the ring in his lip. 'When I was inside you, were you glad I had the piercings?'

Her attention is drawn to his tongue as he asks the question. Memories of what he did with the piercing come back to her with a shiver.

'I'll take your flushed cheeks as a yes.'

'So, you got your tongue and dick pierced so you could... pleasure people better? Really?'

He smirks as he picks up another chip. 'It's not like I don't get anything from it myself. And I like the piercings, so it's a win win.'

'I'm not in the slightest bit surprised. It's such a Dillon thing to do.'

'What does that mean?'

'It means you just do what you want. And I don't mean that in a bad way at all. I've always admired that about you. You've always been yourself no matter what.'

His smile fades slightly. 'Doesn't always work in my favour. I've pissed off a lot of people doing things my way. Ended up inside because of it.'

'From what I read you were protecting Luke, but his bitch of a wife twisted things her way. You should never have been in there. I can't imagine what it must have been like for you.'

He shrugs, but his expression darkens. 'It wasn't good.' He rubs his ribs in a move that appears nearly subconscious.

'What happened?'

He quickly drops his hand from his side. 'Nothing.'

That's a flat out lie, but as much as she wants to push him, she doesn't. Someone had hurt him. If he'd been in a fight, he would have said. He was never shy about telling her when he'd gone up against someone.

'Water under the bridge.'

It's not, but she lets it go. Talking about that isn't going to help his frame of mind. 'When did you get her?'

'Get who?'

'The Mustang.'

And there's the huge smile again. 'About a year after we were signed.'

'It must have taken you a while to find the right model.'

He turns to look at her. 'You remember?'

'Are you kidding? That car is all you talked about for months! It was on your bucket list.'

'Top of my bucket list. I found her in the UK and brought her over. Cost a fortune to restore her and to keep her going, but I love her.'

'She is so you. Loud and in your face! You two are a match made in heaven.'

215

His smile disappears again, and she realises it's her fault. 'I've thought that about a few things in my life. I don't always get it right.'

'No one does, Dillon. We all make mistakes.'

'So, I made a mistake? That's what went wrong with us?'

'No! Not you.' Fuck it. She's managed to walk herself straight into a topic she was hoping to avoid. 'It was timing.'

'What the fuck does that mean?'

She has to lie, there's no other way around it. 'I told you in the letter. I wish I hadn't done it that way, but I can't change the past.'

'So, you fell out of love with me? There was no other reason?'

'I'm sorry Dillon.' She's so deeply in love with him it hurts. Telling him that she doesn't care is sickening. But the lie is easier on him than the truth.

She wipes her tears while he focuses on the horizon in front of him.

'Can't do much about that, can I? We better head back.'

He helps her to her feet, then packs away the empty containers. Ash follows him back down the track towards the car park, their last conversation going around and around in her head.

If she thought for one second that he could ever love her again, she'd tell him how she feels. But he's guarded with her. Holding her at arm's length. She's getting part of the real him when they're together, but not everything. The emotion is still locked away from her.

And that's the part she needs.

Travelling to Italy with Dillon is so surreal, Ash nearly has to pinch herself every few minutes. Instead of travelling with a low budget airline, squashed in between two random strangers, she's sitting in a plush leather chair on a private aircraft. He sure knows how to travel in style.

But that's Dillon. No expense spared in any aspect of his life.

In the seat opposite her, Dillon is staring out the window, a pair of impenetrable sunglasses hiding his eyes. A few seats behind, Jace is stretched out in the leather seat, snoring loudly.

No doubt he's exhausted from chasing after Dillon all the time. He can't be the easiest of people to protect. But they seem to have reached an understanding of sorts. Jace is always there, but in the background, giving Dillon the space he needs.

Dillon chews on his lip ring as he looks out the window. He's struggling so much and it's killing her. There's nothing she can do to take away any of his pain. There's nothing anyone can do. The situation is completely out of her area of expertise. Where would you even begin?

What she can do, is be there as much as he wants her to be. And right now, he wants her with him. Somewhere she wishes she could have been for the last decade.

He reaches out and takes her hand, his fingers intertwining with hers on the polished table between them.

There's so much left to say. So much to explain. But now isn't the time. Unfortunately, with every minute that passes, the right time takes a step further away. As much as she disagrees with the length of time the family secret was kept from Dillon, she's hardly in a position to comment, considering all the lies between them. More lies he knows nothing about.

She glances at the screen on her phone and the picture of her daughter. She had planned to talk to him, to clear the air and come clean about everything. Easy to say when the moment has passed. And the next moment. And the one after that.

There will never be a right moment to tell him why she left. It doesn't matter how long she waits, or how carefully she picks the moment, the only truly right time was ten years ago. Each day she allowed to pass since then has been unfair to him.

By leaving as she did, she'd hurt him. By Clara and his family lying for his whole life, they'd hurt him. By telling him the truth now, Clara had hurt him. If she too tells him what really happened, she knows it will hurt him, and she can't bear that. She can't bear to hurt him again.

He rests his chin on his hand as he stares out the window. He's incredible. Every minute she spends with him she falls deeper in love with him. Which is not what she wants.

They've had incredible sex and shared some moments, but there's still a barrier between them, and she has no idea if he wants to get over it, or even if they can. This could just be a fling for him. Some companionship, some out of control sex, and nothing more. Neither of them has spoken about their relationship. And it's infuriating.

She's as much to blame as he is. But if she's being honest, she doesn't want to have that conversation. Whatever is going on between them now, is more than she could ever have hoped for. The thought of ruining all that by talking about it, isn't appealing in the slightest.

They will have to talk at some stage, but not yet. Not while he's still coming to terms with what Clara told him.

She's so ashamed of herself for using his present situation as justification for delaying a conversation she should have had a decade ago. A conversation she could easily have had while at Port Oriel yesterday. Talk about perfect moments. He'd given her the ideal opportunity, but instead she backed away. Idiot!

Dillon squeezes her hand, bringing her out of her thoughts. He pulls off his sunglasses so he can look at her properly. 'You okay?'

'Of course. Why?'

'You looked like you were miles away.'

Tell him. Just say the damn words.

But then she looks at the heavy black rings under his bloodshot green eyes.

Not now. Not while he's already so low.

'I'm fine. I'm just not used to travelling in such style.'

When he smiles it's more sad than anything resembling happy. 'Quickest way to get back. We're not cancelling the show. I need to get back to work. It's what I need to do to get my head straight. Once I'm on stage I'll be grand.'

'Back in front of your adoring fans.'

This time the smile is a bit more genuine. 'You know me. It's what I live for. Before I forget, I've arranged for a car to bring you from the airport to the hotel so you can get ready. I'm heading straight to the venue to meet with the guys.'

'Of course.'

She doesn't know why she expected to travel with him to the venue. Just because he brought her back with him doesn't mean he's going to let her hang off his arm for the rest of the trip.

'I'll see you later for dinner after the show... if you've got nothing else planned?'

'I'd love that. Are you going to tell the guys about Clara?'

'I've got to. It's too big to keep secret, but that's as far as it's going. No one else can find out. Not yet.'

'I understand. Have you spoken to Eva at all?'

He shakes his head. 'I haven't got a fucking clue how to even go there with her. This is probably me hoping for the easy way out, but I'd prefer if Clara told her. I'm too... angry.'

He curses and taps the side of his head. 'It's too fucked up in here to get it out properly. Eva's in the same position as me. I think Clara needs to tell her. If I do, she'll get the seriously fucked up version, and that's not fair on her. She's done nothing wrong. The whole thing is so fucked up. Let Clara deal with it for now. I can't.'

'Give yourself time. It's such a massive revelation. There's no right or wrong way to deal with this, Dillon. Just take it one day at a time. Clara will understand.'

'Right now, I couldn't give a fuck if she does or not. Forty years of

219

lies isn't something I can just forgive and move on from. I'm not even sure I can, full stop. It's a fucking life changing lie, Ash. I honestly don't think I can have her in my life again.'

'Don't rush into any decisions like that today. Or even tomorrow.'

'Listen, can we just drop the subject? I've done enough thinking about the whole fucking sorry situation for the last two days. It's done. I just want to move on.'

He puts on his sunglasses again and looks back out the window, signalling an end to the conversation. Ash leaves him to it. She's on very shaky ground as it is. Forcing him to face his new family dynamic won't do him, or her, any favours.

He can't forgive Clara's lies.

Can't forgive his own sister or mother for the lie that's changed his life.

Is she so different?

The lie she has kept from him since she left is certainly a life changing one. But after what he just said, telling him the truth will mean an end to whatever this is. He'll be furious with her.

Dillon shifts in the seat as he stretches his legs out in front of him.

She'll lose him all over again.

And this time it will be entirely her fault.

Dillon

The fact that Tate, Luke, and Gregg are still staring at him a good minute after he finishes talking, helps him feel a little better about the situation. If they're reacting to Clara's news this way, maybe he didn't blow it out of proportion reacting the way he did.

It's not like his reaction to hearing his sister is his mother was put on or planned in any way. She told him, and he lost it.

Deep down he's still beyond furious, but so far, he's managing to keep it under wraps.

Another minute passes before Tate finally breaks the silence. 'I haven't got a fucking clue what to say to you.'

'What he said,' Gregg adds. 'I'm speechless. Never happened before.'

Luke leans forward and waits until he looks at him. 'Are you all right? The truth, not your usual I'm fine.'

'No. I'm far from fucking all right. But I will be. It answers a lot of questions and that's not a bad thing, but it's just replaced them with a whole load of shit I can't get my head around.'

'Is there anything we can do?' Gregg asks. 'Sorry. Stupid question, but I'm out of my comfort zone here.'

'Join the club. All I know is that I want to get on stage as planned tonight. I need to have a bit of my normal life back. I'll deal with this family shit when the tour is done. I've wasted enough of my life second guessing everything about my family. Enough is enough. This is our time. Ten fucking years is a big deal. No one is going to mess that up for us.'

Tate grips his arm and squeezes it. 'Whatever you want. We'll give them one hell of a show.'

'Thanks Tate.'

'What's the story with Ash?' Gregg asks as he pushes an unruly lock of hair off his face. 'Are you two good now?'

That's something else confusing the hell out of him. 'I don't know. She came over to see me. Helped me get through the initial shit with my... whoever. Anyway, we still haven't talked about what happened ten years ago.'

'Have you slept with her?'

He nods at Luke. 'Yeah. And I know, so don't say it.'

'I wasn't going to say anything. I was just curious.'

'Oh. Right.' He thought Luke would have an issue with that for some reason. Or that was just his fucked-up brain hoping Luke would have an issue. God he's pathetic.

'Are you going to talk to her?'

'No.'

'Dillon...'

'What? There's enough crap in my head without adding more to it. She either wasn't on with the fact I'm bi, or she fell out of love with me, or I drove her away because I'm a dick. It was going to be one of them. What difference is knowing going to make? This isn't anything serious. It's just...' What the fuck is it?

He's still in love with her, so whatever it is, it's not going to end well for him. She'll go back to her life, and he'll be a miserable drunk all alone again.

'Just be careful Dillon. That's all I'm saying.'

Knowing that Luke is worried about his love life pisses him off for some reason. No one worried about his love life. He was the one who was living it up. No ties. Endless emotionless one-night stands, each one taking a little more of his soul every time, until there was nothing left but this empty, moody fucker who has nothing and no one in his life.

He's on the pity train tonight.

'Thanks. Appreciate it.' He grabs a bottle of water from the fridge in his dressing room and swallows a couple of pills. He doesn't care if the others see him do it. It's not like it's a secret, so why is he trying to hide it?

When he turns to face them again, it's like he's back in school being caught by one of the teachers. 'Oh, would you all fuck off with the looks! How about you go back to your own dressing rooms and let me get ready. We've got a show in an hour.'

Tate and Gregg leave without an argument, but the new and improved Luke isn't so easily brushed off.

'Taking pills won't help.'

'Neither will whatever great words of wisdom you're about to spout.'

'I'm your friend and I'm worried about you.'

'Oh, change the fucking record! Everyone is worried about me. I'm really fucking touched, but between you and me, I've had it up to here,' he says, holding his hand a good foot over his head. 'Now please fuck off so I can get ready. We're on in an hour.'

Luke twists the stud in his chin as he gives him an intense look. Dillon doesn't back down, giving as good as he gets when it comes to his own glare.

'Fine.'

That's it. No fight. No more trying to get him to open up. His friend turns around and leaves his dressing room, closing the door loudly behind him.

All alone, Dillon slumps back onto the armchair and stares at his boots. It won't take long for the pills to kick in. After that he'll be grand again. All the thoughts churning around in his head will settle down and he'll be able to think straight. Or not at all. He'll take either option.

Ash

'Hold on. Are you with him or not? I'm confused.'

Ash pulls the brush through her hair a little harsher than she meant to. Taking out her frustration on her own hair won't do her any favours. It'll just add a headache to everything else she's trying to process.

Starting with giving Charlie an answer. If only it were that easy. Is she with him or not?

'Ash? Hello? You're staring into space while you tear your hair out with that brush.'

'Sorry.' She dumps the brush onto the bed and sighs as she gives Charlie her attention. A part of her wants to end the call and not answer him, but he'll just call back.

'You don't know, do you?'

She shakes her head. 'It sounds so ridiculous, but no. I haven't got a clue. We sort of fell—'

'Into bed together,' Charlie finishes.

'No! Okay well maybe a little bit, but it's more than that.'

'Is it really? You don't know if you're with him. I'd hardly call that a deep and meaningful relationship now, would you?'

'I know, okay, but it's Dillon. He's never really been one for talking about stuff like that.'

'Oh, stop it, Ash! Are you telling me that when you were in a relationship with him years ago that you didn't know? Because I'm willing to bet a year's salary that you knew for a fact you were a couple. And that's before you consider the minor detail of you being engaged to him! Who exactly are you trying to kid, cause it's not working for me?'

'That was before. It's different now.' She's fully aware she's making excuses. Each one sounds so ridiculous even to her, so it's not a surprise Charlie isn't buying them.

'It might be different for him, but it's not for you. You're still madly in love with the man. He's still the only person you've wanted to be with for the last ten years. I'm just worried you're going to get hurt.'

He's right. It's going to end badly for her. Dillon may not be emotionally invested in them any longer, but she is. She has been for the last ten years. But is she so desperate to be close to him, that she's willing to put her heart on the line for a few days with him?

'I love you. You're like the crazy sister I never had. You know that. So, you know that when I say-this to you it's coming from the right place. You need to have it out with him, Ash. Clear the air. Talk to him. Tell him whatever you need to tell him.'

'What do you mean by that?'

'I mean tell him why you really left him. Why? Is there something else you need to tell him?'

Charlie raises his eyebrow, but she chooses to ignore the look. 'I have to go. Will you tell Freya I'll call her later.'

'Have to go where? I didn't think they were on stage tonight?'

'They're not. I'm meeting the band.'

'No you're not! You're meeting Dillon for another deep and meaningful conversation. Be careful Ash.'

He shakes his head, then ends the video call before she gets a chance to. She flops back on the bed and sighs at the ceiling.

Charlie is right of course. He usually is. Nothing good can come of whatever is going on between herself and Dillon. Not for her anyway.

There's just short of two weeks left in the tour. That's two weeks of pretending that everything is okay between them, or two weeks of hostility if she tells him the truth.

She pulls up a picture of him on her phone. 'Dillon. I have something to tell you. I didn't leave because I fell out of love with you. I still love you more than I ever did. I left so you could have the career you deserved. I left to have our daughter. And then I kept her from you for ten years.'

She groans and drops the phone onto the bed. That's what it keeps coming back to. Her reasons for leaving are one issue. Her reasons for staying away are completely different.

But at its basic level, the fact she kept Dillon and Freya apart for ten years is what's going to unravel everything for her.

With both Dillon and Freya.

Dillon

'What the hell are you doing?'

Dillon lowers his hands. 'My hair. What the fuck does it look like I'm doing?'

Luke closes the bathroom door. Great. Time for a heart to heart. He's not in the mood for this. Fuck, he'll never be in the mood for this.

He continues fixing his hair, hoping Luke is just hanging around for some styling tips.

Not that he needs them. Luke is naturally stunning.

'Can you stop for a second so I can talk to you.'

Dillon washes his hands then turns to face his friend. 'What?'

'Please stop being defensive with me.'

'You've just shut us in the bathroom together, so I'm feeling fucking defensive. Let me help you out a little. You're wondering what I'm doing with Ash, right?'

'I'm not trying to have a fight with you. I'm worried.'

The long sigh that comes out isn't intentional, but Luke frowns when he hears it.

'Please stop.'

He crosses his arms and raises his eyebrows. 'Go on then. Say your piece.'

'Fine. You're going to attack me whatever I say, so what the hell. Why are you sleeping with Ash when you haven't cleared the air with her? You're both hiding from your past, and it's going to blow up in your faces sooner or later. '

'I'm a big boy, Luke. I'm capable of having sex without getting all emotional about it. It's what I do, remember?'

'You're not having sex with someone you don't know. This is someone you care about. It's completely different. I'm worried this will end badly and you're going to get hurt.'

'I won't.' Dillon pushes off the sink and tries to move past him so he can get to the door, but confident Luke is out today. He blocks Dillon's escape, shoving him back against the sink.

'What the fuck Luke? Move!'

'Why are you running away from this? You don't do that. You're the one who fights. Who always pushes back. Why are you letting yourself get hurt like this? I don't get it.'

'Who's getting hurt?'

'Do you love her?'

'Oh, fuck off Luke! I'm not having that conversation with you. We're fucking each other. That's it. She'll go back to her world, and I'll go back to mine. There's nothing to have a long and heartfelt discussion about, so please let it go.'

'What are you so afraid of?'

'The truth!' He curses his outburst, irritated that he let it escape.

'What truth?'

'If the only other person I've loved in my life besides you, left me because I'm bi, or an asshole, or whatever, I'd prefer not to know. She said she fell out of love with me. I'll take that. It's a lie. I know it is, but I'll take that over any truth. I'm a fucking coward and I hate myself for that. I want her Luke. Goddammit I need her, and I'll take her however I can get her. If that's just sex while she's on this job, I'll take it.'

When Luke hits him with a look of pity, it's like a slap to his face. 'Don't you dare look at me like that! Now get out of the way. It's my night off. I'm going to meet Ash. Feel free to say *I told you so* when she's gone, but for now, I'm asking you to mind your own fucking business.'

Before Luke can respond, he skirts behind him, making his escape. He grabs his jacket from the couch by the door then steps down from the bus. 'I need the keys, Jace.'

His bodyguard peers up from his phone. 'It's my job to drive you. You don't need the keys.'

'I'm heading over to the hotel. It's less than five minutes away. I'll manage.'

Jace narrows his eyes, then sighs and hands him the keys. 'I'm only agreeing because Tate and Gregg are already there with Liam and Ciaran in the gym. Otherwise, you'd be doing what you're told and letting me drive. You get me?'

'Oh, I get you. Forty years old and I can't be trusted to drive my fucking self.'

'I trust you, you awkward git. But you don't know the area.'

'We've been here twice before. I can drive from here to the fucking hotel.'

He slides into the Land Rover and tears away from the bus, leaving tracks in the gravel.

He's not even pissed off at Jace. Or at Luke. It's himself he has the problem with. He's allowing himself to be hurt over and over again, because deep down, he knows it's the only way he'll get what he wants.

Happiness.

He'll deal with the pain later.

27

Dillon

He probably shouldn't be happy, given everything that's come to light over the last week, but he is. Since the minute Ash appeared at his door in Wicklow, it was like he'd gone back in time. Like the last decade apart hadn't happened. Touching her. Tasting her. It was all so much better than he remembers.

She was there while he sang, watching him from the side of the stage as he does what he loves. Never in his wildest dreams could he have imagined how much of a boost that would be. He performed better while she was there. Those last three shows were the best he can remember.

They sat beside each other on the bus as they moved through Europe from venue to venue, talking with the guys and laughing like they didn't have a care in the world.

Then, when they were alone, they'd spend hours together in bed. He had barely spent any time in the bus over the last few days. He was in her hotel room, taking her as often as he could.

Apart from his recent dry spell, his appetite was as insatiable as ever. He can't get enough of her.

It will come to an end at any moment. He knows that. The elephant is still sitting in the corner of the room, refusing to leave them to enjoy their time together. Hiding from their past won't help either of them, but he's not about to ruin what they have. He can't do it.

And it's not like she's eager to thrash it out either.

It's all fake though. Polite conversation followed by sex. It's only when they're in bed together that the strange politeness between them disappears and, for a short time, he can forget how fucked up his life is.

He sits back on his legs and looks down at Ash, lying naked under him. Her skin is covered in a fine sheen of sweat, her cheeks are flushed, and she's breathing heavily. But it's the downright sexy expression on her face that captures him. Her wrists are still secured to the bed by two of his belts and he's in no rush to set her free. Doesn't look like she's in a rush either.

He grips her chin, tilting her head towards him. 'I could look at you tied up like that all day. You're fucking stunning, you know that?'

She smiles lazily up at him. 'Thank you. And considering the fact I'm totally and utterly shagged, that suits me fine. I seriously doubt I could move anyway.'

'That's what I like to hear.' He kisses her before unwrapping the belts, kissing each wrist when he frees it.

He gathers her in his arms, holding her as they both catch their breath. 'Do you fancy getting some food?'

'Mmmm, I'd love to, but I have to meet Sam. She wants to see some of the shots from the concert last night. Ellen is asking for them. Sorry. Speaking of which, I should probably get up.'

A good few minutes later she still hasn't moved. 'I thought you were getting up?'

'I've just decided work is overrated. I'd much prefer to stay put.'

Dillon rolls over, covering her body with his. 'But if you stay, I'll have to tie you up and fuck you all over again.'

'Is that supposed to convince me to get up? Because, for the record, it's not.' She stretches out, taking hold of the headboard again. 'Not in the slightest. I think I need you to show me exactly who is in charge here.'

His dick twitches in response to that. 'Don't tempt me.'

She wriggles under him, rubbing against him. 'You're not tired, are you?'

'You know full well I'm not. Now stop being a brat and knock it off. As much as I want that smart mouth around my dick, I'm not going to get into trouble for you being late. Now get that sexy ass out of the bed.'

'Are you going to get off me so I can get out of bed?'

He smirks and slowly rolls off her, watching as she climbs out of bed. The stunning woman makes sure she wiggles her ass in his direction as she goes into the bathroom, closing the door behind her.

He should probably think about getting up too. He's got a press interview in two hours with the rest of the band. No show tonight though, so once that's done, he can hit the sack.

Even though he's in no rush to get up, he climbs out of bed and pulls on his boxers, knocking the bedside table when he bumps against it. Cursing to himself, he picks up Ash's phone from under the bed where it landed. The screen is on when he places it back on the table, showing a picture of Ash and a young girl as her background.

Why would Ash have a photo of a young girl on her phone? She's an only child so it wouldn't be a niece. Maybe the daughter of a friend.

Dillon brings the phone close and examines the little girl. She must be nine, maybe ten years old. She's pretty. He frowns as he notices her hair colour. It's the same as Ash. In fact, she looks a hell of a lot like Ash.

But then her eyes get his attention. They're the exact same colour as his. And she's got his nose. Does she? He must be seeing things that aren't there. Fair enough the shade of his green eyes is unusual, but he can't be the only one with them. And how the fuck can her nose look like his? It doesn't make sense.

But the longer he looks at the girl, the more similarities he notices.

He's still staring at the phone when Ash comes back into the bedroom, stopping suddenly when she sees him holding her phone. 'What are you doing with that?'

He turns the screen around to face her. 'Who is she?'

'Dillon—'

He gets off the bed and walks over to her, the phone still facing her. 'Don't Dillon me. Who is she?'

The colour drains from her face as she stares at the phone. 'Her name is Freya. She's... she's my daughter.'

Fair enough a decade has passed since he last saw her, but the fact she's a mother hits him hard. 'Your daughter? Why didn't you tell me you have a daughter? Were you ever going to tell me about her?'

'Of course I was. I just... this is... I guess I was waiting for the right time. When I took the assignment, I hadn't planned on this happening between us again. And when it did, I didn't know how to tell you. I wanted to—'

'You have a daughter. That's a pretty fucking big deal. If you wanted to tell me, you would have.'

'It's not that I couldn't. It's more that I was... I don't know. Protecting her.'

'From what? From me?'

She wraps the towel tighter around her body. 'No. Of course not. It's been just the two of us for so long. I didn't want to confuse things for anyone.'

He hands the phone back to her, then crosses his arms as he composes what he's about to say. Freya has his eyes. He has no fucking doubt whatsoever. His eyes. His nose.

Is she his?

Thinking the question is very different to saying the words out loud. 'Who's her father?' It doesn't sound like his voice coming out, but the all-important question is out there.

Ash looks at the photo of her daughter, as she sits on the edge of the bed. He crouches down in front of her, but she keeps her eyes away from his. 'Why can't you look at me? Ash? Why can't you look at me!'

'You probably should go.'

'No way! I'm not going anywhere until you answer my question.'

Instead of answering, she gets up and pulls on her underwear and jeans. He stands, bracing himself against the wall for a second. It feels like his head is about to explode. He has no idea what the fuck is going on.

'How old is she? She's got to be what? Nine? Ten? She has my fucking eyes, Ash. Is she... Is she mine?'

Ash puts on her shirt, then looks down at her phone in her hand.

'Yes or no. That's all I need. Yes or no!'

'Yes!'

He blinks and stares dumbly at her for a second. 'What?'

Ash seems to deflate in front of him, her shoulders sagging. She sighs as she closes her eyes and sits on the edge of the bed. 'You're her father, Dillon. Freya... she's your daughter.'

He takes a step back as if he's been struck. 'Mine? She's mine? I have a daughter?'

Ash wipes her face and nods. 'I'm sorry. I—'

'You're sorry? You're fucking sorry? Are you kidding me! I have a daughter and you didn't tell me!'

'I wanted to, Dillon. I really did. But it was complicated.'

He snorts and walks away from her, dragging his hand through his hair repeatedly. 'Complicated? Complicated! You kept my daughter from me for a decade, Ash. Ten whole years I can never get back. She can't get back. How could you do that to me? To her?'

'I didn't have a choice.'

'Fuck off Ash!' He grabs his jeans and pulls them on. 'I thought leaving like you did was bad enough, but this is a whole new level of fucking with me. What did I ever do to deserve this? I get if you didn't love me, but I should have known about her. I had a right to know!'

The tears are pouring down her face, but he honestly couldn't care less. All he knows is that he can't fucking breathe and it's getting worse.

'I know you did, and I can never fix that. And you didn't do anything, Dillon. It was just... I don't know how to explain it.'

He puts on his boots then searches for his t-shirt. 'Don't bother explaining. Why change the habit of a fucking lifetime?' He grabs the notebook and pen from the dressing table, the hotel logo printed on the top of the page. 'Here.' He throws them on the floor at her feet. 'That'll make things easier for you. Try writing me a note.'

'Can you please just sit down, and we can talk about it.'

'You must really fucking hate me to do something like this.'

'I don't. I could never hate you.'

He slams his fist against the headboard, cracking the polished surface. 'I have a daughter and you didn't tell me!' The realisation hits on another level when he says the words again. He's a father. Him. Fucked up Dillon Ryan is a father. 'Does she know? Does our daughter know I exist?'

'I thought it would just confuse her.'

'Fucking perfect. Not good enough for you, so how can I be good enough for her, right?'

'Why would you think you're not good enough? I've never said that!'

'You left me! You kept my daughter from me! What the fuck do you expect me to think?'

'I know and I'm—'

He rounds the end of the bed, charging right up to her, driving her back against the wall. 'Don't you dare say you're fucking sorry, Ash! Sorry won't fix this. Sorry can never fix this.' Then another thought hits. 'You were given this assignment. You didn't ask for it.'

'I'm sorry?'

'Did you ask for this assignment?'

'Well, no, but—'

'You never planned on telling me, did you?'

'I don't know.'

'Bullshit! If you hadn't been given this assignment, I'd still be in the dark. I'd just have carried on with my life having no idea I had a kid.'

She doesn't reply, but she doesn't need to. He can see the truth all over her face.

'Fuck you, Ash!'

He hurries from her room before she can throw any more lies at him. He needs a drink. Badly. Hurrying past the room where the bodyguards are hanging out, he goes downstairs and out to the car.

He can't remember ever being this angry before and he's had some raging tempers. How dare she! What right did she have to do this to him? And to Freya.

He slams the car into gear, then speeds out of the car park. He has no fucking idea where he's going. All he knows is that he needs to get away from her, away from everyone, so he can kick the living daylights out of some inanimate object.

28

Ash

'How the fuck did we lose him again?'

Ash buries her head in her hands as Tate shouts. He's not angry at her, she knows that. It's the entire situation with Dillon that's got them all on edge. She knows exactly how they feel. She's worried sick.

Involving the guys was the last thing she wanted to do, but in this instance, she felt there was little choice. After Dillon tore out of her hotel room in a rage, she'd tried to find him, but he was gone. Clearly getting away from her as fast as possible was the priority.

Then she found out he'd given the bodyguards the slip. The thought of him wandering around Prague all alone, angry and pissed off, had her changing her mind.

At that stage, she felt she needed to include the rest of the band. No doubt Dillon would be suitably pissed off with her, but it can't get any worse. He already hates her, so what does it matter at this stage?

The only thing she's worried about is his safety.

'Should we tell Sam?' Luke asks as he sits beside her. 'See if she's heard anything?'

Tate shakes his head. 'No. She'll go straight to Ellen and that'll just get her stressed. Besides, the fucker wouldn't have contacted her. He goes off the radar when he's like this. Best thing we can do for now is split up. Head out with Liam and the others. See if we can find him first. Give it two hours. After that we tell Sam.'

They all agree, so, after deciding on different directions to head in, they file out of the bus. 'You can come with me if you want,' Luke says, shrugging on his jacket.

'I don't think that's such a good idea. He's furious with me. I'm the reason he took off in the first place. If he sees me, it could just set him off again.'

'Are you sure?'

'I want to find him, but this isn't about me. It's about making sure he's okay. I'll go back to the hotel just in case he comes back for round two. Will you let me know the second you find him?'

'Of course. And the same for you. There's every chance he'll go back to the hotel to talk to you.'

She seriously doubts that, but there's no way she can go with Luke. 'Of course.'

'We're heading in your direction anyway, so we'll drop you back on the way.'

She follows him out of the bus and slides into the back seat of the car with Andy and Luke.

The thought of going back to the hotel and doing nothing while Dillon is missing is killing her, but there's no point going with them.

Even if she did find him, he's not going to go anywhere with her. The best thing all round is to stay out of the way and hope the guys can track him down before he does something stupid.

Dillon

Whatever he's lying on is hard and isn't doing his head any favours. He coughs, then groans as he spits out a mouthful of blood. What the fuck happened? Where the fuck is he?

He opens his eyes, then winces, closing them again. Fuck, his head hurts. The second attempt to find out where he is goes a little better, but just adds to his confusion.

He slowly pushes himself off whatever he's face down on and looks around, moving his head slowly so he doesn't disturb the raging headache any more than he already has.

Well, this isn't good!

He's in the car, but instead of a bonnet in front of him, there's a fucking huge tree. Not only is it in front of the car, it's in the fucking car. If he reaches out, he could probably touch the damn thing.

He doesn't remember crashing. Then again, he doesn't remember much after he left the hotel. The anger had consumed him, pushing all other thoughts aside. The only thing he needed to do was put some space between himself and Ash.

It still doesn't explain how he crashed. He's a careful driver. Always has been. He takes a few minutes to check himself out, but apart from biting his lip when the airbag went off, and being fucking sore everywhere, he doesn't think he's broken anything. It's a fucking miracle. If the car had hit the tree a foot or two to the other side, he'd be a goner.

As he looks around, he realises exactly how much of a lucky bastard he is. The roof is buckled above him, and both doors are misshapen. The car must have rolled.

'Fuck!' He winces as his curse pulls at his lip. He's a lucky bastard all right.

His phone rings from somewhere in the car, but he hasn't got a clue where it is. Dillon tries to open the door, but it won't budge. The car is too damaged. If he's going to get out of here, he needs his phone.

It has to be nearby. He always has it in his pocket. He reaches down, feeling his way around his seat. 'Fuck! Where are you?' His fingers brush against something smooth, buried between the driver's seat and the centre console.

It's his phone. He leans over more, trying to get the phone in a scissor grip between his fingers, but something in his elbow isn't on board with that. The pain shoots along his arm, forcing him to take a break.

This is just fucking perfect. He's got himself into some messed up situations over the years, but this must be the best in a long line of stupid mistakes. His head swims again, turning the whole car on its ass for a minute.

It's got nothing to do with the crash. It's the same thing that happened when he had the first fight with Ash. It's the drugs messing with his coordination again. When did he use last? He can't even remember.

It's usually when he's stressed, so he probably took a couple when he was in the car. Things are seriously fucked up if he can't even remember that. Clearly, they're fucking with him more than they're helping. Like leaving him stuck in a car, embedded in a tree somewhere in Prague. How glamorous!

Fuck this feeling sorry for himself shite he keeps doing. It's not going to help him get out of this precarious situation. Without his phone he could easily be here for the next few hours or worse hoping someone would find him. It would help if he knew where he is. He doubts anyone would find the car if they weren't looking. All he can see out the window is trees.

Leaving his injured arm on his lap, he reaches over with the other arm, ignoring the painful complaints from his bruised torso. His fingers brush off the phone, but it slips out of his grip. 'For fuck's sake!'

Shouting doesn't help, but the surge of anger dulls the pain as he tries one last time. He grits his teeth, then leans over as far as he can and finally pulls the phone out from between the seat and console.

The phone slips out of his grasp landing on his lap, as he catches his breath. The screen is cracked, but thankfully it turns on when he touches the sensor.

He hits Luke's contact details and closes his eyes as he waits for the call to connect.

'Where the fuck are you? We've been looking for you for hours! You can't keep disappearing like this. It's not fair to have us running around after you.'

'Yeah. Sorry. I need your help.'

'You mean you're drunk and need me to bring you home again. I'm about done with this shit, Dillon. I've had enough.'

'I crashed the car. I think it rolled. I can't get out of the fucking thing. I need help.'

'Oh my God, Dillon! Are you okay?'

'Yeah. Well, bruised mostly.' He turns on the locator on his phone. 'You should be able to track me now.'

'Great! I'll get Sam to get the emergency services over there.'

'No! Just you and the guys. I don't want this all over the net. Please Luke.' The line goes silent for a moment as Luke thinks about that. The last thing he needs right now is pictures of his sorry ass being cut out of a car by a gang of Czech police.

'Fine,' Luke eventually replies. 'We're on the way. We'll be there as fast as we can. Are you sure you're okay?'

'Yeah. Thanks.'

He ends the call then slowly lies back against the seat. His head is fucking killing him. His eyes drift closed as exhaustion sweeps over him.

Luke

Jace manoeuvres the Range Rover along the road like an expert. Which he probably is. The four bodyguards are seriously good at their jobs. Although, Jace isn't in the best of moods right now. Luke can't blame him. He takes his job seriously, which is why Dillon and Jace bang heads regularly.

Luke glances in the wing mirror. Tate, Gregg, Ciaran, and Liam are following himself, Jace, and Andy. Each of them had wanted to call for expert help, but after a brief argument, they agreed to try to get Dillon out first. But they're not going to be stupid about it. If they can't do it, his friend will just have to deal with the publicity. It might be the final straw, the thing that makes him see how much he needs to get help.

It's not likely, but Luke isn't going to give up on him. No way.

'He should be just around the corner, according to his phone locator,' Jace says, pulling him out of his head. He indicates and veers onto the hard shoulder, then shuts off the engine.

'Where the fuck is the car?' Jace says, as he climbs out of the car. Luke and Andy follow him, running over to the edge of the road, frantically looking for any sign of Dillon's car.

The drop into the forest is only a few metres, but it's still a drop. He continues running up the road, until he finally spots something below him in the trees. 'Found him!'

He jumps off the side of the tarmac, sliding down the bank until he gets to the car. It's upright which is great, but it definitely rolled. The roof and sides are badly battered, its bonnet embedded in the tree that eventually stopped it.

'Shit!' He climbs around to the driver's side, cursing when he jars his knee, irritating the old break.

Ignoring the pain, he peers in the window. Dillon is either asleep or unconscious. He bangs on the window. 'Dillon!'

But there's nothing. He can't see if he's breathing, and there's no movement. He frantically tries to open the door, but it's too damaged and won't budge.

Jace and the rest of the guys join him at the car, testing the other doors to see if they can open them.

'Back door is jammed,' Tate says.

'This one too,' Gregg shouts from the other side of the car. 'Ciaran! Grab the crowbars!'

Jace, Liam, and Ciaran take a crowbar each and tackle the driver's door while Andy, Tate and Gregg try to open the passenger side.

Luke wants to help, to dig his fingers into the metal and tear the door off its hinges, but he can't move. He's stuck to the spot, looking in the shattered windscreen at his unconscious friend.

Please be okay. Please be okay.

His knee is killing him, but he'll deal with it later. Right now, Dillon is the priority.

He has no idea how long it takes the bodyguards to peel the door open, but when he hears the sound of creaking metal he limps over, pushing past the guys to get to Dillon.

The door isn't open fully, but the gap is wide enough to get Dillon out. He reaches out, touching the side of Dillon's neck. He's alive!

He rests his head on Dillon's shoulder as he gets himself together.

'Luke? Come on buddy. We need to get him out.'

He moves away from the car, standing with Tate and Gregg while the bodyguards pull Dillon from the wreckage.

'We've got him from here,' Liam says. 'I want you three back in the car. Now!' he adds when none of them make a move.

'We better go,' Gregg says nudging Luke's arm. 'They've got him.'

Luke nods and turns to follow Tate and Gregg back up the hill, but his leg decides to give up the fight. The pain is like a dagger straight through the side of his kneecap. Tate catches him before he lands on the ground, keeping him upright.

'You okay?'

'My knee. I think I twisted it.'

'Your bad one?'

He nods, clenching his teeth to stop himself from vomiting. The pain is bad, but the queasiness isn't just down to that. When that first spear of pain hit, he was back on his bedroom floor while Pippa kicked him so hard his knee broke. He'll never forget the sickening sensation or sound.

Tate ducks under his arm and helps him up the slope. Gregg opens the car door so Tate can lower him onto the seat. 'How bad is it?'

'It's okay.'

'How bad is it?' Tate asks, his tone firmer.

'It's really sore.'

'Strap in. We'll get you seen at the hospital too. Hopefully you've just pulled something.'

He nods again, his attention on the bodyguards as they slowly make their way up the bank with Dillon.

'Hey!' He looks back to Tate when he taps him on the cheek. 'He'll be grand. Remember, he spoke to you earlier on the phone. You know he's okay.'

'Do you think that's what it was like for him?'

'What was?' Tate asks, crouching down beside him.

'When he found me after I tried to kill myself. That panic? The sensation of something heavy on your chest, pressing down hard so you can't breathe? That helplessness?'

Tate twists the ring on his thumb as he nods. 'Yeah. I'd say so. He's never talked about finding you like that, but he loves you, Luke. It would have hurt like it's hurting you right now.'

'I never meant for that to happen. I didn't think about anyone finding me like that.'

'I never planned on my folks finding me with a syringe in my arm. But finding us like that saved our lives. Just like now with Dillon. Focus on that part. He's safe.'

'For how long? How long until he does something like this again?'

'Fuck knows.'

Tate stands and closes the door, then goes over to help load Dillon into the other car. He wants to go in that car, but he's not about to move his leg again until he has to.

Andy, Ciaran, Gregg, and Tate climb into the car with Luke and follow the others to the hospital.

As Luke watches the landscape speed past, he cries quietly to himself, the tears pouring down his face. If Dillon hadn't saved him that day, he would have died. He wouldn't have this amazing life, wouldn't have Maeve, or a future.

But he never thought what finding him like that had done to Dillon. How much baggage has his friend been carrying around for years? Baggage loaded on him by Luke, his family, the rest of the band. Baggage he had to deal with on top of everything else going on in his life.

29

Ash

She always thought she would be calm and level-headed in an emergency. But as she races through the hospital, calm couldn't be further from how she feels. Ash apologies for the second time after nearly running straight into someone. She glances down at her phone again, then back at the signs on the wall.

The text from Luke had been the worst thing she could have expected. Deep down it wasn't a surprise. Deep down she felt something was wrong. Hours had gone by without any word from Luke.

But when she read his text only a handful of words had sunk in.

Car crash and hospital.

Nothing else has registered with her beyond those pieces of information.

She rounds the corner and breathes a sigh of relief when she sees Luke and Andy sitting outside a room at the far end of the corridor.

'How is he?' she asks when she hurries over to them.

'He's okay,' Luke says, struggling to get to his feet with the help of a pair of crutches.

'What the hell happened to you?'

'I just twisted my knee. It just irritated an old wound.'

She knows exactly what wound he's talking about but doesn't say anything else about it as he leads her into the room where Gregg and Tate are waiting. He closes the door behind her and gestures to one of the spare seats. 'The doctors said he's incredibly lucky. The car flipped. I don't know how, but he managed to escape with nothing more serious than a lot of bruises.'

'It flipped? Oh God. What happened?'

'Dillon doesn't remember. He doesn't remember us finding him or getting him out of the car. There's a chance he blacked out. He thinks he took some pills after he left you, but he's not sure.' Luke rubs his forehead as he shakes his head. 'He wasn't drunk. He wouldn't get behind the wheel after drinking, but what he's taking... it's messing with him.'

'If he doesn't get a wake-up call after this,' Gregg, says, 'he never will. Either way, he shouldn't be driving until he's clean.'

Tate snorts loudly. 'Yeah? How do you suggest we broach that one with him, huh? You know what he's like. We're not going to be able to tell him anything. Unless he sees the problem himself he won't budge.'

Tate is right. They can all tell him to ease off until they're blue in the face. There's only one person who can make him see sense and that's Dillon himself. 'When are they going to release him?'

'They want to keep him overnight just to be sure,' Gregg says. 'After that, he's all ours. Oh yay! Mr. Attitude is going to be worse than ever after this.'

'Can I see him?'

The room falls silent as the three men look at each other. Eventually Tate shrugs. 'Can't say how welcoming he'll be, but it's your call. Go for it.'

Jason opens Dillon's door without asking if he wants to see her. Maybe he knows Dillon won't be on board with it and doesn't care. Maybe he thinks Dillon needs to see her. Whatever his reasoning, she takes the opening, walking into Dillon's room without asking for his permission.

She peers around the corner into the room. Dillon is asleep in the bed, but he's breathing and appears to be in one piece. Moving slowly, she approaches the bed. She may have needed to see him, but that doesn't mean she's ready for another fight with him.

When Luke said he was bruised he wasn't kidding. His chest is battered and bruised, his skin already turning an angry red in colour. The mark of the seat belt is clearly visible. At least he was wearing it. She dreads to think what condition he'd be in otherwise.

It's her fault he's in here. She knew it was only a matter of time before he found out about Freya. By keeping the secret from him she was playing with fire, and he just got burned. He was never going to react well. She knows him well enough to have been sure of that.

The best thing she can do for him at this moment is keep away.

Ash turns towards the door, but a groan from behind her has her cursing under her breath.

'What the fuck are you doing here?'

Talk about bad timing. She looks around at him, not in the least bit surprised at the anger on his face. 'I wanted to see how you are.'

'How the fuck do you think I am?'

'Sore I'd imagine.'

He pushes up the bed, wincing as he tries to get comfortable. 'It's a few bruises. Not a big deal. I'm more fucked up in here,' he says, tapping the side of his head.

'I understand that. I wish there was something I could say to help… but I can't.'

'It's ten years too late, Ash.' He winces again as he rubs his bruised chest. 'You know what hurts more than anything else? You knew what my parents were like with me. You knew how much I wanted them to care about me. Even just to tolerate my fucking existence. Did you not think I'd want to give my own child everything I missed out on? To make them feel wanted?'

She knows that. Without a doubt she knows he would have adored Freya, lavishing attention on her every single minute.

She denied both of them that. Denied them that relationship, and it's something she can never make up for.

He shakes his head and sighs like the weight of the world is on his shoulders. Which, at that moment it probably is. 'You know what? Can you just go?'

'Dillon… we should talk about this. I know I made an unforgivable mistake, but—'

'But what? I can't do this right now, Ash. I just can't. You've had ten years to get used to the idea of being a parent. I've had less than a day. Go! Get the fuck out of here Ash!'

With no other choice, she nods and leaves the room, hurrying past the rest of the band as she makes her way through the hospital to the waiting car.

Dillon

He told her to leave. Didn't give her any choice in the matter. But as he watches her walk away, he wants to shout out at her to stay. He needs to talk to her. There's so much they need to discuss, but he can't see beyond the anger, the hurt, the pain at being betrayed yet again.

'I don't suppose you want to talk?'

Luke slowly lowers himself into the chair next to the bed, stretching his sore leg out on front of him. That's another thing he's pissed off about. Luke only hurt his leg because of him. It's entirely his fault. He's made a right fucking mess of everything.

'I wouldn't know where to start, Luke.'

'Start wherever you want. There's no rush.'

Easier said than done. It's not helping that his head is killing him and every single inch of his body hurts. It could have been worse. He knows that. But even breathing is fucking painful. The seat belt saved his life, but it's not going to let him forget about it in a hurry.

'Ash was pregnant when she left me. I have a ten-year-old daughter called Freya. She wasn't even going to tell me, Luke. I saw a photo of Freya on her phone and confronted her.'

'And she admitted it?'

'Freya has my eyes, Luke. She's got my eyes.'

'I don't know what to say to you. Why didn't she tell you? I don't understand.'

'You and me both. If she left because she didn't love me, I get that. I really do. But that doesn't mean she should have kept Freya from me. Ash must really hate me.'

'You don't know that. Maybe there was another reason she didn't tell you? Have you asked her?'

'I think it's best she keeps as far from me as possible right now.' His ass is going numb, but every time he moves it hurts, and that just fuels his anger.

'I need to ask you something, and please don't get all pissed off. I'm just asking because I care.'

'What?' Anything Luke is going to ask him is just going to grate on his already shattered nerves.

'Did you go off the road on purpose?'

He knew it would piss him off, but he wasn't expecting that. 'Wow! That's great Luke. Thanks for that.'

'It's a fair enough question. Especially after what you just told me. I'm not having a go.' He shrugs and rubs his knee, something he does when he's thinking about his bitch of a wife and how she broke it when he pissed her off. 'I'm not one to judge after what I did.'

He's right. Luke isn't being a dick. He's just being Luke. Trying to look out for him. 'No. I swear. I blacked out and went off the road. That's it.'

Luke nods, appearing to accept his answer. Whatever. He's got too much in his head to worry about whether Luke believes him or not. 'I need to get out of here.'

'No Dillon! They want to keep you overnight. You could have killed yourself when the car flipped. You need to stay here and rest.'

He throws the covers off his legs, swallowing the curse as even that movement is a killer. 'I need to get out of here before I lose my fucking head, okay. Please Luke.'

For a good minute, he's convinced Luke is going to argue with him, but surprisingly, he doesn't.

'I'll see what I can do. Just stay where you are for now. Please. The last thing we need is you falling and doing more damage to yourself.'

'Thank you. Any idea where my phone is?'

Luke pulls it out of his pocket and passes it to him. 'You're not going to do something you'll regret... are you?'

'You know me, Luke.'

'Yeah,' he replies as he hobbles over to the door. 'That's what I'm afraid of.'

He smiles to put Luke at ease, waiting until his friend leaves the room before he scans through his contacts, stopping at Ellen's name. Without pausing to think this through, he taps the screen.

'Dillon! My God! How are you?'

'I'm grand Ellen. Really.'

'I saw a photograph of the car. How can you possibly be *grand*, as you put it?'

'I'm just bruised. Really, really bruised, but I'm in one piece.'

'Thank goodness. You make sure you do as you're told by the medical staff. And I don't want to hear of you even considering stepping on a stage until you are medically cleared. Do you hear me?'

'Yeah. I hear you. I'll do as I'm told.' Like hell he will, but now isn't the time for that argument.

Luke comes back into the room, shaking his head when he notices he's on the phone. Fuck it. He'll have this conversation with Luke here if he has to. He could tell Luke to leave, to give him some space, but he's all out of energy. He's done. Finished. His tank is empty.

'Dillon? Are you still there?'

He'd forgotten about her for a moment. 'Yeah. Sorry. I'm here. I need to ask you a favour.'

'Of course. What do you need?' She's not usually so accommodating with him. Then again, he has a habit of fucking up. But this time it's not his doing. Or maybe it is? Who the hell knows anymore?

He's the common denominator in all this.

'I need you to pull the photographer from the job. Find someone else if you want, but she needs to go. Today.'

Ellen doesn't immediately reply, so he takes a sip of his water, wishing it was a hell of a lot stronger.

'Are you going to tell me why?'

'I've never asked you for anything Ellen. Not once. I'm asking now. Please.'

Well, that display has firmly put him in the pathetic camp. Thankfully Ellen doesn't push him.

'Of course. I'll sort it out immediately. I'll arrange to have her on the first flight out of there.'

'Thank you. But don't put this on her, Ellen. I don't want her in trouble with her boss because of this. It's me. It's just a personality clash. Nothing more.'

'A personality clash?'

'Believable, isn't it? I mean that's what I do, right? Clash with people.'

She falls silent for a few seconds. 'It has been known. Dillon? Are you all right?'

He nods before remembering she can't see him. 'Yeah. All good. Thanks, Ellen.'

He ends the call, fisting his phone and thumping it against his forehead. 'Fuck!' Before Luke can react, he fires his mobile across the room. 'Fuck!'

Luke has the good sense to keep his mouth shut. He's done listening, full stop. What he could do with is one fucking day without someone throwing something else at him.

His life is falling apart. The last thing he's going to do is let them take his career from him. No fucking way. He's going to get on stage tomorrow night and give it his all.

'Can I go?'

'They weren't happy about it, but yes, you can discharge yourself. You have to go to the hotel though. Sleeping on your bunk while you're bruised won't be fun. Sam is sorting it out.'

'Thanks. I mean that Luke. Would you stay with me? Fuck! I hate how pathetic that sounds.'

'Of course I will. Are you sure about removing Ash?'

'Yeah. I'm sure. It's the best for both of us. Now can you get me my clothes so I can get out of here.'

Luke throws him a pair of jeans. 'They had to cut your ones off. I got a new pair from the bus.'

'Fuck. I liked those jeans.' Luke calls for Jace before Dillon can stop him. 'I don't need help.'

Ignoring him, Jace helps him stand, supporting him as he gets his balance.

He didn't feel this wiped out after being beaten up in prison. Tomorrow night's concert is going to be interesting. At this rate he'll be sitting on a stool with his bass on his knee giving a less than lively performance.

'The fans might be getting a more sedate show from me tomorrow.'

'Hang on,' Luke says. 'You're not still thinking of going on? We'll use a fill in for the one night. Or we can cancel it altogether.'

'Look who's talking? Are you going on stage with crutches?'

'I just need to rest it and I should be okay. I just won't move around as much as usual.'

'I'll do the same. I'll be grand. I've got twenty-four hours to get myself sorted.'

Jace stands back and watches as he tries to get his legs in his jeans. 'You're doing a great job of convincing both of us. Are you sure you don't want a hand?'

'I can get myself dressed.' After struggling for a few minutes, he gives in. 'Fine! If you insist, you can help.'

Jace sighs as he grabs Dillon's jeans from him and crouches down to help put them on. 'Right. Like you have a choice! You're a mess, Dillon. I don't know how you expect to walk out of the hospital, let alone prance around on stage.'

'Hey! I don't prance.'

Jace helps to support him as he fastens his jeans then tackles his t-shirt. He should have just walked out topless. Would have been a hell of a lot easier and less painful.

It's not helping that Luke keeps looking at him like he's about to keel over any minute. 'Would you lay off with the looks. I'm grand. You should be concentrating on yourself.'

He stands up and makes it two steps before his head swims again. 'Thanks,' he says, as Jace steps in to support him yet again. 'Okay, maybe I'll be grand after some rest.'

'You can't honestly think you can go on tomorrow.'

'Please Luke. Don't make a big deal about this. I need to perform. I need to.' He hates that he's begging, but if he can get Luke on his side, Tate and Gregg will back him too. He needs to prove to them, and himself, that he has control of even one tiny aspect of his shitty life. Just one.

Luke nods slowly. 'Let's go back to the hotel and see how you feel after some sleep.'

It's the best answer he's going to get for now. Crawling into bed, knocking himself out, and never waking up again, sounds like fucking heaven right about now.

30

Ash

She knew he'd get back at her. Knew he'd lash out in some way. But having her pulled from the shoot hadn't crossed her mind. In hindsight it should have been the obvious retaliation. Why would he want her anywhere near him, after finding out she'd kept Freya from him? He'd want to be as far away from her as possible.

'I'm so sorry Ash.'

She smiles at Sam, taking the folder from her hand. 'It's not your fault.'

'I'm completely against this, but we have to keep the guys happy. If Dillon—'

'Really Sam. It's fine. I'm just embarrassed this happened in the first place. I should be able to make all my clients feel at ease, so I can get the best photographs.'

'You captured some incredible images. We're in no way unhappy with your work. Not at all. It's just a personality clash. Believe me,' she says, lowering her voice. 'That happens quite a bit with Dillon. You're not the first, and I doubt you'll be the last. I better go and let you pack. The car is waiting outside to take you to the airport as soon as you're ready. Your flight details are in the folder. It doesn't leave for three hours so you've got plenty of time.'

'Thanks Sam. And thank you for everything. I've had a... I guess a surreal time would be the best way to describe it.'

'Surreal is right. Take care, Ash.'

'You too Sam.'

She keeps it together until she closes the door and walks over to the bed. Only then does she let the tears out.

So that's it. He's kicked her out of his life. She understands that. The part that's upsetting her the most is that it could mean he's also kicking Freya out of his life.

For too long she had daydreamed about having Dillon in Freya's life. Thought about Freya spending time with her father, about having him love their daughter the way she knows he would.

But she had ruined that. It's all on her. Fear, doubt, and cowardice had all played their part, and there's no going back from that.

She runs her hand over the folder containing her travel documents. All she can do now is respect his wishes and leave.

Luke

'How are you doing sexy? How's your leg?'

Luke smiles at Maeve's face on the screen. Even months later, she still manages to boost his confidence every time she speaks to him. The small detail of calling him sexy means more than she will ever know.

Or maybe she does know and that's why she keeps doing it. Whatever the reason, he'll take it.

'It's okay. Better than it was. I just landed funny on it.'

'You look tired.'

'I am a bit tired. The tour has been full on.'

'That's what you get for being a super popular rock star. You've got no one to blame but yourself.' She winks at him, and he laughs.

'I guess so. How is your own tour going?'

She nods as she twirls her purple hair around her finger. 'Busy, busy, as usual. The theatre has added another date. Seems tickets for the first show sold out in minutes.'

'Well done! That's what you get for being a super amazing dancer.'

'Oh, you are such a sweetie. But yes. I am super amazing. What can I say? So, what are you up to? Resting that leg I hope!'

He turns the phone around to give her a quick peek into the room behind him.

'Is that Dillon flaked out in the bed?'

He brings the phone around again. 'Yeah.'

'Should he not be in hospital? Oh, let me guess. He discharged himself?'

'You know him. He discharged himself after Angel stabbed him. He's not going to stay just because his car rolled, and he hit a tree. I think sedation is the only way you'd get him to stay. Stubborn idiot.'

'Where are you now?'

'I took him to the hotel where the crew are staying. Sam organised a room for us to stay in while he's recovering. He needs room. Being on the bus won't help him recover. He's been asleep since we left the hospital. I have no idea how he's going to have the energy to perform.'

'Hold on! He's not going on stage?'

'Well, he's not sitting it out, so yeah, he's going on stage. I can't really have a go at him about it though, considering...'

'Yeah, well don't get me started on that. But I trust you. If you say you can go on, I believe you. Just no crazy jumping around. You need to give your leg time to heal.'

'I never do any crazy jumping around.'

'Well don't start until you're up to it. How are things going between Dillon and Ash?'

'He asked Ellen to pull Ash from the tour. He found out something and it's really destroyed him. I wish I could tell you what, but—'

'Hey. No need to explain. Is it fixable?'

He's asked himself that question repeatedly. His best friend has a ten-year-old daughter. That's not something he's going to get his head around overnight. Or even in a few days. It's a massive thing.

Something Luke himself can't help but be a little jealous of. He'd give anything to be a father. But after his ex forced him to have a vasectomy, that option was taken from him. Until he met Maeve.

With her support he'd had the procedure reversed. It's still too early to know if it worked, or if he can ever have children, but even a small chance is better than no chance.

'Luke? Talk to me.'

'Sorry. I'm just in my head a little. The situation with Dillon has brought some stuff back. I'm okay though.'

'Do you want me to come over? I can get Dessie to cover for me and get on the next flight.'

He loves her so much for offering. He's still getting used to being put first by someone else. For so long he was made to feel like a passenger in his own relationship, his own marriage. But Maeve isn't like that. She cares about him and how he's feeling.

'Thank you for offering, but I'm okay, really.'

'Mmmm. Okay, so I'm just going to say this. I know you love that moody git to pieces and want to help him. I do too. But don't let what's going on with Dillon get to you. You've come so far, Luke. Be there for him, but not at your own expense.'

'I know. I have a call with my therapist before I go on stage. I promise I'm on top of it.'

'I know you are. But you can't blame a girl for worrying. You know I'm here if you need me for anything. Just call me.'

'I will. I better let you go so you can get ready.'

She pouts a little, but he knows it's put on. 'I suppose so. I miss you.'

'I miss you too. I'll be back soon.'

'And I intend to ravish you repeatedly when I get my hands on you. We have a lot of time to make up for.'

He licks his lips as his dick responds to her comment and the look in her eyes. 'Don't say things like that just before you hang up.'

Maeve giggles as he squirms in his seat. 'Sorry sexy! Tell you what. Call me when you're alone later. We might be able to help each other out,' she says with a wink.

'Now that is a date.'

'Too right it is! I had better go. You give Dillon a hug from me and of course a big one for you too. I'll talk to you later.'

'I love you Maeve.'

'I love you too Luke. I'll see you and your dick later.'

Before he can respond, she blows him a kiss, then ends the video call.

Ash

It's been at least two decades since she's felt so nervous. As she sits in the chair opposite Megan, desperately trying to control her stomach, she could be back at school again. Not that she spent a lot of time in the head teacher's office. She was one of the good students, most of the time.

Megan is going to fire her. Being removed from the Broken tour two days ago is going to end her career. Ash is positive of that.

She wipes her sweating palms on her skirt, wishing Megan would stop reading whatever's on her screen and just get this over with.

'These are... incredible is too weak a word. Spectacular! Out of this world. Well done!'

Ash frowns, wondering what the hell is going on. 'I'm sorry?'

Megan turns her screen around and points to the file of photos Ash sent her from the tour. 'Wow, Ash! Just wow!'

'I'm sorry Megan. I'm a little confused. I thought you called me in here because I'm in trouble.'

Megan dismisses her comment with a wave of her hand. 'Trouble? Far from it. What gave you the impression you're in trouble?'

'I was pulled from the tour.'

'True, but that's not a reflection on you, or your work.'

Now she's so far beyond confused. 'It's not? But I don't understand. How can it not be? You trusted me with this assignment, and I irritated one of the band members so much he couldn't work with me.'

Megan waves her concern away. 'Ellen and the band were singing your praises, excuse the pun,' she adds with a grin. 'They loved you and your work. Apparently, it's the best shoot they've ever had done.'

'It is?'

'Yes Ash. It is. And if you had a personality clash with one of the band members it wasn't mentioned to me. According to the information from Ellen, you were only pulled because Vox decided to call an end to the shoot. They felt you'd get nothing new from prolonging it. There was no other reason. Did they not tell you that?'

He did this. She doesn't know why, considering how they left things, but she has no doubts this fabricated excuse is down to Dillon.

And that just adds to her confusion. He had been so angry with her, and rightly so. It would have been so easy for him to put all this on her, blame her for having to cut the shoot short. Instead, he covered for her.

Or protected himself?

That thought takes some of the wind from her sails. He wouldn't have wanted Vox and the world to know what happened. He either didn't tell them, or they know, and are keeping it private. It's not for her benefit in the slightest.

Wishful thinking yet again. When is she going to let it go, and just accept she's lost him for good?

'Are you all right, Ash? You're looking a little pale.'

'What? No. I'm fine. Sorry. It's just nice to hear such positive comments from Vox.'

Megan gives her a strange look, before slowly nodding. 'Yes, well I must say you don't seem particularly happy.' Megan sits back in her chair and examines her for a moment. 'Since the minute I mentioned Broken Chords to you you've been acting strangely. Is there something going on? Has it something to do with this personality clash you referred to?'

Her relationship with Dillon, however disastrous it is, isn't something she's ever going to discuss with her boss. The shoot with Broken Chords means so much to the magazine and to Megan. She's not going to give her any reason to doubt her professionalism. It could be the end of her career.

'I think I was just thrown by being picked to do the shoot. It's such a big deal and I was nervous about it.'

Nothing she just said is a lie. Not mentioning the connection to Dillon is about protecting herself. He's protecting himself and she needs to do the same.

'Well, that's completely understandable. So, as promised, I'm giving you a week off. Go and spend some time with that beautiful daughter.'

'Thanks Megan. That's great. I'll see you in a week so.'

She leaves the office feeling a mixture of happy and devastated. That went so much better than she thought it would. She was convinced that being removed from the Broken Chords shoot would spell the end of her career. Last night had been spent on the internet, searching for new jobs just in case she was let go today.

Not for a minute did she expect to be leaving here with not only her job intact, but also a glowing recommendation from Ellen and Vox.

She grabs her bag from her desk then heads over to the elevator. As days go, it's a good one. So why does she feel like crying? Why does she want nothing more than to go home, crawl under her duvet and spend the next few hours there, hiding from the world.

Dillon.

Plain and simple. She's yet again grieving for the relationship she lost, wishing she could go back in time and do things differently.

To take a gamble, stay with him, and hope everything would work out. Then they could have spent the last ten years together as a family.

As she steps out of the elevator and crosses the car park, she wipes her face. Crying about it won't do any good. It's done. Finished.

What she needs to do is spend the next few hours getting herself together before she needs to go and collect Freya from school.

Her daughter is her priority and she's going to continue to make sure she gives her the best possible life.

Maybe one day Dillon will change his mind and want to meet her. All she can do is hope.

31

Dillon

However crap he felt when he woke up in hospital, it's nothing compared to today. Nearly a week after the crash his body is still seriously banged up. The bruising had begun to fade to a sickly yellow on his chest, legs, and arms, but the pain is still there.

Every fucking movement hurts. Breathing hurts. Performing was a painful two hours on stage each night, but he was getting through it, mainly thanks to a few extra pills here and there.

He's a fucking joke. There's a strong chance he blacked out because of them, and now he's taking even more because of the pain he's in, thanks to that crash. Vicious fucking circle!

It's also not helping that he's in a shite fucking mood - for a change.

Two more shows after tonight, then they head back home for a week off. They're planning to have the final night of the tour in Croke Park. Tickets to the show had sold out within minutes, which is fucking impressive. The shows they played in Dublin were the ones he really loved. There's nothing like playing to a home crowd.

Hopefully, that time off will help him get his shit together. He doesn't want to do that last show while he's still aching like this.

As he leans over the dressing table, the chain slips out from under his t-shirt. The damn engagement ring spins on the end, the light catching off the diamond.

For some warped reason, he had put it back around his neck after she left. After he sent her away. He just can't throw it away. Can't be without it. Wearing it helps him feel closer to her, as it had for the ten years they were apart.

Regret washes over him again, just like every time he thinks about what he did. Getting her kicked off the shoot was a low move. At the time all he wanted was to remove her from his life, but now there's a chance he regrets it.

Fuck that! When he woke up the following morning in the hotel room with Luke, he'd regretted it. It was a stupid, spur of the moment thing. Fuelled by anger, pain, and a healthy dose of humiliation, he'd reacted in the worst possible way.

He'd reacted in his usual way by pushing her away. Why the fuck can't he stop doing that? Is being alone and miserable better than the alternative? Short term pain for the possibility of a chance at long term gain.

Maybe if he'd taken some time and talked to her, he wouldn't be left with more fucking questions than answers. He doesn't even have a photo of his daughter. Nothing to remind him of her. He knows absolutely nothing about her.

When is her birthday? What does she like? Is she happy?

He could pick up the phone. Get in touch with Ash's boss and ask for her number. But he won't. No way. As much as a part of him needs answers, another part is terrified of what those answers will be.

'Dillon?'

'Yeah. Come in.'

He looks over at the door as Sam steps inside, carefully closing the door behind her. With her clipboard hugged to her chest, she walks over to him, her eyes anywhere but on him.

'You okay?'

She looks up at him, then frowns when something catches her attention. He realises a little too late what she's staring at.

'Is that an engagement ring?'

No point denying it. It's not like it matters at this stage. 'Yeah. Long time ago.'

'Ash, right?'

'What?' How the fuck does she know? The guys wouldn't have said anything. There's no fucking way. He trusts them.

'It's my job to look out for you all. I knew the second you saw her at the first rehearsal that there was history. You're not the most welcoming at the best of times, but your reaction to her was extreme. And you weren't the only one. I lost count of the number of times she had to deal with the tears while she was working.'

'Why didn't you say anything?'

She hugs the clipboard to her chest as she shrugs. 'It's none of my business. It was clearly painful for both of you. I thought drawing attention to it would just make things worse for you.

He can't believe she did that. 'Thank you.'

'I just wish it had ended better for both of you.'

'It's done now. No going back. I guess we just belong in the past. I just can't get rid...' The two of them fall silent.

She tucks the ring under his t-shirt, hiding it from the world again. 'It's a beautiful ring Dillon. You don't have to explain to anyone why you're keeping it.'

Her face drops as she looks down at the ground. 'Okay, I'm getting vibes here. What's wrong?'

'I hate to do this to you now, but your sister and father are here.'

The laugh isn't planned. Deep down he knows she's being serious, but in those first few seconds, he can't allow himself to believe what she's saying. 'What sister?'

'Eva. She said it's important. She desperately wants to talk to you.'

'I've got a show in an hour. I don't have time for this.'

'She only needs a few minutes. Dillon, they flew here to see you.'

He slams his fist on to the dressing table. 'Fuck!' Sam jumps, but right now he doesn't care that he scared her.

What the fuck is Eva playing at? Her coming here is one thing. Bringing *him* with her is out of order. He's seriously pissed off with her and he's not going to hide that fact.

'Fine. Bring them in here.'

Sam hurries from the room without saying anything to him. He shouldn't really have shouted like he did. Fuck it! He'll apologise to her later.

Less than two minutes later there's a knock on his door. Better get this over with so he can get ready for the show 'Yeah!'

Sam opens the door and steps aside to let Eva and his dad... his grandfather, into the room. Before he can get a word out Eva is all over him.

'Where the hell have you been?'

'What the fuck are you talking about? I've been working.'

'I've been ringing you for days! And you know what I've been getting? Your answering machine. Every single time. Which wouldn't be too bad if you ever replied.'

'You came all this way to have a go at me?'

'Well yes! I flew all the way to Sweden to talk to my brother. If you'd just answered the phone my life would have been a lot easier.'

'Yeah, cause that's what I'm all about right now. Making your life easier. I've had a few things to deal with, so I'm sorry if you haven't been my first fucking priority.'

'I've been dealing with some stuff too. We all have. Everything to do with Mum, Clara, you. It's hit all of us. I needed my brother, okay? I needed him, and he just turned his back and dismissed me like I didn't matter.'

'I'm not your brother, so stop saying that.'

She launches herself at him, jabbing him in the chest with her finger. 'Don't you dare go there! You are my brother! I don't care what happened. Well, I do, but it doesn't change how I see you.

'You will always be my brother. You will always be the person who pulled my hair, broke my toys, threw mud on my best dress.' She drops her hand, taking a step back from him.

'My brother who came with me to my school dance when I was stood up. The person who had a quiet chat with my bully in school, making sure they didn't even look at me again. The brother who was always there for me, no matter what. That hasn't changed.'

Now he's crying. He doesn't want to let the emotion take over. Not now. He's been fighting so hard to keep it under control.

'I can't do this now, Eva. I'm on stage in a bit. I need to keep my head straight.'

'Wow! So that's it. Dismissing us as if we don't matter?'

'What the fuck do you want from me? I can't do this!'

'Stop! Both of you shut up and sit down.'

It's been years since he's heard his father shout like that. Eva does as she's told, but he's not sure what to do.

'Dillon Sean Ryan, you sit your ass down right now and keep your mouth shut.'

And he does. Whether it's shock, or being brought back to his childhood, he has no idea. He just sits and keeps his mouth shut, as his father removes his coat and takes a seat himself.

'Right. Now I realise there is a lot of emotion and that's difficult to control. But I will ask the two of you to please let me say what I need to say.'

Dillon's first reaction is to tell him where to go... but he stops himself. Would it hurt to hear what he has to say?

'First, how are you, Dillon? We heard about the car crash. Are you okay?'

''Yeah. I'm fine. Still a bit sore but it's getting better.'

His father nods, looking a little relieved to hear that. 'That's good. I'm glad to hear that.'

He seems genuine, but it's been years since he's been around his father for longer than a few minutes. Who the hell knows what's genuine or not?

At least if he pretends to hear him out, Eva will get off his case. Maybe then he'll be left alone so he can get on with his life.

Dillon drops his head to his chest and squeezes his eyes shut as the pain builds in his gut. What life? He lost the one person he ever really loved. Kicked her out of his life. He's got a daughter he'll never know. Not a lot there to be over the moon about.

Why not add another layer of shit on top of all that? Time to put on the *I don't give a fuck façade* that celebrity Dillon uses daily. He learned a long time ago that if you act like you don't care about anything, it can help to delay the pain. Gives him time to deal with the shit he's had thrown at him, in privacy.

'Thank you for agreeing to speak to me.'

'I'm not doing the speaking. I've got nothing to say to you. Not anymore.'

He nods solemnly, then smiles. 'I understand. Eva? Would you give us a minute please? I need to speak to Dillon alone.'

She gives him one impressive dirty look before leaving them to it. No doubt he'll have to deal with her once this round is done.

When the door has closed behind her, his father lifts his head to look at him. 'I can't blame you for that. I'm just grateful for the chance to tell you my side.'

'Yeah, cause I'd love to hear your justification for lying to me all my life, then disowning me. Bring it on!' He's in a bitch of a mood, and his father is going to get it full force. Not that he gives a fuck. He's done apologising and being ashamed of who he is. It's not like there's a relationship left to destroy. He's got fuck all to lose.

'I deserve that. More too perhaps. When we found out what happened to Clara... our world crumbled around us. But I think your mother... apologies, your grandmother, couldn't move past what happened. He was her friend. That made it so much worse for her. Clara was incredible. So brave. So sure of what she wanted. And she wanted you,' he says with a smile. 'From the second she held you, you were her world.'

He falls silent, but Dillon leaves him to it. Let him talk.

'I am going to tell you this because I feel you need to know. I'll take the backlash from Clara later if I have to. There were complications with your birth. She was so young, and it was difficult.'

'Difficult how?'

'She can't have any more children Dillon.'

He always assumed Clara and Marcus didn't have children by choice. They are both so career driven – always have been. 'I thought they made that decision together.'

His father shakes his head. 'She wanted to be a mother Dillon. She wanted it so badly. That's what makes what your grandmother and I did so much worse. We denied her the chance to be a mother. It's all she wanted.

'And your grandmother tried to love you. I can swear to you that she did. But she blamed herself for what happened. Never stopped blaming herself. And I'm afraid that you took the brunt of that blame. It was unfair. I know it was, and so did she. She did,' he adds when Dillon rolls his eyes.

'But what's done is done. I can't go back and undo what happened.

270

What I can say is that I was wrong to side with her. I was, still am, deeply in love with her. I didn't want to upset her further by not supporting her. But you didn't deserve to be brushed aside as you were.'

'What about when I came out? Was that just an excuse to get rid of me, or is my sexuality another thing you don't agree with?'

'At the time my beliefs were a huge part of who I am. Who I was. They were what I lived my life according to. When you came to us and told us that you...'

'That I'm bisexual. Fuck, you can't even say it, can you?'

His father winces at his words. 'When you came to us and told us you're bisexual, I didn't know how to react. And I let your mother... your grandmother take the lead. I used my faith to justify my actions. We both did. We felt we had no choice but to turn our backs on you.'

'Yeah, thanks. I got all that from the touching *we no longer have a son* letter.'

'I was so very wrong, Dillon. I made an unforgivable mistake, and I lost you as a result. When Clara told me that you had tried to take your life... I'll never forget that call.'

'Yeah, two whopping sins, right? Bisexual son who tried to kill himself. You mustn't have been able to hold your head up in church with the shame.'

His grandfather stops and turns to face him. 'It had nothing to do with that. Aside from her funeral, I haven't set foot in a church since I allowed your grandmother to put my name to that letter.'

His admission shocks Dillon into silence.

'Coming to us that day after school and telling us what you did, was the single most courageous thing I've ever seen. And instead of getting the love and support you deserved, we made you feel so unwanted and unloved that you felt you had no choice but to end your life. We let you down, Dillon. I let you down. And not a single minute has gone by since that day that I don't regret what I did.'

'So why didn't you come and see me in hospital? Or the treatment centre? Or any other fucking day after that?'

'Because I was ashamed of course. I was ashamed and humiliated and disgusted by my actions. I had no right to ask for your forgiveness.'

'So why now? It's been over twenty years.'

'I know twenty years is a long time, Dillon. And I know you can never forgive me. I'm not asking you to. I would like to get to know you though – if you'll let me?'

'Get to know me? As in the *real* me? The real me that has fucked men and women. The real me that takes drugs and drinks probably a little too much. The real me that has piercings and tattoos and has a motorbike? The real me that is the exact opposite of everything you could want in a son or a grandson. Fuck! It's too complicated. This could never work.'

'Why not? I let your grandmother push you away from me. I let her decide to keep this secret from you. I was wrong. I can't fix that. I'm also not here to fix your relationship with Clara. That's between the two of you, and I won't interfere.

'What I will say is that she has only ever put you first. She was left with no choice. We gave her no choice. She was only fifteen. What else could she have done?'

He leans forward and looks Dillon in the eye. 'And you are everything I could ask for in a son. You are brave and strong, and I couldn't be more proud of you than I am. You... well, you'd probably say you *stuck your finger up* at all of us and lived your life the way you wanted.

'And look at you now! You've achieved so much in your life. When I see you on stage with Tate, Gregg, and Luke, I am so proud. I can't keep my eyes off you the whole time. I just want to tell everyone around me that you're my son. Because that's how I see you. You're my son, Dillon.'

'Hang on. What do you mean when you see me on stage?'

He looks away for a moment. 'Please don't be angry, but I have been to some of your concerts. I admit I never told your grandmother. I would go alone. Tell her I was at a pub quiz or bridge game. I just had to see you. Only the Irish gigs mind you, but they are always the best I'm told.'

Dillon knows he's staring dumbly at his father. He can't help it. It doesn't help that he laughs a little at Dillon's stunned reaction.

'You're quite the performer. And your voice. It brings a smile to my face every time I hear you sing.'

'Back up. You've been to every Irish gig?'

'Yes. I signed up to your fan group to receive early access to ticket sales.'

'Come again?'

'If I waited with everyone else for the tickets to be released, I might miss out. I've never missed a show, and that was the best way of making sure I didn't.'

He scrubs his hands over his face, as if that will help whatever is happening here make sense. 'You're in our exclusive fan group. You?'

'Of course. I must admit I haven't worn the t-shirt I was sent, but I kept it.'

He's tripping out right now. He must have taken one too many pills today, and none of this is happening except in his drugged brain. That's the only place this conversation could make sense.

Then his father reaches into his pocket and takes out his keys. Right beside his car key is a keyring with their band logo on it. It's a limited edition one that's only given out to exclusive fans. 'Fuck.' He slumps back in the chair, still trying to figure out what's going on.

Dillon doesn't want to let him back in. He can't. Not after fighting so long and hard to try to get over what they did to him.

'I appreciate you doing that, but it doesn't make things right between us. You turned your back on me when I needed you the most.

I can't forgive that. Sure as fuck can't forget it.'

He nods, then smiles sadly. 'I know, Dillon. And I feel the same, believe me. I'm just asking that you let me get to know you. With Eva there, if it makes you more comfortable?'

'Nothing about this is making me feel comfortable. I don't know if I can do this now, okay. There's too much shit going on with Clara and... I just can't.'

He wants to be a bastard. Wants nothing more than to be able to walk away and not think about anything he said to him. But as much as he may play the heartless dick in public, that's not who he really is.

He's tired of pushing everyone away. Tired of being alone and angry.

Deep down he's a lost little kid who desperately wanted his parents to love him for who he is. When his dad said he's proud of him, he liked it. Those few measly words were the very words he'd been so desperate to hear when he was seventeen.

Dillon curses quietly under his breath and shrugs. 'You're here now. You might as well stay for the show.'

The smile instantly lights up his dad's face. 'Thank you! I'd really like that.'

32

Dillon

The last three days have been spent in his cottage... alone. It's been a hell of a long time since he's spent that much time by himself. But he needs it. It's what they do when they get back from tour. Being stuck on the road with each other for weeks can grate on nerves after a while. They all go into hiding, keeping away from each other while they unwind.

Tate is back with Chloe and his son, Gregg with Bria, and Luke is with Maeve. Everyone is doing their own thing.

He doesn't even have Jace with him. His bodyguard is having a well-deserved break from him for the few days. Apart from the odd trip to Gregg or Tate's place, he had no other plans. No need to drag Jace along after him for stuff like that.

He doesn't even have a sexual partner lined up to meet. He's not interested. His mind is too busy to even consider fucking someone. The only thing occupying his mind is Clara, what his father said, Ash, and Freya. A continuous cycle that's slowly driving him crazy.

Eva had been bugging him again, desperate to come around to be with him. But he's not in the mood for company. He loves her to bits, but time is the only thing that will make any of this better. Talking and hugging it out won't do anything.

When the buzzer at the gate sounds, he groans. 'Fucking Eva!' He rarely closes the gates at the top of his driveway. He's so off the beaten track he's hidden, but the thought of Clara popping in to fix things has him leaving those gates firmly shut.

But it's not Eva or Clara he sees on the security camera. It's Ellen. He opens the gate for her, then goes to the front door. What the fuck did he do? She never calls around.

'What did I do?' he asks as she gets out of her Mercedes.

'Well, that's a welcome and a half. Nice to see you too.'

'You only come here when I've done something I shouldn't have.'

'And have you done anything you shouldn't have lately? Besides flipping a car and finding yourself in hospital.'

He shrugs. 'Not that I can think of, but I've figured out we have different ideas of what that means.'

'Indeed. So, are you going to invite me in?'

He steps aside and gestures for her to come in. Ellen follows him into the living room and places her case on the counter. 'You want a drink or anything?'

'No, thank you. Can I sit?'

'Knock yourself out.'

She takes a file from her case and goes over to the couch. Dillon sits opposite her and waits for her to speak.

Ellen has only been here four times before. Once when he hit a photographer, then again when he punched a hole in a hotel wall, then after he got more than a little drunk, lost his hotel key and kicked the door in, and then when he was arrested.

'Did I forget an interview or something? I thought I was off for a few days.'

'No, you haven't forgotten anything. You're off the clock until Croke Park at the end of the week. I'm here on a more personal issue. I've just spent the morning catching up with Sam. She's been filling me in on you and the photographer we picked for the tour. It's quite unbelievable.'

Too fucking right. 'Small world.'

'Indeed. First, I would like to apologise for any trouble that decision has caused you. I am truly sorry.'

'It was a freak coincidence. She'd changed her name, so I didn't even put two and two together. It's all good.' The words sound hollow as he says them and, as always, Ellen sees right through him.

'I may be about to upset all that.'

'How?'

'Ashling's name struck a memory with me. I've been spending the last few months doing a bit of a clear out at work. My predecessor, Louis, wasn't the most efficient when it came to filing. I've had numerous conversations with various artists about X, Y, and Z that Louis promised them, but there are no records on the system. Hence the clear out. He may not have been proficient on a computer, but he did keep meticulous records, mostly handwritten unfortunately.'

'Okay...' He's not liking the sound of this.

'Right, so while going through these files I found his original details when Broken was initially signed.' She pauses and rests her hands on the brown file on her knee.

'Okay, you're freaking me out Ellen. What the fuck did you find?'

'Before you left on your promo tour, you told Louis about Ashling.'

'How the hell do you know that?'

'Because it's in his notes. He also states that he went to visit her while you were away.'

Dillon has a bad feeling about this. 'What the fuck for?' He swallows heavily. 'He never said. She never said.'

'I don't know what happened during that meeting, but apparently he convinced her that having a girlfriend wouldn't do anything for your career. In fact, according to his notes, he told her she'd ruin your career. Dillon, he told her that if she stayed with you, he'd drop you from the label. He didn't jot down any further details. All he wrote is that *the problem is sorted.*'

'Are you saying he got rid of her?'

'Yes, Dillon. I have no words to describe how I feel about his actions. Louis was always more interested in the figures, than the artists themselves. It's the main reason he was let go, and I was given his clients. In his eyes, four unattached guys would have been a lot easier to market, than three unattached guys and one with a girlfriend hanging off him.

'I know that sounds blunt, but that's all he would have been thinking about.' She pauses and fixes the cuff of her blouse. 'Dillon, I also know he told you to hide the fact you're bisexual. Why didn't you tell me?'

Dillon shrugs absently, his mind still on what Louis did to his relationship with Ash. 'I was used to hiding it for years. All I wanted to do was play music. And it's not like I had to do it for long. You were cool with it, so I just dropped the act, and forgot about Louis.'

Louis wasn't the best of managers, but he had given them the break they had been looking for. But at what cost? Okay, so he had to pretend he was a normal straight guy in public, until Ellen took over and told him to be himself. But what Louis did with Ash is so much worse.

Why didn't she tell him? Why did she make him believe she didn't love him?

'He had no right to interfere in your personal life like that.'

'Yeah, well, he did. Fuck...' Why didn't she tell him?

Because you would have left the band for her.

No question.

But is that so wrong? 'I need a drink.' He gets up and pours himself a glass of whiskey. 'You want something?'

'No, thank you.'

He reaches into the cupboard over the sink, pulling out an old coffee canister. After hearing what he just had, he needs something stronger than a whiskey. With his back to Ellen, he fishes out the plastic bag, but doesn't get any further. Ellen appears beside him and snatches the pills from his hand, holding them behind her back when he spins around. 'Give them back!'

'Not a chance.'

'Ellen, I'm not screwing around. Give them back.'

'And I said no. Have the whiskey by all means, but these won't help, whatever they are. What are they?'

'Ellen, being my manager doesn't mean you get to stick your nose into my private life like this. You following after Louis now?'

'That's incredibly unfair.'

'Yeah, well that's life. We don't all get what we want, believe me. Hand them over.'

'No. What are you taking?'

'This part of the deal now? You keeping track of every drink, every pill?'

'If I have to. You are better than this, Dillon! You all are, but I can't seem to get that through your heads.' She turns away from him, drawing her hand through her hair. He's not used to seeing her flustered like this.

When she turns back to him, she points a finger at him. 'You are four of the most talented musicians I have had the pleasure to work with in my career. I don't say that often. Rarely in fact. But within a few minutes of hearing you perform, I knew how big Broken Chords could be. And I was right. You've achieved more than I ever thought possible.

'So why you feel the need to put this poison in your body,' she says, shaking the bag of pills in his face. 'I'll never know. Do you really think I want to visit another one of you in hospital? Do you think I enjoyed sitting by Tate and Luke's bedsides wondering if they'd wake up? It was the worst thing I've ever experienced.

'And that's before you add crazy cousins and psycho stalkers to the mix. I can't even process most of that, no matter how hard I try. To date I've nearly lost three of you to either drugs, or people intent on destroying you. And for the record, I am done with all this Dillon. Done with worrying about you all.'

'I've never asked you to worry about me Ellen. I can take care of myself. And I'm not going to end up in fucking hospital.'

'You already did. And do you know what? I'm afraid you'll end up in the ground next!' She holds up the packet of pills. 'Tell me what you're taking. You owe me that much at least.'

Fuck it. It's not going to make a difference either way. 'Painkillers. Nothing in particular. Just whatever I can get my hands on.'

She curses under her breath which is a first. He doesn't remember ever hearing her cursing before. Ellen fists the plastic bag and glares at the ground for a few minutes.

Dillon leans back against the counter and resists the urge to grab the drugs out of her hands. But then he realises she's crying. Hard-faced, no-nonsense Ellen is crying. 'You okay?'

'No, Dillon. I'm not okay. When are you guys going to accept that I actually give a damn about the four of you! You're more than a group that I manage. You're my friends and I love you all. I'm disgusted that Louis interfered in your life the way he did. I'm heartbroken that you missed out on spending those years with Ashling and your daughter. But most of all, I'm terrified to leave this house and get a phone call about you in a few hours.'

'I'm not going to do anything stupid, Ellen. I promise.'

'Forgive me if I don't have a lot of faith in that.' She rests back against the opposite counter and looks over at him. 'How long have you been using these for?'

'On and off for a few years.'

'Of course. And I presume you're going to tell me you're in control of it? That you can stop whenever you want?'

'No. I'm not going to lie to you, Ellen.'

That surprises them both. He wasn't planning on saying that. 'Oh. Well I have to admit I wasn't quite expecting that response. Thank you for being honest with me. I appreciate it.'

'No point denying it. Doesn't mean I'll do anything differently.'

She's not thrilled about that response. 'I see.'

He grabs his glass of whiskey and wanders back into the living room. Stuff the pills. He'll get more and have them later. Ellen has been nothing but decent to him. He's not keen on upsetting her more than he already has. Although, upsetting people is his thing at the moment so he's probably fucked either way.

She follows him into the living room, sitting on the couch opposite him. She leaves him to his thoughts as he sips his whiskey. He's not usually a sipper, but he'll take it slowly with Ellen watching him.

'Do you have a plan?'

He shakes his head. 'Nope. Well, nothing different to the plan I had yesterday morning. Or the morning before. I'm fine Ellen.'

She scrutinises him as she taps her fingers on her leg. 'I am going to speak, and I'd appreciate if you would keep your opinion to yourself until I've finished.'

He raises his glass to her. 'Go for it. I'm all ears.'

Her sigh is expected, but she doesn't comment further. 'I'm deeply worried about you. Your mother just died. And yes - I am aware of the background, so I know you may not believe you care, but I think you do.

'The woman you were going to marry has come back into your life with your ten-year-old daughter that you knew nothing about. The man you clearly love has been through hell, and now is settled down with someone else.'

As pep talks go this one is hitting all the wrong spots, but he resists getting up and telling her to get the fuck out of his house.

'You've found out your sister is your mother and are trying to deal with what that means for you. And you clearly have a drink and drug problem. Even one of those issues alone would be enough of a reason for me to be concerned, but all of them...'

'Can I talk now, or do you fancy throwing more juicy snippets of my life at me?'

'That's not what I was doing!'

'What were you doing then?'

'I think you need help, Dillon. Professional—'

'No!' He gets up and refills his glass, painfully aware he's just proving one of her points. 'I've done that and there's no fucking way I'm going back.'

'I had this conversation with Tate when he was using heroin again. Perhaps you should take some time away from the band.'

'No, Ellen! Please don't do this. I need to work.'

'And I need to look out for you. It's my job. You've already collapsed while you were on tour. How long do I let you continue like this? Do I wait until you collapse again? Do I wait until you wake up in hospital the next time? Or crash your car again and take yourself or someone else out? Or maybe you end up on life support in a coma for days like Tate and Luke? How long do I roll the dice with your life, Dillon? Because that's what it feels like.'

She's crying again and he hates himself for it. 'It means a lot that you care Ellen, but I have no interest in opening up to anyone. That's not how I work. I tried it years ago after my parents - grandparents - whatever. I had... I...'

Telling Ash what he did was bad enough. He's not about to share his attempted suicide with Ellen too. 'I needed help, and my sisters arranged it for me. I hated it, Ellen. If anything, it just made me want to keep things to myself even more. Being with the guys, getting on stage, it's what keeps me going. Please don't take it from me! I'll get down on my fucking knees and beg if I have to. I need the band.'

He's not in control here and he fucking hates it. He needs control. Thrives on having it, but Ellen is holding the cards. If she benches him, he's screwed.

She leaves him hanging for a long time. In reality it's probably only a minute or two, but it feels like a fucking lifetime.

Eventually she blows out a long breath and looks at him again. 'Fine, but,' she adds quickly when he relaxes. 'You will remain part of the band if you go to rehab. I am not backing down on that point.'

'Ellen—'

'Enough! I will personally drag you there if I have to. You can't do this alone. As strong as you are, you need help. I'm not going to ask what happened to you the last time you had to get professional help. I'm truly sorry you had a bad experience, but Tate and Luke have both benefitted greatly from the help they received. Speak to Tate. He's not one for talking, but he seems to get on well with his counsellor. Perhaps you can get a two for one deal?'

'What?'

'That was a joke. I was just making sure you're still listening to me. I know you like to zone out.'

He sneers at her before he can stop himself. Zoning out isn't going to help him. She's not going to back down. 'Fine.'

'I mean it, Dillon. I will not jeopardise the band by letting you continue the way you are. It's not fair on Tate, Gregg, or Luke. I won't let you bring them down just because you are being stubborn.' She shuffles closer to the edge of the seat and hits him with one of the most serious looks he's ever seen from her.

'You are also one of the most caring, decent men I have ever met.

Quite the musician too. You are so much more than the *bad boy* of the band. Ridiculous title I'd quite happily rid you of. Just say the word.

'What I'm trying to say is, that you are the backbone of the group. You forced Tate to face his addiction. You went after Angel when she tried to kill Gregg, and we nearly lost you in the process. You found yourself in prison by trying to help Luke escape Pippa. You selflessly give yourself to your friends, to the group every single day. Isn't it time you look after yourself for a change?'

'I thought I was a pain in your ass?'

'Oh, you are! But I wouldn't have it any other way.' She scrolls through her phone. 'What Indian dishes do you like?'

'What?'

'Take-away. Knowing you, you won't have eaten anything substantial for a few days. We are going to have dinner and work out a plan. Stop!' she says, holding up her finger, as she turns her attention back to her phone. 'It's non negotiable.'

Even though he's doing his best to keep up his pissed off front, he can't. This is what he does. He pushes, forcing people to leave him. What he really needs is someone to push back. Just like Ellen is right now.

And he's going to let her.

'I'll have Korma.'

Dillon

All he wants to do is go back to bed and be a miserable git for the next few days. No chance of that with Ellen hanging around his place. She'd stayed with him all night which was weird, but nice in a strange way.

They ate an amazing Indian feast, drank a lot of juice, and watched some cheesy movies she picked out. It was so out of the norm for him. Usually he'd drink, down a few pills and pass out. Instead, he fell asleep without any artificial help.

That hasn't happened often.

He also has steered clear of drink so far today. He'd tried the same with painkillers, but it hadn't gone well. So much for having a handle on it. Within a few hours of getting up he knew he was in trouble. He's operating on half of what he usually would have taken, and so far, so good. Okay so it's barely noon, but it's a start.

This informal rehearsal with the guys is just what he needs to try to take his mind off everything. Slim fucking chance of that but fuck it. It beats sitting at home brooding.

When Ellen first suggested he get them together he wasn't on board, but it was the right decision. He's no idiot. She probably just didn't want him at home alone.

A few hours of this, then he'll contact the centre. Start the ball rolling on the whole *let strangers poke around in his head* thing. He promised Ellen he would, and he doesn't break promises.

With a coffee in one hand and a bag of sour apple laces in the other, he uses his hip to nudge open the door to Tate's studio.

Gregg waves at him as he fills a cup with coffee. 'Want one?'

Dillon holds up his cup. 'Grabbed one on the way.'

He sits on the couch opposite Tate and Luke, both of whom are tucking into a tin of biscuits.

'So,' Gregg says as he sits down beside him. 'What's the plan for today? We just chilling and eating, or having a bit of a session?'

They all look to him for an answer. 'I don't know. I'm not bothered.'

'How about a bit of a session first,' Luke says. 'I kind of miss playing. That probably doesn't make sense after being on the road for so long, but I fancy running through a few songs if that's okay?'

Tate gets to his feet then stretches. 'Sounds like a plan. But how about we stick to something that's not on the tour playlist. I could do with a break from them.'

'Aww, what's wrong buddy? Is your voice getting tired?'

Tate thumps Gregg on the arm. 'Would be nice if your fucking voice got tired every now and again.'

Gregg rubs his arm as he pushes by Tate to get into the back room before him. 'Ouch! And also, it's a good thing we're friends, or I might have been offended by that comment.'

Dillon picks a bass from the stand of guitars against the wall, running his fingers over the strings while he waits for the others to get ready.

'What did we miss?' Bria asks as she joins them with Chloe and Maeve. He was hoping it would just be him and the guys here today, but it's probably to be expected. They hadn't seen Tate, Luke, and Gregg for weeks.

Maybe he had ruined all their plans by calling this rehearsal? He didn't even think about that. Figures. His head was stuck on his own problems.

As the girls get settled in, chatting quietly among themselves, his mind wanders. That's all it seems to be doing the last few days.

'Hey? Dillon! You ready?'

He blinks and nods at Tate. 'Yeah. Sorry.' He needs to get his head on the game, or this last gig in Dublin will be a fucking disaster.

They start with a song from their first album and, for the full three plus minutes, he's distracted. But as soon as he stops playing, he's back in his fucking head, going over that last conversation he had with Ash in the hospital and the phone call to Ellen.

'Yo Dillon! Hello?'

He glances at Gregg as he lowers his bass. 'I made a mistake.'

'You what?'

'I made a fucking mistake Gregg.'

Luke turns around to face him. 'What mistake Dillon?'

'I let her go. Fuck! Why did I let her go?'

'Because you were hurt and scared,' Luke says.

'Yeah but now I'm hurt, scared, and missing her. Why didn't I just talk to her? Why did I get her kicked off the shoot?'

'I think that's what everyone is wondering!'

He glances over at Meave. 'I couldn't handle being around her Maeve. Or I thought I couldn't.'

'So, what the fuck are you doing here?' Maeve rests her hands on her hips as she glares at him. For someone a good few heads shorter than him, she can throw the attitude around. 'Yes! You!'

Leaving Maeve to her glaring for a few seconds, he lowers onto the other couch. His damn legs feel like they're made of jelly. Instead of responding to her, he takes a long drink from his coffee. He needs the help to get his head in gear today.

What he doesn't need is Luke's feisty girlfriend ruining his calm. Which he gets the impression she's about to do.

'You know,' Tate says, resting his arm over the mic stand. She's got a point. If that's how you feel, what the fuck are you doing here?'

He groans and glares at Luke and then Gregg. 'I suppose you're both going to chip in now too?'

'Yep buddy. That's absolutely right,' Gregg says, twirling his drumstick in his hand. 'Should you not be in the UK with the lovely Ashling and your daughter?'

'It doesn't matter what I want. I fucked it up. She's where she needs to be and so am I. Can we drop this now and get on with playing some music? I'm just in my head today. Ignore me.'

But Maeve isn't in the mood for ignoring anything. She charges right up to him, jabbing him in the stomach with her finger. 'No! One hundred percent no! Any idiot can see you're crazy in love with her. And she's crazy in love with you. Then on top of all that, you have a ten-year-old daughter who needs her fucking stubborn, argumentative, irritating pain in the ass father in her life.

'What in the name of all things sweet and pure are you doing Dillon Ryan? I mean I knew you had your head up your ass most of the time, but this is a whole new level of stupid.'

The room falls silent as she brings her rant to an end. For the first time in a hell of a while, he's speechless.

He glances at the guys, each one looking anywhere but at him. Only Luke is smirking over at Maeve. Fucker.

'Well?'

He turns his attention back to her. 'Well what? I didn't want to interrupt. You were on a roll.'

'Why did you send her away?'

'Back off, Maeve. I'm not—'

'In the mood,' she finishes, in a whiny put-on voice. 'You're never in the mood. You can't just switch off when you don't feel like talking.'

'Oh really? Watch me!'

'Okay, okay!' Gregg says, getting in between the two of them. 'There's just a little too much tension in here and we're not even recording an album. How about we all sit down and take a minute to stop shouting at each other.'

He wants to shove Gregg out of the way, tell them all to go fuck themselves, then leave. But he doesn't. If he runs, Maeve will just come after him.

Dillon sits on one of the couches while everyone else follows suit. Gregg grabs a couple of soft drinks from the fridge, passing them around. 'Well, isn't this nice,' he says as he sits down.

'No, Gregg. Not really.' Dillon opens the bottle of coke but doesn't take a drink. It's kind of difficult to do anything with Maeve throwing daggers at him from across the room. He came here for a distraction. To give himself something other than Ash and Freya to think about.

Or Clara.

Or drink.

Or drugs.

Or anything to do with his life as a whole.

He should have stayed at home instead. He should have kept his mouth shut and not mentioned anything.

After a few minutes of seriously awkward silence, he's about had enough of Maeve glaring at him. 'Would you give it a rest with the dirty looks. I like you Maeve, but don't fucking push me.'

'I just don't get it. Why didn't you fight for your family?'

He rolls his eyes as he turns to face Luke. 'Taking over from your girlfriend?'

'Why don't you shut the fuck up for two minutes and listen!' Stunned into silence by Luke's outburst and his out of character curse, Dillon does just that.

'You told me so many times that I had to fight for Maeve. That you regretted not fighting for Ash.'

'Just to add my two cents here,' Gregg says. 'You kinda said the same thing to me about Bria. And she said you mentioned the same thing to her too.'

'What's your fucking point?'

'I think Luke mentioned the point.' Tate raises his eyebrows and hits Dillon with one of his trademark no-nonsense looks. 'Why aren't you fighting? Why are you here with us instead of with them?'

'Because I'm not good enough for them, okay! Fuck!' He slams his fist against the wall beside him, putting a nice dent in Tate's expensive soundproofing.

'I've messed up so many things in my life. It's what I do. I'm an alcoholic. I'm addicted to painkillers. I have a very public sex life with both men and women. I've been arrested for losing my temper. Spent time in prison for assault. I never cared about any of that before. I was doing what I wanted to do and fuck everyone else.

'But now there's a ten-year-old girl who deserves so much better. Deserves more than I could ever give her. She should have a father she's proud of. Someone she can look up to. And that's not me. I can't even get my own head straight with all the shit going on in my family. The best thing I can do for her is to keep the hell away.

'And as much as I appreciate whatever the fuck is going on here, I'm telling you all to leave it alone. Please. Everything is as it should be. As it has to be.'

Before any of them can offer advice he could do without hearing, he gets up and leaves the studio. He's unbelievably grateful he gets to his car and out of the driveway without anyone following him.

They probably haven't got a clue what to say to him. Or they agree. Everything he said is the truth. Every single word. He's not fit to be a father to Freya. Maybe in a few years if he manages to get himself clean, but by then it will probably be too late. She won't want to know him. She'll have moved on. Ash would have met someone else, and Freya would have a new family.

A new father.

He curses to himself.

He doesn't want that, which is messed up. He won't step up to be there for her, but he doesn't want anyone else near her. He's never even met Freya and he's already more than willing to protect her.

That's probably how it should be.

He pulls into the car park of the first beach he comes to and hides his car down the far end, so hopefully no one will see it. He can't go home. If he does, he'll do something stupid and, even though he's only a few hours sober, he'd like to add a few more before he messes up.

After walking for a good ten minutes, he sits on the rocks near the water and curses to himself.

Maeve is right.

He shouldn't have let Ash go, but he stands by what he said too. They're better off without him in their life.

'Can I join you?'

He groans as Luke sits beside him. 'How the fuck did you find me?'

'I followed you. If you want to hide or do a runner, best to use a less conspicuous car.'

'Okay, look I know what you're going to say, but it's for the best. I'm adamant about that. Can you just leave it now?'

'I love you, Dillon.'

He looks over at his friend. 'You what?'

'I love you.'

'Right. Thanks.'

'But you can be a selfish, stubborn, immovable ass at times. Make that most of the time.'

'I think you could have left that at the *I love you* part.'

'I'm being serious.'

'So am I.' He goes to stand, but Luke grabs his arm, yanking him back onto the stones again. 'You're going to sit there and listen to me.'

'Oh, am I now?'

'This has nothing to do with protecting Ash and Freya. This is about you doing your usual bullshit.'

While he's grateful that Luke has found himself again, this new *take no shit version* is harder to argue with. 'Go on then. Enlighten me.'

'You're terrified of getting hurt again, so you're pushing them away. It's easier for you to be alone and miserable, than take the risk of being rejected. I understand that. I know you better than most people do. Probably better than you think I do.

'I know what your parents - sorry, grandparents did, destroyed a part of you. I know that every time something good happened in your life, you lost it. But that doesn't mean it was because of you.

'Sometimes bad things just happen. Weren't you the one to say that to me when I was in the centre? That what Pippa did to me wasn't my fault. You are such an incredible person Dillon. You're protective, loving, supportive, and go out of your way to help people. Nothing about you, past or present, should make you think you're not good enough for them. Ash loves you. Anyone can see that. And as for Freya. You'd be such an amazing father. I know you would.'

'Oh, you know that?'

'Yes, I do.' Luke pauses and looks out at the sea. 'I'd give anything to have what you do.'

That surprises him. 'What part of what I have do you want? Cause you can fucking take it.'

'You're a father.'

With those three words Dillon understands why Luke is on his case about this.

'I'm sorry.'

'I'm not trying to guilt you. I haven't given up on that dream. I could still be a father one day. I guess time will tell if the reversal worked. You have this amazing girl out there who is a part of you. She's a piece of you Dillon. And I guarantee her life will be made better having a father like you in it. Your life will be made better having her in it.

'All you've ever wanted is a family who love and support you the way you are. Now you have one. Doesn't Freya deserve the same? Her mother and father are decent people. Why wouldn't her life be so much better with both of them in it?

'Whatever your feelings for Ash, that's your business. But Freya is different. You know that.'

'So, you think it's that simple? That I can just pop into her life and be her dad after all this time?'

'It's ten years. In the grand scheme of things, it's nothing. It's never too late to find happiness Dillon. Let them love you.'

'I'm scared Luke. I've just got over...' he stops himself from finishing the sentence. He swore Luke would never find out how heartbroken he was when Maeve arrived on the scene.

'Me?'

'Forget it. We better get back.'

'No! Don't do that. I can't stand it when you do that.'

'Do what?'

'Brush all that away as if it didn't matter. Your feelings matter. It's not like it's a secret or anything. I thought we were okay?'

'We are okay.'

'No, we're not. You've been off with me since I got back from Wales. Probably a bit before too.'

'We're fine Luke.' They're not fine but it's his problem.

'You either act all weird around me or avoid me completely. You barely talk to me. Don't call me anymore. What's going on?'

'Nothing Luke.'

'It's Maeve, isn't it?'

'I love Maeve, you know that.'

'I don't mean that you have a problem with her. I... it...I don't know how to say this without sounding terrible and so self-important.'

'Just say it.'

'It's because I'm in love with Maeve, not you?'

Well clearly he's shite at keeping things from Luke. Talk about being handed the truth along with a massive kick to the guts. 'Fuck!'

'I'll take that as a yes. Why didn't you tell me?'

'Tell you what? It's my problem. Or it was. I'm over you so it's all good.' He's not sure if that's the truth or not. Who the fuck knows how he feels about anything? He sure as hell doesn't. It's all just a jumble of pain and confusion.

'Just for once can you please stop trying to protect me and be honest.'

'Fine! You want honest. I'll give you honest. It broke my fucking heart when you fell in love with Maeve. There. I said it. I'm a complete bastard I know, but that's how I felt. I want you happy. I love Maeve. The two of you are so fucking perfect for each other and the change in you since being with her is... well, after where you were, it's a fucking miracle.

'But *I* wanted to be the one to help you like that. *I* wanted to be the one to make you happy. I know you're straight and it was never on the table, but that's how I roll. Nothing like torturing myself in as many interesting ways as possible. Give myself a kick in the gut as often as I can.'

He stops talking and waits for Luke to say something, anything. But nope. He leaves him hanging for a hell of a long time, mortified and downright pathetic.

'Thank you.'

Not quite how he thought Luke would break the silence. 'For what?'

'Loving me that much.'

'Yeah well, like I said. It's my problem.'

'Why do you keep calling it a problem? Your feelings aren't a problem as long as you don't bottle them up.'

'I didn't want to bring a downer on you and Maeve. I honestly couldn't be happier for the two of you. I mean that.'

'I know you do. But I don't want to lose you because you can't be around us. You've been my best friend for decades. You're a massively important part of my life. That hasn't changed. But... okay to put it bluntly, you have to get over this. I need my friend. I need you in my life. Stop pining over me and move on to someone better. Someone who loves you the way you love them. Besides, I'm not that great - believe me.'

He looks over at Luke, then breaks out laughing when his friend grins. It feels so good to just laugh like that again. 'Is that right?'

'Absolutely. We're much better as friends.'

'Yeah. You might have a point there. So, you reckon I should just stop being an ass and get on with my life?'

'I'm suggesting you give it a try and see how it goes. You never know, it might be a better option.'

He kicks at the stones by his feet as he thinks about that one. Sounds easy enough in theory, but it's the practice he's not so sure about.

But Luke is right about something. He doesn't want to lose his best friend because he's caught up in his feelings for him. Old feelings. If he's really being honest, he's probably more over Luke than he wants to admit. Hanging on to that love gave him an excuse to push the happy couple away. Or keep himself alone.

'I just want to be happy Luke. That's it. Really happy. I can't remember the last time I felt that way. There's always something in the back of my mind saying it won't last. Something will go wrong. I guess I've just got used to thinking like that.'

'Maybe it's time to change that.'

'Yeah. Maybe it is.' He lies back and stares up at the clouds. 'Could you forgive her?"

Luke lies down beside him. 'I honestly don't know. I guess you have to ask yourself if the mistakes she made in the past are reason enough to walk away from the woman you've loved for a decade.'

Ash

Of all the things to be assigned to her after her week off to recover from the Broken Chords tour, why did it have to be a lovey dovey happy couple madly in love with each other? Nothing like getting slapped in the face with a good dose of true love after losing Dillon yet again.

But this is her life. He's gone and she needs to get on with things. Which right now, means convincing herself to get out of the restroom and do her job.

She's not in the slightest bit surprised when she finds Charlie leaning against the sink beside her. 'Were you hiding?'

'You know this is the ladies, right?'

He waves away her comment. 'Like I care about that. Answer the question.'

'Of course not.' He gives her his best attempt at a *yeah right* look. 'Okay, so maybe I was. I just needed a minute to build up my wall against the tide of happiness that's about to head my way.'

Charlie pulls her into a hug. 'I know. If I could slap that sexy rock star I would. I can't understand why he walked away. I know that he was upset about Freya, but he shouldn't have just walked away. Talk about it. Sort it out.'

'It was self preservation, I think. Anyway, I don't want to think about him. I just need to get out there, smile at the happy couple, then go home and give Freya a huge hug.'

Charlie holds her at arm's length. 'Well first you need to fix your hair and makeup. You look like you've been crying.'

She dumps her bag on the counter beside the sink and searches for her make up bag. 'That's because I was. God! I am so done crying over that man. Where the fuck is my makeup?'

Charlie gently manoeuvres her aside, finds her makeup, then helps restyle her hair, as she tackles her face.

'Close your eyes and do some deep breathing. This is a wedding.'

She does what he suggests, and it seems to work. She's a professional. She can do this.

'Now you look stunning. Are you ready to get out there and wow everyone?'

'I'm ready. As long as my wingman is going to stick with me.'

He holds out his arm so she can link hers underneath. 'Always.'

About an hour later, she is beginning to enjoy herself. This is what she loves. Because of her, this couple will have lovely memories of their special day. Her work will be a part of their life together. How can she not be proud of that?

As the food is cleared away and the room prepared for the band, she wanders through the crowd, snapping natural shots of the guests, before making her way out to the huge, terraced area overlooking the garden.

298

Okay, so she survived. That's all she can do. She did it before when she left the first time. She can do it again.

But she doesn't want to merely survive.

She wants to live, to thrive. But she's not sure how she can do that without Dillon in her life.

Behind her she can hear the band giving it their all. The first dance had been covered by Charlie. He offered and she wasn't going to turn him down. Blubbering in front of the guests wouldn't do her career any favours. She'll give it another few minutes then call it a day. Most of the guests are either too drunk to be photographed in a complimentary way or have left for their beds.

Charlie joins her on the terrace and hands her a glass of juice. 'You did it babe.'

She clinks glasses with him. 'Thanks. I'm glad it's over though. I need to detox from all this happiness.'

He nudges her in the side. 'Oh, would you stop it. You're a happy person, so stop all this gloominess. You know I'm a firm believer in fate. If you and Dillon are meant to be together, you'll be together. Nothing in the world can get in the way of fate. Not even Dillon Ryan's notorious stubbornness.'

'I know. I'm sorry. I'll snap out of it. I just need to give myself a good kick. I got over him once. I can do it again.'

He smirks as he nods.

'What?'

'You didn't get over him.'

'Are you trying to help or pull me down again?'

'Sorry. But we both know you will always be in love with him. We can only hope he comes to his senses and realises he feels the same about you.'

She nods but isn't put at ease by Charlie's words. If he can't forgive Clara for her lie that was designed to protect him, there's no way he can ever forgive her for keeping Freya from him.

Dillon

'You're in withdrawal, aren't you?'

Of all the people to notice, he was hoping it wouldn't be Tate. He takes the coffee from Gregg and settles back into the couch in Tate's studio. Chloe had ordered half a dozen pizzas which Gregg, Tate, and Maeve were doing a great job of devouring by themselves.

He's got no appetite. His stomach is in knots, he's got a raging headache, and it's only getting worse. And that terrifies him.

All these years he'd convinced himself he had a firm grip on his drug use. He told himself repeatedly he was in control of it, not the other way around. A few fucking hours without anything and he's already in bits. 'Yeah, Tate. I think I am.'

'How long since you took something?'

'Last night. Nothing since. I didn't think I was this bad.'

Tate turns the ring on his thumb and hits him with his trademark glare. It's not directed at him. He knows that. It's the situation he's not happy about. The fact he's not saying anything is more than a hint at how uncomfortable he is with the topic.

'I've got a handle on it, and I'm not just saying that. I booked an assessment for a few days' time. Ellen was with me when I made the call, so you can check with her if you don't believe me. I'm heading to rehab, but if I have to go away for a while, I don't want this thing with Ash hanging over me. I need to put things right with her first. I'm not putting off getting my shit together. I want more from my life than drink and drugs.'

'You can't come off the painkillers without help. It'll mess you up.'

'I know that Gregg, but I don't have a choice. I'm blacking out.'

'I can't believe I'm going to say this, but maybe you should just keep going as you have been - with more restraint and with us keeping an eye on you? Coming off both at the same time could be too much for you to cope with, without that professional help.'

Gregg is right. He's already struggling, and it's barely been a few hours. He needs to do this one last show. There's no other option. He's not going to let his fans down. 'Can you help me, Gregg?'

'Of course.'

'I will too,' Maeve says. 'We'll make sure you don't take things too far.'

'Thanks.'

'We all will,' Tate says. 'We're all here for you.'

'Tate, I don't want you to get dragged—'

'I said this to Luke a while ago, and I'll say it to you now. Let me help. I'm not saying I have a fucking clue what you're going through, but I know the hold drugs can have on you. Use me. I'm not going to relapse by being there for my mate.'

He's not usually stuck for something to say, but facing the guys, Maeve, Bria, and Chloe, each one willing to step up and help him, he can't think of anything to say. Chloe, Maeve, and Bria are massively protective of their partners.

Each woman has been through some serious shit with Tate, Gregg, and Luke. They nearly lost them at one stage so he can't blame them for being like that. But they're standing next to their men, each one of them offering to support him while he gets his shit together.

'We're a family Dillon.' Chloe reaches across and takes his hand. 'You're not alone in this.'

He nods, completely mortified when he can't stop the pathetic tears. Chloe is instantly on her knees in front of him, pulling him in for a hug.

Fuck, he is so tired of being an emotional basket case. He used to have a handle on all of this. People could be falling apart around him, and he'd be the cool, together one. Not anymore. He's like a broken shell of himself and he's so scared he'll never his life together again.

'So do you have any ideas on how to sweep the lovely Ash off her feet?' Maeve asks once he's got himself together again.

He wipes his face then shrugs. 'No fucking idea. Everything I say or do, just makes things worse. We just fight when we're together. I need to do something... big.'

'Big how?' Bria asks.

'I can't just waltz up to her and ask if she wants me. She's gone back to her own life, and I pretty much told her I didn't want anything to do with her.'

'Ah you say that to us all the time,' Gregg jokes, popping a gummy bear into his mouth and chewing on it. 'We still love you, buddy.'

'Thanks... I think.'

'Just go to her and tell her how you feel.'

Chloe laughs at Tate's suggestion. 'Oh really? Do you remember when you first asked me out? You fumbled the whole thing. It was like you were a teenager asking someone out for the first time.'

Tate glowers over at his wife. 'Laugh all you want. You married me didn't you, so it must have done the trick.'

'I fell for your boyish charm,' she says, blowing him a kiss. 'But Tate is right. Just get on a plane, go to her, and tell her how you feel.'

'I've messed up so many times. I want to show her how I feel. She likes romantic gestures. Always has. I'll need to do something that shows her I'm being serious. Words are great and all, but she'd want me to prove myself.'

'Hang on. You? Romantic?'

'Yes Gregg. Believe it or not, I'm not all about restraining people so I can to fuck them. I can be seriously fucking romantic.'

'Well, I have to admit you've sold me with that deeply moving statement.'

'Fuck off Gregg!'

'That one too. How about we take your word for the whole romance thing? You're not really selling it.'

'Yeah well, thankfully he's not trying to romance you,' Bria says, shutting up her boyfriend before he can keep arguing. 'Do you have any ideas on what you can do? You're talking about something more than a fancy dinner, aren't you?'

'Yeah. I think so. I'll need to go to the UK to her. Doubt she'd be interested in coming over here after I got her kicked off the shoot.'

'What time scale are you thinking about?' Luke asks. 'We've got the final concert in town this weekend. Do you want to sort things out before that?'

It's going to be one hell of an end to their tour if the ticket sales are anything to go by. The Dublin date had sold out within minutes of going live, but that wasn't a surprise. The home dates tended to be the popular ones. Playing a few miles from where they all grew up helps make the Dublin dates even more personal for everyone.

He smiles as a thought comes to him. 'I have an idea.'

Ash

This can't be good. That thought hits Ash as soon as Megan's message appears on the screen of her phone. *I need to see you now.*

Better get it over and done with. She straightens her top, then makes her way through the office and knocks on Megan's door.

'Ash. Come in and have a seat. So how was your week off?'

'Yeah. Thanks, it was great.'

'Good. So, you're feeling rested? Ready to get back to it?'

'Absolutely. Do you have something for me?'

Megan's grin doesn't put her at ease in the slightest. 'Oh, I have something for you. A rather exciting something in fact. I've just been speaking to Ellen at Vox.'

Shit. 'Okay. Is there a problem?'

'No. Not at all. In fact, quite the opposite. The band are back in Ireland and are scheduled to play in Dublin on Saturday night. It's the last night of the tour. It's going to be quite the show from what I hear. They always sell out, but apparently the shows on home soil tend to be the best ones.'

'So I heard.' Ash has no idea where this is going, but she desperately wishes Megan would get there.

'Ellen wants you to be there so you can finish the shoot.'

That wasn't what she was expecting to hear. 'I'm sorry?'

'You're heading back to Ireland to cover the last night of the tour with the band. What part wasn't I clear on?'

'I just wasn't expecting that after the way Ellen ended the shoot.'

'She insisted. She wants you and your style of photography. It is the final date of the ten-year anniversary tour in front of home fans. I'm sure she only wants the best photographer there. And that is you. So, I'll book the flight for you?'

No way. She can't go back. Leaving his life once had nearly killed her. Being shown the door the second time had compounded that. Having to see him again, then walk away after, will be too much for her. She knows that.

'Oh, and just to make sure you say yes, Ellen has offered you a bonus of an additional ten thousand pounds to cover that one night.'

'Ten thousand! Really?'

'Oh, I never joke about money, you know that. Say yes, Ash. Get on the damn plane. Do an amazing job as usual. Take the money. Then come home. Put it in a college fund for Freya. Go on a shopping spree. It's all yours for one night of work. What the hell are you thinking about?'

Megan is right. Ten thousand pounds bonus would go a long way. And he'll be on stage doing what he does best. There won't be any time for anything else.

'Yeah. Book the flight.'

Dillon

Nerves have never got to him. Whether facing a camera, an interviewer, or thousands of fans, he never flinched.

Yet here he is, crouching in front of the toilet after emptying his stomach. This is what she does to him. As much as he fights Ash, she always manages to get through all the shit and bravado to find the real him underneath.

And it appears nerves are part of that. Who knew?

But it's not the thought of getting on stage in front of all those people that's getting to him. It's knowing that she's back, only a stone's throw from where he's throwing up. Which has him wanting to throw up again. He needs to get a grip, or this whole thing is going to be a fucking disaster.

'Oh God! What's wrong?'

He gestures to Luke, waving him away as he groans into his arm. Fuck he feels rough.

'Are you sick?'

He shakes his head as he pushes to his feet. 'No. I'm fine.'

'You haven't had a drink, have you?'

'Fuck Luke! I haven't. All I've had today is too much coffee and a couple of pills. No drink.' Which probably isn't helping the queasiness. Maybe it's not just the thought of facing Ash again.

Who is he trying to kid? His body is craving one of its two poisons. Denying it whiskey isn't doing him any favours but fuck it. If he's to have any chance of a future longer than a few weeks, he has to keep control.

Luke passes him a glass of water then sits beside him on the couch in the dressing room. 'We've got an hour. Are you going to be up for it?'

'Yeah. No problem. I guess I'm just nervous.'

'That's a good sign. You never get nervous.'

He frowns over at Luke. 'Why is that a good sign?'

'It means you really care about this. About her.'

'Yeah. I do.'

'Good, because she's here.'

The water nearly makes a comeback when he hears that. He knew she had accepted the job to photograph the show. No doubt the ten thousand he paid to get her here had been a deciding factor. He doesn't care. He would have paid ten times that amount to convince her to take the job again. And he knows her. He knows that money would have gone straight into an account for Freya.

For his daughter.

For her future.

'I've only loved two people in my life. You and Ash. I lost you. And yes, I know I didn't have you like that, but in here,' he says rubbing his chest. 'In here I did. I can't lose her too, Luke. Not again.'

He looks up as Luke grabs his hand and squeezes it. 'If you love her you've got to fight for her.'

Dillon smiles at that. Hearing his own words being thrown back at him helps. 'Yeah. I have to fight for her.'

Luke pulls him up off the couch and hugs him. 'You haven't lost me Dillon. You never will. It doesn't matter who I'm with, or where I am, I will always be there for you. I love you.'

'I love you too.'

Luke steps back and looks him up and down, the frown growing. 'What?'

'I think you need to pull out some of that infamous Dillon Ryan energy and go clean yourself up, because right now you're not the larger than life, stylish bassist people are expecting to see. You look shite.'

'Wow. Great motivational speech there.'

Luke grins at him and Dillon can't help but notice how gorgeous he is when he smiles like that. Which he's doing more because of Maeve. He's smiling because of the risk he was willing to take to let her into his life, after he'd been so brutally hurt for so long.

If Luke can do that, what the fuck is he whinging about?

'Welcome back!'

Ash barely has time to turn around before Maeve launches herself at her. 'Hi!'

Luke's girlfriend hugs her tightly, squeezing hard before she finally releases her. 'I'm so glad you decided to come back. I didn't think I'd see you again.'

'I didn't think I'd be seen again either. It was quite a surprise to get the call from Megan about this job. I thought I'd seen him for the last time.'

'Ah but you didn't want that, did you?'

'What do you mean?'

Maeve steps closer to speak in her ear. 'You are crazy in love with that irritating bassist.'

'I'm not sure that means anything.'

Maeve takes her hand, leading her to one of the backstage rooms set aside for the band and their families. Maeve grabs two bottles of water from the table and passes one to her. 'This may surprise you, but I'm a bit of a romantic at heart. I'm a strong believer in the *meant to be* thing. I mean look at me and Luke! It took us twenty years, but we got there in the end. It's all about timing.'

'I think the two situations are different. You didn't do anything to hurt Luke.'

Maeve snorts loudly. 'All in the past. What matters is the here and now. And right now, that means getting ready to watch those four incredible men own that stage. I mean that's one of the best parts, right? Watching them perform.'

'Yeah. You couldn't be more right about that. Are Chloe and Bria here too?'

Maeve nods as she takes a drink. 'Full house tonight.' She holds out her hand and nods towards the door. 'Let's do something about those pesky tear tracks.'

Ash wipes her face, irritated she can't seem to stop crying. This isn't what she wanted from tonight.

Maeve takes her hand and leads her out of the room. 'We've got an hour before they blow the roof off this place. You and me are going to chill out with the rest of the girls. Get you all relaxed so you can go out there and kick ass.

By the time the band are ready to hit the stage, she's a lot more together and ready to do her job. Spending that time with Bria,

Maeve, and Chloe had absolutely done the trick. It's something she's going to miss when this assignment is done. Her relationship with the Broken Chords women had grown over the length of the tour - especially Maeve. While she hopes they can stay in contact after she's finished, she doubts it will happen. With Luke and Dillon being best friends it would probably be difficult.

Ash wipes the tears from her face again, as she watches the band step on stage to a nearly painful scream from the crowd. Their fans love them and it's not difficult to see why. Even if she wasn't in love with their bassist, she knows she would be a fan of the band. Tate is an incredible songwriter, and when he sings, she gets goosebumps every single time.

But hearing Dillon in the background is what really sends shivers through her. Watching him on stage, seeing that enormous, genuine, real smile while he performs is completely addictive. He was born to do exactly what he's doing.

Walking away from him to make sure he got his chance at realising the dream he'd had for years, was absolutely the best thing she's ever done. Not for her, but for him. And that's what's important.

Remembering she's here to do a job, she gives her face one final wipe, then picks up her camera. If she was the one chosen to document their ten-year anniversary tour, she's going to make sure it's the best work she's ever done. He deserves that. They all do.

Beside her, Maeve, Bria, and Chloe sing along with their partners. Watching them won't help her deal with being so close to him again, so while they drool over their men, she moves closer to the barrier holding the screaming crowd back from the stage. It gives her an unobstructed view of the whole stage. And of Dillon.

The fact he hasn't even glanced in her direction once hurts so badly. It's understandable, but that doesn't ease the pain.

They finish the first song, so she decides to use the brief pause to check her phone. Leaving Freya with Charlie again after just getting back wasn't what she wanted. Freya understood work sometimes took her away, but she had been hoping for a few weeks at home before she had to leave again.

The lights dim slightly, then Tate plays the intro to the next song. As with every song, the fans scream when they recognise it, but there's something different this time. The excitement seems to be on another level. Before she can lift her head, she recognises the song.

It's not one of Broken's songs.

It's *their* song.

It's what Dillon used to sing to her all the time.

Almost too scared to look, she slowly lifts her head, and her breath catches in her throat. Instead of Tate taking centre stage, it's Dillon. He's exchanged his bass for an acoustic guitar, and he's looking directly at her.

Those incredible cool green eyes are on her, and only her.

Then he sings, and the tears pour out. She can't stop them.

He's singing their song to her.

He's even facing her on the stage, dismissing the thousands of fans in front of him, so he can sing to her and her alone.

In that moment, it's just the two of them. Tate, Luke, and Gregg are hanging back, giving him the stage. None of the fans behind her exist anymore. She's back in their bedroom, lying on the bed as he sings that song to her.

And she doesn't want it to end. Not ever. His voice is spectacular, deep, and rich, and so much better than she remembers. But it's the way he's looking at her that has her desperate to live in this moment forever. He loves her. She has no doubts about that fact whatsoever. Dillon Ryan loves her.

The song ends far too soon, the crowd erupting behind her. But he's still looking at her like she's the only person on the planet. His eyes never leave hers as he passes his guitar to Tate, then jumps down from the stage and makes his way over to her.

The stunning rock star stops in front of her, then slowly reaches out to brush the tears from her cheeks. She knows the crowd are going nuts behind her, but she couldn't care less. Thousands of people are watching her crying like a baby, but she's far from embarrassed. The excitement, the love, the pure elation she's feeling is all that matters.

'Hey.'

She laughs as she wipes her face again. 'Hey yourself. God, I love that song so much.'

'It's our song. Always has been.'

'I never thought I'd hear you sing that again.'

'I'd only sing it for you.'

'So can I presume you didn't just decide to sing that song out of the blue?'

He shrugs, something that makes him appear a little less confident than usual. 'I made a mistake, hurt someone I love, and I needed to do something to show her how much she means to me. I thought a big romantic gesture might convince her to give me a chance. To hear me out at least.'

She sniffs and wipes her face again. The damn tears are refusing to give her a break. 'Is that right? Do I know this person?'

He closes the gap between them and slowly cups the side of her face, his thumb wiping away the tears. 'I am completely in love with you Ashling. I have been for the last ten years. I'm so sorry for not fighting for you. It was a mistake. I should have gone after you. I would have given all this up for you in a heartbeat.'

The silence in the venue is deafening. All eyes are on Dillon, probably wondering what is going on, and why he's left the stage.

'I know you would have. That's why I had to leave. I couldn't let you walk away from your dream.'

'But you were my dream, Ash. You still are. I don't want this unless I can share it with you.'

'Really? You mean that?'

'Too fucking right I do. I love you, Ash.'

'I love you too.'

He leans down and kisses her, his hand wrapping around the back of her head, his fingers brushing through her hair to hold her tight against him.

Dillon rests his forehead against hers, his smile incredible as he looks down at her. 'I suppose we both better get on with our jobs.'

It's only then she comes back to the real world and turns around to face the crowd of Broken Chords fans, all clapping and chanting Dillon's name. 'Ah. I forgot about all of them for a sec.'

He grins as he takes her hand and leads her back up the steps at the side of the stage. She blushes as he stops at his mic, her hand still firmly in his. 'Sorry about that. I owed this stunning woman an apology, and it had to be a good one.'

He pulls her close and kisses her again as the crowd erupts cheering.

Dillon waves, then leads her over to the side of the stage. 'I better get back to it before there's a riot. And you have a job to do. We'll talk properly after the show if that's okay?'

'I'd love that.'

He crushes his lips to hers one more time, before rejoining the others and picking up where he left off.

She's not going to get too carried away yet. They're in love with each other. That's such an amazing start, especially after she thought she'd never hear those words from him again. But there's still a lot to talk about. A lot to work through.

But, for the first time since she left him, there's hope.

36

Dillon

As he puts on the kettle and takes two cups from the cupboard, he can't stop glancing over at his guest, standing at the window looking out at the sea. He's never been a fan of company, preferring to be alone, especially when he's at his cottage. But he likes having her in his space. It's something he could easily get used to.

The plan may have worked, but he's still a long way from the finish line. All he's managed to do is win himself a chance to talk to her, to see if they can somehow find a way through everything that's happened over the last ten years.

It will mean being honest with her, in a way he's never been with anyone before. But he'll do it. If it means having her in his life again, he'll do whatever he has to, no matter how painful. Unless he puts all his cards on the table, opens up to her fully, they haven't got a chance.

He glances at the cupboard where he usually keeps his whiskey, before picking up the two cups of coffee and taking them in to the living room. It's been a long time since that cupboard has been empty. It's all part of the winning Ash back part of his plan.

It's not a part he's coping with all too well though. He'd been telling himself he'd got a strong hold on drink and drugs. If he's learned anything over the last few days, it's that it's the other way around. He's an addict. He's been living in denial for too long.

Another achievement to add to his list.

Ash sits opposite him, looking just as uncomfortable about this whole thing as he feels. When he was with her at the show, he couldn't have been happier, but now she's here, he's unsure what to do, how to act around her.

The car ride from the venue to his house had been awkward and polite. They'd passed the time with meaningless small talk, leaving the more serious topic until they were here, where they could talk in private.

But she's here.

He frowns and looks down at the table as he chews his lip ring. It takes him another few minutes to get himself sorted. 'I haven't got a fucking clue where to start.'

'Thank God,' she admits with a relieved smile. 'I thought it was just me. I know we need to talk, but there's so much to talk about it's a little overwhelming. Why did you change your mind? Why did you get me to come back?'

That's an easier place to kick this off. Leave the other shit for another few minutes. 'Ellen was sorting through some paperwork from our old manager. Why didn't you tell me he came to see you?'

Her face drops and she falls silent as she stares into her drink. 'He told me not to.'

'What?'

'Louis gave me two options. I could walk away from you. Just disappear, and he'd leave things as they were with the band. But if I stayed, or if I told you anything about his visit, he'd drop you from the label, and end your career.

'I didn't leave you because I fell out of love with you. I wanted to marry you, Dillon. So much. But Broken, the guys, your dreams... I couldn't be the reason you lost that. You'd worked so hard for so long. I'd only been in your life for a few months. I couldn't be the reason your dreams didn't come true.'

She's crying and he hates it, but they need to get all this out. 'Did he threaten you?'

'Not in so many words, but he was far from pleasant. Actually, he was a bastard. All smiles and oozing fake compliments. I believed him though. I believed he'd ruin your career. The way he was speaking about you... vile little man.'

'What way?'

'Dillon...'

'Please Ash.'

She wraps her hands around the mug and stares into the coffee for a minute. 'He made your sexuality the issue.'

'What did he say?'

'He said it would be difficult enough to market you because of *what* you are. I won't tell you the term he used but I'm sure you can guess.

'Anyway, apparently having me hanging off you would make it so much harder, if not impossible. At least if you were single, he could promote Broken as four unattached guys. Three single straight guys and one who couldn't make up his mind, but was also in a relationship, wasn't going to work for him.

'I hated what he was saying and how he talked about you, but all I kept hearing was the part about you losing your place in the band. He said he'd say horrible things about you in the industry, so no one would ever give you a break.'

He reaches out and takes her hand. 'If it came down to you or Vox, I would have walked away from Vox.'

'But don't you see? I didn't want that.'

'Broken would have still existed with, or without Vox. We made a deal a long time ago that it was a *one for all* kind of thing. We're all in, or none of us are. The four of us would have walked.'

'That's worse. I would have been to blame for all of you—'

'Stop! Louis was the only one to blame. He fucked this up.' Hearing what he just did infuriates him. He's downright fucked off. Hiding his sexuality was shite and he hated that, but losing Ash was so much worse.

'Broken Chords began in Tate's barn. If we were doing regular jobs and meeting up every weekend in that same barn, that would have been fine with all of us.'

'But you've achieved so much. All the fame, the awards. You and the guys are known all around the world. You have an incredible career.'

'All the fame, the money, the craziness - it's great, don't get me wrong. But...'

All I wanted was you. All I've ever wanted was you.

This is his fault. Had he not told her often enough how much he loved her? She shouldn't have doubted how much she meant to him. If she did, that's on him. 'What about Freya though? Why didn't you tell me about her? All the other stuff I get. I really do. But I don't understand why you kept her a secret.'

Ash puts her cup on the table. 'I was scared.'

'Of what? Me?'

'Yes, but not in that way,' she adds quickly. 'More that I was scared of seeing you again.'

'Why?'

'Because leaving you was the single most difficult, heartbreaking thing I've ever had to do. I didn't think I could survive seeing you again. It was selfish I know, but I was scared. And then Broken hit the top of the charts.'

She smiles as she looks up at him. 'I was so proud of you Dillon. So proud you were living your dream. I knew then that I'd done the right thing for you. If I had showed up on your doorstep with a child, that would have messed everything up for you. I thought it was better to leave us in the past.'

'But you were never in the past. Do you have any idea how this messed me up? I thought you left because I'm bi. Louis didn't help. He told me you probably left because I *fucked* men. What woman would want to be with a guy who had been with men too? His words.'

'Bastard! Your sexuality has never been an issue for me. Not for a second. Please tell me you know that?'

'I thought you were okay with it, but then you left. I didn't know why you left. Maybe it was because of that? Maybe it was because you didn't love me? You weren't there to ask, so my mind went on its own fucked up adventure.'

'I can't ever make this up to either you or Freya. I know that. I've kept you both from each other for ten years. Kept her father from her, and your daughter from you. It was unfair and cruel. All I can say is that I thought I was doing the right thing. For both of you. And as the years went on, I couldn't come clean to either of you.

'I know you'll never be able to forgive me for that, and you shouldn't. Freya may never forgive me either and I'll have to deal with that. Whatever happened between us is separate to you and Freya. I had no right to do what I did to both of you. And I did think of telling you about her. When I got this assignment, I tried so many times to tell you, but I chickened out.'

'It probably didn't help that I was a dick.'

'It was deserved.'

'No Ash. It wasn't.' He leans forward, resting his arms on his knees. 'After my parents disowned me, I blamed myself. I've been doing that

317

for as long as I can remember. Every time something shit happened, it was my fault. I've been pushing people away for years. It was easier to be alone than risk fucking things up.

'When you left like you did, it killed me, Ash. And now I get why you left. I'm not having a go about that. I'm just explaining. I turned into a complete dick who used and abused everyone in my life instead of letting anyone close.

'But I never stopping thinking about you. Never stopped loving you. But this thing with Freya... it fucking hurts Ash. I know what it's like to have parents who didn't give a fuck about me. Her father hasn't been there for her. How do I fix that? Should I even try?'

'What do you mean should you try? Do you not want to meet her?'

He chews his lip ring. Yes, he's a father, but that doesn't necessarily mean he should be a dad to her. Maybe keeping out of her life would be the best thing he can do for her.

'Don't shut down now. We need to get all our cards on the table. Please Dillon.'

'I'm not exactly what you'd call a half decent role model. All she has to do is stick my name into any search engine, and she'll get a long and very detailed breakdown of my life. She'll find out about my sex life, the drugs, and drink. That I have a criminal record. That I was in prison for a month. There are pictures of me with guys, all over the net, Ash. Details about what I do with them.' He scrubs a hand over his face and groans to himself. 'Fuck, that's going to get her kicked off any play date lists.'

'Dillon—'

'I spent my entire life feeling like an outsider. Like I wasn't normal. I don't want that for my daughter. I'd prefer to keep away from her altogether than to fuck up her life like that. I'll support both of you no question. You know that. I'll make it official if you want. Child support or whatever. I want to do right by you both.'

Then just be with us.

318

'I'm not interested in your money. Never have been. It's you I want and have always wanted. The fantasy of the three of us being a family has played on my mind for a decade.

'I'm not going to force you to be part of my life and I'm absolutely not going to force you to be a father to Freya. But don't for one second suggest that you're not good enough to be an incredible father to her. Don't you dare!

'Your life experience is what makes you such an amazing role model. You've seen and done so much. You'll be able to talk to her, with the experience behind you. That's invaluable, Dillon. We can address each point as it comes up with her. Discuss it with her together.'

'And what about having a father who's bi?'

'So what? It's a different world to the one we grew up in. That will not be an issue. I promise.'

'And what about all the shit with Clara? How do I explain that? I don't get it myself. How the fuck am I supposed to help her understand when I don't?'

Ash grabs his hand, squeezing it firmly. 'Look at me.' She waits as he meets her eyes. 'We will deal with your family stuff together. What matters right now is you and Freya. You are a caring, thoughtful, loyal, incredibly strong, resilient, massively protective man and I know Freya will be just as proud of you as I am.'

'What about us?' He wants her. Dillon has never been more sure of anything in his life. He wants Ash and Freya in his life. Wants to be a family with them.

Ash runs her thumb over his hand. 'I think that all comes down to whether you can ever forgive me for leaving you and keeping Freya a secret.'

He's thought about that a lot over the last few days. Leaving him and the whole Freya situation, are two different things. But if he's to have any chance of a future with her, he needs to move on.

'I get why you left. I'm not going to lie, I'm fucked off it happened, but there's nothing we can do about that. And Freya... we can't change that either. What I do know is that I love you, Ash. I want to be with you, and I'd like to try to be there for our daughter... if you'll let me?'

'Let you? You have as much right to be in her life as I do. Not that it means much after this long.'

'I forgive you. Can you forgive me?'

'Forgive you? For what?'

'Letting you go.'

'There's nothing to forgive. I made sure you couldn't find me.'

'Do you think you could love a stubborn, seriously messed up asshole like me?'

'That's an easy question. I've never stopped loving you for one single minute of the last ten years. I love that you're stubborn, and you are not messed up. What you are is a survivor. Someone who sticks his finger up at life and just carries on. You're strong, and loyal, and without doubt the sexiest man I've ever met. Why wouldn't I be head over heels in love with you?'

Now for the part he's not looking forward to. The part that may change her mind about being with him. 'I need to do something before I can be with you, and definitely before having anything to do with Freya.'

'What is it?'

'I'm heading to rehab tomorrow. I just wanted to get the tour out of the way. And fix things with you of course. But I can't put it off any longer.'

'Tomorrow! Oh. I mean that's great. Sorry, I just wasn't expecting you to say that. What made you decide to get help?'

He doesn't know if it's a good or bad thing that she's not surprised.

'Ellen threatened to bench me otherwise. But it was said for the right reasons. She really cares about the four of us. Fuck knows why! All we seem to do is give her trouble.'

'If Ellen hadn't given you the ultimatum, would you have suggested it?'

'No. But that's because I'm in so deep I don't realise how fucked I am. Part of the whole addiction game, I guess. I think I needed her to give me no choice.'

'I'll be with you every step of the way.'

'No.'

'What do you mean?'

'I don't want you anywhere near me while I'm getting my shit sorted. I can't do it if I know you're there, watching me fall apart like that. The only way I'm going to get through rehab is if it means I get to see you again once I'm done - not before.'

'So, no contact at all? For how long?'

'When I had my assessment yesterday, they said maybe two months? Depends how I get on. It's not just painkillers I've to get off, there's drink too. Really fucked myself over. It won't be a quick fix. But I have to do it and stick with it. For you guys, the band, and for me.

'I'm sick of just existing, Ash. Sick of drinking and using, just to get myself through the day. I'm forty now. It's about time I stop blaming the world for screwing over my life and take ownership of it. That starts with getting clean, so then I can be a half decent father to Freya, and someone who deserves to be loved by you.' He reaches out and wipes her face. 'Hey. Why are you crying?'

'You have no idea how happy I am to hear you say all that. But are you sure about doing this alone? I want to be there for you.'

'Just wait for me. Be there when I get out.'

She gets up and sits on his knee, wrapping her arms around him. 'I've waited for you for ten years. I think I can manage a few more months.'

Dillon

Eighty long, fucking painful days.

Tate hadn't mentioned much about his time in rehab, and now he knows why. Nothing about what happened over the last two and a half months will ever be mentioned again. Humiliating doesn't even come close to describing the experience.

But that's what it took to undo all the crap he'd done to himself over the years. It took longer than he thought to be discharged, but he'd survived. He'd done everything they asked of him. He talked, he cried, he opened up about all the shit he'd desperately kept buried for decades.

And survived is the right word. He hated it. Every single second was hell, a torture he never wanted to experience again. The doctors and therapists are happy with his progress. But he's not. Far from it.

Fair enough he's clean. No drink. No drugs. That part worked a treat. It's all the other stuff he hadn't even thought about that's giving him the problems.

He lost a piece of himself in the process. He thought he was lost before, wandering through his life, living from day to day. But stepping out the door of the centre, he has never felt more lost, more alone, more unsure of himself than ever before. It's like his armour has been stripped from him, and it's not a feeling he likes. He fucking hates it.

But then all that gets pushes aside.

She's here!

Standing beside Jason's car, leaning on the bonnet, looking more gorgeous than he remembers. She came! She waited for him.

She said she would, but that didn't mean he believed she would. He wouldn't have blamed her if she'd made a run for it again.

Positive thinking.

Fuck positive thinking! He's not exactly a prize. More like the booby prize if anything.

Great to see the positive thinking part is going a treat so far.

She smiles and waves at him. God she is so beautiful. And she's here for him. Dillon takes a deep breath and walks towards her. As he gets closer, he can't help but smile. She's more than a sight for sore eyes. The woman is fucking stunning. 'Hey.'

She races towards him, jumping into his arms and wrapping her legs around his waist. 'God, I missed you!'

Before he can say anything, she kisses him, groaning against his mouth as she tugs at his hair.

'You taste incredible. Sorry,' she mutters, pulling away from him. 'Got a little carried away there.'

'Don't apologise. What are you doing here? Not that I'm not glad to see you. I just wasn't expecting you. I thought you'd be in the UK.'

'Why would I be over there? The man I love can come home today.

I've been counting down the hours, Dillon. There's nowhere else in the world I'd be except here.'

'Really? You still love me? Still want me?'

'Of course I do you stunningly irritating man. I told you I'd wait for you.'

'Yeah, but I didn't...'

She shuts him up by taking hold of his face in her hands and touching her nose to his. 'Look at me. I fucking love you.'

Dillon laughs then kisses her. 'I fucking love you too.'

'Good. Fancy getting out of here?'

'Please. I'm done with this place.'

Once she dismounts him Jace walks over and hugs him. 'Good to see you. Damn it! Never thought I'd say that,' he adds with a grin.

'I've been a bit of a dick, haven't I?'

Jace nods. 'No worse than some I've been assigned to. You good?'

'Yeah. Getting there. Can you take me home?'

Jace opens the back door of his car. 'It would be my pleasure.'

The drive back to Dillon's cottage is strangely polite. The conversation flowed easily enough but it wasn't *her* Dillon she was talking to. The man she picked up from rehab is far more subdued, more in his head than he was before.

She knew the two and a half months away from his friends, from his family, would take their toll on him. But she wasn't prepared for how quiet he is.

Maybe he just needs time to readjust? He's all about his privacy so no doubt being in a situation where he had to talk would have been exhausting.

He unlocks the door to his cottage and goes inside, taking a few minutes just to look around. 'It's a lot bigger than I remember.'

'It's not exactly a small house.'

'Yeah. I guess after spending the last two and a half months living with too many other people, it seems bigger.'

Ash rubs his arms, waiting until he looks at her before she speaks. He's exhausted, the impressive black rings around his eyes can be seen from across the room. 'Are you hungry? I can order us some take away?'

'Yeah. That sounds good. I'll just grab a shower and get changed first. I can still smell that place on me.'

She wraps her arms around his neck and kisses him. 'Oh. You're right. There is a bit of a strange smell off you.'

'Okay. I'm going before you throw another insult at me.' He smirks and grabs his bag off the floor.

She finds the pile of take away menus in a drawer in the kitchen, but has second thoughts. Leaving them on the counter, she follows him to the bathroom, watching from the corridor as he strips out of his clothes, then examines his reflection in the mirror.

He's far from happy with what he sees, but to her he's every bit as gorgeous as ever.

His hair needs a cut, and his beard isn't as closely trimmed as usual, but he still looks incredible. He was in shape before rehab, but he's put on a fair bit of definition since he was gone. No doubt he was taking advantage of the well-equipped gym at the centre.

Ash watches as he gets into the shower and turns on the water before she takes off her clothes and joins him in the bathroom. He rests his hands against the wall then drops his head to his chest as the powerful water pounds into his shoulders running down the huge wings tattooed onto his back.

He's spectacular, even slightly withdrawn, and unsure of himself as he is right now. He needs to be pulled out of his head, but she doesn't want to be with him his way. Not today.

Sex with Dillon is always energetic and extreme, but being with him like that right now wouldn't feel right. It's not what he needs.

He smiles at her over his shoulder when she opens the shower then holds out her hand.

'Come with me.'

He takes her hand and allows her to lead him, still dripping wet, into his bedroom. She pulls him onto the bed, then lies down with him, holding him in her arms for a few minutes.

She missed him so much over the last two months. Going on tour with Dillon and the band has spoilt her to a certain degree. Over the time on the road she'd become used to having him around all the time.

She went from that to no contact at all and that was the hardest part. She missed seeing him, missed talking to him, missed having him there.

And she desperately missed being with him.

The last time they were together was just after Clara told him the truth. The night he sang to her in Croke Park had been spent in his bed, just holding each other and talking until he left for rehab the following morning.

She shuffles back from him and tilts his head. God, she missed those eyes. But she wishes there was less sadness in them.

Ash kisses him, slowly and tenderly, just familiarising herself with him again. He still tastes of apple, and it brings a tear to her eye.

'Hey, why are you crying?'

'Oh, ignore me, Dillon. I just missed you so much. I think it's just sinking in that you're back with me.'

He brushes his fingers through her hair. 'I missed you too. Thank you for waiting for me. I honestly didn't think you would. It was such a fucking relief to see you when I walked out of the centre.'

'Yeah well, I'm not going anywhere Dillon. Never again. I swear I'll never let anyone, or anything drive me away from you. I love you.'

'I know. I love you too. So, so much.'

He gathers her in his arms, rolling her onto her back as he kisses her. Their hands move slowly as they gently caress each other. This isn't about control or dominance. This is two people, madly in love with each other, reuniting after being apart.

She takes a condom from his drawer, desperate to feel him inside her again. Desperate to have that connection with him. He slides in, his powerful body hovering above hers as he moves slowly, giving her time to adjust to him.

He feels better than she remembers, those addictive piercings rubbing against all the right places. He lowers onto her, kissing her as he moves, his tongue and hips keeping perfect time with each other.

He's being so careful, so tender with her and she loves it. His slow, steady thrusts are nearly more intense than when he's being dominant. The tenderness of his touch, of his movements is a side to him she's never seen before but could get used to.

His firm body presses against hers, the rhythmic movement of his hips increasing as they both near orgasm.

Dillon's hand slides between them, his thumb massaging her clit, pushing her over the edge. His own orgasm follows soon after, sending an impressive shudder through his body.

When she comes down, she opens her eyes to find him looking at her, a huge smile on his face. 'Hey.'

She laughs, kissing him again. 'Hey yourself. What's that grin for?'

'Just happy.'

'That's a good answer.'

He slides out and deals with the condom before pulling the duvet over them and gathering her in his arms. 'Can I just hold you for a bit? I just want to lie here with you.'

'You never have to ask.'

As she lies on his chest, listening to the steady, reassuring beat of his heart, she realises what just happened.

Dillon Ryan made love to her.

Dillon

He'd thought about this moment every minute of the last two months. Even though she said she'd wait for him, he didn't really believe it or expect it.

When you're at your lowest, barely able to control your own body, you think the worst possible things about yourself. In his head, he was sure she'd leave him again. She'd take Freya, find someone better, and he'd be in the past yet again.

But this time it would be entirely down to him.

If he had been able to resist, or even keep control of his drink and drug use, he wouldn't have had to go to rehab. If he'd been stronger, he wouldn't have had to go through the most painfully humiliating experience of his life.

If he'd been better at dealing with all the shit in his life instead of hiding behind drink and drugs, he wouldn't have been lying awake at night wondering if she would be there for him when he got out.

She sighs contentedly, snuggling closer to his side. But not only had she waited, she's asleep in his bed now, after helping to bring him out of his head.

They'd made love. It wasn't sex. It wasn't a fuck. It was love and that's a first for him.

He'll be grand. It'll take time, but he's sure he'll be back to his old self in no time. If he can even remember what that was. Maybe, a new improved old self, if there's such a thing? He won't go back. Not after everything he just went through. No fucking way.

Moving slowly, he opens his bedside drawer, smiling at the

engagement ring on the chain safely tucked away. He wasn't going to wear it to rehab in case he lost it, but he's also not going to put it back on again.

It's been a part of his life for so long, a constant reminder of what he lost.

He doesn't need to wear it any longer. He's got something so much better. He's got Ash. He slides the drawer closed again and smiles to himself. He still wants to marry her, no question of that. But not yet.

There's time. For now, he just wants to enjoy getting to know her all over again.

Ash stirs, cupping the side of his face as she wakes up. 'Morning gorgeous.'

He hugs her close, then kisses her. 'It's dinner time. Haven't got to the morning yet! Are you okay?'

She stretches then smiles up at him. 'Okay? No. I'm so far beyond that. I'm happier than I've been for a long time. I've got you back.'

Hearing her say all that brings a fucking huge smile to his face. 'Same. All thanks to you. I'm sorry about the last few months, about not keeping in touch with you much, but I had to do this on my own.'

'Hey! Stop that. I understand. That time was about you one hundred percent. I can't put into words how proud I am of you. Unbelievably proud. And I promise, I am here for you from now on. Talk to me, or not. I know you. But just use me whenever you need to. Let me help you keep hold of this.'

'Thanks. I will. I'm not saying I'm now an expert on talking and sharing my feelings, or anything like that. Far from it. But I have a therapist to help with that. I just need you to give me a good kick if I turn into a moody shite again. I'm done with that.'

'That sounds good. But don't lose all that attitude. I like it.'

'Fuck no! I'm still me. No changing that. I'll always have a little too much attitude for my own good.'

'Phew!' She falls quiet as she strokes her thumb over his cheek.

'Okay, I'm just going to say this, but I'm honestly not putting any pressure on you.'

'Sounds ominous.'

'Yeah, it does a little with that lead up. Okay, so I was wondering, would you like to meet Freya? There's no rush. I just thought it might be as good a time as any. I could bring her over next weekend. But if it's too soon I understand.'

That's another thing he's been thinking about nonstop. He wants to meet her. Desperately does. But he's fucking terrified too, for so many reasons. But there's one thing that is so much stronger than any fear he's experiencing.

His parents fucked him over. There's no way he's doing that to his own daughter. No fucking way! 'How about tomorrow? I'm off the clock for another few weeks. I could fly over with you to meet her on her own turf. Might make things a little easier on her. If that's okay?'

'Tomorrow? But there's no time to arrange a flight?'

'Of course there is. I'll organise a helicopter or private plane to bring us over to the UK.'

She laughs at that. 'Of course you will! I forgot who I was talking to for a minute. But seriously, that would be amazing. She'll be so excited to meet you.'

'You think?

'I know. It'll be fine, Dillon. I sat her down a few weeks ago and told her everything.'

'How did she take it?'

Ash grimaces. 'She's your daughter. How do you think she took it?'

'Not great I'm guessing. Is she okay with you?'

'I got the silent treatment for a few days after a lot of shouting and slamming of doors. She was angry I didn't tell her about you. Of course she was. But I told her the truth. I told her I was trying to do the best thing for everyone, and I got it wrong.

'It took a lot of talking but she understands. We're good now. Not only that, but she really wants to meet her dad. Trust me.'

He wants to believe her, but this is such a big deal. And as little as he knows about kids, he knows one thing. A ten-year-old girl isn't going to be so easy to win over.

38

Dillon

This is ridiculous. He can sing in front of thousands of people. He can handle tough interview questions. Completely nail TV performances. He can do this.

Dillon gets off the chair and paces the small living room of Ash's house, keeping his focus on the large pot plant in the corner. That'll be his go-to spot in case he needs to throw up. Not ideal in any way, but the way his stomach is churning it'll do as an option.

'Yeah, real classy, Dillon. Throw up in a pot plant. Idiot!'

He shakes his head and continues to pace, but it's doing nothing to settle his nerves. Nothing he does will help with that.

He's meeting his daughter for the very first time in a few minutes, and he couldn't be more unprepared for something if he tried. How can you prepare to meet your daughter? And it's not like he's meeting a baby. Freya is going to talk to him. She might ask him questions. Possibly awkward questions he won't be able to answer. Or won't want to answer.

Ash had done her best to put him at ease, but for the entire helicopter flight, he'd been running through every single possible scenario. What if she didn't like him? What if she didn't want to meet him at all? What if he got to the house and she refused to come out of her room? What if the whole rock star celebrity thing freaked her out?

Jace was keeping his distance for that very reason, staying in the car outside Ash's house. Knowing that her father needs a bodyguard to protect him when he's in public isn't exactly reassuring.

He just wants to make a good first impression. He needs to make a good impression. He straightens his t-shirt again, grimacing at his reflection in the mirror over the fireplace when he passes by.

Ash may have insisted he be himself, but he'd still made a bit of an effort. His t-shirt isn't as tight and doesn't show as much of his chest as it usually does. His jeans are less ripped, and his boots aren't as scuffed. As his wardrobe goes, it's his Sunday best.

Dillon straightens his t-shirt again and wipes his damp palms on the legs of his jeans. This is a fucking joke. He eyes the pot plant again as his stomach threatens to embarrass him. Nerves had never affected him. But this is so much different. This is meeting a whole new person that he created with Ash.

He moves towards the plant pot but stops when Ash opens the door a little and peers into the room. 'You okay?'

'Yeah. Great. Perfect.'

'Really? Cause you look like you're going to be sick.'

'Me? No. It's all good.'

Ash smiles, then opens the door wide, leading Freya into the room. Ash sits on the armchair and he sits on the one opposite. Freya perches on the arm of her mother's chair and examines him.

She's even more beautiful than her photo. He can see a lot of Ash in her, but he's definitely in there too. Her eyes are the exact same shade of green as his, and she absolutely has his nose. Dillon smiles at his daughter, but he feels completely out of his depth.

Fuck that! He's in some alternative universe and he couldn't feel less comfortable if he tried. What does he do now? How do you begin a conversation like this?

As father and daughter examine each other, Freya crosses her arms and gives him a no-nonsense look. She's got a bit of his attitude too, and he fucking loves it.

Before Ash or Dillon can say a word to help get things going, she takes charge of the conversation. 'Mum said you're famous.'

'Me? Yeah. I am. I play bass in a band.'

'Broken Chords, right?'

'Yeah. You've heard of us?'

She laughs as she rolls her eyes. 'Eh, yeah! Of course I have. I like Gregg. He's my favourite band member.'

Ash covers her face. 'Seriously, Freya...'

She turns to give her mother an exasperated look. 'What? He is. I like the drums. There's not a lot to playing the bass is there?'

'Not a lot to it? There's a hell of a lot to it actually.'

'Dillon!'

Now it's his turn to give Ash the look. 'What! There is.'

'I never said there wasn't,' Ash says.

'There are only four strings, Mum. How hard can it be?'

He shuffles forward to the edge of the seat. 'Hang on. Do you have any idea how many hours of lessons I took to play those four strings. I'll give you a hint. A lot!'

Ash slumps back in the armchair, covering her face. 'I can't believe the first conversation you two are having is an argument. Actually, I don't know why I'm surprised. I should have been expecting it.'

'We're not arguing, Mum. We're debating whether he picked an easy instrument instead of something more challenging.'

'Easy! Okay. I'll teach you the bass. Give me a week and I'll prove to you it's not as easy as you think.'

Ash laughs and shakes her head. 'You walked right into that one, Dillon. That was her plan all along.'

Freya grins as she crosses her arms. 'It might have been.'

Fuck! She is one hell of a firecracker. Freya is so much like him it's scary. He was just like her when he was a kid. 'Well played! You manipulated me. Good one.'

'Thank you. I'll need a bass too of course.'

He laughs. 'Figured as much. I'm sure I can give you one of mine for now.'

Freya nods her head. 'I guess that will work for now. So, are you mega rich or just moderately rich?'

'Freya,' Ash scolds. 'You don't ask someone that.'

'It's fine, Ash. I guess I earn a fair amount, yeah.'

'So you have houses all over the world? Flash cars and things like that?'

'No. I own a few houses in Ireland, but nowhere else. I do like cars though. I have six and a motorbike.'

'Six! Nice.' She leans a little closer, then frowns. 'Does that ring in your lip hurt?'

'No. Well, at first it did, yeah. But not anymore.'

'Do you have any more piercings?'

Ash flashes him a look. Yeah, like he's going to be honest about that one. 'My tongue too. That's it.'

'Ouch! Can I see it?'

'Freya!'

'No, it's fine, Ash. Really.'

Freya gets up and walks over to him. He sticks out his tongue and she grimaces. 'It looks sore.'

'It's just like getting your ears pierced. Once it heals you don't feel it anymore.'

'Mum won't let me get my ears pierced yet,' she mutters, glaring over her shoulder at Ash.

'I said you can when you're a little older.'

'That's what you say about everything. Hey! Do you want to see my Guinea pigs?'

'Your what?' Her mind is as quick as his. Piercings one second, the next, Guinea pigs.

'My pet Guinea pigs. I have two outside.'

'Sure.'

He follows Freya outside to the patio and watches as she takes a brown and white guinea pig from its hutch. 'This is Riggs, and the other one is Murtagh.'

'Bit young for Lethal Weapon, aren't you?'

'They're Mum's favourite films. She's always talking about them, so I called them after the two guys.' She hands him Riggs, then picks up Murtagh and sits on the ground rubbing the Guinea pig. Dillon sits beside her and crosses his legs.

He's letting her take the lead in this. His experience talking to kids is non existent. Eva has two kids but they're not that close. He has no idea how to be around kids.

'Mum said that you knew her years ago. That you were her boyfriend.'

'Yeah. We dated for a few months.'

'Did you love her?'

He nods, his throat suddenly drying. 'Yeah. A lot.'

'She said you're my dad.'

Dillon swallows and nods. 'Yeah. I am. You okay with that?'

She nods, as she rubs the Guinea pig on her lap. 'I think we look alike.'

'We do. We've got the same colour eyes.'

'Mum always said that. She used to say that she was reminded of you whenever she looked at my eyes. I think she liked that. She wouldn't tell me anything about you, but I think me having eyes like yours made her happy. It made her sad too. I heard her crying sometimes. I think she really missed you.'

'I missed her too.'

'How do you feel about having a ten-year-old daughter?'

'Honestly, I'm nervous. Excited to get to know you of course. But this is very new to me. I'm not great with kids.'

'You'll be fine. And you're my first dad so I'm nervous too. I've always wanted a dad. I never thought I'd have a famous one though. That's pretty cool! When Mum told me who you were I Googled you.'

Fuck!

That's not what he wanted to hear. He was hoping to have a few years to get to know her before he had to broach any of that shit.

'You're bisexual, right?'

He nods, wishing Ash would come out of the house and save him. 'You know what that means?'

She rolls her eyes again. 'I'm nearly eleven. Of course I know what it means. You're attracted to men and women. So have you had boyfriends and girlfriends?'

Where the fuck are you, Ash?

'Yeah...'

He desperately wants to change the subject, needs to change it fast, but he doesn't know her well enough to have the first clue what to change it to.

'That's cool.'

'It is?'

'Sure. My friend in school, Gabby. Well, her dad is married to another man now. They got married a few months ago.'

'Right.'

'Love is love, right? That's what Mum keeps saying.'

He can't help but smile at that. 'Yeah. Love is love.'

'And you've been in prison.'

'I have.'

'Actions have consequences. That's something else Mum says. You must have done something you really shouldn't have.'

'I've done a lot of things I shouldn't have. I've made a lot of mistakes over the years.'

'I get in trouble a lot too. I'm not a fan of being told what to do.' She shrugs as she strokes the Guinea pig. 'I suppose I get that from you too.'

'Maybe.'

'I wonder what else we have in common?'

'Would you be okay with meeting up again? Maybe getting to know each other a bit more? See what else we share.'

Her face lights up at that, which is such a fucking relief. He's making this up as he goes, completely out of his depth.

'You want to be my dad?'

The best he can do initially is a nod. He wasn't expecting her to get to him on this level so fast. 'Yeah. I do.'

'Me too. And you don't have to look so scared talking to me. You're not going to do or say the wrong thing with me.'

'Like I said, this is all new to me. I don't want to mess it up.'

'You won't. And I know Mum didn't tell you about me. I know it's not your fault you didn't see me until now.'

'Things were complicated. Your mum did what she felt was right for you. For me too. Things are different now though and it's all good.'

'Hey, if you're famous and you're my dad, does that make me famous too?'

Dillon laughs at that. 'Sure, why not!'

39

Ash

'He's really nice.'

Ash smiles as she tucks Freya into bed. 'I'm so glad you like him. I know you were nervous about meeting him, but you did brilliantly. Although, that whole Gregg and drums part was unnecessary.'

'It got him talking.'

'Hang on. Was that why you did that?'

'He was nervous too. I thought he was going to be sick. I was trying to distract him.'

She can't believe Freya did that. When she called her to say Dillon would like to meet her, she'd instantly fallen silent. Freya only does that when she's not sure about something. While she was excited to finally meet her father, nerves had taken hold as expected. It was a massive moment for both Dillon and Freya. For herself too.

Watching father and daughter having a go at each other like they did was incredible. It's not difficult to see where Freya gets her argumentative streak from.

'Well, it certainly worked. Just remember, it's important you keep being honest with me, okay? If you're not sure of anything, or if you've any questions please ask. This is new for all of us. We're going to take things slowly. Give all of us time to get used to things.'

'Is he staying?'

'Here? In the house?'

'Yeah.'

'We hadn't planned for him to stay. He needs to go back to Ireland in the morning for work. I think he's spending the night at a hotel near the airport.'

'Oh. Can he not stay here? I wanted to make him pancakes in the morning. His bodyguard can stay too.'

'His bodyguard?'

'Yeah. The guy sitting outside in the car watching the house. I'm not an idiot. I know Dillon would have someone minding him. All the famous people do.'

'And you're okay with that?'

Freya shrugs. 'Can you ask Dillon to stay?'

'No problem. I'll talk to him, but right now I want you to get some sleep. Dillon and I have a lot of things to discuss. Goodnight.'

'Night Mum. Make sure he stays!'

Ash laughs, then closes the bedroom door. That went a lot better than she could have expected. The fact Freya wants him to stay is a big plus.

After making a coffee for each of them, Ash brings the drinks into the living room and places them on the coffee table. Seeing Dillon lounging on her couch is a sight she could easily get used to.

The last two months away from him had nearly seemed longer than the previous ten years. Knowing that there was a possibility they could finally be together as a family when he was discharged, had made the time crawl. Every single hour had felt like a lifetime.

Not being allowed to contact him hadn't helped pass the time any faster. He'd written to her a few times. Brief letters just saying he loved her and couldn't wait to see her again. Asking about Freya and saying that he was working hard to be a decent dad for her.

Working hard was the only mention of his treatment, or how he was dealing with being in the centre. That nearly said more to her than if he had told her all the details.

He had struggled. One look at him as soon as he stepped through the doors, had told her that much.

But he stuck with it and came out the other side, and she couldn't be prouder. He was different though. More subdued perhaps. Or was, until Freya had stepped into the room. The man sitting on her couch is different to the one she collected from rehab yesterday. And that's all down to Freya.

She hoped father and daughter would hit it off but watching that stunning rock star sitting cross legged on the grass in her garden, with a Guinea pig on his lap while he talked to his daughter, was a sight she will never forget. It brought tears to her eyes for all the right reasons.

'Everything okay?'

She shakes herself out of her thoughts and tucks in beside him. 'Couldn't be better. She knows about Jace. Spotted him in the car outside.'

'Fuck!'

'No! It's fine. She knows he keeps you safe. That's all she said about it. She was more concerned with making sure I ask you to stay the night. She plans on making you pancakes in the morning before you leave. Jace too of course.'

'Do you think that's a good idea?'

Ash shrugs as she sips her coffee. 'It's up to you and Freya. I told her you have to head back to Ireland tomorrow, so there's no pressure.'

'I'd like that, but I'll stay on the couch.

She nods, relieved he got there before she had to mention anything. 'I think that's for the best. Not that I don't want you in bed with me—'

'But it's too soon for her,' he interrupts. 'Is there a hotel or something nearby for Jace?'

'I've got a camp bed he can sleep on in my office. It's a tiny room but it's big enough for a bed.'

'I'll text him and let him know.'

As he sends Jace a message, Ash can't stop looking at him. Can't quite believe he's finally here.

'Stop staring at me.'

'I can't help it. You're here. You and Freya met each other. I still can't quite believe it.'

He lowers his phone, resting his head back against the sofa. 'I think it went okay. Did it?'

'It went more than okay.'

'I'm just fucking thrilled she wants to have anything to do with me. I was freaking out beforehand that she'd be off with me or tell me to fuck off.'

'If she told you to fuck off, she'd be up to her neck in trouble, believe me. But as for not wanting to have anything to do with you, that was never going to happen.' Ash smirks as she runs her finger along the rim of her mug. 'So, did you notice anything about her?'

Dillon nods and smiles proudly. 'She's me. Fucking attitude and not a fan of backing down.'

'Oh, so you picked up on that?'

'Picked up on it? It's hardly subtle.'

'You're telling me! She has this uncanny way of getting exactly what she wants, without you realising you've agreed to it.'

'Like me teaching her the bass?'

'Like that. Don't worry though. She won't hold you to that. I think it was just a test.'

'But I'd like that... if she meant it?'

'Really?'

'Too right. I can't have a daughter of mine preferring the drums to the bass. Not happening.'

'I should have guessed it would come down to that. But I really do think she'd love that.' They fall silent, so she decides to broach the subject she's been dreading for the last few hours. 'Dillon?'

He lifts his head, and his green eyes look so serious. 'What now, right?'

'You read my mind. I'm not trying to put pressure on you, but I'm just curious.'

He sits back and chews on his lip ring for a moment. 'I'm happy to move over here while we see how things go with all of us. I don't mean here, as in your house, but I could rent somewhere nearby. I want to be here for Freya.' He reaches out and takes her hand. 'I want to be here for you. For our family.'

'But your life is in Ireland. I'm not going to ask you to leave.'

'My life is with you two. Ash, I love you, and I want to be a father to Freya. I can't do that from the other side of the Irish Sea. I can still fly back to Ireland if I need to do anything with the band.

'Luke manages to live in a camper van driving around fucking Wales, so I think I can manage from here. I can do video calls with my therapist and fly back for any other appointments. If that's what you want? I'm happy to just go back and forth to see you both if you prefer?'

Hearing that he's more than willing to move his life over here to be with them, leaves her speechless. It's what she's always wanted. From the minute Freya was born, she'd wanted nothing more than for Dillon to suddenly appear on her doorstep and take them under his wing. Wishful thinking considering she'd been the one to stop that from happening.

But she's not going to take him from his life in Ireland, or away from the guys. Not now when he's just been discharged and needs stability, his friends, and professional support.

'How about we do it the other way around? Freya is on holidays in two week's time for the summer. I'm not saying we come over for the full three months, but we could go back and forth.'

'But what about your job?'

'I can do it remotely.'

'You... you'd do that?'

'In a heartbeat. I love Ireland and I really want to show Freya what it's like. She's never been. It would be a win for all of us. She gets a holiday. You get to stay near your therapist, and we can spend time together as a family.'

When he smiles, she nearly bursts out crying again. This man is so beautiful she can barely believe it at times.

'One condition.'

'Go on.'

'You both stay in the cottage. I'll use the apartment in town to give you both space. It's only an hour away, so I can spend as much time with you both as you want.'

'You'd let us stay there?'

'In a heartbeat,' he replies with a smile. He lifts her up, pulling her onto his knee. 'So, we're doing this? You're coming over to Ireland?'

She leans down and kisses him. 'Oh, we're doing it. It's time this family gets to know each other.'

'Starting with pancakes in the morning.'

His fingers trace down the side of her face, but he doesn't say anything. He just looks at her, almost as if he's committing her face to memory.

No one has ever looked at her the way he does. She can see so much love in his eyes, feel it in his touch. There's no doubt in her mind he adores her. Even after everything she did to him. After all the hurt she caused him, he still loves her.

'I'm sorry Dillon.'

'For what?'

'Everything. I'm so sorry.'

He cups her face in his hands, making sure she's looking at him. 'No apologies. It's done. All that matters is from today onwards. Our future. Nothing else.'

'How can you say that? I mean really say it and mean it?'

'Because I am completely in love with you Ashling. That's how I can say it. And come on, it's not like I've been a saint or anything. I'm less than two days out of rehab. I've fucked up so many times. Monumental fuck ups too.

'But it's in the past. I want you. I want Freya. I want to be happy. We can't do that if we keep beating ourselves up about what we did ten fucking years ago. If we're to have any chance, we need to move past all that. It's the only way.'

'Listen to you being all sensible.'

He smiles as he runs his thumb along her cheek. 'That's what very expensive therapy will do for you. I'm all deep and meaningful now.'

'Are you now? Deep and meaningful Dillon Ryan. That sounds interesting.'

'Loads of surprises to come.' He moves back a little and meets her eyes. 'So? We all good?'

'Yeah. We're all good.'

'Glad to hear it.'

When he pulls her close so he can kiss her, Ash finally allows herself to accept that he means what he's saying. It starts today, and she can't wait to see what the future holds.

40

Dillon

Time flies when you're having fun.

He's heard people say that so many times, but he never understood it. Time goes by. It doesn't go fast or slow. It just goes.

His family arrived in Ireland a week ago, but it seems like it was only yesterday when he collected them from the airfield.

He can't remember the last time he had fun. He's enjoyed things in the past. Being on tour, getting on stage, singing. They're all things he enjoys. Fucking loves in fact. But even messing around with the guys, he'd been trying to keep that wall up, that guard to protect himself.

He doesn't have to do that with Freya and Ash.

Shielding the guys from what was going on in his mind was his decision. Each of them had shit to deal with. Shit he tried to help them get through. There's no way they could have done that if they were worrying about him at the same time.

But this is his time. His time to find happiness. To find peace. To find love. So far so good.

As Dillon places the dirty dishes in the dishwasher, he realises how easy it would be to get used to this He'd spent the day with his girlfriend and daughter, then cooked them dinner. God, he loves cooking for them. He's going to have to up his gym workouts if he keeps cooking like this. His diet is a hell of a lot better than it used to be.

But more importantly, he's still clean and sober. Heading towards the four-month mark. He's not going to fall. No fucking way. Ash and Freya deserve a half decent boyfriend and father.

He'd prefer he didn't have the baggage he does, but there's fuck all he can do about that now. All he can do is keep heading down the right path from here on in.

Having his family so close is amazing. Really fucking amazing. Sharing his space had never been something he enjoyed but leaving them at the end of the evening to go back to his apartment in town is so hard.

But it's an arrangement that's working for them all. Freya needs time to get used to him. She can't do that with him hanging around all the time.

He turns on the dishwasher and leans against the counter, looking out into the living room. Freya's sweatshirt is lying on the couch. Her shoes are under the coffee table. And he fucking loves it.

The longer they're here with him, the more convinced he is that he wants to make this permanent. He wants the three of them to be like this all the time. He'll move to the UK if that's what it takes, but he'd love if they moved here. He wants them to live right here with him.

But how does he even go there with Ash? It's too much to ask. It would mean uprooting Freya from her friends, her school, her life. He can't do that to her.

'What time are you meeting the guys for rehearsals tomorrow?' Ash asks as she joins him in the kitchen.

Dillon puts a bag of popcorn in the microwave and sets the timer. 'About one, I think. Gregg has a doctor's appointment in the morning.'

'Is he okay?'

'Yeah. Well, I think so. He hasn't said otherwise. As far as I know it's just his regular diabetes check. He has them every now and again. The late start will give the coffee time to kick in with Tate too. He's a grumpy fucker otherwise.'

He grimaces when he remembers Freya. He's trying so hard to cut down on the cursing when she's around, which is proving difficult.

'She's still on the phone to her friend. Relax.'

'I'm trying to ease up, but it's fucking hard. See. Can't stop.'

She reaches up to kiss him on the cheek. 'Be you. Don't try to do anything different. So, I was wondering if we could meet you after you're finished. Maybe grab dinner or take out?'

'Do you both want to come to rehearsals?' He wasn't planning on just dropping that in like that, but it's out there now.

Introducing the guys to Freya is something he's been wanting to do for a while, but he's got no rule book when it comes to this. He's making it up as he goes.

'You mean meet the band? You want to do that?'

'Freya is part of my life now. They should meet her. I want them to. Is that okay?'

'Of course it is. I love them. And you're right. They should meet.'

'Who should meet?'

He can't help but smile when Freya appears, opening the microwave to take out the popcorn.

'I was wondering if you want to come to rehearsals with me tomorrow. Maybe meet the rest of the band?'

She turns around slowly, totally playing up the dramatics. 'You mean I can meet Gregg!'

'Oh fu—' He grunts when Ash elbows him in the ribs. 'Ouch!'

'She did that to stop you cursing around me,' Freya says matter-of-factly. 'I am ten. I have heard cursing before. And you do it a lot., Mum.'

'Yeah, well tell me off if I do.'

'I'd always be doing that,' she replies, grabbing a handful of popcorn and stuffing it in her mouth.

'Freya!'

She smiles sheepishly but takes another handful of popcorn. 'So I can meet the band?'

'Yeah,' he says. 'We'll probably head out for dinner when we're done. We usually work up an appetite.'

'The drums are hard work.'

He sticks out his tongue at Freya as she laughs at him, then disappears into the living room. 'Am I going to have to watch her idolising Gregg all morning?'

Ash wraps her arms around him, pulling him close. 'Drums are hard work.'

He picks her up and pins her back against the wall. 'You want to say that again?'

Ash kisses him, biting on his bottom lip as she pulls away. 'Drums are hard work. All that exertion. Getting all hot and sweaty like that. But I much prefer bassists. Big, strong, stubborn bassists.'

'I am not stubborn.'

She kisses him, gently tugging on his lip ring. 'Are too.'

'Not again!' Freya mutters as she walks back into the kitchen. 'Can you two not stop for even a minute?'

Dillon quickly places Ash back on the ground and smiles at his daughter. 'Sorry. Have you picked a film?'

'I have three options. I just need the popcorn and you two to stop smooching like that.'

He empties the popcorn into a bowl and passes it to Freya. 'Don't eat any yet. We'll be with you in a sec.'

'I'm timing you.'

'She will too,' Ash says, taking some glasses from the cupboard over the sink. 'Go on. I'll be there in a sec.'

He takes a packet of apple laces from the cupboard before going into the living room, sitting in his usual spot on the couch. As soon as he sits, Freya surprised him by shuffling closer to him. When she lies against his arm, his surprise gets ramped up to plain old shock.

What the fuck is he meant to do now? He wasn't expecting her to get so close. It's the first time she's really latched on to him like this.

Okay, so not freaking out would be a good start. If Clara or Eva did what she just did, he'd probably hug them closer. He can do the same with Freya. There's no doubt she'd push him away if that's not what she wants.

Moving slowly, he slides his arm out from under her. But she beats him to it, tucking under his arm and snuggling in against him. He lowers his arm, holding her close. This feels so good. It feels so right.

He looks over to the kitchen when he feels someone looking at him. Ash is quietly watching the two of them, her eyes shimmering with unshed tears. She's not the only one. He's fucking close to having an emotional moment himself.

'Hey, stop standing there, and sit down with us.'

Ash sits on his other side, helping herself to some popcorn from the bowl resting on his lap. He wraps his arm around her shoulder, kissing the top of her head before he starts the film.

'She'd like to say goodnight to you?'

Dillon swallows the apple lace he's chewing, barely avoiding choking on it. 'She wants to what?'

Ash drops onto the couch next to him. 'She'd like to say goodnight to her dad.'

Sounds easy enough, but he just wasn't expecting it. Freya is taking to their new relationship a lot faster than he is.

He knocks on the spare room door and waits until he hears the *yep* before he steps inside. Freya is tucked up in his spare bed, her things scattered all over the room. Ash is a clean freak, so clearly, she gets her messy streak from him too.

'Your mum says you want to say goodnight?'

Freya pats the bed beside her, so he sits down, completely out of his depth. His parents would do this with Clara and Eva, but never with him. He was told to go to bed and that was it. Just him alone in his room, crying himself to sleep every night. There was never any big, emotional display.

'You need anything?'

'Are you kidding? I've got my own bathroom! With a bath! And it's the size of a swimming pool. I love this room. It's so much bigger than my room at home.'

'Glad you like it. I better let you get some sleep.'

'Dillon? Can I ask you something? You don't have to say yes.'

'Go for it.'

She twirls the corner of the duvet cover around her finger. He hasn't seen her come across as nervous as this before.

'Would it be okay if I called you Dad instead of Dillon?'

His heart beating loudly in his ears is the only thing he can hear for however long he takes to process what she just said. It's probably only a few seconds at the most, but in that moment, it could be a lifetime.

He knew this is what he wanted in his life. Ever since he held Tate's son in his arms, he knew he wanted... hoped, to be a father. Hoped he could someday give his own child everything he missed out on.

But hearing his daughter ask to call him dad is nothing he could have prepared for. No fucking way.

'Dillon? Are you okay?'

He nods, or at least he thinks he does. Everything is still a little surreal.

'Are you going to faint? You're not going to throw up, are you?'

'No. No, I'm good.' He's more than good. He's fucking flying. 'You really want that?'

Freya nods, seeming a little unsure of herself. Join the club. 'It's okay if you don't want that. I've just always wanted to call someone that. And you are my dad, so I thought I'd ask.'

'I'd love it. As long as you're sure, I'd really, really, love that.'

Her face lights up as she emerges out from under the thick duvet. She hugs him, wrapping her arms tight around his neck. Dillon hugs her back, unable to stop the tears that make an appearance. Thankfully, he's got them under control again by the time she releases him.

Freya tucks back under the duvet, the huge smile still on her face. 'Goodnight Dad.'

He stands up, needing to get away so he can break down in private. 'Goodnight Freya.'

He turns away but she stops him as he gets to the door. 'Dad?'

Now he's smiling like a fucking idiot. 'Yeah?'

'Nothing. I just wanted to say that again.'

Dillon blows her a kiss before closing the door and leaning against the wall to get himself together.

'Hey? What's wrong?'

He smiles at Ash as she rubs his arms. 'Nothing. It's all fucking perfect. She wants to call me Dad.'

Ash covers her mouth, her own tears joining his. 'What did you say?'

'I said yes. Of course I said yes.'

Ash

He's distracted. Has been all evening, but she didn't want to push him. The movie night was amazing. He'd even laughed and joked quite a bit with Freya, but as soon as she went to bed, he withdrew into his head.

Freya asking is she could call him dad had been such an incredible moment for him. For Freya too. But something is pulling him away from her every now and again. He stares into space, his thought dampening his mood again.

She had hoped he'd want to be with her tonight, but his head isn't in the right place for that either. At least he agreed to stay the night. She hates the thought of him staying late, then driving an hour back to his apartment.

His fingers trace up and down her arm as he stares at the ceiling. She can feel his heart racing in his chest, the rapid beating echoing as she lies on his chest. While she combs her fingers through his hair, she hums to him. It's worth a shot.

He turns his head and smiles at her. 'What are you doing?'

'You're over thinking something.'

He pulls her closer. 'Yeah. Probably always am. I like when you do that though. The humming thing. It relaxes me.'

'Do you want me to keep going?'

He nods, so she does as he asks, hoping it will help. It takes about five minutes, but he eventually relaxes a little.

'I think I need to talk to Clara.'

Dillon's sudden statement takes a few seconds to sink in. Well, that explains why he was in his head so much. She's been tempted to broach the subject with him a few times since they arrived, but she wasn't sure how to do it. Or even if it was a good idea.

She has no doubts it would have come up during his time in rehab. He wouldn't have kept it to himself and no therapist worth their money would have brushed over it without trying to help him.

Not that she's sure how that would even be possible. The entire situation has been going around in her head since he told her, and she still can't process it.

'Okay.' She's not sure what else to say to that. Knowing him, he'll either want to put things right with her, or put some space between them.

'Everything with you, me, and Freya has kind of made it hit home a little differently.'

Ash pushes onto her elbow and looks down at him. She hates that he seems to be struggling even talking about her. 'Hit differently how?'

'Ever since I was a kid, I've been fighting something. Whether it was fighting for attention, fighting my sexuality, fighting the crap in my head, fighting drink and drugs.' He pauses before continuing.

'Fighting my feelings for Luke and for you. Right now, I don't think I've any more fight left to give. I just want a bit of peace. Some time to get my life sorted. I'm barely clean four months. I can't let anything knock me off track. I've got too much to lose.'

She brushes her fingers through his hair, instantly calming him. 'What do you mean when you say you've no more fight to give?'

He looks out at the sea for a moment before turning his attention back to her. 'I can't have her in my life right now. I thought about it a lot while I was in rehab. Talked about it a lot too, but it doesn't matter how many times I thrash it out, I can't do it Ash.

'I can't accept what happened. I can't forgive what happened. And I don't think I can forgive Clara for lying to me for so long. I get why. I'm not a total dick. I do get it, but that doesn't mean I can forgive and forget. I have to shelve the whole thing for a while.'

'Shelve it? Really? Are you going to tell her?'

He nods as he looks up at her. 'I have to. It's not fair to have her waiting for something that I might not be able to give. It doesn't matter how much we want things to go back to the way they were - they can't. It's impossible.'

'I understand. I'm sorry for both of you, but you're right. You have to put yourself first.'

'I want to get it over with sooner rather than later. I'll talk to her in the morning before I go to rehearsals. Will you come with me? You can just stay in the car with Freya, but I don't think... '

She wraps her arms around him, resting her head against his chest. 'I'll be there. I'll always be there.'

Dillon

'Do you want me to go in with you?'

Dillon looks at Clara's house and shakes his head. 'It's better I do this alone. You get in the car and stay with Freya. She can spend some time with Jace. He's loving having two Ryan's to deal with.'

'I'm not so sure *loving* is the right word. He's still recovering from yesterday.'

Watching his daughter and bodyguard have a heated debate about whether football or rugby is better, went on for a good hour. Freya won of course. 'Yeah. He might still be a little sore after that.'

Ash takes his hand, lacing her fingers with his. 'Hey, Clara will understand. This is so much to process. It's understandable you need time.'

'I know, but it's going to hurt her. I know it will and I hate that. She's been through so much and I don't want to make things worse for her. I just can't deal with all this yet. I've just got you back in my life. I need to concentrate on you, Freya, and staying clean. That's all that matters right now.'

Ash leans over and kisses his cheek. 'Go on. I'll be here for you when you're done.'

Dillon waves at Freya as he pushes off the car then walks up the driveway. He's doing the right thing - for himself, for his girlfriend, and his daughter. He knows that. As tough as he thinks he is, even he can't handle everything that's been thrown at him lately. He missed out on ten years with Freya. He won't lose another second with her. She deserves a father who is there for her.

Marcus opens the front door and smiles when he sees him. 'Dillon. It's so good to see you. Come in.'

'Is she here?'

'In the living room. I'll give you some privacy.'

'Thanks, Marcus.'

Dillon takes a few seconds to get himself together before opening the living room door and facing Clara for the first time since that moment on the beach when the truth came out.

She smiles and closes her laptop, getting to her feet. 'Dillon! I'm so glad you're here. How are you?'

'Can I sit?'

'You don't have to ask.' He takes the armchair leaving her alone on the couch. 'How have you been?'

'Okay, considering. You?'

She nods. 'The same. I didn't think I'd see you again.'

'That's why I'm here.'

Her face drops. 'Oh. Okay.'

'A lot has happened to me over the last few weeks and it's only right I fill you in. Okay, so I have a daughter. She's ten and her name is Freya.'

Clara stares at him for a long few seconds before she breaks out into a large smile. 'You're a father! I'm a grandmother? Really? How? I mean obviously I know how. Sorry... this is all a bit of a shock.'

'I didn't know about her until recently, but to cut a long story short, I was in love with her mother when I was living in the UK. Things didn't work out and we lost contact until recently. We're together again, and I'm going to be the best fucking father that little girl could ever have.'

Clara wipes her tears and nods. 'Oh, I don't doubt that for even a second. I'm so happy for you, Dill. I really am.'

'Thanks.' And now for the part he's not looking forward to. 'Clara, I need to be there for Freya now. I have a lot of time to make up for - with both her and her mother. I can't deal with what you told me right now. I can't do it.'

She swallows and nods, wringing her hands together on her knees.

'Right. Okay, so what does that mean for us?'

'It means there is no us. Not for a while. I understand why you did what you did at the time. I really do. And I'm heartbroken for what you went through, but everything I thought I knew about my life was a lie. Everything. I need time to get my head around that.

'I've got a lot of shit to deal with, Clara. A lot to sort out. I've been to rehab. I've been clean and sober for ninety-eight days and I plan to keep adding to that tally.'

She smiles when he says that. 'That's great Dillon. I'm so proud of you. I really am.'

'Thanks. I need to focus on my daughter and getting my life straight again. But while I'm working on that I need space, Clara.'

'From me?'

He nods. 'I'm not saying we'll never sort this out. I hope we do, but I'm asking you to give me time.'

'Of course. Whatever you want. I love you Dillon and all I've ever wanted is what's best for you. I know I messed up. Believe me I know. Take as much time as you need. I'll be here when you're ready.'

'Thanks.' He pushes to his feet, hating how awkward this entire situation is. Before he found out who she really is, he'd lounge on the couch, completely relaxed with her. Now it's so uncomfortable. He's not even sure time will be able to fix this.

He doesn't want to hurt her, but right now, he can't give her what she needs. He can't hug her and say they're fine. Because they're far from it.

'I'll leave you to it.'

Clara nods, then wipes her face again.

'I'm sorry, Clara.'

'Hey. You have nothing to apologise for. Nothing at all. Can you just remember one thing for me?'

'What?'

'I love you, Dillon. That's never changed for one second since you were born. I love you and I am so unbelievably proud of the amazing, beautiful, strong, ridiculously stubborn man you've become. Whenever you feel like you're ready, I'll be here. I'll always be here for you.'

And now he feels like he's about to cry. 'Thanks, Clara. Goodbye.'

She nods and does her best to smile, but like him, there's not much to smile about. Dillon waves at Marcus, sitting at the kitchen table, but doesn't speak to him. Instead, he leaves the house and gets back in his car.

'So, Freya. You want to meet the guys?'

'Sure. Sounds good.'

Ash smiles at him as he starts the engine, but she leaves him to his thoughts, silently supporting him as he pulls away from the house.

When Freya reaches out to take his hand, he nearly stumbles and lands face down on Tate's expensive lawn. Fantastic impression to leave her with. On the other side, Ash walks beside him, her stunned expression telling him she was as surprised by what Freya did as he was.

He opens the door to Tate's garden studio and holds it back for Ash and Freya, then points to the couch at the side of the room. 'Sit here for sec and I'll get the guys.' He opens the inner door, closing it behind him after he goes inside.

'At long last,' Gregg says, lowering his drumsticks. 'We've been waiting for you.'

'Yeah. Sorry. I went to see Clara. I had to tell her I need time.'

'Damn. Sorry buddy,' Gregg says. 'How are you doing?'

He shrugs. 'I'm not sure. It was harder than I thought.'

Luke hugs him, holding on to him for a good minute before releasing him.

Enough. He'll deal with Clara when he's ready. For now, he has to concentrate on his family. 'So, Freya and Ash are here. Outside. Sitting out there,' he says, pointing over his shoulder.

'Holy shit!' Gregg points a drumstick at him. 'You're nervous. How cute!'

'Go fuck yourself Gregg.'

'Watch that language. There's a minor outside.'

'You really want me to punch you, don't you?'

Gregg grins, but Luke steps in front of him, blocking his view. 'Are you going to bring them in?'

'Is that okay with you guys?'

Tate lowers his guitar, letting it hang from its strap. 'Why wouldn't it be okay? Chloe and Bria are in the house with Brandon. They'll be over in a minute. Is Maeve joining us?'

'Do you think I'd be able to stop her?' Luke asks. 'She's just visiting her brother. She'll be over after. Ash and Freya are your family. Of course they're welcome. Tate will just have to watch his mouth while they're here.'

'I already have to do that around Brandon. Chloe is convinced his first word will be *fuck*. If it is, I'm a dead man.'

Dillon doesn't doubt that for a moment. Both himself and Tate need to cut back on their cursing now they're fathers. Easier said than done. He's already put his foot in it a few times.

'Don't leave them sitting out there. Let them see a master at work.'

He grimaces at Gregg. If only he knew how right he was. Freya is going to be in her element. He opens the door and beckons them inside.

But instead of racing over to Gregg like he expected, she stands beside him, her small hand slipping into his again. His little firecracker is nervous.

'Freya, this is Tate, Luke, and Gregg. Guys, this is my daughter, Freya.'

Saying those words aloud still has his stomach doing somersaults.

She lifts her hand and waves at them. So confident Freya is only like that in familiar circumstances. She's more like the younger him than he thought.

The guys say hi to her and Dillon notices the blush when Gregg takes her hand and kisses it. Fucker.

After a bit of banter between Ash and the guys, they get the rehearsal underway. Having Freya watching him is such a buzz. She seems to be enjoying it too. Her eyes are glued on what he's doing.

She even mouths a few of the chords as he plays them. Someone has been doing their homework. Take that Gregg Egan and your drums!

About an hour in, Bria, Chloe, and Maeve make an appearance along with a tray of pastries. Gregg chooses one of the diabetic offerings, stuffing it into his mouth in one go. He grunts when Bria elbows him in the ribs.

'Where are your manners?'

'Lost them,' he says around a mouthful of pastry.

'You'll have to excuse him,' she says to Freya. 'He's still learning how to be a human.'

'You love me.'

'How could I not? You're simply marvellous!'

'Too right I am,' he replies, his mouth still full of pastry.

Dillon sits back and watches his friends, his family, interact with Freya and Ash. It's so strange to him. He's used to having the other girls around. They're part of the band as much as he is, but he never imagined this for himself.

He always thought it was too far beyond his reach. That it was something he didn't deserve.

But he does.

He's made some fucking massive mistakes, but none of that matters anymore. All that matters are the people in this room right now.

He smiles when Ash takes his hand, lacing her fingers with his. 'Penny for them?'

'I'm just happy.'

She leans over and kisses him, stopping and laughing when Freya and Gregg both say *eww* at the same time.

Ash

As she paces his luxurious penthouse overlooking the Liffey in Dublin, Ash keeps glancing over at the door. Dillon should be here any minute.

This moment is one she's been planning for a while and today is the day. Today is when she turns the tables on him. Puts him exactly where she knows he wants to be. Where he needs to be.

He's been at a photo shoot all day with the guys, dressed up and looking sexy no doubt. But that wouldn't be difficult. Even just out of bed he takes her breath away.

Ash gets to her feet as the door opens and Dillon appears, and there he goes taking her breath away again. The man who walks in the door is in another league. Wearing tight fitting leather trousers, a black t-shirt with a deep V neck teamed with silver chains around his neck, the rock star just arrived home.

Her rock star.

'Hi,' She clears her throat and tries again. 'Hi.'

He grins, clearly noticing her slight fumble. 'Hi yourself. I've got to say, you look happy to see me.'

'Always.'

He leans over to kiss her. The taste and smell of apple mixing with his cologne is instantly intoxicating.

'So why are we meeting here? Where's Freya?'

'She's with Maeve and Luke. They're going to take her to the movies then dinner. They'll bring her back to the cottage and stay with her if we're not back by bedtime.'

'They are? Why?'

Ash laughs at the suspicion on his face. 'Relax. I just thought it would be nice if we had some time alone. Just you and me. I've got dinner lined up and the table is set on the balcony. We're going to have a bit of romantic adult time. Just you and me.'

He smirks and licks his lips. 'Adult time, huh? I might be interested in that.'

She traces her finger along his neck, following the line of the t-shirt. 'I thought you might. By the way, you look incredible. Did the shoot go okay?'

He nods. 'Same as always. A lot of posing and having to look like I either want to fight or fuck someone. Depends on the mood they're going for.'

'Wow. Nice imagery. Thanks for that! I have to say I've never asked a client to do either of those when I photograph them.'

He lifts her chin, wrapping his firm hand around her jaw. 'You ask anyone to give you a *fuck me* look and I'll have to make sure they don't even consider it.'

'Such a tough guy.'

'You know it.' He grins and tilts her head back, capturing her mouth with his.

'So, did you do as you were told?' she asks when he finally breaks the kiss that was clearly telling her she is his and his alone.

'Yeah. For the most part. I find it gets the damn thing over with faster if I behave and do as I'm told.'

She presses her body against his, not surprised when she can feel his hard dick against her stomach. 'So would you do as you're told if I was in charge?'

He tilts his head to the side as he looks down at her. 'Why do I get the impression you weren't talking about photos?'

She unbuttons her shirt dress, dropping it to the floor at her feet.

'Jesus, Ash!'

She smiles, glad her leather corset, thong, and heels got the reaction she was looking for. Dillon reaches out to touch her, but she pushes his hand back against the wall. 'You didn't answer my question.'

'Yes. No. Fuck knows. What was the question?'

'I asked if you'd do as you're told if I was in charge?' She slips her knee between his legs, widening his stance.

Then his face changes, the cocky grin disappearing as he realises what she's saying. 'Hang on. You want to be in charge? Over me?'

'Yes. I want you under my control. I want you begging for release. I want to fuck you for a change.'

Then the cocky grin comes back. 'You really think you can handle it?'

'Handle you, you mean? I think so. Give me some time and I'll have you begging for release.'

'You won't get me to beg. I don't beg.'

He grunts as she grabs him through his trousers and squeezes. 'We'll see about that.'

She takes his hand and leads her rock star into his playroom. She'd spent the last two hours here, exploring and familiarising herself with the set-up.

She knew he was a fan of bondage, but when she saw his playroom, she realised it was more than just being a fan of it. He is living the lifestyle. Or was.

He hasn't been here since they've been together. And that's not right. This is a part of him. A part she has no intention of taking from him. If he's willing, it's a part she wants to share with him.

Starting now.

She stands him in the centre of the room then takes a step back to just look at him. He's nervous, his eyes darting around the room, finally settling on the bed and the pile of chains at the bottom of it.

'Do you want me to do this?'

Dillon looks at her again and nods.

'Dillon?'

'Yeah. I want you to do it.'

Hearing his verbal confirmation is all she needs. Time to get this underway. 'Strip.'

There's the briefest of pauses as he thinks that over, then he does as he's told. Once he's naked, she slowly walks around him, taking a minute to marvel at the man in front of her. This is going to be fun. 'I see you're enjoying yourself already.'

He glances down at his dick, then back up at her. 'It's your outfit.'

'Or maybe it's the thought of what I'm about to do to you.'

He swallows but doesn't say anything. She's never seen him like this. She's taken control before, but this is going to be so much more.

Ash fastens a leather cuff around his wrist while he intently watches her. She might have to do something about that too. Having him watching her as she does this might throw her off her game.

She fastens the second cuff around his other wrist then walks over to the far wall, picking up the long length of heavy chain attached to

366

the wall.

'Fuck,' he mutters more to himself than her as she padlocks the chain to the first cuff, pulling his arm out to the side. Once she's dealt with the other side he's firmly pinned, arms outstretched and unable to move.

'Are you okay?'

'No,' he answers with a slight smile. Oh, he's definitely beginning to enjoy himself.

Ash walks around him, rubbing her hand over his ass, before giving it a hard slap. He tenses under her touch but recovers quickly. He's going to fight this. But she's prepared.

She chains his ankles to the rings on the floor, keeping his legs spread and every inch of his powerful body on show.

His breathing is slow and steady, but his dick betrays how turned on he is. The circle of black metals balls piercing the tip glisten with pre-cum.

She traces her finger over the piercings, coating them before slowly licking the crown. Dillon bucks and curses. 'Fuck...'

She circles him, running her fingertips across his body, loving the way the muscles tense and relax under her touch. 'Do you remember our safe word?'

'You'll call it quits before I do, babe.'

Challenge accepted.

Ash opens a cupboard and runs her hand along the line of floggers hanging inside. As she takes her time choosing, she glances over her shoulder to Dillon. His eyes are wide, his chest rising and falling rapidly as he waits. She starts at the left of the line with the smaller less sever floggers and he relaxes a little.

She smiles and moves her hand to the right dismissing the next few as she keeps watching him. He's frowning now, but his dick is betraying him. It's standing proud, eager for whatever is coming his way.

Ash picks the heavy black leather flogger next to the chain one. He may use that on others, but neither of them are ready for that. Not yet anyway.

Ash runs the thick leather tails over her palm, her attention on Dillon as he watches her every move. As she gently brushes the tails over his skin along his chest and back, his breathing quickens at the anticipation of what's about to happen.

Ash places the flogger at the end of the bed before picking a blindfold from a drawer and reaches up to buckle it in place over his eyes. She doesn't want him to see what she's about to do. Each stoke needs to be a surprise.

It also helps that he can't try to unnerve her while she's doing this.

She beings with light strokes, focusing on his hard ass initially, eagerly waiting for a flinch or groan from Dillon.

But he's being stubborn, standing tall and straight, defiant to the last. He may want this but he's not going to give in easily. It's not who he is. But that's just fine by her. She's got all day with him.

She's going to have to up her game.

Ash draws her arm back and braces herself as the flogger meets with his flesh, the harsh slap sounding so much louder in the room. But it works.

He grunted. but composes himself again.

'You really don't want to admit you're enjoying this.'

'Because I'm not,' he replies, but his flash of a smile encourages her.

Ash draws her arm back and strikes him again and again, the skin on his ass and back gradually reddening under the contact. Dillon's reactions increase too, his ability to hide the gasps, groans, and curses failing as the sting builds.

She pauses as he breathes heavily. 'Just breathe, sexy.'

'Easier said than done.'

She has no doubt behind the blindfold he's glaring at her. She runs

368

the leather straps along his chest, his ab muscles rolling as she makes contact.

'I love the way your body moves.'

'Stop talking. I'm concentrating.'

She laughs as she rubs his warm flesh. 'Let go, babe. Stop fighting. Stop concentrating. This is your time to just feel.'

He swallows heavily but doesn't say anything.

She swings the flogger again, the leather straps snapping against his chest, harder, and faster until she's gasping for breath herself.

She stops and caresses his hot skin as he composes himself. 'You're holding your breath again.'

'I am fucking breathing...'

'Now you are.'

He curses as she traces her nails along his chest. His skin is warm under her fingers, his body tensing as she caresses him. Her hand traces a path down his chest to his stomach to wrap her hand around his hard cock.

Dillon groans and thrusts his hips forward.

'Oh, you are liking this.'

He bites his lip ring, refusing to answer. 'So stubborn. Let's see if I can change that.'

She drops the flogger on the bed then takes bottle of lube from the drawer, coating one of the butt plugs. His entire body tenses when her slick fingers brush against his hole.

'Ash?'

She spreads his ass cheeks then rubs the tip of the plug over his ass, teasing him with what's to come. 'Relax.'

'Easy for you to say.'

Ash slips the tip of the plug inside, loving the groan he releases as it slides in. 'Oh, you do like that.'

She could swear he growls and then his hips move towards her. It's subtle and barely noticeable, but she sees it. Seems he does want this.

Ash pushes the plug further into his ass then stops. 'Do you want this?'

'Fuck,' he mutters in a low voice, but she can feel him push against her hand again, trying to take it further. 'I want it,' he grinds out, his voice deeper than usual.

Ash smiles to herself. One step closer. 'Let me in, babe.'

Dillon relaxes and Ash slides the plug home until just the stubby end is showing. 'Holy fuck, Ash...'

She flicks the switch on the remote and his entire body jerks as the vibrations work through him.

She picks up the flogger again, moving around to his back again. But this time she doesn't hold back. The stubborn man is still holding back, fighting to keep control of his body and not give in. But she's not giving up.

She pauses long enough to turn the plug up a setting before striking him again.

Then it happens. A small shift in his stance. Instead of tensing against the contact, his shoulders drop every so slightly, and he groans loudly.

As she continues, his movements become more animated, jerking to either side to lessen the sting of the leather tails. Seems his chest is more sensitive than his back.

'Ah fuck!'

He shouts out in frustration, jerking his arms towards him, trying to get free. His broad chest heaves as he struggles to control his breathing. A fine sheen of sweat covers his skin, the sensitive flesh still red from her efforts.

She never thought she'd see him like this. Dillon had always held the reins in the bedroom. Even a decade ago, he'd always been the one to take the lead, although without the fun toys he has at his disposal now.

Doing this with him is so much more than seeing if he can submit.

It's about him dropping his walls for the first time. About trusting her to take him somewhere he's never been before. Restrained as he is, he's handed himself over to her in a way he's never done before.

Leaving the flogger on the bed, she grips his dick as she massages his balls. The instant she touches him, Dillon drives his hips forward, trying to move against her and build some friction, but she keeps the pace, holding him back no matter how hard he tries to convince her to go faster.

His body vibrates, his movements becoming desperate. She gently pushes against the plug in his ass as she moves.'

'I need to come Ash...'

He growls and throws his head back as his hips push against her. 'I'm going to come!'

Ash lets go of his dick, keeping her hand clamped around his balls.

'Fuck, Ash!' He pulls against the restraints, his body shuddering as his release slips away from his reach. 'Damn you.'

'No coming yet.'

Ash unbuckles the blindfold, and he blinks a few times before looking at her, a seriously hot fuck me look in his eyes.

Starting with his ankles, she unlocks the chains from the cuffs. He sways slightly as his arms are released but straightens his legs before he falls over.

'On the bed. Lie down on your back.'

Dillon stretches out on the bed, then watches her as she walks over to the bottom and picks up another length of chain already attached to the bed. Dillon is nothing if not prepared. This room is set up to go without any delays.

She clips a link into a catch on the side of the bed, shortening it so his legs are bent at an angle.

Once she's happy with the positioning, she locks each ankle in place. 'Arms over your head.' She locks his wrists to the metal headboard, making sure he secured.

Ash runs her fingers down his arms, loving the way the goosebumps appear when she touches him. 'Comfy?'

'Comfy isn't a word I'd use right now.'

She opens a drawer in one the cupboards beside the bed and takes out something that has his eyes opening wide.

'Fuck, Ash...'

She slides the thong down her legs, replacing it with the strap-on harness. Ash slips on the harness, tightens the straps before lubing the thick dildo.

He blinks, then chews on his lip ring. 'Where the fuck did you get that?'

'You're not nervous, are you? It's not like you haven't had anything up there before. I want to fuck you for a change. You're not going to tell me that's not what you want.'

'No! I do.'

'Trust me, Dillon.'

'Always.'

Ash takes hold of the base of the plug, gently teasing it out of him. She leans over, rubbing her fake dick on his real one and he whimpers. The sound drives her crazy, instantly soaking her.

Dillon is the ultimate control freak. Seeing this side of him, this secret vulnerability is such a turn on. She doesn't want to think about how many people have been with Dillon over the years. But she doubts any have seen him like this, seen his submissive side.

He's still eyeing up the dildo, but she knows he can take it. That he wants it. Ash positions the dildo against his asshole, and he whimpers again. Doing this to him while he's on his back means she can watch as his impressive dick flinches against his stomach, the black piercings gleaming with precum.

Ash takes a deep breath, trying to calm down. Her pussy is buzzing under the harness, every movement she makes rubbing the leather against all the right places. If she doesn't relax this could be a short fuck.

She holds his cheeks apart while she nudges up to his hole, then gives the dildo a gentle shove, pushing the head inside him.

Dillon arches off the bed as much as the restraints will allow. God he is spectacular. The way his perfect body reacts to what she's doing is stunning. He closes his eye as she slides deeper inside, using her hips to slowly guide it in.

She grips his thighs, digging her fingers into his flesh as she pulls back then thrusts in.

'Fuck! Fuck! Fuck!' His dick twitches against his stomach with each thrust of her hips. The headboard creaks as he yanks his arms down, but the chains hold. Watching him like this, controlling him, is all she needs to come herself.

'Ash I'm going to come.'

'No, you're not! Hold it.'

He curses, turning his head to the side, burying his face against his arm as he groans to himself. His entire body is trembling now, his breathing hard and fast as she fucks him.

She wants to take his thick pulsing dick in her hand, but she resists. If she does that he'll come. No question. He lifts his head, glancing down at the thick dick disappearing inside his ass. 'Oh fuck! That feels so fucking good...'

She moves between his legs, adjusting her position as she aims for his G spot. It takes less than a minute to hit the right angle.

'Jesus Ash! Holy shit!'

As if his shout wasn't confirmation enough, his dick jumps wildly, precum leaking onto his abs.

'Do you want more?'

He nods quickly, moaning and writhing his hips, trying to push the dildo in further.

Ash grips his waist, digging her fingers in as she fucks him hard, pushing the dildo in as far as it will go. She leans forward, pressing his dick between them, the slick piercings sliding against her each time she thrusts into him.

'Fuck me, Ash. Please fuck me!'

He doesn't have to ask her again. She fucks him harder, the sound of his guttural growls of pleasure driving her insane. Her body is tiring, but there's no way she's going to stop. Each groan, growl, and moan of pleasure from her man keeps her hips working hard, driving her dick into him hard and fast.

'Please Ash. I need to come. Please...' His whimper is the sexiest thing she's ever heard. As much as she wants to keep going, she's nearing the edge herself.

'Come for me Dillon. Come all over yourself for me.'

His eyes lock onto hers as he comes, his cum shooting out, coating both of them. She keeps up the pace, their flesh slick with his orgasm.

It takes less than a minute before she comes, her orgasm tearing through her. She screams out loud, her own shouts combining with his.

Dillon

He has no idea how much time has passed since she collapsed on top of him, her head resting on his stomach. All he knows is that he's in no rush to move. He'll stay here all fucking day, no problem.

She fucked him, and it was so much better than he imagined it would be. And he's so proud of her. She did everything right, pushing him to his limits while making sure he was okay through it all.

What she had done to him was everything he wanted... and more. Watching his stunning woman fasten that harness on her, seeing her lube up the thick dildo... fuck he'd nearly come in that moment without her touching him. But when she'd fucked him with it, she'd thrown him into a whole new fantasy he'd only dreamed of.

'Are you still alive down there?'

He flashes her a brief smile before groaning. Her dildo is still buried deep inside him driving him crazy every time he moves.

'Don't tell me I've finally tired you out?'

He grunts, unable to form anything resembling a coherent sentence. He has never been like this after sex. Never been so wiped out he couldn't move.

'Poor baby! Are you worn out?'

When she laughs, he looks down at her. 'What's so funny?'

'Nothing at all. I'm just giving myself a pat on the back. I broke Dillon Ryan and got him to submit. I honestly didn't think that was possible.'

'You temporarily knocked me off balance. Don't get carried away.'

She ruffles his hair, and he glares at her. 'Whatever you say Sexy. It's still a win for me.'

Oh it's a win for her all right. She's got him wrapped around her little finger. Always has. He knows without a doubt he'll be putty in her hands every time she produces that strap-on. 'Are you going to unlock me or leave me here all day?'

She rests her arm across his stomach and props her chin up on it. 'I haven't decided yet. I like having you like this. The bad boy of Broken Chords is naked and chained to a bed. You have no idea how wet that makes me.'

'If you call me a bad boy again I'm going to have to chain you up and fuck an apology out of you.'

'How are you going to do that if you're still chained up?' She moves her hips, pushing the dildo inside him.

'Fuck... Fine. Okay. You win. Call me what you want.'

She taps him on the cheek. 'Good boy. You know, I might have to make this a regular occurrence.'

'That's good to know, because there is a small chance I might have really fucking loved every single minute of that.'

'I know you did. But as much as you look seriously hot chained up like that, I probably should let you go.' She slowly pulls out, removing the harness before unlocking his restraints. Ash snuggles in beside him. She feels so right in his arms as he hugs her.

'Thank you, Dillon.'

'For what? Giving you a workout?'

She laughs at that. 'Not just that, but yes. It's damn tiring after a while. But I meant for trusting me to do that to you.'

'You're the only one I would let do that to me. Sex has... well I guess it's never meant much to me. It was just something I did. Something I needed to do. But there was never any emotion in it for me. You know that, right? I mean with other people, not you.'

'It's okay. I know what you mean.'

'I've always wanted someone to take me like that. I've wanted it for so long Ash. Just to be restrained and not have to think about what I was doing. No planning. No wondering if the person I was with was enjoying themselves. Putting it in plain terms – I just wanted to be fucked.'

'And no one ever has?'

He shakes his head. 'That badge of honour is all yours. Will only ever be yours.'

'That sounds absolutely perfect. I'll take it.'

He shuffles around to face her, brushing her sweat soaked hair back from her forehead. 'Will you stay with me?'

'Of course. I told you. I've got dinner planned too. This was the appetiser.'

'Fucking amazing one too, but that's not what I mean. Will you stay with me, long term? You and Freya.'

The way she looks at him has him second guessing the timing of his question. He wants his family with him all the time. He needs them with him, but maybe it's too soon? Maybe he's just rushed headfirst into this.

'Can you say that again?'

He smiles as he cups the side of her face. 'Ashling, will you and Freya please move in with me?'

'Yes!'

She said yes. Just like that. No thinking, no pause. Just a yes. 'What? Really? You didn't even think about it. What about talking to Freya? She might not—'

Ash places her finger over his mouth silencing him. 'We've already discussed it just in case it ever came up. I didn't want to get my hopes up if Freya wasn't on board. But she couldn't want this more. She loves her dad and wants to be with him.

'She also loves Ireland so it's not a difficult decision. It's a huge, massive, absolute definite yes from both of us.'

'We're really doing this. We're moving in together? We're going to be a proper family?'

'Yes Dillon. We're really doing this. We have a sister magazine in Dublin so I'm sure I can transfer there. If not, I'll just have to find a new job. I've recently photographed a rather well-known band. I doubt that will have done my reputation any harm at all. Quite the opposite in fact.'

'Speaking of that. I might have demanded that my hot girlfriend is made our official photographer. Ellen usually gives me what I want. I can be an awkward ass at the best of times. It's easier to let me get me way. Besides,' he says as he pulls her against him. 'She was going to ask you anyway. Apparently, you're the best photographer she's used.'

'Oh my God! Are you being serious?'

'You might even get their moody bassist to smile every now and again. He tends to go for the serious vibe when he's photographed.'

'So I've heard. Thank you for this Dillon!'

'This wasn't me. It was all you, Ash. You deserve it. Now I believe you mentioned dinner. I'm fucking starving!'

43

Dillon

If someone had told him a year ago that, not only would he be clean and sober, but that he would be a father and a boyfriend, he wouldn't have believed it.

But that's his life now.

Four months without drink and drugs is a lifetime considering how addicted he was. Soon it will be five months. Then six.

Every single day is an achievement, and he plans to keep marking the days off on his calendar.

As for the other new and exciting part of his life. Well, that's just fucking amazing. He's sitting in Tate's massive back garden, the sound of the sea in the background, all his friends around him, watching his stunning girlfriend and amazing daughter fill their plates with food from the barbecue.

He can't believe Tate and Chloe's son is one. Where the fuck did that last year go? Most of it was probably at the bottom of a bottle of whiskey. Fucking waste. How much of his life was lost that way? Too much probably.

At least he's got a handle on it now. It's not an iron clad handle, but it's one he is confident he can maintain. His very expensive therapist is helping. Not that he's fully on board with the whole *opening up* shit he needs to do, but he's determined not to mess this up.

Freya needs him and there isn't a chance in hell he's going to let her down.

She waves at him from across the garden as she shovels a spoonful of rice into her mouth. Luke was right. Missing out on the first ten years of her life was shitty, but it didn't take away from what they have right now. He adores her. Would quite easily kill anyone who hurt her. Good luck to any boyfriends she may have when she's older. Much older. He's going to be the father you don't mess with.

'What's that grin for?' Ash asks as she slips onto his knee to straddle him.

'Oh nothing. I was just imagining all the fun ways I can scare off future boyfriends.'

She slaps him on the chest. 'She's only ten. I think we have a few more years before we need to worry about anything like that.'

'Too damn right. Is she okay? She seems to be getting on with Tate's nieces.'

'She's having a ball. You know, I think our daughter has settled into the celebrity lifestyle a little too well. She's like a duck to water. Then again, you did too.'

'I've always been a fan of nice things,' he says as he pulls her down for a kiss.

'Speaking of that,' she says when he eventually releases her. 'After Freya is asleep tonight, I am going to chain you down and fuck you hard with my strap-on. I got a new one today. I'm dying to try it out.'

'Is that right? I thought it was my turn to take control tonight?'

She grins as she shrugs. 'What can I say? I like having you helpless while you beg for release. Which I will hold off as long as possible of course. I want to have a little fun with you first.'

'Like to torture me more like.'

'That wasn't a complaint now, was it?'

'Fuck no! Just an observation.'

'Good. And I promise I'll let you be in charge tomorrow... maybe.'

God he fucking loves his life now. 'Tell you what. You stay where you are for another minute until my hard on is less obvious and you can do whatever the fuck you want later.'

She laughs as she runs her fingers through his hair. 'Sorry about that.'

'Doing that to my hair isn't helping the situation. Actually, how about you put some distance between us. Otherwise, I'll have to take you home right now.'

'If Freya wasn't enjoying herself so much, I'd let you.' She glances around when someone shouts her name. 'Looks like Maeve wants me. I'll leave you and your dick to calm down.'

'Thanks,' he replies, sarcastically, but he doesn't let go of her hand when she climbs off him. 'Ash?'

'Yeah?'

'I love you.'

When she smiles at him, he can't help but smile back. She is fucking gorgeous.

'I love you too.'

She squeezes his hand before releasing it so she can join Maeve at the far side of the garden.

'I never thought I'd see that. Dillon Ryan is all lovey dovey.'

He lifts his middle finger, directing it at Luke as he sits beside him. 'Fuck off.'

'I'm not having a go, really. It's great to see. I mean that.'

'Thanks, Luke.' He watches as Tate and Chloe mingle with their guests, their son Brandon, in Tate's arms. Gregg and Bria are on the patio, wrapped in a blanket as they laugh with each other. 'I guess we're all grown up now, huh?'

Luke laughs. 'Getting there. We're all happy which makes a change.'

'Did you ever see us like this? I mean if you thought ahead years ago, would you have pictured this?'

Luke pauses before slowly shaking his head. 'I hoped we'd be happy, but it wasn't like this. This is better. The other version has me with Pippa.'

That's a version Dillon would rather not think about. Her threat when he visited her in prison, still plays through his mind when he can't sleep. She pretty much told him she's coming for his head as soon as she gets out. Something to look forward to.

Luke turns to face him, a huge smile on his face. 'I wanted to tell you first. I had some tests to see if the vasectomy reversal worked. I just got the results back.'

'And?' he asks, sitting up straighter in the chair. Luke would make a fucking awesome father. His friend has wanted kids as long as he can remember.

He smiles widely. 'I should be able to have kids.'

Luke grunts when Dillon pulls him into a tight hug. 'I am so fucking happy for you. And for Maeve.'

'Breathe...'

He releases him. 'Sorry.'

'It's all good. Everything is great in fact. We're not planning to start trying yet. It's too soon. But at least I have the option when the time is right.'

'I am so fucking happy for you Luke. I really am.'

'Thanks. Maeve has been asked to choreograph another show in the UK, so I'll be heading back there for a while. It's only for a few months. After that we're going to settle down here. Touring around like that with Maeve has been amazing, but we both just want to settle down. And I'm sure Andy would appreciate not having to trail around Wales after us.'

'You'll be living in Wicklow full time?'

'Once we find the right place. What about you and Ash? Have you made any plans?'

'Actually, they're both moving here. She's looking at schools for Freya. I haven't got a fucking clue what's good or not, so I'm leaving that to her. But as soon as that's sorted, we'll all be living in the cottage.'

'That's amazing! You're going to be like a proper family.'

'I know. Never thought it would be possible, but it's happening. It'll be one hell of a learning experience for a while, but I'm looking forward to it.'

'And Clara?'

He shakes his head. 'Not yet. I'm being selfish for a while. The right kind of selfish. All of this is too new. Ash, Freya, staying clean. I can't lose my grip on any of those points, or I'm fucked. Clara will just have to wait.'

Luke nods. 'We all need to be a little more selfish from time to time. Nothing wrong with that.'

'Hey! Luke! Dillon! Get over here!'

Luke laughs as Tate shouts over at them, a guitar in each hand. 'I think that's our cue. How about we show your daughter what her father can do? She's never seen the trad side of Broken Chords, has she?'

Dillon pushes to his feet, gesturing at Tate to say they're coming. 'In fairness, I don't think anyone outside this family group has. It's a private part of us.'

'Freya and Ash are part of this family group now. Let's show them what we can really do.'

He stops beside Ash as he walks up the garden, pulling her into his arms and kissing her hard. 'I fucking love you.'

'Oh, you old romantic. Sweeping me off my feet with your sweet talking.'

'You're not with me for my sweet talk.'

She grins, dragging her fingers through his hair again. 'Too right I'm not. So, I believe you're going to give us a little show?'

'It's what we do at these things.'

'I can't wait. And later we'll have our own little show.'

She smirks as she steps back when Freya runs over to him. He doesn't know how Ash does it, but she can get him hot under the collar just by looking at him.

'Hey Dad! Are you all going to play?'

'Yeah. You fancy joining in? We have a few spare bass guitars lying around.'

She jumps and squeals, clapping her hands together. 'Are you serious! Of course I want to.'

Freya hurries over to Tate who hands her one of the bass guitars, then stands next to Luke who talks her through a few of the chords she'll need to play.

Dillon blows Ash a kiss then joins the rest of the band and Freya, feeling like nothing in the world can take him down.

Gregg passes him a bass and stands to his other side. When they do these more Irish traditional sets, it's all about the guitars and lots and lots of singing.

They launch into the first song, everyone joining in with them when they sing, Maeve and Chloe dancing in the middle of the garden with the rest of the guests.

He looks down at Freya, doing a fucking amazing job at hitting the right chords.

'Am I doing okay Dad?' she shouts over the music and singing.

'You're doing amazing, Freya. I'm really proud of you.'

She beams up at him, then looks back at the bass, concentrating on her chords.

He's got this. For the first time in as long as he can remember, he's got this.

Epilogue

Gregg

Breathing slowly through his nose helps calm him a little, but he's still on the verge of freaking out. Gregg rubs his clammy palms on his jeans as he looks out at the sea a few feet from him. Even the sound of it makes him nervous and he hates it.

Since the minute Angel kidnapped him and chained him to a jetty so he could slowly drown, he's been a nervous wreck. Therapy is helping. Bit by bit, he's feeling more like his old self.

But he's not there yet.

Nowhere near.

'Are you okay?'

He jumps as Tate's voice startles him. 'Damn it Tate! You scared the hell out of me. Do you have any idea how many horror movies start with scenes like that?'

His best friend stands beside him, smiling sheepishly. 'Sorry. I saw you head down here so wanted to check you were okay. I thought you'd be happier after what happened today.'

Gregg takes a few steps back up the beach, putting a bit more distance between himself and the water, before sitting on the sand. 'I am. I'm over the moon.'

Tate peers across at him, his eyebrows lowered. 'You don't look it. Thought having the sale go through on your old house would lift a weight off your shoulders?'

'It has. I just...' He's not sure why he's not happier. He loved his old house. It was the first thing he'd bought for himself... well, with the help of the bank, once he was signed.

But then Angel moved in next door and the stalking began. When she held him captive in her house, it had kind of ruined the *home sweet home* feeling for him.

But now it's no longer his problem. As of today, it's gone. Sold. Someone else's house.

'You know I'm not going to kick you out of my Blackrock house, right? You and Bria can live there as long as you want. I have no plans to sell it.'

'I know Tate, and we both appreciate that.'

His friend pulls his legs up, resting his arms on his knees. 'You thought selling the old house would get rid of all the crap in here,' he says, tapping his finger against the side of his head.

'Busted.' He sighs, scrubbing his hand through his hair. 'No quick fix, huh?'

Tate shakes his head. 'I wish. Believe me. That whole *time heals* shit we keep hearing seems to be true.'

'Is it? Really? I mean that. Will it get better? I'm getting a little tired of nearly breaking my neck to get in and out of the shower before

I have a panic attack.'

'Fuck, Gregg! You never said it was that bad? I thought it was just the sea that freaked you out.'

Busted again. He forgot he'd been playing it down with Tate. His buddy is still dealing with his own shit. The last thing he needs is another friend he has to worry about. 'I'm being dramatic.'

'You're being honest. What the fuck Gregg? Why didn't you tell me.'

'Because...'

'Well, that's answered that question.'

'I don't know. It's not too bad anymore.'

Tate hits him with his trademark glare. His friend has an incredible talent of speaking without saying anything. And right now, that look is saying plenty.

'We've all got our own stuff to deal with. This is my problem Tate.'

'First of all, you're my best mate so that's bullshit. Second, you're with my sister. If you weren't family before - which you were by the way, you are now. If you're struggling, you tell me.'

'What about you?'

'What about me? I'm fine.'

'Are you?'

Tate pauses, then blows out a breath. 'Fuck. Fine! This thing with Dillon might have hit me harder than I thought it would. Seeing him going through rehab, knowing what he was dealing with while he was in there. It was hard. I know we went through it all with Luke, but that was different. Luke was a cry for help.

'Dillon and me... we both made the conscious decision to use drugs and drink. If I hadn't got my shit sorted, I might have lost Chloe for good, Brandon wouldn't exist, and I wouldn't be a father or a husband. I can't imagine that, Gregg. It's scary as fuck.'

'You've done really well, buddy. I mean that.'

'Thanks. Hey, are you going to be okay? I know I'm not the best one to offer advice like this, but are you talking to Bria about things?'

'Sometimes. It feels never-ending at times.'

Tate laughs. 'Oh, I get that.' He curses as he pulls out his phone. 'Sorry. Message from Chloe. She needs help with the cake. You coming?'

'Can you give me a sec? I'll be right after you.'

Tate squeezes his shoulder before walking away, heading back up the beach.

Gregg jumps as a particularly loud wave crashes against the stones, his heart speeding up as the panic build.

Just breathe. You're safe.

He thought he was getting better. He really did.

Hours and hours of therapy and he still feels like he's in the exact same place. Tate is moving on better than he ever could have imagined. For a while there he thought he'd be visiting Tate in his grave, not at his house with his wife and son. Luke has Maeve and is experiencing all the amazing things a new relationship offers - along with a healthy dose of feeling safe and loved which he had been missing out on for so long.

And now Mr. Never Settling Down, has settled down. They're all happy. All safe. All getting on with their lives.

All except for him.

He's so deeply in love with Bria. They're building a life together. Being with her is better than anything he could have imagined.

So why can't he get out of his head? Why can't he move on and be happy?

Why does he still not feel good enough?

For the band. For Bria.

He reaches into his pocket and takes out the small black leather box. He's been carrying it around with him since they finished the last date in Dublin. After having a quick check to make sure he's alone, he opens the box and looks at the engagement ring.

He's had it for months. Had this whole big romantic proposal planned. But he kept talking himself out of it.

He'd be all psyched up, then he'd get freaked out when he heard water running, or he had a nightmare. Whatever it was, something would happen to convince him it wasn't the right time.

Maybe in another few months he'd be on top of it? Maybe with more counselling he'd feel more like his old self? Maybe...

Who is he kidding? Maybe nothing. He's never going to get over what Angel did to him. Never going to be able to forget being chained to the jetty watching the water slowly covering him.

He shuts the ring box, squeezing it in his hand.

All he wants is Bria. She's everything to him. Everything he's wanted for years. He adores her. Loves her more than he could ever put into words. She deserves everything she could ever want out of life.

But right now, he's not so sure that should include someone like him.

Thank you for reading **Shattered Rock.**

I hope you enjoyed catching up with the band again. There's plenty more to come!

The next book, **Damaged Rock**, is coming soon.

Do you fancy staying updated with news about my books?

• Join my mailing list at: **www.kafinn.com**

• Like me on Facebook: **www.facebook.com/kafinnauthor**

• Follow me on Instagram:
www.instagram.com/kafinnauthor

• Keep up to date with new releases:
https://books2read.com/ap/nE2Kdj/KA-Finn

Also, if you have a moment, I'd appreciate if you could review **Shattered Rock** at the store where you purchased it. The band and I would love to know what you thought of the book.

Thanks for your support!

K.A. Finn

Coming next...

Broken Chords # 6

DAMAGED
Rock